Praise for

Shepp

MW01502700

"Another fascin...   r
and a fitting sequel to his first. His seamless blending of historical fact
and fiction brings alive the maritime engagements of World War II so
vividly that it almost makes us seafarers want to get on to a plotting
sheet and recreate the maneuvers of the gripping Fleet actions. The
skillful portrayal of Captain Sheppard of the *Argonne* battling his own
insecurities and yet rising to the occasion is so typical of good leadership
at sea and all those who have driven warships and submarines would
see a little bit of themselves in him.

"G. Wm Weatherly has indeed emerged as the foremost author of
authentic naval action and on par with some of the best before him."

—**Commodore A Jai Singh**, IN (Retd), Vice President, Indian
Maritime Foundation

"Well, he's done it again—G. William Weatherly that is—or his
avatar CAPT Sheppard McCloud, Commanding Officer of the storied
Battle Cruiser *USS Argonne*, as they continue their extraordinary
exploits within an alternative history of World War II—the way things
might have been, given that a different butterfly was accidentally
stepped on at some distant place a long time ago.

"Although it certainly helps if this book is read after reading its
precursor, *Sheppard of the Argonne*, this is not a requirement, since
. . . *The French Rescue* stands well on its own. What makes these series
of books so unique is that they are not just another "action" piece full
of sound and fury (although there is certainly plenty of that!), but that
the author captures as only one who has been there, the nature not only
of Command itself, but the agonies of difficult decisions, the politics
of a military hierarchy, and the almost paternal pleasures of watching
subordinates blossom under your tutelage. Those who have 'been there,
done that' will recognize all of these nuances, and those that haven't will
learn from them.

"Although I remain amazed at the detail to which this submariner has captured not only the engineering, mechanical details, and tactics of major surface warships, but also the innovative manner in which he employs what was then cutting edge technologies. For example, the VT (Variable Time) or "proximity" fuse. Vannevar Bush, the head of the Office of Scientific Research and Development (OSRD), which initiated, controlled funding, and coordinated all wartime weapons development during WWII (including the Manhattan Project), declared that the most significant war-winning development of the conflict was not the Atomic Bomb, but rather the proximity fuse. CAPT Sheppard employs this then very secret device in ways probably never envisioned by its inventors.

"I would highly recommend *Sheppard and the French Rescue* regardless of whether the prospective reader does or does not consider him or herself relatively knowledgeable about history or naval matters. You can be assured that those areas about which you do not feel knowledgeable are indeed accurate—which is not always the case about other works in this general genre."

—**CAPT Jim Patton, Jr.**, USN (ret), Naval Submarine League

"As I finished *Sheppard and the French Rescue*, I sat in stunned silence contemplating what I had just read. I am a retired submarine officer, but have not commanded a ship. I came up through the ranks and so have experience on both sides of the demarcation line between enlisted and commissioned. Following my years in submarines, I surfaced to serve on submarine rescue ships, and later on NOAA research vessels, so I have a broad seagoing background from which to draw.

"Most people know nothing about war at sea. Their view of a ship's captain is that he is just the guy in charge. Anyone reading *Sheppard and the French Rescue* will learn the truth, that a warship's captain is the body and soul of an integrated fighting machine, that he is an extension of his guns, torpedoes (and in the modern world, his missiles). The captain fights his ship, aided by the men he has trained, relying on their expertise to carry out his battle needs, trusting them, relying on them, and leading them. I have never seen this concept so clearly laid out as in this novel. G. William Weatherly, a former warship captain, knows his stuff and has the skill to bring it to his readers in a way they can understand – not only the big picture, but what is happening in gun turret 4, or wherever else the immediate action is taking place.

"Beyond this, Weatherly takes his reader into the minds of the forces opposing *Argonne* and Captain Sheppard McCloud: German submarine skippers, Italian capital ship commanders, German aircraft pilots, and even the field grade officers urging their troops into frenzied battle. The reader also gains insight into the bigger picture: the British allied vessels, French senior officers, and French resistance ground forces.

"Weatherly has recreated World War II battles, but with a twist. His story takes place within the larger picture of a world at war, but his ships and the people manning them are constructs he employs to tell his fascinating story. The backdrop is real, the nature of the battles is authentic, the infrastructure is accurate, but the actual story originates in Weatherly's fertile mind. Far from lessening the impact of this novel, this technique allows Weatherly to explore his flawed hero, his less than perfect participants, as they play out one strategic situation after the other, keeping the reader turning pages, while educating him or her to what it is really like in the throes of heated battle at sea.

"This book is a bit technical, but without this detail, it would be much less of a book. It is a must read for anyone interested in WW II, war at sea, fighting capital ships, and the role submarines played in the sea-battles of WW II."

—Robert G. Williscroft, PhD
Author of the Bestselling *Operation Ivy Bells*
and *The Starchild Series*—modern hard science fiction

"Having read G. William Weatherly's *French Rescue,* I can congratulate him to another superb book after *Sheppard of the Argonne*! Again I suffered and hoped with Sheppard, and again I enjoyed the author's outstanding style of writing that does not circumvent problems or technical or tactical details, but elaborates on the stuff that was and still is the essence of our wonderful naval profession. Again Weatherly lets his protagonist, the commanding officer of the monstrous battle cruiser *Argonne,* apply unconventional tactics, be it to save his ship and the people entrusted to him, be it in high risk maneuvers to outwit the enemy. And with every line and with great subtlety, he achieves to bring Sheppard's warmhearted character ever closer to the reader.

"I feel inclined, however, to admit that—as a German and as a submariner—my emotions interfered with my pleasure of reading another of Weatherly's thrilling novels. It's the Germans he describes, getting obliterated by Sheppard and his men, be it at sea or ashore. It's 1942, the heyday of actual history's "Operation Drumbeat"—and still the author does not grant the German U-boats any chance of even the smallest success. I would understand if it had been 1944/45, when even getting to the U.S. east coast had been an achievement in itself, let alone the sinking of a ship . . .

"Emotion wells up in me, because—like most Germans of my generation—I have fallen uncles to mourn, two of the three having perished in the theaters of war which this splendid book deals with. Every "swine" (in French Résistance fighter César's words) among those Krauts was a deplorable individual seduced into a war of aggression, their ideals and their bravery exploited by a ruthless band of brown-shirted criminals . . . But still they were humans—and in a way Weatherly does them justice by letting Sheppard always have morality in the back of his mind when he goes through all the dilemmas he is thrown into by having to kill the enemy."

—Raimund Wallner
Captain German Navy (ret.)

"William Weatherly's *Sheppard and the French Rescue* is a worthy and most readable sequel to his first novel *Sheppard of the Argonne*. The author adeptly and skillfully continues to develop the character of Captain Sheppard McCloud, giving the reader an insight into the thoughts and private life of a brave but very human captain who, in his super-capable battle cruiser, is pitted against the odds. However, McCloud's competence, innovation, and resourcefulness, supported by a first-rate crew, enable him ultimately to achieve success.

"Continuing the theme of an alternate history of the Second World War, where there had not been the constraints of the Washington Naval Treaty upon warship building, this novel focuses upon a scenario where the US has developed battle cruisers of great size, phenomenal speed, and immense firepower. Weatherly, with ever an eye to detail and realism, vividly and grippingly describes the shock and awe of gun actions between capital warships.

"The plot is centred upon the avoidance of the French fleet from falling into the hands of the Axis Allies at a critical time early in the Second World War. McCloud in *Argonne* has a pivotal role in achieving this. Weatherly skilfully develops a sequence of events and characters which grip the reader's imagination and attention.

"In sum this book is a superlative narration of the complexities and demands of warfare at sea and is very much in the mould of C.S. Forrester's *Hornblower* series. William Weatherly is to be congratulated in delivering a novel which has all the ingredients of a first-rate read which describes maritime warfare in the WWII era in a very comprehensive but understandable style."

—**Captain Dan Conley**, OBE, RN, co-author, *Cold War Command*

Sheppard and the French Rescue
by G. William Weatherly

Published by

BATTLE FLAG BOOKS

An imprint of

◄ köehlerbooks™

210 60th Street
Virginia Beach, VA 23451
800-435-4811
www.koehlerbooks.com

SHEPPARD

AND THE

FRENCH RESCUE

Volume I of Allies and Enemies

G. William Weatherly

VIRGINIA BEACH
CAPE CHARLES

AUTHOR'S NOTE

Sheppard and the French Rescue continues the story of Sheppard McCloud begun in *Sheppard of the Argonne*. Though this novel will stand on its own and lays out the strategic situation for the next volume, I would encourage my readers to enjoy *Sheppard of the Argonne* first. This work makes reference to many events from the first work as well as character development contained therein. I have included the prelude of the first work as an end note to outline how I arrived at this alternative history with its larger ships and more difficult strategic situation.

Writing alternative history presents a plethora of choices. In this series of books, I chose to accelerate some technology development such as ship building, metallurgy, ordinance, and radar, while keeping others such as aircraft close to the actual timelines since that development was not restricted by treaty. Using fictional names for ships can be confusing where a ship of that name actually existed in WWII. For American ships, I slavishly followed naming battle cruisers after famous American battles grouped by ships of the same design, to battles of the same war, aircraft carriers after famous sailing frigates, cruisers after cities appropriate for their size, and destroyers after historical naval personnel, mostly Medal of Honor recipients. Battleships are not named, but would follow historical traditions. Nation designators (USS, HMS, FNS, or KMS) are only used where the historically accurate named ship actually existed. Names for allied and German warships followed their conventions to the best of my limited abilities.

To my several editors' frustrations, I have mostly followed naval usage and style from the early 1940's period, so please forgive the deviations from *The Chicago Manual of Style*. Spelling and usage of the rank and position of the ship's captain as a reference or in conversation may have driven them to drink.

War in the twentieth century was dictated by technology. Presenting that without detracting from the battles and struggles of the protagonist and other characters, I hope, leaves the reader with an understanding of why events can be shaped by the tools of war as much as by the men that controlled them.

PROLOGUE

HE WAS ALMOST HOME. Not his home, but close to Evelyn's arms. For the moment the memories of what he had done; the screaming wounded as the white phosphorous burned into them—could be forgotten. He knew that the images would return from dark recesses of his memory that everyone wished were not there. They would haunt him in the night when his conscious mind was not occupied or distracted by Evelyn's beauty. The men, thousands of them screaming in German; writhing in agony as his shells exploded above them, the only relief to throw themselves into the sea. Oceanic swells left no tombstones, no markers for young lives snuffed short at his order. At least this time, in this battle; the men were not his.

Sheppard had succeeded in preventing Schröder from raiding Great Britain's lifeline—the convoys. But had he? Those ships still served Germany—would be repaired to raid again. Was the price of temporary success too steep? Was he never to enjoy a peaceful respite away from Evelyn's arms? When would his men learn the truth of his tormented soul? At what critical moment would they question his judgment—*his sanity*? The only certainty was that there would come a time. It would be his men that screamed, bleed, and died. It would be his fault—all his fault. There would be no one else to blame for his sailors' deaths.

Had they already guessed the price he was paying? Were the accolades only an attempt to ease his tortured mind? If they were, they failed. He knew what he had done. Nothing would change it. The war would continue. That was a given. More war, more battles, more death; would that be the only future for the "great" Captain Sheppard McCloud and the battle cruiser *Argonne*?

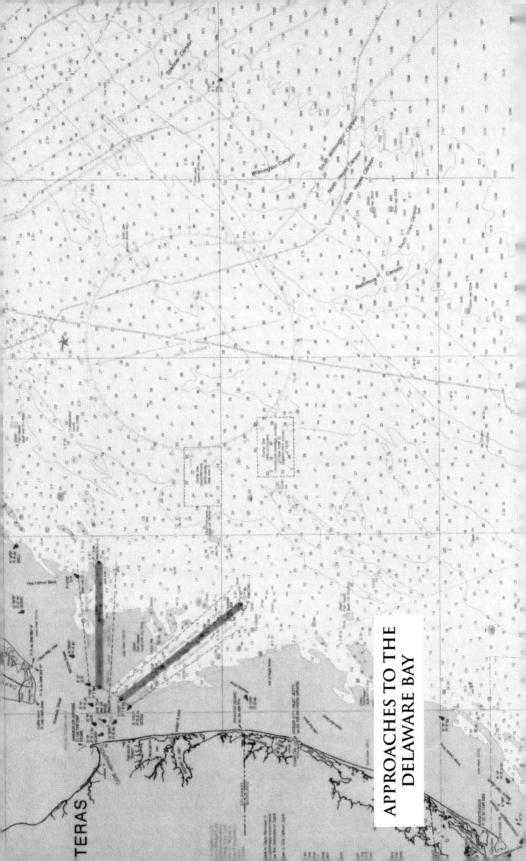

APPROACHES TO THE
DELAWARE BAY

1

CONTINUANCE

"CAPTAIN IS ON THE CONN," boomed the Boatswain's Mate of the Watch.

Captain Sheppard Jackson McCloud, hero of the raid on Pearl Harbor, savior of the West Coast from air attack, victor of the Battle of Cape Vilan, and war criminal had slowly made his way up to the secondary conning station of his ship—the battle cruiser *Argonne*. Tall, at an inch over six feet, and still athletically trim, he was dressed in his khakis with black tie and his usual spit-shined black shoes, but his steward, Petty Officer First Class George Washington Carver Jefferson, was already hanging his number two set of blues in his sea cabin, appropriate for entering port later on what should be a beautiful May morning tomorrow. The only problem was that to meet the tide and current constraints at the Philadelphia Navy Yard south annex, his ship would have to begin the transit up the Delaware River on a very dark night.

He had to admit that even though he had been able to rest his leg for the transit back to the East Coast; his surgically repaired left leg had not gotten better. Sheppard resigned himself to the fact that his limp was a permanent part of his gate just as his slightly bent nose was a reminder of his time on the Naval Academy boxing team every time he shaved his black but now flecked grey whiskers. As usual, his Marine orderly Corporal Pease in his open necked khaki shirt and blue trousers with the brilliant crimson strip on each leg, followed behind in tow. Where able, Pease would follow on Sheppard's left, slightly behind, but matching his step precisely—right leg moving slightly further than Sheppard's left allowed.

When they reached the O-12 level of the command tower, Pease opened the joiner door to the secondary conning station, allowing Sheppard to pass and be greeted by the emphatic words of the Boatswain's Mate of the Watch. Sheppard was surprised that Commander Arthur Roberts, his Command Duty Officer, was not availing himself of the padded leather high back swivel chair of the conning station. Set slightly to starboard so that the helmsman had a clear view of the bow, that chair had been Sheppard's home for the voyage to the northwestern coast of Spain and the battles with *Vizeadmiral* Schröder's German raiding fleet. Now it was his welcoming respite from the long climb on his damaged leg.

"Good evening, Commander," Sheppard casually said as he surveyed the condition of the watches on the conning station with his pale blue eyes, squinting against the brilliant sun close to the western horizon. A slight smile crossed his face as he noted the same formal watch-keeping practices that he used. Such small observations spoke volumes about Art's readiness for command of his own ship. As Sheppard's Command Duty Officer for the tow of the badly damaged battle cruiser *Belleau Wood*, Art had acted as *Argonne*'s captain in almost everything. His skill at ship handling and tutelage of the conning officers to keep the fragile tow line from breaking had been the official reason for Sheppard's decision. His other reason would forever be a secret shared only with his Executive Officer Ted Grabowski, was to test Art in command and instill that thrill in Sheppard's Navigator.

"Good evening, Captain," came a cheerful greeting from Art, a barely suppressed smile and twinkle in his eyes telling Sheppard as much as the successful tow of *Argonne*'s sister ship across the Atlantic under Art's supervision. Sheppard had never really asked Admiral Hamilton, Commander Task Force 48, if he should tow Hamilton's second battle cruiser or not. When the tow had rejoined the carriers, smaller cruisers, and destroyers of Task Force 48, more than a few messages were exchanged subtly implying that *Belleau Wood*'s crew should abandon her and the floating, burned hulk of a ship scuttled. Sheppard had to admit *Belleau Wood* was a wreck, but a wreck that could be repaired in much less time than building a replacement. After all, none of the German 410 mm shells had penetrated her armored belt and deck. It had taken all of Sheppard's tact with Hamilton and the good will engendered by saving his flagship, the aircraft carrier *Sabine*, from a similar fate for the unprecedented rescue to proceed.

Part of Hamilton's decision was undoubtedly the intelligence gained from *Argonne*'s POWs on the specifics of the German submarine deployment, and the ineptitude of the *Luftwaffe* searches. Two more German plane symbols graced *Argonne*'s directors as they had flown within range of her 5"/54 caliber guns on the first day of the tow. After a fresh water wash down of her aircraft, *Raritan* had then kept a combat air patrol of F4F Wildcat fighters up—destroying or chasing off more of the FW200 Condors using *Argonne*'s fighter direction capabilities and Jonathan Becker's skills to make intercepts well away from the Task Force.

"Captain," Art began, "*Belleau Wood* has disconnected her anchor chain from the tow wire and we are recovering the wire onboard now."

"Good, where are you putting it, Commander?"

"The easiest place is to fake it down just aft of the Number III turret. It will be clear of the hanger hatch and allow Lieutenant Commander Burdick's men enough room to handle and launch all the Kingfishers we have onboard. I checked with him before committing us to that course of action."

Another smile crossed Sheppard's face. Art was doing everything he himself would have done to arrive at the best possible decision. "How long do you anticipate you will need until we are ready to proceed on our own?"

"Captain, it shouldn't take more than ten or fifteen minutes at the rate Chief Boatswain's Mate Donnelly's men are bringing it onboard using the two winches aft."

"Very well, Commander, I relieve you as Command Duty

Officer. You may return to your duties as Navigator—and well done on the tow!" Smiling at Art's identification of the men who actually accomplished the ordered tasks, Sheppard punched up the signal bridge on the 21MC, "Signal Bridge, Captain, make to Commander Destroyer Squadron Thirty, 'Detach two destroyers to escort *Argonne* to port.'"

"Signal Bridge aye, Make to COMDESRON 30, 'Detach two destroyers to escort *Argonne* to port.'"

Sheppard smiled at the unmistakable voice of Chief Signalman Evan Bryce.

— —

He was a tall man. Really too tall for what he was about. Already the scars on his forehead served as a reminder of previous encounters with the various pipes, valves, and hatchways of each of his U-boats when new to an assignment. Now as *Kapitänleutnant* in command of the Type IXB submarine *U-182*, there were fresh red indentations on his head above the hair line of his thick wavy black strands. But he had learned. He had also learned his profession as a killer of ships well under the tutelage of Günther Prien. Fate had detached him from the *U-47* prior to her loss. Now he wore the white cap cover of a Commanding Officer in the *Kriegsmarine*, backwards as he prepared to look through the search periscope again, the sweep of the sky and horizon completed.

"Kruger, mark this bearing."

"Two-six-seven, *Herr Kaleu*"

He lowered the scope, dropped into the control room, and went to the chart converting the relative bearing called out by Kruger into a true bearing in his head from the U-boat's course of two-seven-zero. The leading capital ship had hardly moved, in fact at 3 knots his boat was moving ahead of this large group of ships. Perhaps even at the slow speed dictated by the need to conserve his battery, while remaining submerged in daylight, he might yet reach a firing position. It was the two capital ships that had his attention in the faint haze, however. Beside their high command towers, he could see a dozen masts, mostly moving around the second of the two major warships. Others were spread ahead and astern of those larger warships—probably escorts.

Suddenly his sound man interrupted. "*Herr Kaleu.* Heavy screws rapidly increasing in revolutions."

Kapitänleutnant Alfred Kuhn leaped into the conning tower, grabbed the periscope hoist control lever and started the search periscope up until it was a bare 10 centimeters above the waves, riding it up the last meter with his eye glued to the rubber eyepiece, motioning to Kruger to halt the rise at the proper height above the light chop and gentle swells.

"Mark this bearing!"

"Two-seven-one!"

The right hand capital ship was moving swiftly away toward the entrance to the Delaware River. Why wasn't the other one following? Only a few of the other mastheads had moved away with the first rapidly opening to the west.

Stepping back from the periscope, Kruger immediately lowered it below the waves—preventing all but a fleeting radar return even if the American's had equipment good enough to detect the miniscule target of the scope.

Why wasn't that other capital ship moving?

— —

Captain Harvey Jensen's brown eyes stared out at the fleet tugs and destroyers surrounding *Belleau Wood.* He wasn't sure if his squint was the result of the bright evening sun or weeks with little sleep and the resulting puffy eye lids. There was little good news that he had received—even Admiral Calhoun's abbreviated left arm had required additional shortening as septicemia had taken hold. At least now that seemed to have abated, but Harvey guessed the Admiral's stump was too short now for a prosthetic. He had personally reminded his friend several times that losing an arm had not slowed Admiral Horatio Nelson. Harvey hoped it would help as he watched his friend slip deeper into a depression. He guessed the Admiral regretted more than anyone not taking action earlier to correct *Belleau Wood's* fundamental problem.

Captain Kevin Bailey had been relieved for cause—cowardice and incompetency. He was now confined to his quarters under Marine guard until Vice Admiral Ingraham (Commander Scouting Forces Atlantic) determined whether to court-martial him or not.

Harvey had done everything he could to rally the remainder of his crew to the task of trying to restore propulsion to *Belleau Wood*. It had proven impossible to overcome the training deficiencies, let alone the devastation of the battle cruiser's unarmored uptakes and intakes. The hardest blow to overcome was the fact that there was barely one boiler-room's worth of water-tenders and firemen remaining fit for duty, none senior enough to divine the complex piping cross connections required. If he had been able to restore one boiler, he might have been able to steam on two engines across the ocean adjusting course by the revolutions on one shaft or the other since the rudder machinery room had been burned out and flooded. *Belleau Wood* was a floating wreck, down by the stern, the only command space left intact was the secondary conning station in the fire-control tower. *Thank God, at least the rudders had died amidships.*

Daily on the trip across the Atlantic at the end of *Argonne*'s tow wire, more of *Belleau Wood*'s crew had to be buried at sea. At first hundreds, then only a few, as infection claimed more despite the best efforts of the overworked doctors, dentists, and hospital corpsmen. At least those medical personnel had suffered comparatively few casualties in the after-battle dressing station, despite the devastation wrought by the Germans and Bailey's incompetence. The worst part for Harvey was that he now knew the burial-at-sea service by heart. The suffering of the crew hadn't been their fault.

— —

Evelyn McCloud followed the two Steward's Mates who carried her luggage into the house on the grounds of the Philadelphia Naval Shipyard away from the prying eyes of the press. It had been a whirlwind few weeks with first the cross-country flight to have lunch with the President's wife (Eleanor she had insisted) after a quick shopping trip to Washington's premier boutique for an appropriate tea dress and hat. Her lithe frame, creamy complexion, blue eyes, and auburn tresses made her an instantaneous celebrity. The press had been everywhere snapping photographs and asking questions about her husband. At lunch Eleanor had complimented her deft handling of their questions and her obvious love of her husband and family.

Another cross-country flight back to San Diego to pack for the transfer to the East Coast was now just a swirling memory.

Sheppard's and her belongings were being shipped to Norfolk where *Argonne* was homeported, but Admiral Ingraham and his staff also arranged to make available a house here at Philadelphia while the battle cruiser would be undergoing repairs from the Battle of Cape Vilan. Sheppard's letters had emphasized that his men had all survived the battle, but also warned that his return might not be as pleasant as when *Shenandoah* had docked in Long Beach and he was transferred to Balboa Naval Hospital. Should the service and the President decide to court-martial her husband, life would immediately become less pleasant for her entire family.

As she surveyed their new temporary home that the Navy was providing, this was obviously beyond quarters that a mere captain could hope for. There was a silk upholstered settee, an ornate rug, coffee table and two wing backed chairs tastefully done in colors hinting at the Navy's blue and gold motif. To one side a secretariat and upholstered chair matching the settee, where a standing lamp nicely balanced the end tables and ornate lamps in the room. As the stewards carried her luggage to the second floor, she sat and opened the secretariat. It was very clear that the admirals had arranged flag quarters for Sheppard. Evelyn prayed it was an indication that her husband and her family had a future in the service.

There were more immediate concerns though as she took out a fountain pen from her purse and began to write on the embossed stationary in the secretariat. The first letter was to Cindy Trotter, wife of Commander Scouting Forces Pacific and a close friend. She began by thanking her and the Admiral for arranging her rail travel and more importantly taking in three of her children while they finished the current school year. She was not worried how Bonney and Heather would behave, but Sean, her youngest, was not that far out of puberty and the Trotters had a similarly aged girl Katherine. Katie as she was called was a tomboy and those two were going to require continuous supervision living in the same house, even if everyone had separate bedrooms.

Her second letter was to a man she knew well from when he was her husband's Commanding Officer on the battle cruiser

Ticonderoga. Now a Vice Admiral, Jonas and his wife, Becky, had been mentors to them both and suspected that it was he that had arranged the flag quarters in Philadelphia as well as the more appropriate but still large house in Norfolk on the grounds of the Naval Station, away from harassment by the newsmen and photographers. That secluded abode was the destination of all her household goods. Evelyn knew that this gypsy life she now faced would only get worse as her husband jumped from one command to another or this close knit support group that was part of service life would evaporate with his pillorying.

— —

The train whistle announced the arrival of the private express from Germany. On the platform at Roma Termini to greet the distinguished *Admiral* Klaus Schröder, decorated hero of the fight at Cape Vilan (the Ritterkreuz now hanging around his neck) against overwhelming odds and victim of unspeakable war crimes on the part of the Americans was *Grand' Ammiragilio* Aldo Dragonetti commanding admiral of the Italian Navy. Klaus knew that he was really only the titular head of the Regia Marina; Mussolini had to approve every operation of the fleet. But Dragonetti's presence confirmed Klaus's new status as the *Führer's* direct representative.

Klaus waited in the private rail car that *Großadmiral* Raeder had loaned for the occasion; just long enough to make sure the Italian *Ammiragilio* knew who was waiting on whom. As he stepped off, followed by his loyal Chief of Staff, *Fregattenkapitän* Fritz Bodermann, he pointedly did not salute his host. He knew that Dragonetti would be upset, but Raeder had made a point of impressing Klaus with who was the very junior partner in this alliance.

"This point must be made crystal clear to the Italians from your first meeting," Raeder had emphasized. Well, Klaus might be upset with being sent to this backwater now that the British had been cleared from the Mediterranean with the sole exception of Malta; however, he knew how to obey orders.

Following forced pleasantries, both men entered the open Mercedes limousine for the ride to Italian naval headquarters (Supermarina). The two men chatted as Aldo pointed out the sights, their trip not being by the quickest route. Passing the Colosseum, there was an unspoken reminder of Rome's past glories when it had ruled the known world.

— —

"Kruger, mark this bearing."

"Two-six-two!"

"Down scope!" He would continue with only short intermittent observations suspecting the allied advantage in radar might make him detectable.

Alfred dropped down into the control room to look at the navigation chart where his quartermaster was already laying down the true bearing. Marked with a heavy line, the western boundary of his patrol area had to factor into his plans. *Vizeadmiral* Dönitz did not prohibit one boat entering an area assigned to another boat of Operation *Beckenschlag* (Cymbal Crash), but his patrol report had best contain an excellent justification when he returned to Saint-Nazaire. This capital ship was clearly that justification. He knew that *Korvettenkapitän* Conrad Kluge in *U-197* had the area to the west and suspected that he would be as close to the mouth of the Delaware Bay as he could safely get or have moved away to throw off the increasing American air patrols and occasional patrol craft or ancient destroyer.

From his last observation, that remaining capital ship was moving at under his 3 knots, he could make a submerged approach but he had to get closer. He was running out of time as the sun dipped ever closer to the western horizon.

"Come left, steer course two-two-five."

"*Jawohl, Herr Kaleu*, steer two-two-five," came the quick reply from his helmsman.

"*Steuermann* Schmitt, what time does the moon rise?" Alfred asked as he turned back to his quartermaster.

Schmitt busied himself with his nautical almanac making notes and calculations on a scrap of paper. "Moonrise is zero-seven-zero-eight Greenwich, *Herr Kaleu*." "Ah . . . , zero-two-zero-eight local," he added not quite sure of the calculation.

That matched what Alfred remembered of when he had surfaced last night for the battery charge and hunt. The moon would still be a last quarter waning crescent, just enough for him to make out his target on the surface. Now the issue was how to make an approach on the surface against all those ships milling about the capital ship.

— —

It was Squadron Leader Rupert Wythe-Jones's turn. There had been so many deaths before the King was able to honor members of the armed forces that the traditional New Year's and birthday ceremonies, on December 14th, had been expanded. The Central Chancery of the Orders of Knighthood had organized today's ceremony specifically for members of the Royal Air Force and Royal Navy. There were the usual fighter pilots and bomber pilots, who had the shortest life expectancy, one senior Air Marshall, and two Royal Navy officers, but Rupert was the only member of Coastal Command. That distinction was lost on him as he desperately hoped he would not forget the detailed instructions he had been given.

It helped that he did not have to go first. That honor was given Admiral Bruce Hardy, being elevated to the order of the Bath. Both he and Rupert were being honored for their actions in the Battle of Cape Vilan. The two men had, at great personal risk, made singular contributions to the battle which saved the British from certain defeat at the hands of the *Kriegsmarine*.

"Squadron Leader Rupert Wythe-Jones, your majesty," the Lord Chamberlain intoned.

Rupert stepped forward and knelt before the dais. King George stood in the center guarded by five wicked looking members of the Gurkha Regiment in their dress uniforms. Two Gurkha officers had escorted the King into the ornate room in Buckingham Palace. *Mustn't look directly at the King*, Rupert tried to remember all the instructions. Keep your head down, don't react to the sword touching your shoulders. It was so much easier commanding a squadron of Sunderland flying boats and attacking submarines. He would rather face German anti-aircraft fire any day.

First the touch on the right shoulder. *I hope he doesn't cut my throat*, now the touch on the left shoulder. *Is the King going to comment on my hair? I know it is too long, but I would never hear the end of it from Lois if I cut it to regulation length.* Now what, Rupert had forgotten!

"A-Ah-Arise, Sir Rupert," George the sixth stammered to help out his most recent knight.

My God, the King is just another human being with his faults like the rest of us.

The King took the red and white ribbon with the gold Cross Patonce and pinned it on the left breast of Rupert's dress uniform. "Tha-Thank you, for main-maintaining contact." He then took the Cross Flory and white ribbon with alternating broad purple diagonal stripes of the Distinguished Flying Cross and pinned that to the left of the Most Excellent Order of the British Empire. "May-May you sink many-many more U-boats."

Now what? Oh, yes, I need to back away. Don't turn around, mustn't show my back to the King. God I hope I don't stumble on something. How far back do I go?

The ceremony now complete, Rupert had been last, the King turned his back and left escorted by his two Gurkha officers. With that the assembled group of recipients and invited guests were free to mingle.

Admiral of the Fleet Pound came over and greeted the squadron leader, "Sir Rupert, let me be the first to congratulate you. You have no idea how critical your reports were to our victory. Let me introduce you to Admiral Hardy"

"Thank you, First Sea Lord, and congratulations, Admiral Hardy, on your honor." Admiral Hardy smiled and gave a quick nod of acknowledgement. "Admiral of the Fleet, I understand you had a hand in my honor today—thank you. May I introduce you both to my wife Lois?" Rupert self-consciously said turning to the woman tastefully dressed with long blond hair, creamy skin, and warm brown eyes.

"Good afternoon, you should be very proud of your husband. I can't tell you the details, but his bravery and insight into the unfolding battle was critical to Britain's and our ally's great victory."

"Thank you, Admiral, for your kind words," came the voice that had melted Rupert's heart years before.

"If you will excuse me, I must get back to Gibraltar as soon as possible," injected Admiral Hardy.

Both admirals departed engaged in hushed conversation. Rupert was congratulated by the other senior RAF officers present. As the crowd thinned, Rupert and Lois looked at each other. Lois planted a red kiss on his cheek, "And what shall we do for the rest of the day?" she seductively added.

As they walked out of the palace Rupert congratulated himself on not embarrassing himself or the Royal Air Force too badly in front of the King. He was oblivious to the red lipstick on his cheek.

— —

"Schmitt, how hard would it be to quickly rig a green light over a white light after we surface from one of the periscopes?" *Kapitänleutnant* Kuhn asked.

"It will not be hard, *Herr Kaleu*," Schmitt quizzically answered.

"Good! Let me know as soon as the electrician is ready." He knew he would never be able to get to an attack position before the sun set. But the blackness of the night could be used as a weapon.

"Schmitt, what does the chart say for the depth of water?"

"About one-hundred-fifty meters, but shoaling fast, then it will flatten out on the shelf starting at about one-hundred meters."

Leutnant Dieter Werner, the first watch officer entered the control room looking like he had sensed something was up. "*Herr Kaleu*, you seem to be formulating a plan of attack. Should I wake the crew and get a meal ready?"

"*EinsWO*, yes we are going to attack that capital ship after the sun has set and before the moon has risen. The hard part is not going to be getting into an attack position. The hard part will be trying to escape."

"*Herr Kaleu*, how are we going to see on a moonless night?" Dieter asked wondering if his *Kommandant* had the unthinkable in mind.

Smiling Alfred told his second in command, "*EinsWO*, we will attack on the surface. I want you to prepare a torpedo tube load of garbage and items that will float, but do not load it until after we attack."

"Helmsman, come right to course three-two-five."

"*Jawohl, Herr Kaleu,* Come right to course three-two-five"

Now certain his new captain was in fact mad, Dieter, nevertheless, went off to carry out his Captain's wishes thoroughly confused on what *U-182* was about to conduct.

— —

Captain Jensen was pleased that the tow had been resumed. It was an odd arrangement, dictated by still being in the open ocean, but two fleet tugs *Potawatomi* and *Wenatchee* were now both pulling on the *Belleau Wood*. From the smoke gushing from their stacks, both tugs were at maximum power. The resulting 3 knots of progress was disappointing to Harvey, but adding another fleet tug would make it impossible for them to avoid collisions as they all pulled from the same point on his battle cruiser's bow.

Four other fleet tugs were standing by, in company. They also would begin pulling once his ship entered the mouth of the Delaware Bay and ocean swells no longer created an untenable risk of damage for the tugs secured alongside. Harvey hoped that would bring the speed of the tow up to 7 knots as the assemblage of ships worked their way up the Delaware River to Philadelphia. Only then could Jensen relax.

He idly wondered who the service would tap to take over the *Belleau Wood* for what would inevitably be a long yard period to repair all the damage. He desperately hoped it would not be him—he hated shipyards.

— —

"Surface," Alfred yelled from the conning tower.

"Blow main ballast, full rise on both planes, both two-thirds power," Dieter commanded in the control room, the roar of high pressure air filling the ballast tanks quickly making further communication difficult. As the sea water was forced out the bottom of the tanks, *U-182* rose; the fair-water and conning tower breaking the surface.

Kruger spun the hand-wheel of the conning tower hatch and pushed it open to a drenching shower of cold seawater. Both he and the *Kommandant* scrambled up to the small bridge of the U-boat. Alfred had a pair of Zeiss binoculars swinging from his neck as he climbed the short ladder.

"Send up the electrician with the lights." Alfred screamed over the noise of the two diesel engines starting to a full throated rumble. Their exhaust would first quickly empty the last of the sea water from the ballast tanks.

"Raise the attack periscope to my mark," he ordered as soon as the lights had been lashed to the scope. "Mark! . . . On running lights, on new lights." Soon Alfred was satisfied that he had turned his surfaced warship into something far more innocent to fool the stupid Americans.

He shouted down the hatch to his first officer, "Action stations."

— • —

"Surface lookouts report a trawler bearing three-four-zero."

"Very well," Harvey Jensen acknowledged. *I guess I should expect that there might be a few still out trying to make a living, especially if they are too small to be of use to the Navy.* There was no need to worry.

T . . . twang! startled him. What had happened? He turned to his JA phone-talker, "Forecastle report status of tow."

It wasn't long in coming and the news was not good. *Potawatomi*'s towing hawser had parted where it had left *Belleau Wood*'s bow chock. *Wenatchee*'s was also fraying. The tow was going to have to stop while new hawsers were rigged or other fleet tugs in company would have to take over pulling his battle cruiser to safety.

Harvey turned to his JA talker, "Do you have the signal bridge on the circuit?"

"No, sir"

There was nothing to do except grab a signal pad and write out what he wanted sent to the tow master. "Messenger of the watch, take this to the signal bridge and have them man the JA phones." Another example of the lousy training and micro management of Kevin Bailey, without a functioning 21MC, the signal bridge had not seen the necessity of manning the phones continuously or perhaps there were just not enough signalmen left. Shortly though the one remaining signal light on *Belleau Wood* began clattering out the message.

"Signal bridge is on the phones," reported the JA talker. "Tow master is ordering *Lakhota* and *Navajo* to take over the tow. *Potawatomi*'s towing winch was damaged by the rebounding hawser. It will take about a half-hour for the new tugs to prepare their hawsers. He requests that our forecastle be lit with the signal light to assist."

"Very well, Make to DESRON Thirty. Tow will have to stop while towing tugs are changed." After this message was sent, his only signal light would have to be trained on the forecastle for illumination. His ability to command the tow would have to wait until the replacement tugs had passed their hawsers and were ready to proceed.

— —

So far, so good, thought *Kapitänleutnant* Alfred Kuhn, those stupid Americans must have bought my ruse, as he clipped his binoculars into the bearing transmitter on the bridge. He could just make out the capital ship before him. There was a destroyer on his port bow about fifteen hundred meters away and he dared not approach it closer.

Suddenly a blinding light illuminated the bow of his target. *God this ship was huge!*

"*Herr Kaleu*, that destroyer is moving off," Schmitt reported.

Alfred looked up, but his night vision had been destroyed looking at the magnified illuminated bow of his target. He could not see the destroyer. He would have to rely completely on Schmitt as his lookout.

"Attack procedures," he yelled down the hatch. He wanted to get closer but dared not for fear of other escorts. Based on size alone, he judged he was within range of the G7e torpedoes he had onboard.

There was another shape moving past his field of view illuminated by the light. What was it? The silhouette did not remind him of any warship. How far away was it? Were there others? The few other surface attacks he had made were on moonlit nights. Even in that dark, he had been able to see much better. How much should he risk? Should he get any closer?

Suddenly another light illuminated the aft end of a small ship off the bow of his target. What was that? What were they doing? Why did these ships suddenly need lights?

Dieter yelled up from the control room, "Ready, *Herr Kaleu.*"

"We will fire four torpedoes spread from aft to forward two degrees offset between torpedoes. Set running depth at fifteen meters!" Alfred hoped that running depth which was the deepest setting available would be sufficient to run under his target and detonate under the torpedo defenses.

"*Jawohl, Herr Kaleu*, aft to forward, two degrees between shots, run depth fifteen meters," Dieter answered barely audible above the diesels trying to cram as much power into the battery as time on the surface would allow.

"Set target speed at two knots."

"Target speed set."

"Final bearing; *Mark!*" Alfred pressed the buzzer on the bearing transmitter. The next command was the simplest. "*Torpedos Los!*"

— —

"Captain, that trawler is still on a collision course." *Belleau Wood*'s Officer of the Deck reported. "Should we turn on navigation lights red over red to have them bear-off?"

Harvey Jensen thought for a moment. Yes it was a good idea; with his forecastle brilliantly illuminated two red lights even though high up on his mast would not make much difference even if they were only on for a few minutes. "Energize red over red navigation lights."

Captain Jensen went out on the port walkway and raised his 7 x 50 binoculars to gauge the trawler's reaction to his navigation lights. What was he looking at—a low pilot house with a mast; the trawling lights clearly visible, but was the foredeck that low, were the swells actually breaking on it? There was something dimly visible ahead of that pilot house, what was it? Harvey was wracking his brain when suddenly those navigation lights went out. Was it his imagination or did it seem that the masthead lights had gotten lower?

Why did that trawler suddenly turn off their navigation lights just after he had turned his on? *It was a deck gun!!!*

He leaped into the secondary conning station. "JA talker. Signal bridge use anything and make to COMDESRON Thirty. Submarine bearing three-four-zero. Range four thousand yards." Officer of the Deck, "Man battle-stations, sound the collision alarm." He didn't even have a functioning announcing system; well maybe the alarms still worked.

— —

"*Alarm!*" Alfred yelled down the hatch. The bearing transmitter was below and the electrician had just dropped into the conning tower with the "navigation lights". Schmitt was next, then Alfred too dropped into the small conning tower, pushing the electrician out of the way. Schmitt pulled the lanyard of the hatch until it shut with a clang and the *Kommandant* spun the hand-wheel to lock it shut against the inevitable depth charges.

"Depth fifty meters. Full ahead both."

"Fifty meters, aye, *Kapitan*," Dieter answered as both planesmen had their control surfaces on full dive.

"Motor room answers both full ahead," the helmsman next sang out.

Alfred had to wait half a minute until *U-182* was fully submerged before he could order the rudder over and a course change to three-zero-zero. "Quartermaster, take a sounding."

"Ah . . . depth of water seventy-five meters, *Herr Kaleu*," as Kruger converted the depth beneath the keel from the fathometer into water depth based upon the depth gauge reading at the time of the sounding.

"Torpedo room load the garbage, mattresses, and floatable objects into tube one."

"On ordered depth *Herr Kaleu*," Dieter reported a smile growing on his face as he realized what his *Kommandant* had been planning all along.

Alfred and Dieter stared at each other. Would the course change be enough to get clear? Would the Americans think that they would try to escape to the northeast rather than to the west-north-west? The move to shallower water was illogical. Only time would tell and what of his four torpedoes, each with two hundred kilograms of hexanite wakelessly running toward that capital ship?

— —

Commander John Badger had been in command of the destroyer *James Lawrence* for a little less than a year, since he had formed up the new construction crew, taken his ship through shake down, and finished the training program specified by Rear Admiral Gregory Tuttle (Commander Destroyer Force Atlantic) under the critical eye of Captain Jones and his team. The *Lawrence* had done well enough to now be assigned to Destroyer Squadron Thirty.

That was all behind his ship and he was currently snoozing in his cubbyhole of a sea cabin aft of the bridge, fully dressed in long sleeve khakis but without tie and shoes; he lay under a grey blanket. His current assignment was to patrol on the aft starboard quarter of the battle cruiser *Belleau Wood*, while the fleet tugs *Lakhota* and *Navajo* rigged towing hawsers to recommence moving the capital ship toward the entrance of the Delaware Bay.

The buzzer near his head woke him. Instantly alert, John grabbed the sound powered phone handset from its metal holder and spoke, "Captain" as the mouthpiece came near his lips.

"Captain, Commodore is signaling," his Officer of the Deck reported.

"Very well, I am on my way," was all he needed to say; quickly replacing the handset in the dull red illumination of his sea cabin. He slipped on his black leather sea boots (much faster than shoes that needed tying), opened the cabin door and was on his destroyer's bridge in less than thirty seconds.

"Captain, the Commodore has ordered us to investigate the trawler bearing three-one-eight and warn them off of the tow."

"Very well, acknowledge! What do we have on the SG radar?"

"That's odd, the trawler's lights went out and the radar contact has disappeared," his OOD reported.

"Man battle stations." John Badger knew that it had to be a submarine and a German one at that since he had used a ruse to get close on the surface. He punched the sonar button on the 21MC (Captain's command announcing circuit). "Sonar, search a sector forty degrees each side of the bow. Officer of the Deck, come to course three-one-eight at two-thirds speed." The last thing he did was start his stop watch.

— —

This was the hard part. It was easy when you could see what was around you. On the surface, everything was clear and his U-boat's small silhouette made an easy assumption that what he could see would not, in all likelihood, see him. Even submerged at periscope depth, he could see and gain that priceless perspective on what was around *U-182*; but now, at fifty meters, everything was guesswork. His ears, actually those of *Oberfunkmaat* Ehrlichmann, now could only estimate the actions of his enemy.

"*Herr Kaleu*, one contact is growing louder, bearing about two-two-five. Probably one of the escorts, but he is not increasing speed. I only get a turn count of about eighty."

That would be a destroyer, investigating and searching. "Can you tell how the bearing is changing?"

"The contact is drawing to the left I think. I can't tell for certain, but he appears to be on a steady course."

Alfred knew from experience that this was actually bad. He could not tell if his enemy had contact or not. He was acting as if he did not, but now the British had learned not to charge immediately—lull the U-boat into thinking they did not have contact while they carefully evaluated attack options.

— —

"Battle-stations manned and ready", the new OOD reported.

"Very well," John Badger answered. He had moved over to the plot where one of his petty officers was marking the destroyer's position on a sheet of paper taped to the top of the DRAI (Dead Reckoning Analyzer Indicator) as the "bug" moved in response to inputs from the gyro compass and the underwater log for his course and speed.

"Conn, Sonar, contact bearing three-four-five relative, range one-six-hundred yards, down Doppler."

"Sonar, conn, aye", the Officer of the Deck answered while John looked at the location laid down from his own ship's position on the DRAI. *What to do, he could turn and run right at the submarine and immediately attack or could he lull his enemy into thinking that he had not been found?* Doctrine

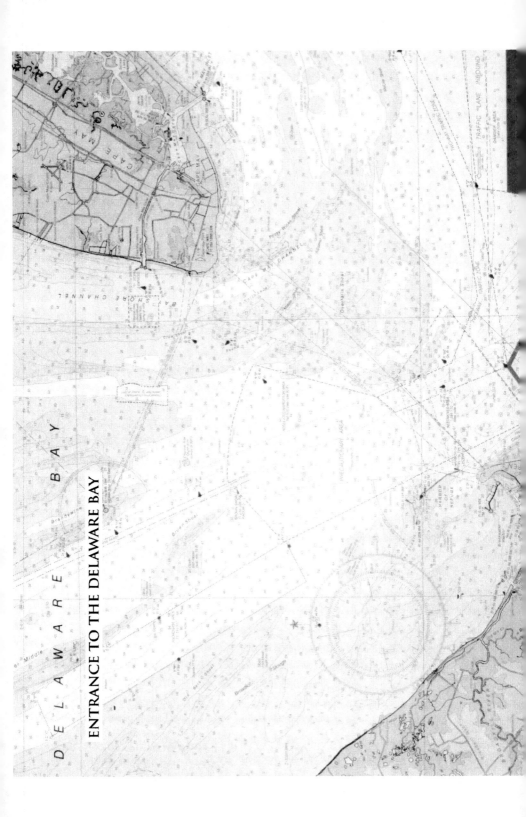

DELAWARE BAY

ENTRANCE TO THE DELAWARE BAY

recommended an immediate attack.

He punched the 21MC for the signal bridge. "Signal Bridge, make to *Belleau Wood*. Submarine bearing three-three-five from you. Make to COMDESRON Thirty. Submarine contact bearing three-zero-three, range one-six-hundred from me; request additional destroyer."

"Conn, Signal Bridge, *Belleau Wood* and COMDESRON Thirty acknowledge."

The TBS (Talk between Ships) speaker began to bark. It was the Commodore of Destroyer Squadron Thirty, "Foxhound (the call sign for the *James Lawrence*), Beagle (the call sign for the *Jesse Elliot*), this is Hunt-Master, coordinate, prosecute the contact."

John Badger waited a moment to be sure the Commodore had stopped talking and then keyed the mike for the TBS, "Foxhound roger."

Quickly he heard Mike Siegel's voice, "Beagle roger." The Commodore had picked the *Elliot* even though she was on the other side of the formation so that the remaining destroyers could cover the gaps. It did not matter to John, but he was senior and would do the coordination.

"Beagle, this is Foxhound; come up on my port side. Expedite." It wouldn't take Mike long at the 24 knot stationing speed the Commodore had specified earlier. He just prayed that the *Elliot* didn't collide with anything as she wove her way through the maze of the tow and escorts.

— —

"No!" Harvey Jensen inadvertently screamed as the first towering water column rose just forward of Number I main battery turret. *Belleau Wood*'s deck heaved and shook as the force of the explosion dissipated into her bowels. No sooner than the first column of water began to fall on the main deck, than it was replaced by a second farther forward, and then a third nearer still to the bow. "JA talker, is Damage Control Central on the line?"

"Yes, Captain."

"Pass to DC Central. 'Report status.'"

It seemed like an eternity, before the report came back as

Belleau Wood slowly began to list to starboard. Harvey had to think, what else did he need to worry about immediately? "Pass to the forecastle. 'Report status of personnel and the progress of replacing the towing hawsers'."

It was the JA talker trying to catch his attention, "Captain, forecastle reports that some personnel caught up in the lifelines, cuts and abrasions, but nothing serious. They are double leather wrapping the hawsers now where they go through the fairlead."

"Very well." Was it his imagination or was the list to starboard starting to lessen.

"Captain. DC Central reports flooding in the forward hold and second platform storerooms. The forward Damage Control party is shoring bulkheads and decks. DC Central is pumping liquids to counteract the list. Turret Number I magazines are dry."

— —

"All ahead one third," *Argonne*'s Conning Officer ordered as they approached the entrance to the Delaware Bay. "Captain, lookouts are reporting the pilot boat in sight."

"Very well, Officer of the Deck. Prepare to take the pilot onboard on the port side." Sheppard would soon be able to relax a little in the confines of the Delaware, safe from German torpedoes.

"Conning station, radio central, 'Commander Destroyer Squadron Thirty reports that *Belleau Wood* has been torpedoed and requests release of our escorts,'" the 21MC shattered Sheppard's illusion of safety. A quick answer on the squawk box and a curt. "Quartermaster, report the depth of water." Sheppard could see Cape Henlopen fine on the port bow with Cape May light house, dark but visible through his binoculars bearing zero-zero-five.

"Captain, Navigator, depth of water is eighty feet, but the approach to the Delaware was sixty to sixty-five feet."

Another indication that Art Roberts was a good officer; he was telling Sheppard not only what he had asked for, but more importantly, put it in context of what was important to a submarine. "Very well." He took the microphone for the TBS, "Akita (call sign for the *John C. McCloy*), Coonhound (call sign for the *George Charrette*), this is Panther; Detach, return to Hunt-Master, expedite; acknowledge."

"Akita, roger."

"Coonhound, roger."

Sheppard watched as both destroyers peeled outboard, their sterns settling in growing phosphorescent wakes, their bows climbing the pressure wave ahead—accelerating toward 40 knots. *Had he made the wrong decision, was Argonne still in danger?*

— —

"Beagle, this is Foxhound. U-boat bears two-nine-five from me, range one-two-hundred yards.

"Beagle, roger"

"Beagle, I want you to lay a sixteen charge pattern on the contact. Set charges at one-fifty, and two-hundred. Set the charges from your K-guns at one-seventy-five.

"This is Beagle, roger, set charges at one-fifty, two-hundred, and one-seventy-five."

"Beagle, approach at twenty-four knots, I'll provide vectors and course corrections. Drop on my mark."

"This is Beagle, roger."

John Badger hunched over the chart table as the DRAI bug slowly moved. The quartermaster now on a sound powered phone headset to cut the noise on the Conn, laid down bearings and ranges to the U-boat every minute on the minute. Another plotter was marking the range and bearing to the Jesse Elliot from the SG radar. It wasn't the greatest system, but it was the best that John and his officers had come up with. He owed a lot to Commander Johnny Walker of the Royal Navy. He had managed to spend several weeks with him while on a liaison tour to Vice Admiral Ramsey's staff in Dover.

"Beagle, come to course three-two-four, submarine is one-oh, double oh yards ahead."

"This is Beagle, roger."

— —

He had made his attack well. As the torpedo run time had reached three-minutes fifteen-seconds, the first explosion of two-hundred kilograms of hexanite had detonated. With each explosion his control room had burst into cheers. Now as the reverberations of his success began to die away, the success was over, he was now the hunted with no more ability to counter his approaching tormentors.

"*Herr Kaleu,* there is a second set of high speed screws bearing about one-five-zero. There is not yet a bearing drift."

These Americans were being very smart about their approach. "Ehrlichmann, is the first destroyer still echo ranging and drawing to the left?"

"*Jawoll, Herr Kaleu*"

Sweat began to form on the brow of *Kapitänleutnant* Alfred Kuhn. He had expected the American destroyer to immediately charge him and wildly throw depth charges at the *U-182*. That would give him his opening to exploit their naiveté in anti-submarine warfare. But this American, the one in the first destroyer had not taken his bait. He doubted that his three hits on that massive ship would sink it. It obviously had already been damaged. Had he been foolish, had his own inexperience as a captain and his ego gotten the better of him?

— —

The submarine was maneuvering. It was accelerating and turning rapidly left. "Quartermaster, lay down bearings and ranges to the sub every thirty seconds." *Now what, he had to guess—factor in the turning radius of the Jesse Elliot. Would a maneuver at the last instant slow her so much that her own depth charges would damage her? If the first attack was going to disable that U-boat he had to make a change.*

"Beagle, this is Foxhound, come to course two-seven-zero sharply, increase speed."

"This is Beagle, roger, coming to course two-seven-zero. Will roll and shoot charges on your mark."

In his mind, Commander John Badger drew a circle around the plot of Jesse Elliot's position—the lethal radius of her depth charge attack, moving it invisibly as his estimate on his sister-ship's position changed second by second. It always boiled down to the skill of the commanding officer—the years of experience at sea. The time spent thinking through the problem, training the crew, integrating the pieces. It all came down to this moment.

"Mark, mark, mark!!"

"Beagle, open to the west about one-five-hundred yards, slow to ten knots and attempt to gain sonar contact. Foxhound will make the next attack."

"This is Beagle, roger."

— —

Ka-boom!!! The first depth charge exploded aft of the *U-182*—then another to starboard. More and more rained down on the U-boat. Light bulbs shattered. Bolt-heads ricocheted about every compartment. Water sprayed on electrical equipment producing a shower of sparks as dead-shorts caused by the seawater sprayed molten copper. Some men screamed—others silently prayed.

Alfred Kuhn knew that he had made a mistake. He should have changed depth as well as altered course. The depth charges were detonating at the same depth his boat fought to remain under control. "Fire tube one," he screamed. He was desperate to stop the damage being inflicted on his submarine.

The order was quickly relayed to the torpedo room and the load of flotsam and jetsam headed toward the surface contained within rapidly expanding bubbles of air.

"Engineer, release five-hundred liters of fuel." Alfred did not know but that order was unnecessary as one of the fuel ballast tanks had ruptured and tonnes of diesel were on the way to the surface. He looked over at the depth gage slowly winding its way deeper as the boat grew heavier from the in-rushing sea.

"Stop both." It was time to settle to the bottom and complete his ruse. His thoughts were interrupted by reports of flooding in the motor room and the after torpedo room.

— —

"Foxhound, this is Beagle, gained faint contact bearing zero-eight-five, range one-two-hundred, no doppler."

"This is Beagle, roger." Now it was the *James Lawrence*'s turn.

"Quartermaster. report sounding at the contact's position from the *Jesse Elliot*."

"Forty-two fathoms, Captain."

"Officer of the Deck, set depth charges two-hundred-twenty-five feet. I am going to use an eleven charge pattern." Glancing at the chart, guessing his turning radius and acceleration, his next order would send them to the attack. "Come to course two-four-seven, and increase speed to full."

"Aye, aye, Captain."

What had he forgotten? This was a new feeling—this attempt to kill. This enemy had tried to sink the ship he had been guarding. Was his attack revenge for the sailors killed or wounded on *Belleau Wood*? Was it just another ugly event in an infinite series of ugly events called war? Did that absolve him of the deaths of his enemy?

"Roll charges!" The first one silently fell into his destroyer's wake but the thunder of the K-guns heralded others thrown to port and starboard matching others rolled from the stern racks. Each charge had 600 pounds of TNT. It was lethal to any submarine if it exploded within 28 feet of the hull—extensive damage if within forty.

Another set of depth charges were detonating around *U-182*. Reports from the aft torpedo room and the motor room stated that seems in the pressure hull had been broken. There was no hope of lifting his submarine off the bottom.

In a way it was a blessing when a depth charge exploded close to the control room rupturing the hull. Alfred Kuhn's last conscious thought as his lungs rebelled against the sea water entering them was, "*I was foolish to attack!*"

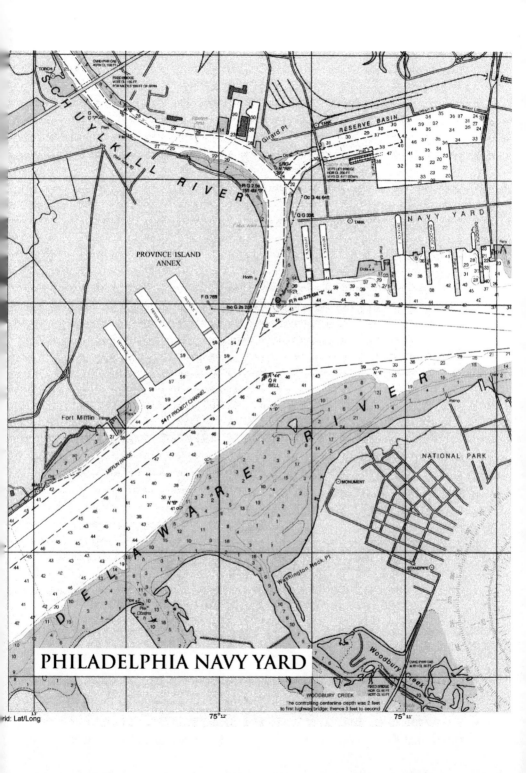

PHILADELPHIA NAVY YARD

2

HIDING IN PLAIN SIGHT

SHE LANGUISHED IN THE sublime knowledge of their love. She luxuriated in the respite they had together. She knew she had to share his affection, share his attention, his devotion. She intuitively guessed that she always had; but it was a small price to pay for their magnificent life together. He could promise nothing but pain, ask anything of her, demand her best, and she would willingly comply. Fate had brought them together. It would take fate to tear them apart.

As she rested, rejuvenating in his support, she knew her skills to support him were improving. She was becoming the perfect companion for a rising star. As he succeeded in his career so did she. It was invigorating being with him, but there was still the dark side of his troubled soul. Oh, if she could only heal the pain, remove the guilt, restore the indomitable spirit he once had, all would be perfect.

— —

"*Torpedo Los!*" *Korvettenkapitän* Conrad Kluge gave the order sending his last G7e electric torpedo on toward a median sized freighter. Snapping the periscope handles up, he grabbed the hydraulic hoist lever sending the attack scope back down to rest on the boat's keel. Conrad was disappointed that this was not a significant target, just one more allied merchant in the war of attrition on Britain's lifeline. He looked at his second in command carefully timing the torpedo run. Three seconds before the stop watch reached zero, a loud explosion reverberated through *U-197*. His crew cheered and clapped each other on the back—another kill, another success.

He had been off on his estimation of the target's range—not by much but enough that the hit was probably in a forward hold rather than the engine room he aimed for.

The swishing noise of the periscope hoist stopped at his action on the control lever of the attack scope, just high enough to clear the water from the head-window for an observation. Bending over, quickly he grabbed the handles and swung the periscope around covering the horizon and searching for any aircraft in the vicinity alerted by his attack.

Finally satisfied for the safety of his boat and crew, Kluge allowed himself the pleasure of a lingering look at his target. Well down by the bow, the crew was feverishly working to take the canvas cover off a lifeboat. Other men were starting to swing the davits outboard and lower their only hope into the ever decreasing distance to the sea. They were only about 40 nautical miles from the mouth of the Delaware River and those men should be able to row ashore in a day or two if they were not picked up by another ship.

Another sweep of the horizon and air space in his vicinity as the freighter's bow slipped beneath the waves. Her stern rose and then began accelerating in the inevitable plunge to the bottom. She must have been carrying a heavy cargo to plunge so quickly—perhaps tanks or other armored vehicles. Conrad wondered what he had just saved Germany from; that ship's contribution to the allied war effort. Well it would have been easy to surface and question the survivors, perhaps throwing them some bread to loosen their tongues. But the intelligence was not worth the risk so close to the American coast.

Lowering the periscope, Kluge ordered 50 meters. At that depth, with the dark paint on *U-197's* horizontal surfaces he had nothing to fear from air patrols. Dropping into the control room, the quartermaster's chart commanding his attention now—each kill had been carefully plotted with a dark black *X,* seemingly spread well around his patrol area. That was his intent. Conrad Kluge was no fool. His Knight's Cross left in the cubbyhole of a stateroom proved his prowess not only at sinking ships, but seeing to the safety of his command.

The observations he had made of shipping too distant to attack were also plotted, though not as boldly and color coded to show daylight observations or those at night. The numerous sightings clearly showing the shipping lanes merchant captains inadvertently followed trying to please the ships' owners with quick and efficient passages.

Well, all he had left for his few remaining days on station before his fuel supply dictated a long return to his base in France was his 10.5 cm deck gun. Surface attacks trying to sink ships with shell fire dictated being on the surface at night. Even those could be tricky if an unseen warship suddenly arrived. This far from Le Havre though also dictated not returning before he had expended his ammunition as well as his torpedoes. However successful he had been, Admiral Karl Dönitz would criticize the patrol for wasting fuel carting cannon ammunition to the shores of America only to bring it back.

— —

Sheppard and Evelyn had just returned from the memorial service for the officers and men of *Belleau Wood* that had perished in the Battle of Cape Vilan. Lori Ingraham had arranged for them to stay in the guest house on the grounds of the Philadelphia Navy Yard, which gave Sheppard respite from the reporters that always seemed to know where he was going when off of Navy property. Sheppard was at a loss to understand what all the fuss was about. Evelyn understood the need of the American public for good news and the hero that created it. Trying to explain it to her husband; however, was beyond even her considerable abilities.

Evelyn was removing her hat and Sheppard his cover when a gray Navy sedan pulled up in front of the house and a petty officer jumped out. He ran around to the right rear door and opened it as an officer with four rings of gold braid circling his left shoulder jumped out of the left rear door. An elderly gentleman in a gray worsted suit wearing a fedora stepped out of the right side and headed up the path to the front door. Medium height, but still reasonably slender with neatly trimmed nearly white hair, Sheppard wasn't sure who the distinguished visitor might be.

"Good afternoon, Sheppard. And this lovely woman must be Evelyn. Your picture at the luncheon with Eleanor Roosevelt doesn't do you justice," he began. "I am John Hamblen."

"Admiral, I am sorry that I didn't recognize you out of uniform. Would you please come in and have a seat."

"Thank you." Turning the admiral addressed his aide, "Lieutenant Halverson, please wait outside, I'll only be a few minutes."

"Admiral, may I brew you some coffee or tea," Evelyn offered.

"Yes, coffee please," Admiral Hamblen said as an excuse for Evelyn to leave the room.

As she left, he began, "Sheppard, I wanted to personally thank you for what you have done for my son. I have not seen him this enthusiastic about the service since he was a boy."

"Admiral, he saved all of us from a potentially disastrous situation. He is a good officer. I just had to undo some things that happened to him on the *Boone*."

"I know; I am sure Junior told you about how that came about."

"Yes, sir."

"Sheppard, what I really wanted to talk to you about was the business of you being a war criminal. I have investigated with Navy JAG, and you acted within the Geneva conventions. Whatever you may personally feel, the blood of those German sailors you killed is on the hands of that madman Hitler. Unfortunately, raising that issue in your report has allowed your enemies an opening to spread rumors and prevent the Senate from immediately promoting you to Rear Admiral."

"Admiral, I understand what you say. I didn't want the German propaganda machine to make an issue of something about which our government didn't have the facts."

"Sheppard, trust me when I say, that was appreciated in Washington. Rear Admiral Richard Troubridge must have quite an axe to grind with you to start the rumors that he did with Senator Russell."

"Yes, sir, he does. When I was at the Bureau of Ordnance, he made a proposal for a rocket propelled mine clearing device that would run up on a beach and clear out any land mines that might be there. I opposed it. He swore he would never forgive me."

"I remember the proposal. I agree with you, that damn thing would never have worked, but Admiral Troubridge is one hard headed SOB. He is also a good officer, when he is sober. You are not the only one that he has unjustifiably hurt. His inebriated memory destroyed my friend Husband Kimmel."

"I am sorry to hear that. I always thought Admiral Kimmel was railroaded as a scapegoat for Pearl Harbor."

"Well, Sheppard, what is done is done and nothing can be accomplished about it now. I just wanted to let you know that the service will see to it the Admiral Troubridge is assigned somewhere he can't start any more Washington rumors. I also wanted to tell you that when the next Flag Selection Board meets, I for one will write a letter on your behalf. I know there will be others."

"Thank you, Admiral."

"Please give my apologies to Evelyn for not staying. I really need to get back to Washington. The President has called me to a meeting tomorrow about a mission for the new strategic intelligence service that I head. Good luck and thank you again for helping my son."

"Please don't mention it, Admiral," Sheppard concluded as he walked the Admiral to the door. Lieutenant Halverson was holding the sedan door open for the Admiral. As soon as John Hamblen the 3rd got in, his aide climbed in the left side and the car sped off.

As if on cue, Evelyn came in with a silver tray of coffee cups, saucers, sugar bowl, and cream server. "Where is the Admiral?"

"He had to leave, something about a meeting with the President."

"Darling, you know these walls are paper thin." Evelyn ran her fingers through his hair—more grey at the temples now than the last time they had been together, though still black and full.

"Yes, dear, but let's not get ahead of ourselves. It is going to be a long war and anything can happen between now and when the Board meets."

"Well, darling, I am just as glad he left. I have something else planned for a lazy May afternoon," she said with a come-hither look, her lithe frame arched, allowing her auburn tresses to frame her creamy white complexion. She kissed him full on the lips, her tongue meeting his. Sheppard smiled, took the tray and set it on the coffee table, sweeping her off her feet, and carried her upstairs as smoothly as his game leg could manage.

— —

Corporal Pease was waiting at attention when Sheppard came out of the guest quarters at 0700 on Monday May 18th. Evelyn stood at the door to wave goodbye with her usual total lack of propriety. Dressed only in Sheppard's uniform shirt from the previous day, there wasn't a man on the planet that would not look lustfully at her beauty. Corporal Pease, however, was too disciplined a Marine to start any rumors of the Captain's wife's attire or the Captain's virility, contrary to Evelyn's intentions for the latter. Sheppard had long since stopped trying to tame his wife's wild side. Getting her to conform to the Navy's white gloves and hat etiquette in their personal life was impossible. Besides, he reveled in it. Most men away at sea would worry about faithfulness, but Evelyn had spurned every advance and was completely at peace with the mate she had selected. Sheppard had always been amazed at the faithfulness of her correspondence since the first day they met his senior year at the Academy. She had picked him but it took two years and a Pacific assignment for him to realize that she was a jewel and he needed to make their relationship permanent.

The superintendent of the yard had been kind enough to provide a sedan for his use and the Marine orderlies were assigned as his drivers. Corporal Pease gave a smart salute with his usual, "Good morning, how is the Captain today?" as he held the right rear door open for Sheppard.

"Fine, thank you, Corporal Pease; and how are you today?" Sheppard enjoyed teasing his orderlies about the Marine tradition of addressing people in the third person. Corporal Pease smiled in response but refused to answer. Sheppard knew the standard return was "Yew, what do I look like a female sheep;" but they would never tell him that. Still the morning exchange brought smiles to both of them and set a pleasant tone for the day.

Corporal Pease shut the door and accelerated off toward the Platt Bridge and Province Island where the West Annex to the Philadelphia Navy Yard was located with its immense construction docks—numbers 7, 8, and 9. Each dock was well over a quarter mile long, the better part of a football field wide, with 54 feet over the sill at mean low water. Designed and constructed to support the fleet expansion authorized in the mid 1930's, the latest battleships were already beginning to tax their dimensions. *Argonne* was currently located in number 7. Aligned to a bearing of 325 degrees, the dock was adequate for the main battery realignment that Sheppard wanted to conduct. Any orientation would do for a batten beam procedure, but Sheppard had directed his Gunnery Officer, Commander Chuck Williamson, to align the 18-inch guns to the North Star.

There were some benefits to being a national hero and Sheppard had made sure that his personal status translated to benefits for his crew and ship. The Shipyard Superintendent had promised any support that he could as long as *Argonne* left the dry dock on time. The four new ice cream machines installed in each of the crew's messes, the chief's quarters, and the wardroom would contribute more to morale than any non-sailor would ever understand. There was one personal luxury that he was allowing himself by having the yard install a standard shipboard bunk for his personal use in his cabin. A bed even if the same size just didn't feel right aboard ship.

Argonne's repair would only require about two weeks of the dry dock's schedule for the propeller change, turret alignments, and repair of the damage suffered in the Battle of Cape Vilan. *Belleau Wood's* repair would delay the next battleship by the better part of a year to repair her hull damage and rudder machinery. That would give Captain Greg Anderson, formerly of the light cruiser *Colchester*, a chance to learn his ship and start a training program undoing the damage done by Kevin Bailey. *Colchester* had performed well in the battle and Sheppard in his reports had made certain to commend Greg's leadership and tactical acumen in the employment of *Colchester* and *Burlington*. It was ironic that Greg's reassignment meant the loss of Sheppard's Engineer Officer Andy Scott. He was transferred as soon as *Argonne* was docked to relieve Greg on *Colchester*.

As Corporal Pease drove up to the brow, Sheppard could see the side-boys forming up. Despite his urging, his Executive Officer Ted Grabowski had not relented to Sheppard's request to do away with the quarterdeck ceremonies that he hated. Ted had a good point—that Sheppard would notice any errors and correct them before *Argonne* offended an important visitor. He knew it was good practice for when it counted in making an impression. Nevertheless, Sheppard did not have to enjoy it.

Sheppard started across the aft starboard brow to the quarterdeck. About half way Coxswain Jacob Bergman started the call *Over the Side* on his boatswain's pipe, "sssssssssssssss sssss sssssssssss"; all four side boys and the officer of the deck saluted on the first note of the call. The pipe was timed so that Sheppard had sufficient time to reach the quarterdeck and salute the Officer of the Deck before it ended. Since it was earlier than the 0800 colors, the national ensign was not flying at the stern and a salute to it was not rendered by Sheppard before he raised his right arm and hand, ramrod straight, to the bill of his gold braided hat in salute to his watch officer. The only imperfection in Sheppard's appearance, a slightly crooked nose, was a continuous reminder of the day he won the light-heavyweight intercollegiate boxing title. Alone among all the sailors and officers who were assigned to *Argonne*, as the Commanding Officer, he did not have to, "Request Permission to Come Aboard!" By tradition and fact, *Argonne* was *his* ship and the deck officer was his representative.

The moment that Sheppard's foot hit the deck, a signalman watching from the signal bridge lowered the *Third-Repeat* from the port yardarm indicating to all ships and the yard that the Captain was back onboard. Sheppard paused for a moment to allow Petty Officer Bergman to remove himself and the side-boys as Corporal Pease followed him across the brow.

"Good morning, Lieutenant Hamblen, I see that you have a new officer under your instruction this morning."

"Yes, Captain, may I introduce Ensign William Fairchild. He reported aboard shortly after we docked and the Commander assigned him to me for orientation and instruction."

"Good morning, Mr. Fairchild, I look forward to meeting you officially later today." Bergman had gone to the microphone for the General Announcing system or 1MC as it was called. He keyed the system and gave the call, *Word to be Passed*, s$^{\text{s-s-s-}}$^{ssssss}, followed by, "*Argonne* arriving." Now everyone onboard knew that Sheppard had returned to the ship.

Scared speechless by this national hero, Will Fairchild was unable to respond. Sheppard sensed his difficulty and promptly asked John Hamblen if anything of significance had occurred during the night. When John responded in the negative Sheppard left with Corporal Pease in tow. He knew that John would give Will the correct perspective on how to deal with Sheppard in the future. It was not the first time nor would it be the last that a brand new Ensign, his head filled with horror stories from his instructors concerning the power of ship Commanding Officers, had been rendered incapable of the simplest actions when introduced to their first.

Corporal Pease fell in one pace behind and to the left of Sheppard as they walked forward along the starboard side of *Argonne's* main deck. In port, the starboard side was reserved for the commanding officer's use and any official guests that he entertained. On most ships, if the crew had a limitation on paint or time, the starboard side still got the most attention and remained the best maintained by the deck gang. Sheppard, though, made sure that both sides of his ship were maintained the same. He was not going to create a false impression of the true nature of his command.

When they arrived at the passage door to Sheppard's in-port cabin on the starboard side forward, just aft of Number II main battery turret, Corporal Pease posted himself at parade rest outside. Sheppard entered and was greeted by his steward, Officer's Steward first class George Washington Carver Jefferson, "Morn'in Cap'n, It is another fine Navy Day," holding a steaming mug of black coffee for the Captain.

"That it is, Petty Officer Jefferson, and good morning to you too." Sheppard smiled, he never tired of this morning ritual that he had with Jefferson ever since he had met him on his second command, the light cruiser *Lancaster*. Jefferson, by hook or crook, had managed to remain with Sheppard on each of his ships since that time. If what Admiral Hamblen said was true, Sheppard could make their relationship permanent as a flag officer.

"Captain, would you like the usual for breakfast, or something special? I whipped up some blueberry muffins this morning."

"Jefferson, those muffins sound wonderful, I'll have them along with the usual."

Corporal Pease made a loud knock and ushered in Radioman first class Sinnett with the morning message boards. As was his custom, Sheppard would read and initial each message that had come to *Argonne* during the night. Usually, Ted Grabowski, Sheppard's executive officer, had seen them already and designated any action that was needed to be taken by *Argonne's* officers before they got to the Captain. Sheppard could then serve as a double check that everything, as it was this morning, had been properly assigned. In addition to messages directed only to *Argonne*, there were also messages that were sent to AIGs that included *Argonne*—in the case of one this morning sent to Scouting Forces Atlantic by Admiral Ingraham.

Jefferson entered Sheppard's stateroom and set out a plate of ham, two eggs fried, corn beef hash and bacon, as well as a dish with three hot muffins wrapped in a linen napkin and a plate with a stick of butter. Jefferson always marveled how Sheppard could eat as much as he did and remain fit and slender.

Sheppard took his time eating as he knew this would be the only peaceful period of his workday. In addition to the morning message boards, he was given a copy of the local morning newspaper, the *Philadelphia Enquirer*. The war news was getting worse. General MacArthur had been forced to retreat off of Luzon onto the Island of Corregidor. Sheppard knew that with the Pacific fleet bottled up in Pearl Harbor, where the narrow channel was blocked by wrecks; there was no hope of relief. It was inevitable that the Japanese would soon have possession of the Philippines and with that conquest, have a free hand throughout Southeast Asia.

No sooner had Jefferson cleared away the breakfast dishes and place setting than his personal yeoman Petty Officer second class Brewster entered with the Captain's schedule for the 18th of May 1942. Sheppard noticed that the first meeting was with the shipyard concerning the installation of the new propellers on *Argonne*. Officially the reason for the docking, he wondered why an additional meeting was needed beyond the routine daily progress meeting with the Engineer.

Corporal Pease knocked and announced *Argonne's* new engineer, Commander Christopher Peterson, who entered with a short stout man in a tweed jacket and bowler hat, whose identity Pease did not know. Sheppard rose greeting his guests with a smile, hand shake and a warm, "Good morning, gentlemen. Would you like a cup of coffee?"

As expected both men nodded. Before Sheppard could say anything, Jefferson entered carrying a gleaming silver tray of mugs and a thermos pitcher of hot strong coffee with a sugar bowl, creamer, and spoons.

Chris started. "Captain, this is Mr. Arthur Hess, the yard supervisor assigned to oversee *Argonne's* refitting here in Philadelphia."

"Mr. Hess, it is a pleasure to make your acquaintance. How can I help you this morning?"

"Captain, may I say that it is a genuine honor to meet the hero of the Battle of Cape Vilan."

"Mr. Hess, the real heroes of that battle are all around you. It was the crew of *Argonne* that achieved the victory in conjunction with the fine crews of the other ships of Admiral Hamilton's task force." Embarrassed, Sheppard wanted to change the subject quickly. "What brings you to *Argonne* this morning?"

"Captain, I am not really the yard supervisor to oversee your refit—that would be Mr. Gregg Feldman. My job in the shipyard is supervisor of the propeller foundry and machine shop. As you know all the propellers of the Navy are made right here at the Philadelphia Navy Yard. We are very proud of that distinction, and with the Superintendent's and Bureau of Construction and Repair's blessing have embarked on an extensive research project to improve the durability of your propellers."

"Mr. Hess, that sounds very interesting but how does it affect *Argonne?*"

"Captain, I know from talking to Commander Peterson that you are aware of the erosion problem with the propellers on this class of battle cruisers. When the lead ship of the class, *Santiago,* came back to Fore River for her post shakedown availability, everyone was surprised at how badly her propellers were eroded and her speed affected in only six months. The Bureau began an immediate investigation to find a better material with which to make large high power screws. There were two promising alloys. The first was a nickel, copper, aluminum, iron and manganese alloy with some other elements in small percentages called Monel K500. The second was a high chromium stainless steel. Both are believed to have much better erosion characteristics than the aluminum bronze with which your old propellers were made."

"Mr. Hess, that is very good to hear, but how can *Argonne* help you in this effort?"

"Captain, the Bureau contracted with us to make a full set of four of each material. We finished the Monel ones last week. I'll tell you that K500 is tough stuff to work with. We went through a full year's worth of tool bits smoothing down the casting. The stainless steel was much easier to work. Let me get to the point.

"Captain, we are going to put one set on *Argonne,* and the other set on the next *Santiago* class battle cruiser to dock. It may well be *Belleau Wood,* but having seen the extent of her damage it probably will be one of the others. Since both sets are currently available, the Bureau thought that since you are here, you might as well get your choice."

"Mr. Hess, do you have a background in metallurgy?"

"Yes, Captain, but I am a little behind the latest research on these alloys erosion characteristics. My expertise is more in casting than those details of alloy metallurgy. I really can't give you any more information except that we have seen Stainless Steel tend to crack in solutions with chloride salts at high temperature. That should not make a difference in this application."

"Well, Mr. Hess, if it is my decision, I would like to try the Monel propellers, solely on the basis of how tough they were for you to machine."

"Captain, that would have been my choice also. Both materials are stronger than the old bronze ones. As a result they are somewhat thinner at the tips. The only change you will notice is the onset of cavitation being at a slightly higher speed.

"We hope that you will give them a good trial and spend as much time as you can at high speed. When you get back, we'll send divers down to inspect and take measurements on the blade wear."

"Mr. Hess, we on *Argonne* will be happy to do what we can to support your trial." Sheppard asked, "When do you think the propeller change will be completed?"

"Captain, you have the highest priority in the shipyard. My orders are to have the change completed by early tomorrow night. We will have four gangs of men simultaneously installing your new screws. The old ones are already removed and the tail shaft surfaces inspected. New keys have been manufactured of the same K-monel. We have been varnishing the mating surfaces of your current tail shafts to minimize the electrical connectivity between the Monel and steel.

"Whoa, Mr. Hess, I am afraid you are way beyond this gunnery specialist's understanding. I trust you to do your best for *Argonne*."

"Thank you, Captain, but from what your officers tell me, you are far more than just a gunnery specialist."

Embarrassed, Sheppard changed the subject. "Is there anything else?"

Taking their cue, both men got up to leave. As Mr. Hess left, Chris Peterson hung back. "Captain, I am sorry that I introduced Mr. Hess incorrectly. He has been here every day fussing about the propeller removal, making sure that everything else was also being addressed. We have all gotten comfortable in going to him with our problems with any of the work being done by the yard. I assumed he was the supervisor in charge of our yard period."

"Chris, it would be an easy mistake to make. Unfortunately, it does lead to something I need to address with the superintendent though. If Mr. Feldman is an unknown to you as Chief Engineer, his absence does not speak well of his capabilities.

"How have the repairs to the hanger, side protective system and bridge been progressing? Will everything be finished with the completion of the propeller change, or will we need additional time alongside in the yard?"

"Captain, everything should be finished by midnight tomorrow, but there will still be a lot of wet paint in the morning."

"Very well, Chris, but make sure the yard does not paint the hanger!"

"Yes sir." Commander Peterson turned and left Sheppard alone with his thoughts of the fire that raged in *Shenandoah's* hanger, betraying his location to the Japanese and leading to the deaths of so many of his men. *I have to focus on the here and now!* Nothing will bring those men back.

"Corporal Pease, please send for Petty Officer Brewster."

Shortly, Sheppard's personal yeoman entered, "Brewster, please coordinate with Commander Grabowski and the Superintendent's office to find a time that is convenient today for me to call on Rear Admiral Utley."

"Yes sir."

Sheppard looked at the schedule that Brewster had coordinated for him today and noticed that he had ten minutes before his Gunnery Officer, Commander Chuck Williamson, was scheduled for a meeting. He went across his stateroom from the large table that sat almost amidships to the desk in the alcove formed by the barbette of the number three six-inch three gun turret. There he took out a pen and some of the "Commanding Officer USS *Argonne*" personal stationary to write a few quick letters.

> *Dear Admiral and Mrs. Ingraham,*
>
> *I can't thank you enough for the kindness that you have shown to Evelyn and I in arranging housing for us in both Philadelphia and Norfolk. It has made a world of difference for the two of us in being together while Argonne has been docked for repairs. I am sure you have had to pull strings to get housing this nice for a battle cruiser captain. I remain in your debt.*
>
> *Sincerely,*
> *Sheppard McCloud*

The next several were to each of his five children. His oldest son, David was flying F4Fs now assigned to the aircraft carrier

President in the Pacific out of San Diego. He knew the rumors about an impending push by the Japanese to finish the job that they had started at Pearl Harbor and hoped that David would survive, but more importantly, be courageous when the time inevitably came to face an enemy bent on killing him. The country needed a victory in that theater of war as badly as it had needed one in the Atlantic. Writing to his son Peter was much easier. At least Peter was still safe at West Point, though Sheppard expected that as an upper-classman Peter and all of his classmates would be accelerated, graduating early to fill officer billets in the rapidly expanding Army. It would not be long before Evelyn would have to worry about two of her sons being at war, as well as her husband.

Corporal Westbrook, having relieved Corporal Pease for the morning watch, knocked and announced Commander Chuck Williamson, showing him into the Captain's stateroom.

"Good morning, Chuck! How is the main battery alignment going?"

"Captain, it is going very well. It is nice to do it in a Navy Yard where everyone is only interested in doing the procedure correctly. The shipyard managed to come up with a few more bore-sight telescopes, breech adaptors, and muzzle targets to let us do an entire turret at once. That has been saving us considerable time and allowed us to get an exact parallel for the guns. We also found that the shimming of the trunnion bearings was off. That error undoubtedly also contributed to the poor alignment done in New York Ship.

"Captain, I may have overstepped my authority invoking your name with respect to the trunnion bearings. I didn't want to disturb you over the weekend."

"Chuck, it is all right. If it was to improve the accuracy of the alignment, you have my blessing. What of replacing our expended special anti-aircraft common projectiles with the radar fuses?"

"Captain, on that issue, I have nothing but good news. The Bureau of Ordnance was so pleased with the results from the Battle of Cape Vilan that they are going to give us replacements up to a total of five thousand of the new five inch shells. I managed to talk them out of another five hundred fuses with adapters that we can use for our six inch or eighteen inch high capacity projectiles. They had wanted to exchange some of our contact fused projectiles for the radar fused ones. Again, I didn't want to disturb you even though the Bureau wanted an immediate answer. When I told them I could not give them one, they suggested a solution allowing my gunner's mates to do the work onboard."

"Chuck, I think it is a good one, as long as your people are comfortable making the fuse changes onboard."

"Captain, Senior Chief Hancock has assured me that we have several gunner's mates who did that very job at an ordnance depot in the past."

"Very well, Chuck, how long would it take to change the fuse on a projectile?"

"About five minutes, Captain, ten if we were careful and had to swap the gains from the contact fuse to the radar fuse."

"Okay, but don't change any of the contact fuses until I tell you. I can't say ahead of time how we would have to use our high capacity shells and you know the restrictions against firing them over enemy held territory."

"Aye, aye, Captain. There is one more thing. The Bureau of Ordnance believes that the flight paths of shells from a turret are still interfering with each other even with our current delay coils. They have new ones that fire the two wing guns simultaneously and the center gun a full two seconds later. I have the Ordalt package but need your permission to install it. We will be the first battle cruiser with this and it should improve the accuracy of our salvos even more."

"Okay, Chuck, install the modification but keep the old delay coils if it doesn't work out."

— —

Almost 4,000 miles to the east-northeast, the last of the 19 gun salute was reverberating from the steel hulls of the German battle fleet anchored in the Jade Bay. *Großadmiral* Erich Raeder, the *Kriegsmarine's* highest ranking officer, had come to meet with *Generaladmiral* Günter Lütjens, *Flottenchef* (Fleet Commander) and Commander of Battleships. Both men knew that the strategic situation was at a critical point. The English newspapers, obtained through Switzerland and Spain, were filled with reports of scrap metal drives and citizens growing victory gardens for food. It was clear to both men that the British were near to starvation and defeat.

The only real question was how best to convince the British Prime Minister that further resistance was futile. The *Luftwaffe* under that fat egomaniac Goering had failed to break the Royal Air Force in almost two years of trying. The vaunted German Army had attempted a landing but when the Royal Navy's destroyer squadrons had attacked, just before dawn, 59,000 soldiers had been killed last year, drowned as their landing barges sank. Lütjens had made certain that the destroyers had paid a heavy price, but the landing force was cut off and eventually surrendered before they could reach London. What damage that had been inflicted on the *Kriegsmarine's* Battle Fleet had been repaired. Unfortunately, the same was true for the Royal Navy. The building race that had been going on for almost two decades was still essentially a tie for their strategic situation, with neither nation able to achieve any clear superiority in the North Sea. At least Hitler was still enamored with the ever larger battleships and battle cruisers that were being constructed at the new building yards in Danzig, Wilhelmshaven, and Hamburg.

The damage done to *Vizeadmiral* Schröder's fleet at the Battle of Cape Vilan had destroyed the plans to use his battle cruisers and carriers to raid the British convoys. There were the outlines of two options now open for discussion. The first appealed to both admirals. If the German battle fleet sortied from the Jade and sought a decisive encounter with the Home Fleet before American reinforcements arrived, German submarines and mines just might be able to ambush the English and bring the two fleets to parity when they fought. The only problem was that *der Führer* did not want to risk his splendid battleships in a fleet action.

The two admirals, both veterans of World War I, marveled at how similar these two wars were being fought. Both Kaiser Wilhelm and Hitler would rather risk millions of men in the Army to unending slaughter than use their navies for a decisive blow to the English supply lines. Germany did not need a navy to survive, but Great Britain did. Conversely, Germany needed her army. For naval officers it was lunacy to risk what was needed and hold back what was not.

That only left the second option. If the fleet sortied as a ruse to cover sending a replacement force for Schröder's fleet north of Iceland, the English Admiral Tovey would not be able to cover both. To protect his base and the British eastern coastline, he would have to keep his fleet concentrated in the North Sea just as Jellicoe had in the first war. What was different this time was that Germany had captured Norway. Despite Raeder's efforts to build bases there, it would still be at least a few months before the battle fleet as a whole could base in Trondheim or a full year if the Vestfjord was used.

There remained the questions of what ships to send and who should command the fleet. Günter did not want to lose the very able commander of his scouting forces, *Admiral* Kummetz. It seemed easier to settle on the ships. *Peter Strasser* and *Manfred von Richthofen,* the two oldest carriers still with the fleet in the Jade, were available for air support. Raeder overruled Lütjens and decided to send the *Freiherr von Seydlitz* class battle cruisers of the 3rd squadron rather than those of the 4th squadron. Taking a lesson from the Battle of Cape Vilan, they decided to send four armored cruisers *Barbarossa, Hansa, Vineta,* and *Freya;* and six light cruisers and two full squadrons of Z.49 class destroyers would provide anti-submarine protection and screening. A few of the remaining scout cruisers would provide reconnaissance and support to the destroyers if ordered to conduct a torpedo attack.

Unspoken was the concern that the main fleets were being too depleted. That left the thorny issue of command of this now rather considerable force. The various candidates were debated for over an hour. Those officers who were sufficiently "air minded" were too junior in comparison to *Konteradmiral* Pauli Hartmann, the commander of the 3rd battle cruiser squadron. Eventually they settled on *Vizeadmiral* Joachim Moeller. Joachim was not an aviator, but had demonstrated a good understanding of the use of aviation in the last tabletop war game that *Generaladmiral* Lütjens had conducted for his flag officers.

Raeder assured Lütjens that *der Führer* had approved the operation in principle, though Lütjens still had his doubts. His predecessor had been summarily dismissed for using the fleet contrary to Hitler's orders. He was not going to make that mistake. His last comment to Erich as he got ready to depart the flagship, *Frundsberg,* was that he would make the arrangements necessary, but would not sail a ship until he received an order directly from Hitler's headquarters.

— —

"Alard, it is so good to see you. Will you please come in out of the rain?" Madame D'Aubigné extended her ivory right hand for her guest to kiss. Of medium height, still slender and strikingly beautiful with her green eyes and raven tresses even in her mid-fifties, Daphne D'Aubigné was lord of all she surveyed in the absence of her husband.

"*Merci, madame.*"

"Welcome to Chateau D'Aubigné. It has been too long since your last visit. I only wish my husband could be here to welcome an old friend."

"*Oui, madame,* but I would wish the circumstances of my visits were different. Perhaps one day we can meet without the need for me to smuggle your prized art to Switzerland."

"Yes, Alard, but our brave sailors must eat and the *les bosches* continue their efforts to force my husband into surrendering his fleet."

"If only France had more patriots such as your husband. One day the sacrifices that your family is making will be known and he will rightfully take his place with Dusquesne, de Grasse, Picquet de la Motte, and Suffren as the great admirals of France."

"*Merci,* Alard," Madame D'Aubigné turned to a servant. "Gérard, bring our guest a Cognac"

"*Oui, Madame.* The Courvoisier?"

"No, bring the LaFontaine de La Pouyade."

— —

It was late afternoon by the time that Sheppard returned to the *Argonne* from his meeting with Rear Admiral Utley. It had been a pleasant enough conversation with the Admiral agreeing that Mr. Feldman was not doing a good job as the shipyard's liaison and supervisor of *Argonne*'s refit. On a better note he was pleased to hear how helpful Mr. Hess had been and how well the propeller change was progressing. The two men parted company with an agreement that a Mr. Wozniak, an experienced ship supervisor would be assigned to oversee Mr. Feldman's support and offer suggestions as needed. Mr. Wozniak would meet with Sheppard daily to insure that everything was being addressed adequately. As he left Sheppard could not understand why the Admiral was smiling. Utley never smiled.

As soon as Sheppard entered his stateroom, Ted Grabowski was waiting for him. "Afternoon, Ted, I thought I was done for the day. What gives?"

"Captain, I know how much you hate ceremonies, but you are not going to be able to avoid this one." With that Ted handed him the message board containing the afternoon traffic on top. "The top one is the one of immediate concern."

Sheppard started reading, skimming past the addressees lines and concentrating on the text. "Captain Sheppard Jackson McCloud will attend an award ceremony at the White House at 1300 local on the 19th of May following a luncheon in his honor served promptly at 1100. At the ceremony Captain McCloud will be presented the Navy Cross by the President—uniform service dress blue able. Mrs. McCloud's presence at the ceremony and luncheon is specifically requested by the First Lady." Sheppard sat down . . . stunned.

"Congratulations, Captain!" Ted gushed with enthusiasm. "I am afraid that this is the worst kept secret on *Argonne* I have ever seen. Your yeoman Brewster told me he heard it from a boatswain's mate not five minutes after the radioman returned with the afternoon message traffic from the yard communications center."

"I'd better call and tell Evelyn."

"Captain, please forgive me but in your absence I already have. I knew she would want to go shopping in the downtown stores before they closed and sent the sedan to pick her up. I know that I am not supposed to do that, but Captain; *it is the White House* and she did say that she didn't have anything to wear."

"All right, Ted, but we had better let Admiral Utley's Chief of Staff know in case someone complains about one of the yard's sedans being seen in downtown Philadelphia in wartime."

"Way ahead of you, Captain. The only hard spot was making sure that Admiral Utley could get through your meeting with a straight face. The yard acquiesced to our request to let us tell you first."

"Captain, if you will follow me there are a few people who want to congratulate you before you leave for Washington tomorrow morning."

Ted turned and left holding the stateroom door open for Sheppard. He then led his Captain through the superstructure of *Argonne* until they exited into the fading sunlight just forward of the Number III 18-inch three gun turret. The turret had been trained to starboard in preparation for the evening alignment to the North Star, or so Sheppard thought. Ted climbed the ladder to the top of the turret as Sheppard wondered what was going on. By the way, where was his orderly? Since the days of sail, captains of ships of the line always had an armed marine with them, ostensibly for protection from mutineers.

As Sheppard's head came into view of the fantail he heard Major Morris Jenkins, the commander of his Marine detachment sound off, *"Present Arms! Hands, Salute!"* It was an impressive sight. Lined up in front of Sheppard must have been the entire compliment of *Argonne* all saluting. At Morris's command, *"Ready to; Order arms."* Chief Turret Captain Hancock, the senior chief petty officer onboard stepped forward.

"Three cheers for the Captain; Hip, Hip *Hurray; Hip, Hip, Hurray; Hip, Hip, Hurray!"*

Sheppard looked at Ted who was clapping and hooting like the rest of the crew, with tears in his eyes. Sheppard was obviously not the only man who knew of this old sailing navy tradition that had fallen out of use about the turn of the century. He climbed down on the right side of the turret to shake as many hands as he could. Fifteen minutes later as the last of the day faded into night, Commander Grabowski rescued his Captain; sending him home in a borrowed sedan.

— —

It was so good to finally rest in his arms. He was nervous about what lay ahead, but happy in what they had accomplished. Perhaps it would ease his pain to know that a great victory had

*been won; more importantly that it had been achieved without
costing the lives of his men. Were they being rewarded for all
the struggles and hardships, the secrets and desires that had
been overcome? Oh if it could only stay as it was now.*

*But she knew it would not. She could feel that their rest was
coming to an end. Everyone about them seems frantic with
effort to complete something too soon. What lay ahead, why the
secrecy and subterfuge? Would he be called away from her, or
would they both be asked to do something new—something for
the country—something with great risk? Whatever lay ahead
she was confident in his abilities to protect and guide them. She
could rely on her love—on this Shepherd.*

— —

Admiral Jonas Ingraham, his face lined with the heavy
responsibilities he bore, sat in the morning briefing with
his principal staff officers. The subject was the continuing
deterioration of the situation in the Mediterranean. There was
no good news. General Erwin Rommel was moving quickly. He
would conquer Algeria and Morocco before anything could be
done by Great Britain or the United States. The French had a
powerful fleet at *Mers el Kébir*, but they had no supply line for
food, fuel, or ammunition now that all of metropolitan France
proper had been occupied by the Germans. The French Foreign
Legion in Algeria were tough fighters but lacked the tanks
and air forces needed to hold against the panzers of Hitler.
Montgomery's army in Palestine would need at least three
months to reequip before they could launch an attack on the
Italian forces guarding Rommel's strategic rear in Egypt.

The briefing officer continued with what was known of the
Italian situation. *Grand' Ammiragilio* Aldo Dragonetti had
redeployed the Italian fleet from Taranto to Naples and LaSpezia
following the British evacuation of Alexandria. The damage
inflicted by the Fleet Air Arm attack in 1940 had been largely
repaired with Mussolini's Regia Marina currently possessing
twelve modern battleships and six modern battle cruisers. They
had numerous cruisers and destroyers of all types and a large
well trained submarine force. Though they only possessed four
aircraft carriers, the Italians excelled in maneuver, gunner and

torpedo attacks. The Italian air force was large and well equipped with fighters and bombers. The Regia Aeronautica possessed an exceptional bomber in the S.M.79 Sparviero as well as the bombs and air launched torpedoes to make the aircraft a formidable anti-ship weapon. However, the coordination between the two services was poor. Detection by one would not necessarily mean an attack by the other.

The only British forces in the Med consisted of Force H under the command of Admiral Bruce Hardy RN, VC, KCB, KBE, DSO based at Gibraltar. Decorated and knighted a second time for his role in the Battle of Cape Vilan, he had demonstrated exceptional capabilities in command. Force H though, only possessed two damaged aircraft carriers HMS *Ark Royal* and *Splendid* and two ancient battle cruisers, the damaged HMS *Renown* and her sister *Repulse*. With the damage that *Argonne* had inflicted on the battle cruisers in Brest, the Admiralty was contemplating sending Hardy reinforcements in the form of an additional destroyer squadron and the *Invincible* class of battle cruisers. Those heavy ships with their nine 16.5-inch main guns might arrive in a few days. Slow by modern standards they were nevertheless well armored and reliable. Even with the reinforcement of the battle cruisers, Force H was still not a match for the Italian fleet, if it sortied in strength.

— —

As Sheppard and Evelyn stepped out of the sedan at the White House, Evelyn, stunning in her new floral print dress and matching wide brimmed hat, garnered admiring looks from all in view. The colors she had chosen perfectly matched her complexion, eyes and hair. Sheppard was always at peace in her company and today was no different. The Marine sentries in their impeccable dress blues and blazing white trousers rendered synchronized salutes that Sheppard awkwardly returned with Evelyn on his right side. As they entered, they were greeted by a Naval aide to the President and an officer's steward who took Evelyn's hat and gloves, as well as Sheppard's cover.

The aide, Commander William McClintock guided them to a waiting room where Evelyn excused herself to freshen her makeup. Commander McClintock engaged Sheppard in small talk about the weather and the service. Out of the blue, he asked if Sheppard might be looking for a new Gunnery Officer in a few months when his tour at the White House was up. Sheppard said that he probably would be, knowing that Chuck Williamson had been with *Argonne* since before her commissioning. Bill McClintock was smiling as Evelyn came back, but Sheppard would never know if it was because of her beauty or his conversation.

Commander McClintock then ushered the McClouds to a small dining room. Shortly, Secretary of the Navy and Mrs. Knox, Admiral and Mrs. King, Secretary of State Hull, and surprising both Sheppard and Evelyn, Admiral and Mrs. Hamblen entered. Everyone located their place cards just in time for the President and Mrs. Roosevelt's arrival. Sheppard, ill at ease separated from Evelyn, sat at the President's right with Mrs. Roosevelt (Eleanor she insisted) next to Sheppard on his right. Evelyn was at the other end of the table seated between Admiral King (the new Chief of Naval Operations as he had renamed the job) and his predecessor Admiral Hamblen (the former CINCUSFLT). The President and Eleanor wanted to hear all about the Battle of Cape Vilan, which Sheppard was delighted to discuss having a subject he knew something about. He left out the details of the use of the secret anti-aircraft fuse only saying that he used his secondary armament to suppress the enemy fire attempting to down his Kingfisher aircraft.

Secretary Knox interjected. "Captain, what is your opinion of the German Navy as a fighting force?"

"Mr. Secretary, they are well trained, but rather rigid in their adherence to doctrine. The only reason that *Argonne* was successful was because we used our capabilities in an unorthodox manner. They did not react to what we were doing until it was too late. They couldn't understand what was happening with my spotter aircraft and the use of smoke projectiles in a naval battle." Sheppard did not say that he had no choice in lieu of the terrible accuracy of his main battery. Admiral King smiled that he had managed to avoid that issue with the Secretary.

It wasn't long (too long from Sheppard's perspective) before the desert of baked Alaska was finished and the President said, "Ladies, if you will excuse us, the men are going to adjourn for a smoke. We will rejoin you shortly. Captain would you please give me a push?"

"Yes, sir," was all Sheppard could think to answer as he got up to push the President's wheel chair into an adjoining room.

Secretary Hull began. "Captain you will have to forgive us for getting you here under the pretense of presenting you with the Navy Cross."

Sheppard's heart sank envisioning returning to *Argonne* sans the blue and white ribbon that the crew was expecting. "Mr. Secretary, I am afraid I am not following."

"Captain, we really needed to meet with you to discuss your next assignment. Your medal was the excuse to get you here without raising suspicions in the press. In Washington, the best way to keep a secret is to do it in the open."

"I understand, Mr. Secretary," Sheppard said, trying to hide the relief in his voice.

The President jumped in. "Sheppard, I have formed a new organization, the Office of Strategic Services or OSS to accomplish missions without the use of military force directly. Their current mission is to keep the French fleet in *Mers el Kébir* out of German hands. Neither Winston nor I have the resources to stop General Rommel's advance. Our only hope is to convince the French to move the fleet for us."

"Yes, Mr. President. How can *Argonne* or I be of assistance?" Sheppard was really confused but couldn't think of anything else to say.

"*Argonne* is the fastest big ship we have," Admiral King stated. "You are going to take an agent to *Mers el Kébir* and support him with whatever he needs to deliver a message from the President to the French Admiral." He paused before continuing, the trepidation clear in his voice. "Sheppard, we are well aware of the risks involved, but have no choice but to use a *Santiago* class ship. Yours is available and Jonas Ingraham has assured me you have the greatest chance of success."

Secretary Hull started. "Captain, I think you need a little background to understand the delicacy of your mission. You see the British attacked the French fleet in 1940 and not surprisingly the French are loath to assist the English in their war with Germany. It wasn't until the Germans occupied the rest of France in forty-one, just before the invasion attempt against England, that there was even a hope of preventing the French fleet from falling into German hands eventually. From the French perspective they have two equally hated enemies. That is where we come in. At the moment they have no reason to hate or distrust us. We think a skilled operative may be able to convince the French Admiral by the name of D'Aubigné to either move his fleet out of German reach or better yet, join us in the fight against them."

"Mr. President, you seem to be placing great faith in the abilities of this agent."

"Captain, you are correct I do have great faith in his abilities and his personal relationship with the French Admiral. He will need both to accomplish the mission."

"Yes sir." Sheppard was beginning to grasp the significance of what he was going to be tasked to accomplish and that there would be great risks involved. "Mr. President, may I ask whom you wish me to take to *Mers el Kébir*?"

"Sheppard, that's easy. I am the agent!" Admiral Hamblen volunteered.

Surprised Sheppard concluded, "That seems fairly straight forward."

Now it was Admiral King's turn. "Not really, Captain. No escorts or aircraft carrier can keep up with you. You are in a race with Rommel. We are going to stage some tankers in Gibraltar to refuel you and the French if need be on the way out of the Med. Those tankers will arrive soon after you're underway. As soon as we can scrape up a replacement for *Sabine* Admiral Hamilton will sortie to cover your withdrawal. *Chateau Thierry* is just finishing up her post shakedown availability and will replace *Belleau Wood,* if she is ready before we find another carrier. Your old friend Admiral Hardy will be tasked by Churchill to provide you with distant cover if the Italians try to intervene. We are hoping that you can get in—and out—before the Germans or Italians can mount a significant air attack."

Sheppard began to think through what they were asking him to do. *Argonne* despite all her capabilities would be alone. There would be no fighter cover and no anti-submarine screen. "Admiral, I assume that there is a plan to get *Argonne* through the British defenses at Gibraltar."

Secretary Hull provided the answer, "The British Admiralty has provided an officer with a copy of the relevant charts, codes, and signals that will go with you to get you through the strait."

"When is *Argonne* leaving?" Sheppard needed to make plans.

"As soon as you cross the sill and head down the Delaware River, you will be on your way." Admiral King began to fill in the details. "Your crew is loading supplies and ammunition today. The main battery alignment was finished last night. As soon as the ammunition load is complete we will start fueling *Argonne* from a tanker moored to the approach dock. Hopefully that will be finished before dawn."

Sheppard paused. He understood what was planned, but more so, he knew his respite with Evelyn would end, far sooner than he wished. Far sooner than he knew he needed! Again he was being picked for a vital assignment by men unaware of how damaged he was—how that damage to his psyche could affect this mission. Sheppard was certain of failure; failing his men— failing his country. The gnawing doubt was back.

"Admiral, if you don't mind my asking, how have you arranged all this without involving *Argonne?*"

"Sheppard, Captain Feldman of my staff is a master logistician. He was masquerading as your shipyard representative."

"Admiral, how do you expect me to keep Admiral Hamblen's and a Royal Naval Officer's presence a secret? Nothing happens in the shipyard that doesn't quickly find its way into the *Enquirer.*"

"Sheppard that is the easiest part of all," President Roosevelt smiled as he answered. "The easiest way to keep a secret is to leave it in plain sight. Admiral Hamblen is coming to visit his son and watch your gunner trials on the way to Norfolk. You have already met his aide Commander Halverson."

Sheppard had to smile. The President's plan to hide his mission had been well thought out.

"Gentlemen, I think it is time we rejoined the ladies and get on with decorating our hero. Captain, would you be so kind as to give me a push."

"Certainly, Mr. President"

This time Sheppard actually felt honored by the President's

PORT AT MERS EL KEBIR

request. The photograph of Sheppard shaking the President's hand with Evelyn hanging on his left arm made the front page of all the evening newspapers. Evelyn's look of love and admiration was clear to everyone, and brought a smile even to that noted sundowner Admiral Ernest King standing in the background.

— —

Amiral Phillipe D'Aubigné of the French Navy sat in a briefing aboard his flagship, the cuirassé *Languedoc* moored to the mole stern first in the port of *Mers el Kébir*. The situation was grim. *Général de division* Henri Laroque of the French Foreign Legion had just concluded his brief on the military capability of the Legion to resist the German onslaught that was engulfing Algeria. Everyone present knew that there was no force with greater *élan* than the Legion, but the absence of armor and air support made the situation hopeless. The only question that Phillipe needed to ask was one that he did not dare.

Henri answered it for him. "I can hold for a week, perhaps longer if you will use your ships as artillery to support my troops. If I fall back to the hills to the south and abandon the city of Oran, perhaps two weeks. After that we will run out of the supplies we have and there are no more to be had."

"*Les Boches* are worse than the English who stabbed us in the back in 1940," he added and spat on the deck for emphasis.

Phillipe knew he was referring to the attack by Force H at the direction of Winston Churchill after negotiations had broken off to transfer the French Fleet to a location where it could not fall into German hands. He felt fortunate that he had been able to move his damaged ships to Toulon for repairs. All the warships there had managed to flee, with what stores and skilled yard workers from the base that they could carry, only hours ahead of the Germans moving to occupy the Arsenal. The work had continued here and was as complete as it would ever be as long as metropolitan France was occupied.

— —

The huge dry dock number 7 at the Philadelphia Navy Yard Annex was more than half flooded when Admiral Hamblen's limousine pulled up at the brow of *Argonne*. Alerted by the shipyard gate guard force, Sheppard was standing by with the eight side boys, the ship's band and his quarterdeck watch standers. Ted Grabowski had kept the bandsmen up most of the night practicing the *Admiral's March* and *Ruffles and Flourishes*. Chuck Williamson had made certain that the black powder charges for the 6-pounder saluting cannons were dry and that he had more than enough available. Deck division had held a contest to determine which Boatswain's Mate could best pipe *Over the Side*. Sheppard was pleased that his coxswain, Boatswain's Mate Second Class Raymondo Cruz had won. Now it was time to put it all together as Sheppard crossed the fingers of his left hand.

Cruz's pipe twittered, "~~ssssssssss~~s^sssssssssss^s~~sssssssss~~s^s^." On the first note everyone on the quarterdeck and topside on *Argonne* rendered a hand salute to Admiral Hamblen. The Admiral saluted the National Ensign at *Argonne's* stern, and then rendered his salute to the Officer of the Deck. Unlike for mere mortals, when the pipe was finished everyone held their salute except the Admiral as the band sounded off with four *Ruffles and Flourishes* followed by the *Admiral's March*. No sooner had the march ended when Senior Chief Hancock ordered, *"Fire One!"* The blast of the black powder charge in the 6-pounder, split the normal roar of the shipyard. Everyone within miles stopped what they were doing and looked at *Argonne*. Senior Chief Hancock one deck below *Argonne's* signal bridge was reciting the age old phrase to exactly time the guns to the required five second intervals, "If I wasn't a gunner; I wouldn't be here; *Fire Two!"* He repeated himself fifteen more times until the required 17 gun salute for a four star Admiral had been executed perfectly. At the last gun, the halyard for the Admiral's square blue flag with four white stars arranged in a diamond, which had been balled up with rubber bands, was jerked, breaking the rubber bands and immediately showing the world that *Argonne* was now the flagship of a full Admiral of the United States Navy.

With the echo from the seventeenth gun reverberated from the shipyard's buildings, Sheppard and his watch standers dropped their salutes and Admiral Hamblen stepped aboard his flagship.

"Good morning, Sheppard. I see the dock is filling nicely."

Sheppard knew the use of his first name was a sign that the Admiral was pleased with the arrival ceremony. He uncrossed the fingers of his left hand as he responded, "Good morning, Admiral. The brow will be lifted shortly and we should be able to cross the sill of the dock in about an hour."

"Thank you. Would you please accompany me to the flag quarters?"

Sheppard smiled that even admirals could be lost aboard a new ship as he fell in step to the left of Hamblen guiding him to the flag cabin.

As soon as they were out of sight and hearing of everyone except Commander Halverson, still masquerading as an American Lieutenant, and Corporal Pease, following behind; the Admiral added, "Nothing like hiding in plain sight."

3

UNDERWAY

ADMIRAL KLAUS SCHRÖDER OF the *Kriegsmarine* was still smarting over the loss of his command. *Großadmiral* Raeder may have sent him to this backwater assignment in Rome, but he was determined to return to the real battle being waged in the Atlantic. Those fools in the high command just did not understand that a sustained raid against the convoys for only a few months would force Great Britain to capitulate. At least he was able to bring his Chief of Staff, *Fregattenkapitän* Fritz Bodermann, with him to Italy. Fritz's younger brother Karl was a *Gruppenführer* in the SS with responsibilities for all of France. The bond between the two bothers was strong and Karl had proven very accommodating in keeping the skilled French shipyard workers off of the list of Jews in Brest. Raeder would see that he needed Schröder to get anything done in France for the *Kriegsmarine*.

The task at hand was to meet with the Italian Supermarina (Headquarters) officers, be briefed on their plans and find out why they were not being more aggressive in destroying the British bases at Gibraltar and Malta. Germany needed the fleet of her axis partner in the Atlantic. Klaus was also officially calling on *Grand' Ammiragilio* Aldo Dragonetti, but had not made much headway in understanding the complexities of Italian politics other than it seemed Mussolini did not want to risk his fleet unless Aldo could assure him of overwhelming superiority. Klaus did not understand what it was with these leaders that had experience only in the army. Did they not understand that naval combat was as much a war of attrition as a land campaign? It really didn't matter if you lost ships as long as your enemy lost proportionately more.

After a half hour, it was clear to both Klaus and Fritz that the Italians were only concerned with the French. It did not matter that the fleet in *Mers el Kébir* did not have any source of supplies or repair. The Italian staff was only concerned about the size of the ships, the number and type of guns. They were delighted that Rommel would capture the fleet in a week or less without any Italian intervention. There was only one staff officer who demonstrated an offensive spirit. *Capitano di Vascello* Dario Pettinato was in charge of special operations, involving something called *maiale,* which translated as *pigs.* It did not make much sense to Klaus until Dario explained that they were two man submersibles that carried a huge charge into enemy harbors and then attached it to an enemy ship. Later, a time fuse detonated it sinking or crippling the ship. The human torpedo only had a range of 24 kilometers; getting them within range was the problem. Dario whispered to Klaus that they were building a secret base in Algeciras Spain. When completed they would be able to attack the British in Gibraltar.

— —

Madame Daphne D'Aubigné, sat in the great hall of *Chateau' D'Aubigné* crying softly. The faded cloth above the ornate wainscoted walls everywhere contained brighter rectangles of red velvet, painfully reminding her of her missing Rembrants, Manets, Renoirs, Degases, Donatellos, even her favorite Cézanne—all were gone. What more could France demand of her. There was nothing left to sell to those barbarians. However much Alard could get from the Germans would be the last deposit in her husband's Swiss account unless the chateau itself could be sold.

"*Maman?*"

"*Oui, Étienne,*"she said wiping a tear from her eye.

"Don't cry. You are as much a patriot of France as papa. Tomorrow I will travel and visit our friends. I am sure they too will help keep the fleet from the *Boches*."

"No! No son of Philippe D'Aubigné will beg." The fire in her eyes silencing her son. "If there is begging to be done, I will do it." Softening she added, "Besides, you must stay with Marie. The birth of your first child is too close for you to be away."

— —

The dock was finally filled; the special sea and anchor detail was set: and Chris Peterson's electrician's mates had completed the transfer of electrical power from the shipyard's shore power cables to *Argonne's* own turbine generators and diesel generators. Not as easy as it sounds, all the coolers and condensers in the Engineering spaces had to be vented inboard until filled with water after the level in the dock had risen high enough. Boilers had to be lit and temperature raised to the normal steaming range for 600 pounds per square inch pressure. Only then could sea water flow be started and vacuum drawn in the turbine-generator condensers and the diesels started.

It was too dangerous to warm the main engines or test them in the dock. One false move on the part of any of the four throttlemen or a casualty to a portion of the complex machinery could send *Argonne* crashing into the dry dock wall or worse the caisson closing the entry. The main engines would wait until she was clear of the dock but still under the control of the fleet of tugs standing by to assist.

As soon as the water levels both inside and outside the dock matched, the water filling the ballast tanks of the caisson was pumped out. Once afloat the caisson was moved out of the way clearing the opening for *Argonne's* exit. Timing was critical. Even though the range of the normal tide was only a little less than 2 feet, since the shipyard was on a river, there could be tremendous variation both in the range of the tide and the timing of slack water. Both were dependent on the rainfall in New York, New Jersey, and Pennsylvania. The period of slack water was the time that was the goal to get *Argonne* across the sill. Too early or too late and the tugs would have to fight the river's full force exerted on the entire nearly 1,300-foot waterline length of the ship crosswise to the river. Every evolution that *Argonne* needed to accomplish had to be timed to the projected sill time, even Admiral Hamblen's arrival.

Because of the delicacy of the maneuver to leave or enter the dry dock, Sheppard was not responsible for the safety of his ship. He was a mere spectator, officially, until the ship's bow crossed the sill outbound. A very experienced officer, normally from the construction corps, assigned by the shipyard, called the docking officer, would be held accountable if *Argonne* was damaged during the undocking. Fortunately for everyone and her mission of grave importance—she was not.

Clear of the dock at last, the tugs turned the battle cruiser parallel to the Delaware River pointed downstream as the main engines were warmed and tested by the Officer of the Deck with Sheppard's permission. One long blast of her whistle indicating a change in status to any vessels within hearing distance, and her powerful engines started rotating her four shafts with their new propellers each over 24 feet in diameter. The Delaware River astern of her began to swirl in acres of moving water as *Argonne* majestically gathered way down river. Standing next to Sheppard and Lieutenant John Hamblen IV was a civilian upper Delaware River pilot. An advisor to the Captain and Conning Officer, who actually issued the orders to the Helmsman and both Lee Helmsmen at the engine order telegraphs, he knew the river better than anyone. Pilots spent their lives learning the vagaries of a constantly changing harbor or a stretch of a river and then assisted ships with their intimate knowledge of currents and shoals to avoid disaster in mother-nature's ever changing seabed. *Argonne* would change pilots several times as she journeyed down the Delaware River into the Delaware Bay.

When she finally left the area of the bay where the channel or water depth restricted her motion, it was time for the last pilot, called a bar pilot, to leave the ship. No sooner had he started down the ladder behind the conning station than Sheppard turned to his Officer of the Deck Lieutenant Commander Gerry Archinbald and directed him to, "Prepare to answer bells for maximum speed!" Gerry looked back at Sheppard wondering what was on his mind as he relayed the order via the Captain's Announcing Circuit or 21MC to Chris Petersen in main control.

For a normal underway *Argonne* only used four of her sixteen boilers, with four more in 'hot standby'. That was all she needed to drive her at 40 knots. With a clean hull and the new propellers, she might well be able to go 10 to 12 knots faster on all sixteen. Only three men aboard *Argonne* knew why she would need her best speed and two of them were eight decks below on the flag bridge watching the sights, and casually discussing the mission ahead.

Sheppard observed the bar pilot acrobatically climb down the Jacob's ladder against the hull to the waiting pilot boat. The ladder was hoisted aboard as the Captain turned to the Officer of the Deck and directed him to secure the starboard anchor for sea. Kept in readiness to drop in the unlikely event of a rudder or engine casualty, that 'emergency brake' was no longer needed in open water. Once secured, the regular underway watch was set, and material condition *Yoke* was established below the second deck. The vast majority of watertight doors and hatches in the spaces below where the crew lived were shut and dogged. If Sheppard's ship was hit by an unexpected torpedo, *Argonne* was in the best condition to limit the damage yet still routinely function.

Lieutenant Commander Jonathan Becker called up from the combat information center fourteen decks below just under the heavy armor. "Captain, combat, no sign of our destroyer escort on radar"

Sheppard answered on the 21MC, "Roger, combat."

Gerry Archinbald's look of incredulity at taking a capital ship to sea, with the German U-boat offensive in progress off the East Coast, and not having a destroyer escort caused Sheppard to smile.

"Boatswain Bergman, pipe the word."

"s^s-s-s-sssssss," echoed in every manned space.

Sheppard reached for the press-to-talk switch on the General Announcing System (1MC) squawkbox. "This is the Captain speaking. *Argonne* is in a race. We have to get to the Mediterranean before Rommel captures the French fleet at *Mers el Kébir*. There is not another ship in the fleet that can keep up with us. Accordingly, we will make the trip unescorted and rely on our speed alone for protection."

Sheppard turned to his special sea and anchor detail Conning Officer, Lieutenant John Hamblen. "Let's get going."

John gave the order to send them on their way to both Lee Helmsman at the engine order telegraphs, "All Ahead Flank!" As more boilers came on line, *Argonne's* speed rose beginning her race with Rommel.

— —

"Heavy screws, *Herr Kapitän*, bearing two-six-five degrees," Georg Bachmeier, the sound man on the *U-197* reported to his Commanding Officer *Korvettenkapitän* Conrad Kluge. Conrad had deployed to the Delaware Bay entrance as part of Operation *Beckenschlag* (Cymbal Crash) in early April. His patrol had been very successful with six merchant ships and one old destroyer to show for his twelve G7e electric torpedoes. Tonight would be his last night on station. He still had thirty-two rounds of 10.5cm ammunition for his deck gun. With luck, he might be able to sink one last merchant before his fuel situation demanded the start of his return to Brest at 0400.

Conrad went to the conning tower of his Type IXB submarine. Raising the search periscope he looked on the bearing that Bachmeier had reported. A masthead, silhouetted, against the western sky, a large warship from the looks of what he could see. He slowly swung the periscope around the horizon looking for the escorts. Not surprisingly he did not see any. That only confirmed in his mind that his contact must be a large cruiser or battleship with the escorts too far below the horizon to be seen. Too bad he had used all his torpedoes; here was a contact worthy of his largest salvo.

As Kluge trained the periscope back in the direction of the contact, he could not believe that the superstructure was now visible. What had it been two minutes? No ship could move that fast.

"*Achtung*, action stations on the double."

He took an observation on this unusual contact—bearing two-six-eight, range seven-two-hundred meters, angle on the bow starboard five. *Course zero-eight-three degrees* true, he calculated mentally. He swept around the horizon again—still no sign of escorts. Conrad knew that there was nothing he could do about this contact, but if he got an accurate course and speed, perhaps one of the boats farther to the east could.

He took another observation; bearing two-seven-nine, range two-three-hundred meters, angle on the bow starboard sixteen. No! He had done something wrong. No target could move almost five thousand meters in three minutes. This time he lowered the periscope. Even though the light was fading, he did not want to risk a lookout seeing him. Kluge reviewed his thoughts. He was certain of his classification. It was a *Santiago* class battle cruiser. He had seen the two secondary triple turrets clearly abreast the bridge. After she passed he would surface and report her to Uncle Karl as the German submariners called their commanding admiral, Karl Dönitz in casual conversation.

Georg Bachmeier was alarmed. The contact was moving to the right so quickly, there must be a danger of collision. "*Herr Kapitän*, contact very close!"

Conrad knew that he was six-hundred meters from the track of the battle cruiser, but could not resist the temptation to take one more look at this tempting target. He raised the periscope as his target flew past at what must be close to 50 knots. What a sight! The curl of white foam at her bow reached all the way up to her main deck and as far aft as her forward turret. He could not rotate the elevation of the periscope high enough to see the top of the mast. The battle cruiser covered his entire visible horizon. Awestruck he watched the sight of a lifetime, mentally preparing the message he would send to Admiral Dönitz. Kluge did not realize the danger *U-197* was in from the wake generated by the battle cruiser's over a half-million shaft horsepower.

— —

"Skunk 'ABLE,' bearing two-four-one degrees, range two-oh-double-oh yards," the Sugar George or SG radar operator sang out. Screamed was more like it. Sheppard knew that *Argonne* had just passed that point without spotting anything. It had to be a submarine sucked to the surface by *Argonne's* wake.

He jumped to the 21MC, "Guns track skunk 'ABLE' bearing two-four-one—illuminate!"

Lieutenant Commander Gerry Archinbald, now the on watch gunnery officer in the top level of the command tower, began barking orders in response to his 1JC sound powered phone talker. The telephone talker immediately relayed them to the directors and mounts.

"Sky eight, track skunk 'ABLE'." "Mount five-two-two load one star shell." Mounts five-one-three, five-one-nine and five-two-one load high capacity. "Sky eight control mounts five-one-three, five-one-nine, five-two-one, and five-two-two."

The wisdom of Sheppard keeping two Mark 37 directors and eight of his twenty-two five inch twin mounts manned underway was clear as he ordered, "Commence firing!"

Fifteen decks below in the after anti-aircraft plotting room, the fire-controlman at the Mark 6 Stable element closed the firing key. The gathering dusk was broken by the flash and sharp crack of mount five-two-two's right hand 5"/54 gun. Gerry immediately passed, "Mount five-two-two load high capacity."

Sheppard went out on the starboard open conning station and fought the wind to raise his binoculars as the magnesium flare and parachute from the illuminating shell deployed and turned night into day around the exposed conning tower of the U-boat.

No sooner had the illumination round burst, than Gerry ordered, "Continuous Fire, master key!" Now the gun crews in the mounts and the handling rooms that served them raced to load and fire as quickly as they could. The submarine was trying to dive. "Load armor piercing," Sheppard passed hoping the delayed action of the fuses would allow better penetration of the enveloping sea.

Sheppard ordered the Conning Officer to come left and put the target directly astern in order to unmask mount five-two-zero. Soon he saw the flash of a hit among the water columns of near misses. Then another and another as the operators of the Mark 37 director and the Mark 1 Ford computer refined their solution of the exact course, speed, and range of the target. Within sixty seconds of the first high capacity shells exploding on contact with the conning tower of U-boat, Sheppard ordered, "Cease fire". The target had disappeared beneath the waves. The burning magnesium flares lighting the spreading pool of burning diesel fuel. That fire might be the only tombstone for forty German sailors.

Sheppard sought protection from the wind created by *Argonne's* passage inside the conning station as he breathed a sigh of relief that his ship had escaped the German wakeless torpedoes and just as if not more importantly, hopefully silenced any report of his passage.

— —

Admiral Klaus Schröder was having breakfast with his Chief of Staff when the idea first began to form in his mind. If Raeder and Lütjens would not provide him with ships, then he would have to get some of his own. There was clearly too much political control of the Italian Battle Fleet for him to ever convince the Supermarina to let him command a foray into the Atlantic. That left the French Fleets in *Mers el Kébir*, Casablanca, and Dakar. Rommel was closest to the one in *Mers el Kébir* and would capture that one first.

"Fritz," he began, "how can we convince the French to give up their ships in Algeria without scuttling them or getting them damaged in a fight?"

Fregattenkapitän Fritz Bodermann looked at his Admiral as if the stress of the Battle of Cape Vilan had finally manifested itself in lunacy. "*Herr* Admiral, surely you don't think the French would ever consider such a thing—particularly if it was Germany that was making the demand?"

"Fritz, that is just it, what if we could convince them that they didn't have a choice? What if we could offer something that they would want, to do as we say? Of course, that would not be enough. We would also have to make the consequences of not doing it too painful to consider."

"*Herr* Admiral, I have no idea what you are contemplating! Beside we are only two men, how are we going to operate a fleet of French warships?"

"I agree, Fritz, there are lots of problems to overcome but first we have to get the ships under our control. Do you think your brother would help us?"

"*Herr* Admiral, if it meant capturing a French fleet and adding them to the *Kriegsmarine*, of course."

— —

The men all around Sheppard were screaming in agony. Blood had splashed over his uniform and was dripping from his Navy Cross. Suddenly white smoke enveloped them and the phosphorous began to burn its way into flesh and bones. Those who were not badly injured rose and limped or ran to the lifelines hurling themselves over the side into the beckoning sea—anything to put out the terrible burning phosphorous. One by one the men on the deck around him whimpered pitifully, then fell quiet.

But they rose and began screaming louder. They forced themselves to their feet and began inexorably to come in his direction, zombies from the night ghostly in the white fog. Their outstretched arms were reaching for him. In unison they screamed like harpies, "Why did you do this to us?"

Sheppard woke. He sat bolt upright in his bunk aft of the conning station bathed in sweat. Had he cried out in his sleep? Did his men know of his nightmare? How long had he slept? What time was it? Was his ship, were his men safe? Where was Evelyn to comfort him now when he needed her? Was he ever going to be free of this terror that awaited him in the dark reaches of his guilt ridden subconscious? The clock on the bulkhead chimed three bells. *It must be* 0130, he thought.

— • —

Admiral Hardy watched from the flag bridge of HMS *Renown* as the tugs began to gather at the caisson for the Prince of Wales Dock at Gibraltar. This was the largest dry dock remaining under allied control in Europe and the west coast of Africa outside of Great Britain—at least until the King George Dock was finished at the northern end of the harbor. Sir Bruce was pleased that the smaller dock would finally be clear for the emergency repairs to battle damage suffered by his ships at Cape Vilan. With short whistles sounding more like chirps than blasts, the tugs acknowledged the orders of the master pilot to maneuver the deep slab of the floating gate out of the opening.

No sooner was the caisson made fast to the mole than the tugs spun about and raced back to catch heaving lines thrown from the stern of *Splendid,* the second aircraft carrier assigned to Force H. It had taken over two months to repair the damage to her starboard side caused by a German torpedo hit just under her bridge. Slowly the carrier moved out of the dock. First only under the force generated by the two capstans turning near the entrance of the dock pulling on hawsers attached to the carrier's bow. As *Splendid* came further out more tugs were made up amidships and the pilot onboard took control of the undocking from the dock master. With the orders to the tugs now coming from the pilot the hawsers were cast off and the tugs alone provided the forces needed to maneuver the carrier clear of the dry dock and against the aviation loading pier.

Sir Bruce saw the first belch of smoke rise from her stack as her engineers lit the fires in a boiler. He smiled. He would soon have an operational carrier again. HMS *Ark Royal* needed to enter the dock next to patch the few holes in her hull caused by a German bomb that hit her in the Battle of Cape Vilan. Most of the internal damage to HMS *Ark Royal* that could be repaired without the docking had already been completed. Two days; three at the outside, and the pumps onboard his second carrier would finally be silent.

— —

The bulkhead clock in Sheppard's sea cabin struck one bell in the morning watch (0430) when Petty Officer Jefferson knocked and entered.

"Good morning, Cap'n, it is another fine Navy day."

"That it is, Petty Officer Jefferson, that it is and good morning to you also," Sheppard smiled at the pleasant ritual that had been part of his sea going life for, what was it—four years now.

"Cap'n, would you like the usual for breakfast?"

"That would be very nice."

Jefferson turned and left to make the eleven deck decent to the Captain's pantry and begin the task of cooking up Sheppard's breakfast.

The two men had worked out the timing of the morning events perfectly. By the time Jefferson returned with Sheppard's meal in his 'Jim Dandiest' carrying rig as Jefferson had described it, his Captain would have finished washing, shaving and brushing his teeth in the fold out sink that was part of the forward bulkhead of his cabin. Sheppard would then change into a clean uniform for the new day, placing the one that he had slept in neatly stowed in a laundry bag that would periodically be collected. After washing, his khaki uniforms would be starched, pressed and folded. Jefferson would see to it that, when returned they were all carefully stored in the correct drawers with the cleaned fresh items on the bottom of each stack.

Sheppard had time to finish his breakfast in his usual place, the high upholstered chair on the conning station. After Jefferson had cleared away the tray and dishes it was time for the morning battle stations. A request from the Officer of the Deck followed by an order from the Captain and the Boatswain's Mate of the Watch went to the 1MC microphone sounding the pipe *Word to be passed*, "s$^{\text{s-s-s-sssssss}}$;" followed by, "General quarters, general quarters, man your battle stations." The general alarm was then sounded, "*Bong, Bong, Bong, . . . ,*" fourteen in total. Sheppard wondered why the designers had selected fourteen; any single *bong* would wake the dead. Then a final, "Man your battle stations!"

Most of the crew and officers were already up, but now the race began. If you had to move down or aft in the ship you did that on the port side. Up or forward was done on the starboard side. With that system collisions between running men were rare and injuries even less so. As soon as the running men had finished passing through the watertight doors and hatches in *Argonne*, those openings were shut and dogged tight. If she was damaged, the damage would be contained to the smallest possible area of the ship, whether it was explosion, fire or flooding. Once all men were present at any given station the phone talker would report, "Manned" to the next supervisory watch station in the ship. When all equipment had been prepared for action, ammunition hoists filled, machinery started, electric switchboards split or any of thousands of other items completed, the spaces would report, "Ready."

Sheppard would punch his stopwatch when the Officer of the Deck in the armored command tower reported on the 21MC, "Battle stations manned and ready!" Five minutes twelve seconds—Sheppard wasn't that pleased. *Argonne* had done better, but some of the rust needed to be worked out by everyone as well as the new crew members becoming familiar with their assignments and this was the first routine GQ (General Quarters) that had been exercised in almost two weeks. There was only two minutes to spare before first light.

Always the most dangerous time for a warship at sea, as the visibility began to improve unexpected enemy forces could be near and have approached unseen in the dark. Modern radar was making it less likely, but radar would not detect a submarine lurking to ambush a ship silhouetted against the eastern horizon. A wise sailor was always prepared for the unexpected and *Argonne* was filled with wise intelligent seamen.

All this mattered little to the engineers in *Argonne's* boiler and engine rooms. Regardless of the watch condition, they oiled, wiped, adjusted, and tuned the engines and machinery to keep *Argonne* racing toward Gibraltar with every bit of power they could coax out of her massive engines.

———

Ammiraglio di Armata Gugliehno Romano the commander of the Italian Battle Fleet based in Naples was enjoying a cup of cappuccino with *Ammiraglio di Squadra* Leonardo Moretti the commander of the Italian scouting forces on board the Battle Fleet flagship *Italia*. It was a closely guarded secret that Mussolini had approved an operation in the Mediterranean for the entire Italian fleet. *Generaloberst* Rommel had asked that the Italian Fleet make a show of force off *Mers el Kébir* to convince the French that there was no alternative to surrender. That would be the official reason for the Italian fleet to sail, but the real purpose was a secret. Not even the representative of Italy's ally, Admiral Schröder, was to be informed.

Both Italian admirals knew that this war would eventually end. Inevitably when it did the French fleet in *Mers el Kébir*, if under German control, would represent a threat to Italian naval hegemony in the Mediterranean. However close the axis alliance was now, it might not last. Even worse, the Germans might decide to return the fleet to France as the price for a bilateral treaty guaranteeing an alliance with France once the war in Europe ended. Italy had faced French aspirations in Mare Nostrum for a century and was not about to allow the Germans to control a sizeable fleet that could challenge Italian supremacy regardless of which flag they flew. As long as the British controlled the Straits of Gibraltar, Italian thinking was that the French fleet would remain in the Med. Italy could not allow that potential challenge to remain.

Mussolini recognized that there was no other answer than the complete destruction of the French fleet before the Germans could capture it or it could escape to a port outside Italy's reach. If the Germans succeeded in capturing the ships, Italy could not attack them nor demand that her ally turn them over to Mussolini. The only solution was to capture them or destroy them before Rommel arrived. The entire Italian Battle Fleet sailing off *Mers el Kébir* before Rommel arrived might convince the French admiral to surrender his ships to Italy rather than Germany. If *Amiral* D'Aubigné did not surrender, then the Italians would spark a fight resulting in the total destruction of all the French warships. That thinking was the genesis of Operation *Guardare al Futuro*.

— —

Admiral Klaus Schröder was pleased with the plan that he and Fritz had come up with. Fritz was telephoning his brother in Paris at that very minute while Klaus was drafting the cable to the German Embassy in Switzerland. In a telephone call earlier *Großadmiral* Erich Raeder had given his approval to implement the plan, but Klaus knew that he was not optimistic of its success. Raeder didn't know of the part that Karl Bodermann was going to play. That was the real key to the success of the plan.

Schröder thanked God that the Swiss could provide a channel of communications to the French in Oran. There had to be a way to send messages to the French *Amiral* D'Aubigné and to receive his answers. Schröder's first cable read:

My Dear Amiral D'Aubigné,

I am certain that you and your fleet recognize the hopelessness of your situation. Generaloberst Rommel has assured me that within a week's time his panzers will have occupied Oran and captured your fleet. I am certain that you do not have the fuel or supplies to reach another more distant port or you would have left already.

As one professional naval officer to another, there is honor in the preservation of the lives of the men under your command. I am prepared as the Führers direct representative in Italy and with the full cooperation of the German Army, to offer you a safe passage to Toulon were you and your men can be repatriated to your homes and families without bloodshed. Germany is not interested in the useless slaughter of brave sailors. We only wish that your ships not fall into the hands of your historical enemy, the British, whom have cowardly attacked your fleet once with considerable loss of life.

I cannot delay Generaloberst Rommel's progress even one day. I fear that once your ships are under his guns there is no hope for an outcome satisfactory to all concerned. I require your answer no later than 1600 GMT on the 22nd of May 1942.

Klaus Schröder
Admiral Kriegsmarine des Führers
representative to the Italian Navy

That would give the French about 2 days to consider the proposal before the deadline. Fritz had assured him that would be more than enough time for his brother Karl to complete the research needed in the records of the old French Naval Ministry. Klaus already could guess at what answer the French would give. It really didn't matter what they said this time. It would be the next cable that would be more demanding—with consequences.

— —

Gibraltar Harbor
soundings in meters

Detached Mole

GIBRALTAR HARBOR

South

Mole

Prince of Wales Dock

The little net tender was pulling on the line of floats supporting the anti-submarine barrier across the south entrance to Gibraltar Harbor. Composed of interlocking steel mesh the barrier prevented submarines or torpedoes from gaining access to the warships berthed inside the moles. Effective as it was, the net was a considerable inconvenience when ships were trying to enter or leave. In the roadstead Admiral Hardy's reinforcements moved slowly toward the entrance, delaying until the net could be removed.

His Majesty's Ships *Invincible, Inflexible, Indomitable,* and *Indefatigable* were perhaps the oddest looking battle cruisers ever constructed. They were on a par with other ships built in the early 1920s being armed with nine 16.5-inch guns in three gun turrets and a secondary armament of sixteen 6-inch guns in two gun turrets. Their anti-aircraft armament was limited to 4.7"/40s in single open mounts and 2pdr pompoms in eight gun octuple mounts. Only the 20mm Oerlikons were a recent improvement. What made these warships so unusual was the arrangement of their main turrets. From the bow, turrets *A* and *B* were conventionally arranged before the tower superstructure, but *Q* turret was located aft of the tower nearly amidships but forward of the machinery spaces. As a result main armament fire could not be directed aft.

At 32 knots they were the equal of the remodeled HMS *Renown* and *Repulse* but slow by modern standards—barely able to outrun the newer battleships. They would have been modernized after the 'Admiral' class had the war not come to Britain in 1939. However, their armor was exceptional with a sloped belt of up to 14 inches of face hardened steel internally and deck armor of 9 inches protecting the magazines. When it came to protection, the British had learned the supposed lessons of Jutland, where three of their battle cruisers had been destroyed by internal explosions.

Sir Bruce wondered if they were going to remain attached to Force H or would the First Sea Lord send them back to the Home Fleet when the repairs to the German ships in Brest completed. Speaking of repairs, the *Ark Royal* would need two days in dock to patch her hull. He was going to lose time as the supports in the bottom of the dry dock, called blocks, were repositioned for the

Renown to repair the holes in her starboard anti-torpedo bulge caused by the American armor piercing shell. It would take a day to reposition the blocks and then another to repair *Renown*. The real question on his mind was to sail on the night of May 23rd, with five battle cruisers or wait until the 25th when he would have all six. If he waited he could keep his flag in *Renown* and gain the advantage of his exceptional Flag Captain Sir Phillip Kelley RN VC KBE DSO Commanding Officer of the *Renown*. Sir Bruce would also gain a second of his most capable anti-aircraft assets. He had a few days to decide. After all, the Americans had not requested Force H to meet the *Argonne* off of *Mers el Kébir* until the afternoon of May 24th, but a request was not an order and there were exceptional reasons to delay. Sir Bruce directed his communications officer to draft a message for the Admiralty, outlining his need for the delay with a request that it be forwarded to the Americans. If the Admiralty really wanted him in a support position on the 24th, it would be their decision.

— —

The message arrived about 1200 from the *Führer's* headquarters authorizing Operation *Doverübung*. There were a thousand things for Günter Lütjens's staff to accomplish. The Operation order specified a breakout through the Denmark Strait on or about May 30th, at the full moon. German optical range finders and directors would be at the least disadvantage in comparison to the allied radar then. Everything that had to be accomplished had to be backed up in time from that point. An advanced location had to be selected for the final fueling rendezvous before Moeller's Fleet sailed for the breakout into the Atlantic. Supply tankers had to be positioned in the Atlantic to keep his ships supplied with fuel, food, and ammunition. The position of the supply ships needed to be coordinated with a general plan for the raid. Ranging far in the North and South Atlantic would use significant fuel, but staying in one area would make the allied task of hunting Moeller much easier.

The first question was the jumping off point. The closest was Trondheim with Narvik and Bergen slightly further away. The construction of basing facilities at Trondheim was well advanced which made the decision all the easier. From Trondheim it was about 1,100 nautical miles to the Denmark Strait. Two days steaming at 24 knots. Moeller would have to leave Trondheim on the morning of the 28th to arrive at dawn in the Strait, though dawn was relative since at that latitude daylight lasted nearly 24 hours.

It would take two full days to replenish Moeller's fleet in Trondheim which meant he had to arrive no later than 1600 GMT on the afternoon of the 25th. It was two days steaming from the Jade to Trondheim. That set Moeller's underway time as 1600 on the 23rd. Sufficient tankers would have to leave tomorrow as they did not have the speed to get there in time otherwise.

The problem of coordinating supply ships and rendezvous was easier. Schröder's supply ships still had all of their cargoes intact and when Schröder had been defeated, they had remained on station instead of being recalled to Spain. The plan to support Schröder would be adequate to support Moeller since the numbers of major warships was the same. Just as Schröder needed to conserve his major caliber ammunition so too would Moeller. Lütjens's staff had yet to come up with a viable way to transfer ammunition heavier than 60 kilograms at sea.

That settled, the remaining issue was how best to deceive Admiral Tovey into thinking that the Germans were seeking a major fleet engagement. It was the only way to draw him to the east and leave the Strait of Denmark unguarded. The English coast was too well guarded by minefields to close and bombard a city as Hipper had done in the first war. There had to be a way to threaten a vital interest of the allies that would leave him no choice but to sail from Scapa Flow and come east while Moeller skirted Iceland to the northwest.

— —

Argonne had settled into Sheppard's normal underway routine. At least as normal as it could be with the battle cruiser charging across the Atlantic as fast as she could go. Following the morning 'Battle-stations' the forenoon and afternoon watches were devoted to drills and evolutions. All of the gun crews were required to spend time on the loading machines to maintain or develop the rapidity with which they could service the guns.

Loading a 5"/54 caliber gun was not a simple evolution. Breech opened, hot casing ejected, rammer spade drops, fresh brass powder charge placed, shell man-handled ahead, both rammed into the gun, breech closed, shoot. Every day, every mount crew practiced; again . . . 7 seconds, again . . . 6 seconds, again . . . 5 seconds, again, again, again. The 40mm mount crews practiced passing the four round 20 pound clips and placing them in the loading slots at the breech ends of the quadruple mounts. To maintain the firing rate of 160 rounds per minute per gun, a clip had to be loaded every second and a half into each of the four guns. Forty clips a minute for each gun. It was easy to understand why the inside of the gun shields were lined with ready service clips in three rows.

Loading drills for the 18-inch turrets were much more complicated; requiring the efforts of hundreds of men to ensure a steady supply of projectiles and powder bags. The vast majority worked to move the 3,850 pound projectiles or 110 pound powder bags to the hoists. As long as the hoists were full and waiting on the gun captain to load, those legions were doing their jobs well. In any of the three 18-inch turrets it is not hard to imagine the effort required to manhandle forty-eight powder bags a minute into the three hoists during rapid fire. The projectile men also had to move six shells a minute using ropes and capstans in a method called parbuckling into the three pusher hoists that led to the gun chambers.

Each gun had its own separate compartment inside the armored turret. Only four men were with the gun and one more looking at the gun chamber through an armored glass window controlling the upper powder hoist. Bore clearing blast of air, breech open, gun captain inspects bore for cinders, breach mushroom seal wiped, spanner emplaced, shell rammed, rammer withdrawn, breech plug primed, four bags rolled to spanner, bags pushed fore and aft, four more bags, powder carefully rammed (too hard the turret explodes), breech closed, gun captain signals ready, gun elevates and fires. Practice, practice, practice . . . . The Americans were fastest! By regulations, the cycle was not allowed to take less than 25 seconds. Anything over 30 seconds was considered unacceptable. Every one of the nine gun crews on *Argonne* could meet a 27 second mark.

The 6-inch guns for each turret were all in the same gun chamber. Their loading was very similar to the 5 inch, with one important difference. The projectiles at 135 pounds were too heavy to be man-handled and had to be placed (rolled actually) into the gun tray from a loader that took the shell from the hoist, and rotated it on an arc from the trunnion to the gun tray where it was put in place after the 64-pound powder case was positioned next to the spade. The 6-inch gun crews on *Argonne* could reliably load and fire every 6 to 7 seconds; just slightly slower than the 5 inch.

All of the repair parties were manned up in the afternoon watch and had to respond appropriately to simulated fires, flooding, machinery casualties, electronic failures, shell holes, torpedo hits, bomb hits and a host of other potential disasters all under the watchful eye of the Damage Control Assistant and his division officers. If the gun crews and fire-control parties were the offense these men were *Argonne*'s defense.

Even Commander Hugh Blankenship the ship's surgeon and his battle dressing parties were presented with simulated blood and gore to deal with appropriately. Sheppard always enjoyed personally watching his doctor try to cope with whatever mayhem Sheppard could dream up in the most difficult locations in the ship; after all, his own life had been saved by the battle dressing party and skilled surgeons on *Shenandoah*. Sheppard even convinced Admiral Hamblen to simulate a heart attack when Hugh least expected it.

Lieutenant Commander Thaddeus Furlong, *Argonne's* supply officer had to get his storekeepers to run down repair parts that were 'suppose-to-be' located in specific parts lockers and store rooms scattered around the battle cruiser wherever no one else needed the space. That was inevitably the long leg in the timelines to return damaged electronics or fire-control equipment to service.

Only Commander Chris Petersen's engineers on watch in the machinery spaces were exempt from the training schedule. The race was too important. The propulsion plant could not be spared for drills.

— —

Amiral Phillipe D'Aubigné had called a meeting in the wardroom onboard the French *cuirassé Languedoc* of all his admirals and ship captains at 0900 on May 22nd. Normally a pleasant flag officer with kind words of greeting and small talk, this time the admiral's officers were struck by the seriousness of his expression and dark circles under his eyes. They wondered among themselves if it was something more than the approach of the German army and the inevitable showdown.

It had been decided last year, shortly after Hitler had occupied the rest of metropolitan France; that the fleet would stay in *Mers el Kébir*. If the Germans or English tried to take them, they would fight and then scuttle. Neither side would get the advantage of these ships. After the war France could salvage those that she needed and scrap the rest. As far as the officers present were concerned the only issue was how long each of them was willing to fight and take casualties before scuttling to preserve French honor. That was an individual decision that *Amiral* D'Aubigné had left up to his ship's captains.

Phillipe began, "My comrades in honor, we had previously agreed on a course of action to cover any eventuality that we could foresee in the current war. We have been attacked by both sides. Nothing would have given me greater pleasure than to sail into battle against either the axis or the British, but we no longer have the supplies to accomplish anything. You know Rommel is closing in on Oran. It will only be a few days before we will be forced to put our plan into action. I have been meeting regularly with General Laroque who has assured me that the Legion will fight to the last man defending the fleet."

He paused to let his words settle and clear his own thoughts. "I have received a telegram from the Swiss embassy that originated with a German Admiral. He claims to be Hitler's representative to Italy and presents an alternative to our dilemma that we had not considered.

"Let me read the important part to you. 'I am prepared as the *Führer's* direct representative in Italy and with the full cooperation of the German Army, to offer you a safe passage to Toulon where you and your men can be repatriated to your homes and families without bloodshed.'"

Immediately the room began buzzing with whispers,

particularly among the ship captains. This truly was an option that they had not considered. Why would their enemy just let them go home?

Phillipe let the stirring die down of its own accord before speaking. "Let there be no rank or position in this discussion. One man's opinion is to have the same weight as another's. When we finish our discussion and every man has had an equal chance to convince the others, we must decide on what course of action we will follow. I insist that the decision we reach is unanimous, our strength lies in our unity and that we must preserve. Is there any among us who is not prepared to act together as one?"

No one initially rose. Then *Capitaine de Vaisseau* Charles Fournier, Commanding Officer of the *cuirassé Aquitaine,* stood to speak. "Gentlemen, the *Boches* have no honor. Look what they have done in France. They took the rest of our country without provocation. I for one say, Tell them to go to hell!"

Contre-amiral Verne Bertrand of *Le Quatrième Escadron de 'Croiseur Lourd* spoke. "We have a chance to save our men. We have a chance to allow everyone to go home to France. The war is over for us. Let us leave for France and forget the past."

Others rose and spoke, many for leaving the war behind and returning home. Some believed it was more important to preserve the honor of the French Navy and to support the Legion. A few asked what of the officers and men who had their families here in Oran. What was to become of them? Should those men be left behind? The hours dragged on with Phillipe becoming less convinced than ever that his officers could reach a consensus.

Then *Capitaine de Frégate* Destin Moreau of the *Contre-torpilleur Mogador* rose. Though very junior, he had distinguished himself in action against the Italians early in the war. None doubted his courage.

"My friends, someday the war will end and France will rise again as she always has. Whatever action we choose, we must consider how future generations of French naval officers will look back on this day. Will they remember brave men resolute in the face of adversity? Do we sail for France to leave Algeria defenseless for the sake of personal considerations? What plot lurks behind this offer of the German Admiral? What if the Italian battle fleet waits over the horizon? Do we fight then?

There are many unknowns, but I for one believe in duty, honor, and country!"

He sat. The space was silent.

— —

The last glimmer of light was fading in the western sky as Sheppard directed his Officer of the Deck to slow to 42 knots. The loom of the lighthouse at Cape Spartel in French Morocco was on his starboard bow. Soon he expected to see the one from Cape Tarifa fine on his port bow. His Navigator Commander Art Roberts had done an excellent job in bringing them this far. He was exactly where he wanted to be as night began to envelope *Argonne* for the passage through the Strait of Gibraltar.

Commander Oliver Halverson RN VC KCB had stopped the masquerade as Admiral Hamblen's aide and was back in his own uniform. The former Commanding Officer of the destroyer *Swift,* he had been knighted by King George VI and presented with the Victoria Cross for the Battle of Dover Strait. Afire and sinking *Swift* had managed to sink fifteen invasion barges before Ollie had run her aground and continued to fight his guns from what remained above water until captured. When the Germans surrendered he was released, more dead than alive. For the last three days he had been entertaining and educating *Argonne's* wardroom with his firsthand knowledge of the *Kriegsmarine* and the brutality of their common enemy. Unfortunately, Sheppard and his subconscious did not hear him.

Ollie had come up to the conning station where Art had set up his quartermasters to pilot *Argonne* through the Strait. As a precaution, Sheppard had manned battle stations, but was not really expecting any action. Ted Grabowski had taken over the OOD duties from Art and was keeping a watchful eye on things from the armored command tower. Sheppard directed Chuck Williamson to load the hoists with High Capacity shells in the event that trouble came looking. With every gun manned, all radars humming, and condition *Zebra* set throughout the ship, *Argonne* was ready for anything. If they did hit a mine, at least the flooding would be minimized.

Art's quartermasters were taking bearings to both Cape Spartel light and Cape Tarifa using the alidades on the open part of the conning station. The SG radar operator was getting beautifully clear returns from the cliffs in the strait. Crossing the bearings from the two light houses with the ranges reported by radar Art was sure he knew where he was within 250 yards as they entered the strait. Ollie had assured Sheppard that the swept channel was a thousand yards wide in most places.

Sheppard looked at him with a smile, "Most places? Commander, would you care to elaborate?!"

Ollie looked at Sheppard knowingly. He had also listened to the stories of *Shenandoah* at Pearl Harbor and how *Argonne* had pulled a rabbit out of the proverbial hat in defeating Schröder at Cape Vilan. Surely exaggerated in the retelling, nevertheless, Ollie recognized a fellow warrior on whom he might employ a bit of legendary British wit. Ollie smiled, "Well, Captain McCloud, one never knows for sure, does one."

— —

"Welcome home, Madame." The head butler of *Chateau D'Aubigné*, whose family had served the chateau for generations, stood in the doorway as Daphne D'Aubigné returned from visiting friends but more importantly soliciting funds to feed her husband's sailors and marines.

"Thank you, Chevir. How is Marie? Has the baby come?"

"She is resting well, madame, as her time approaches"

"I see, and my son Étienne, is he coping well?"

"No, madame, he is like every expectant father filled with trepidation for Marie and what will come." Mainard Chevir knew all too well the dangers of child birth having lost his first wife during the delivery of a dead son. "Was your trip successful, madame?" he solicitously inquired. The senior staff of the chateau were well aware of what Madame D'Aubigné was doing to preserve her husband's ships, and with it some of the honor of France.

"I fear not, Mainard," breaking tradition, calling him by his first name, "my husband will only have enough to feed his men for another month or two." She sighed as she spoke, "I wish I could be with him and the world returned to the way it was before this horrible war."

— —

Admiral Schröder was frustrated. He did not have an answer. The German ambassador to Switzerland had assured him that the Swiss were trying to make contact with their consulate in Oran but that there were problems with the cable under the Mediterranean. Who knew, perhaps the German advance had cut it. They had sent a wireless message but that had not yet been received clearly according to the Swiss. Well if the Swiss could not carry the mail perhaps the Spanish could. At least they would be more sympathetic to the German position. He sat down to compose the second message. This message the French could not ignore!

4

DIPLOMACY

GRUPPENFÜHRER KARL BODERMANN HAD been very specific in his instructions to *SturmbannFührer* Otto Reiniger. The task had to be completed quickly; not later than 0800 on the morning of the 24ᵗʰ. If there was anything Otto was good at, it was completing a task on time. That skill was the principle reason for his meteoric rise in the SS. It was also the reason that Karl had chosen him to get the information that his brother had requested. Fritz had promised that it would end the war with the English in only six months, if the operation that his boss Admiral Klaus Schröder had devised was successful.

That was all that Otto had needed to enter the former French Naval Ministry with a platoon of storm-troopers and start working. Of course the French had resisted his demands. He had expected that. However, hanging the first two bureaucrats that spoke, questioning his orders had solved most of the problems. It always worked to just throw a rope over a convenient railing or beam at the entrance and hoist the noosed, condemned up without tying their hands or feet. They struggled longer that way to impress the other workers, as slow strangulation eventually ended their protests. All the others were very compliant following such demonstrations of German resolve.

What Otto did not know was that the French were just as resolute in their resistance to the German wishes. As the list of individuals was being compiled, the bureaucrats were making and smuggling out a second list of the same names and addresses to the French underground. The so-called *Maquis* started to notify the named individuals, mostly women and children that they were being put on a German list for some reason and should go into hiding. Before the final list was given to Otto Reiniger, just before the deadline, many were safe in the countryside or soon would be. Only the *Maquis* knew their locations.

— —

The pounding on the door would not stop. Mainard Chevir finally opened the door to this insistent stranger and the two men with him. "Who are you to be pounding on our door at this hour?"

"I am called Commandant César of the *Maquis*, it is imperative that I speak with Madame D'Aubigné immediately."

"I don't care who you are, Commandant, I will not wake Madame on the say so of a ruffian."

"Then get out of my way. We will find her ourselves."

Awakened by the pounding, Madame D'Aubigné dressed in her night gown and robe, entered the great hall. "It is alright, Chevir, I am already awake from the pounding and will talk to these men."

"Madame, it is of utmost urgency that you come with me at once."

"Never! Who do you think you are to order me to leave my home and the people I am responsible for in the middle of the night with no explanation?"

"Madame, you, your son, and daughter-in-law are being placed on a list by the German SS. We believe all of your husband's officers' families are in great danger. Those are the names that the SS has gone to great lengths to quickly acquire. You must come at once."

"But my daughter-in-law can't travel; she is too late in her pregnancy."

"Madame, if she stays, I fear she and her baby will die at the hands of the Germans anyway." A look of horror crossed the delicate features of Daphne D'Aubigné's patrician face.

"Bastards!"

"Madame, we must go now!"

"If you insist, Chevir, get the Grand Renault. Wake Étienne and Marie, tell them to pack light and bring everything they need to be gone for several days."

"No, madame. There is no time. You cannot use the car. We will have to stay off the roads and remain in the woods."

"Impossible, Marie can't walk!"

"Madame, if I may suggest," Chevir interjected, "perhaps a horse cart filled with straw would be acceptable to the Commandant."

"A horse cart would be too big for the terrain we must traverse. My men may be able to pull a small donkey cart. That should be large enough for Marie by herself." Commandant César thought for a moment. He needed to be careful to not betray his real identity. "If Marie needs medical attention, I am sure we can quickly arrange it."

Bowing to the inevitable, Madame D'Aubigné acquiesced, "It appears we have no choice. Chevir, get the cart while I wake Étienne and Marie, but you are coming with us."

— —

She awoke suddenly. What was happening? Was it the strange surroundings since she had left their home? Was it the absence of friends in this strange place? She was bathed in sweat. A gnawing fear filled her with dread.

What of her love? Somehow she knew he was concerned, nervous at their situation, but also confident of their safety. She knew many of his officers and men. They too shared his determination—to do what? She would do everything in her power to see them safe on this new adventure, pray for them; hold them tight in her thoughts.

What more could he ask of her? It was impossible to do more!

— —

NAVAL APPROACHES TO MERS EL KEBIR

GOLFE D'ORAN

ANCHORING AND TRAWLING PROHIBITED

The first hint of dawn was beginning to color the eastern horizon as *Argonne* glided toward the position that Sheppard and Admiral Hamblen had selected off of *Mers el Kébir*. There was no sign of reaction yet from the French as both men prayed that when they finally awoke to the American battle cruiser's presence, the immense stars and stripes flying from both of *Argonne's* masts would also be seen. Sheppard had briefed his crew on what was going to happen, but he could not allay their fears that *Argonne* was too close to the French fleet, and should hostilities start, she would be quickly overwhelmed and destroyed.

The guns, though loaded and ready for immediate action were all trained fore and aft. Even the directors were trained to their normal peace time positions. That did not prevent the fire-control parties deep below the armored deck from using Art Roberts's accurate navigation fixes and observations of the locations of the French warships to generate fire control solutions in the Ford computers. Attached stern first to the mole in what was referred to as a "Mediterranean moor" they were for the most part heading directly away from *Argonne's* location. In a curious application of design more than half of the French battleships and all of their battle cruisers had their entire main armament in quadruple turrets located forward. The heavy guns that faced Sheppard only slightly outnumbered those he could bring to bear with his broadside.

The great armored hatch covering Argonne's hanger on her fantail slowly slid aft, opening the huge space containing the ship's boats and six OS2U-5 Kingfisher aircraft. The aircraft and boat crane lowered its hook into the hanger and Seaman Goldstein put the lifting bridle of the captain's gig over the hook, signaling Chief Aviation Boatswain's Mate Walter Bledsoe to haul away. Rising quickly from its cradle in the hanger, Sheppard was surprised at the fresh coat of dark blue paint that had been applied to the hull of his gig. He raised his 7 x 50 binoculars and saw his smiling coxswain BM2 Raymondo Cruz looking back at him. How Cruz had managed to turn his gig into a shiny Admiral's barge with everything else that had been happening, Sheppard could only guess at. As he looked closer, he saw four large five pointed silver stars neatly aligned in a horizontal row on each bow, completing the transformation of the gig to the barge of Admiral Hamblen. Even the flagstaff was now topped with a halberd indicating that the Admiral was onboard the gig.

Using a bow line to keep the barge pointed into the water flowing past *Argonne,* Fireman Russert started the boat's engine just before it touched the water. Cruz and Russert controlled the position while Goldstein and Seaman Johansen unhooked the lifting bridle from the barge. The moment it was unhooked, the *First-Repeat* pennant was raised at Argonne's starboard yardarm indicating the Admiral's absence from his flagship; as Cruz rang four bells to Russert and then held a fifth clank to make sure Russert gave him every bit of speed possible, The bow line was cast off. Goldstein and Johansen practiced their synchronized routine with the boathooks one last time that would have put smiles on the faces of Broadway's choreographers.

The only item that seemed out of place was the large white flag flying from the flagstaff below the halberd as Admiral Hamblen left with Sheppard's best signalman for his historic meeting with *Amiral* D'Aubigné.

— —

Vizeadmiral Joachim Moeller watched as the last of the four Bf109T fighters left the flight deck of his flagship *Peter Strasser.* Even though his fleet would be off the *Luftwaffe's* base at Stavanger Norway before the RAF reconnaissance patrols would be in his vicinity, he was determined to remain unlocated until the late afternoon. By then he would be north of the latitude of Scapa Flow and Tovey could not catch up using his slow British battleships. With luck the RAF would not even note his sailing until the afternoon photo recon Mosquito had landed at RAF Benson. It would take an hour or two to develop the films and then the interpreters could begin to count noses.

It was good to be back at sea. This raid into the Atlantic had every chance of success. The English had redeployed some of their battle cruisers to Gibraltar; without them, Tovey was not strong enough to detach more squadrons to stop Joachim at the Denmark Strait. The cruiser patrols were too weak to do any real damage. If the weather was fair, his JU87 Stukas would make short work of any attempts to shadow him. With the addition of the four armored cruisers he could even afford to detach two for a gun action in the event of foul weather. No this time Germany would prevail. The lessons from Schröder's foray had all been digested by the Flottenchef's staff. They had assured him that if he could annihilate three east bound convoys of which two had to be mostly tankers, the English would be forced to surrender. The only unknown was the Americans.

What were they up to this time?

— —

Rear Admiral Hamilton was also glad to sortie from Norfolk. Admiral King had made good on his promise to replace *Sabine* and *Belleau Wood* in Task Force 48, *Columbia* (CV-7) was delayed in starting her overhaul. Even though her electronics and anti-aircraft armament were woefully out of date she could still operate her full air group of F4F-3 Wildcat fighters, SBD-3 Dauntless dive bombers, and TBD-1 Devastator torpedo planes. A sister of his new flagship *Raritan* (CV-10), Admiral King's decision had made it easy for Hamilton's staff to incorporate her into all the existing operation plans, particularly the air plan. He was more concerned with the *Chateau Thierry* (CC-48). She was fresh out of her post shakedown availability and undoubtedly would need some time to get the inactivity of the shipyard out of her crew. At least she had all the latest electronics. Dolf Hamilton was counting on her to be his radar eyes and ears.

As he stood on the flag bridge of his carrier, he mused with his Chief of Staff Captain Henry Burke, "Henry, I would feel a lot better, if we had *Argonne* and Sheppard with us right now."

"Yes sir, I too am concerned about the increased wireless traffic originating in the Jade Bay that the Brits have reported."

"Do you think Lütjens is going to sortie, or is it just another feint?"

"Hard to say for sure, Admiral; we gave them a good thumping at Cape Vilan, but they know how vital the convoys are just as much as we do. I was talking to a friend of mine on the CNO's staff. Hardly a day goes by that Admiral of the Fleet Pound doesn't remind Admiral King that the real war is in the Atlantic. King took it personally when the Japs devastated Pearl Harbor. It's clear his heart is in the Pacific and can't wait to divert ships to avenge the attack."

"It is too bad that King could not find us another fighting Admiral to replace Ray Calhoun. He never should have left the armored command tower to override Kevin Bailey's incompetent orders. It is going to take a couple of months before Ray recovers, if ever, from the loss of his left arm at Cape Vilan."

"I know how you feel, Admiral, but it is a blessing in disguise. Sheppard is senior to Jake Gibbons of *Chateau Thierry,* which makes him in charge if you detach the battle cruisers.

"Does Sheppard know that?"

"Not until we tell him, Admiral, but do you really think it will make much difference to him?"

"Only the difference between an order and a request, though Jake would be a fool to ignore any suggestion Sheppard makes."

Both men continued to watch as the *Chateau Thierry's* Kingfishers wove back and forth over the ocean that Task Force 48 was heading towards. Destroyer Squadrons Thirty and Twenty-eight were already deploying into an anti-submarine screen for the heavy ships as they came out of Thimble Shoals channel. Dolf looked at Henry as both men smiled. Sheppard may not be with them now, but his experience was. No German U-boat was going to ambush *Raritan* the way *Sabine* had been hit in these same waters the month before.

— —

To say that the French were surprised by the sudden appearance of the American battle cruiser off the port of *Mers el Kébir* at dawn would have been the understatement of the century. The first lookout spotting *Argonne* had raised the alarm and quickly the fleet was alerted. Sailors ran to their battle stations, boilers were lit, and engines began warming. *Amiral* D'Aubigné briefly considered opening fire as the Americans were allied with the English, but this large warship was not showing any hostile intent. Her guns were all trained fore and aft; not one director was pointed at a French target. The launch with the large white flag had also come into view, dutifully being reported by the flagship's lookouts as battle stations were being manned.

As the launch entered the western gap in the mole, Phillipe saw through his binoculars the four silver stars on the bow and the halberd on the flagstaff. This was significant; the Americans were sending a full Admiral to talk with him. He went below to don his best full dress white uniform pausing to order the *Languedoc's* Commanding Officer to prepare to receive an American Admiral with full military honors.

— —

Boatswain's Mate second class Cruz knew how to handle the captain's gig turned admiral's barge. He put on a show worthy of an Oscar as he darted between ships at high speed. Before they had left *Argonne*, he knew which one was the French flagship. The French tricolor with four white stars arranged in a diamond on the blue field was clearly visible on one of the largest battleships using a long glass. By custom he made directly toward the aft starboard accommodation ladder, backing full to stop no more than 3 inches from the fenders. As had happened before, the rapidity of his approach and landing caused the French boatswain to swallow the last note of the pipe for coming alongside. Admiral Hamblen stepped nimbly onto the landing stage and started to ascend the steps to the quarterdeck. Chief Signalman Evan Bryce also leaped to the landing stage but remained standing on it as Johansen and Goldstein used their boathooks to shove off from the *Languedoc's* accommodation ladder.

Cruz only went a few hundred yards away and then idled the gig to wait. He did not use his usual maximum speed, deliberately slowing enough for Johansen and Goldstein to complete their synchronized boathook routine under the watching eyes of the French fleet. Cruz smiled to himself that a kid from a west Texas border town who grew up with a record and no future was now part of a diplomatic mission of vital national importance. He knew that he had one man to thank for this opportunity. He would make any sacrifice; do whatever was needed, to again save Captain McCloud as he had on *Shenandoah*. When he idled the gig, he personally removed the halberd and replaced the white flag with the stars and stripes.

— —

The echoes from the last of the seventeen gun salute were dying away when Admiral Hamblen stepped forward to greet his old friend *Amiral* D'Aubigné. "Phillipe, thank you for the warm welcome."

"John, I am surprised by your visit and forgive me for not rendering the proper nineteen guns to the Commander in Chief of the United States Fleet."

Raising his hand to reassure his old friend, Admiral Hamblen replied, "Phillipe, you were correct, I no longer hold that position. The seventeen guns was the correct number."

"Let us adjourn to my flag quarters; my steward still knows how to make an excellent cup of American coffee."

"Phillipe, before we do, I have a request of you. My flagship is in a vulnerable position and I wish your permission for her to launch her spotter aircraft for an anti-submarine patrol."

"John, but of course, I will order a signal immediately."

"Phillipe, that is my second request, I brought along my own signalman to avoid the difficulties yours may have with English. He is waiting on the landing stage. If you would be so kind as to have him taken to the signal bridge, he will send the signal necessary to *Argonne*."

Amiral D'Aubigné turned to his flag lieutenant, spoke briefly, and turned back to his guest. "John, you doubly honor me. Not only with your own presence, but you also brought America's most famous ship. I wish my officers could have a chance to meet the famous Captain McCloud. Is he still in command of *Argonne?*"

"Yes, he is, Phillipe, and perhaps your officers will have that chance," Admiral Hamblen concluded as both men turned and walked arm in arm to *Amiral* D'Aubigné's quarters.

— ‐ —

Sheppard's Conning Officer alerted him. "Captain, the French flagship is signaling."

Sheppard turned and began his usual absentminded reading of the Morse code being sent by the signal light. A habit he had developed early in his career, there were very few signalmen in the fleet who could send faster than Sheppard could read. One of them was Evan Bryce, but this time he was slowing his usual blistering pace. When the message was concluded, Sheppard walked to the 21MC 'squawk box' selected the command tower, and ordered, "Officer of the Deck, prepare to launch aircraft." He then walked out onto the conning station platform to look at the fine day that was dawning as the sun began to peek above Montagne de Saint Augustin and Jebel Kahar. Admiral Hamblen's initial meeting had gone well enough for him to be allowed to fly his Kingfishers. It therefore made little sense to keep his crew at battle stations while they talked and he idly cruised off the harbor entrance.

He turned back to the conning station and directed his JA sound powered phone talker to pass. "Officer of the Deck; secure from battle stations with the exception of underway anti-aircraft mounts and directors, set condition *Zebra* below the second deck modified to allow passage of personnel above the fourth deck."

The starting cartridges for the two Kingfishers on his Mark 7 catapults fired almost together as an out of breath Signalman third class arrived on the conning platform with the written out message.

"Is there a reply, sir?" the young petty officer asked.

"No, not at this time, thank you," Sheppard answered. Was there anything he needed to do to insure a safe launch of his aircraft? Sheppard knew they were armed with two 325 pound Mark 17 depth bombs. One was fused to detonate at 50 feet of water depth and the other at 25 feet. That put the Kingfishers at their maximum gross weight. He decided to improve their chances of successful launch by increasing speed and directed the Conning Officer to come to ahead two thirds. With *Argonne's* increased speed, there would be a greater lift for the aircraft relative to the wind at the end of the catapult track.

It wasn't long before the Officer of the Deck reported, "Ready to launch aircraft."

A quick look aft to confirm in his own mind readiness, was followed by Sheppard's order to, "Launch Aircraft!"

— —

The two admirals entered the flag cabin onboard *Languedoc* Phillipe, ever the gracious host that John Hamblen had known when they were both attachés in London, gestured to two overstuffed wingback chairs with a small table conveniently nearby. John sat as the cabin steward politely asked how he wished his coffee. Phillipe made a show of his good memory by answering for John, "Black with one sugar."

Admiral Hamblen began, "Phillipe, I trust that my floatplanes will not find any of your submarines in the vicinity. I would hate to start the relationship between our forces with an unfortunate incident."

"Do not concern yourself, John; unfortunately, I do not have the fuel to support my ships at sea."

"I understand, Phillipe." Slowly Hamblen began to speak seriously. "We have known each other for many years; in all that time have you ever known me to take advantage of our friendship?"

Suddenly serious, Phillipe looked at Hamblen wondering what the destination of this conversation was. "No, John, why are you asking?"

"Because, Phillipe, I am about to."

"Clearly I have not brought a capital ship into the Mediterranean unescorted on a social call. I bring a letter to you from President Roosevelt. I asked him to be allowed to deliver it personally because of our friendship and the hope we could discuss the future honestly."

Phillipe André D'Aubigné leaned back in his chair with a hardened face as he stared at John Hamblen handing him the letter.

— —

The 5-inch cartridge fired when the lanyard on the starboard catapult was pulled. Lieutenant Commander Bronco Burdick USN flying the *Argonne's* OS2U-5 Kingfisher call sign 'mustang zero-one' accelerated down the 80-foot track, became airborne, and cleared the lifelines by two feet. As he flew past the superstructure, Sheppard smiled at the ever present white silk scarf wrapped around his Scout Observation Squadron commander's neck. Sheppard also had to smile at the one broken submarine painted on the side of Bronco's aircraft beneath the single German flag boasting Bronco's 'almost airborne' to air victory in the Battle of Cape Vilan.

Sheppard turned at the crack of the second catapult firing

which hurled Bronco's wingman Lieutenant Barry Jensen off the port catapult in mustang zero-five. With both of his first two Scout Observation aircraft airborne, it was time to ready two more for launch. The plan that Sheppard had discussed with Bronco earlier was for Barry and Bronco to search out to 50 nautical miles while the second group of Kingfishers flew only to a radius of 15 miles, but at a higher altitude. According to the charts the north coast of Africa had a sand bottom and a submarine should be visible against that background as the sun rose higher in the sky.

— ▬ —

Aboard the French flagship Phillipe read:

Dear Amiral D'Aubigné,

I am sure that you know better than I the tragedies that have been visited both on France and your fleet at the hands of Germany, as well as Great Britain. Though I do not condone the actions that the British took in 1940, I understand their motives. Freedom and democracy are in grave peril. If liberty, equality, and fraternity are to eventually triumph, it is absolutely necessary to keep Great Britain in the war. Without the British Isles as a staging base to launch the invasion that will free France from the heel of Nazi oppression, it is likely that the current war will be lost.

Should your fleet become available to the forces of evil, it will tip the balance of naval power in the Atlantic against the cause of freedom. Unless the Americas can continue to sustain Britain by sea, she will starve and surrender within months. I know that it is unlikely you and the men under your command will join us in our righteous cause, but I have sent our mutual friend Admiral Hamblen to persuade you to leave Oran for Martinique in the Caribbean. I pledge the United States of America will supply your men with food, fuel, and what else they may need to await a better and more joyous time when you may return to a free and democratic France with honor.

/s/ Franklin Delano Roosevelt

As Phillipe read, John Hamblen noted that he had begun to cry. "Phillipe, what is wrong? Why do you shed tears? My President is absolutely sincere in his offer."

"John, there are many problems. A year ago I had the fuel to reach Martinique. Now I have neither the fuel nor the supplies. If only the English had offered us such a proposal we would have gladly accepted it, but they chose to insult us and attack us and now it is too late."

"No, it is not, Phillipe. We knew of your situation. I have tankers and cargo ships in Gibraltar to meet your fleet as it leaves the Mediterranean. The United States Navy will make good on our President's promise the moment you decide to sail. The only thing you need to concern yourself with is when you wish to hoist anchor."

"No, John, there is more to this than just America and France." Phillipe rose and went to his desk where he pulled out Klaus Schröder's telegram. He handed it to his friend saying, "Your President is not the only person who wishes me to move my fleet."

Admiral Hamblen sat back in his chair as he thoughtfully read the communiqué. Being able to return to France after nearly two years of exile was a powerful incentive for any group of men particularly men who now found themselves without a country or a government. John knew Phillipe well enough that he would not make these decisions without trying to achieve a consensus of his officers. He noted that the telegram was two days old. His friend and the French officers must have reached a decision already. "What did you decide to do?"

— —

Flight Lieutenant Anthony Pennyman RAF was really a Professor of Paleontology at Cambridge in better times, as he referred to the prewar period. Unfortunately, there wasn't much interest in old bones by the armed services in wartime. His skills of observation and deductive reasoning however, were valuable in his current employment as a photo interpreter at RAF Benson. It was his job to study the photos that others risked their lives over Germany to acquire and try to divine as much intelligence from them as possible.

Sometimes it was not what was seen but what was not seen that was important, as it had been with the immediate assessment of yesterday's photos of the Jade estuary. Other photo analysts were responsible for those assessments. Two aircraft carriers, four battle cruisers, four armored cruisers, twelve smaller cruisers and 16 destroyers were missing from the 1800 photographs. They had to be either in the North Sea or have transited the Kiel Canal into the Baltic. The later possibility was beyond the ability of the RAF to determine with their organic assets. It also really did not matter.

The first possibility would result in an all-out effort to locate the missing warships before dusk. Ultimately successful, the fleet would be located off of Stavanger Norway heading north, but not in time for the Royal Navy to catch it or a strike to be organized by the RAF before dark. These ships represented a dire threat to the fate of Great Britain should they breakout into the Atlantic and countermeasures had to be put in place.

Now it was time for Tony to spend time with his magnifying glass, stereographic viewer and his keen intellect to see what else the original photos contained, in comparison to the ones taken of the same location earlier in the week. His near photographic memory was invaluable in that task. The first thing he noticed was that sixteen cargo and transport ships had been moved into the basin at Wilhelmshaven. They had been idle ever since the failed invasion attempt at Pevensey Bay last year. What were they doing? He used the best magnifying glass he had and wiped it carefully before staring at the wharfs adjacent to the transports. The harder he looked the more convinced he became. Tanks!!

— —

"John, until the Commanding Officer of *Mogador* spoke, the large majority of my officers favored accepting the German Admiral's offer. Destin reminded all of us that service to one's country can never be subordinate to personal needs or desires. History would rightfully judge us harshly, if we gave in. Our comrades in the Foreign Legion have vowed to fight to the last man to defend the fleet and Algeria. We could not do less."

"Unfortunately, I received another telegram from the Germans last night that I have not shared with anyone else." Phillipe rose suddenly looking older, beaten; his shoulders slumped as he walked to his desk and pulled out a second communiqué.

John Hamblen took the telegram from his friend and read it very carefully.

Amiral D'Aubigné,

You have failed to respond to reason. You have failed your men. You have now failed your families. As you read this know that the Gestapo is arresting the families of your officers. Should you not present your fleet intact at the entrance of Toulon Harbor by 0800 on the 26th of May, they will be sent to the slave labor camps in Germany and Poland.

Admiral Schröder
Kriegsmarine

"My God, Phillipe, is there no end to the depravity of our enemy?" Admiral Hamblen suddenly became cold and hard. The steel of a warrior flashed in his eyes as he said, "Phillipe, I have two questions. The first is simple, what can I do to help you? The second is harder, what do you think your officers will say?"

— —

Ammiraglio Romano aboard his flagship *Italia* led his battle fleet out of Naples Harbor. A flotilla of tugs stood by for assistance as his battleships cleared the Molo of San Vincenzo and proceeded in a column turn to a course of 220°. His destroyers and light cruisers raced ahead to form his screen as the fleet passed Napoli Castel dell'Ovo on the starboard beam. Finally clearing Isola d'Ischia, his fleet navigator took a departure fix on the light at Punta Imperatore on Ischia and the peak of Monte Solaro on Capri. More than most Gugliehno knew that Operation *Guardare al Futuro* would determine naval supremacy in the Mediterranean for a generation. He had assured *Grand' Ammiragilio* Dragonetti that the fleet would not fail.

At the same time, *Ammiraglio di Squadra* Moretti onboard *Aquila* was leading his six battle cruisers, light cruisers, destroyers and Italy's only aircraft carriers *Aquila*, *Sparviero*, *Pegaso* and *Falco* past Punta San Teresa into the Gulf of LaSpezia. Also initially in a column he turned his carriers and battle cruisers to a course of 200° until they cleared Isola Palmaria where he altered to 223° until he cleared Corsica on his port side. He would remain well west of Sardinia outside the range of British reconnaissance flights from Malta. It would be his privilege to guard against the intervention of Force H while *Ammiraglio* Romano captured or destroyed the French at *Mers el Kébir* when the sun rose the morning of May 26. Those two old battle cruisers and damaged aircraft carriers of Force H would be no match for him. He had a three to one advantage in gunfire where it counted.

— —

"John, I don't know. It is one thing for honor to demand that we sacrifice ourselves. It is something else for it to demand our families. Before this telegram arrived from the Spanish consulate, we would have gladly accepted President Roosevelt's offer. Now I do not know."

"Are you going to put it to your officers?"

"Yes, I have scheduled a meeting in *Languedoc's* wardroom for 0900. My officers should begin arriving momentarily."

"May I impose on you with a request to attend the meeting myself?"

"Of course, I hope that you have not forgotten the French you learned when we toured France together with our families in '28."

"Phillipe, don't worry, I'll get by. May I send another message to my flagship?"

"But of course, John."

— —

As Bronco and Barry Jensen climbed away from *Argonne,* the first thing they noticed was the absence of Force H. Their escort and heavy support was not where they had been briefed it should be.

Bronco was the first to report, "Panther, this is Mustang Zero-One, big friends and airdales not repeat, *not* present."

Sheppard heard the report from the speaker that broadcast on the spotting network VHF radio into the conning station. So did Commander Halverson. Sheppard gave Ollie an accusatory stare. All Ollie could do was shrug his shoulders, go to the chart table and look busy.

"French flagship is signaling again, Captain," Sheppard's Officer of the Deck reported.

Captain McCloud walked onto the open conning platform, grateful for a distraction to calm his growing concern and anger at being left exposed by the Brits. It would not be long before the *Luftwaffe*'s and Mussolini's Regia Aeronautica's morning searches would be out scouring the Mediterranean for anything new. They may not want to attack and damage the French fleet, hoping to capture it intact, but that did not apply to him. As he looked at the signal light flashing, it was clear that Evan Bryce did not want the French eavesdropping on his message. Sheppard would have to wait until his Signalman first class had read and recorded it before he would know what it said.

Sheppard also had a decision to make. He was prohibited from using the radar fuses where a dud might fall into enemy hands. He understood the reason—the technology was just too devastating to allow the axis to use it against Allied aircraft. He would have to stay as close to shore as he could, cruising off *Mers el Kébir* in order to fire to seaward if search planes were detected. But there, his air search radars were interfered with by the mountains of the western Algeria coast.

The signalman arrived with the message from Admiral Hamblen. Sheppard read it and ordered, "Take this to radio central immediately!" Sheppard turned to his orderly Corporal Westbrook and ordered, "Find the Communications Officer and have him report to radio central on the double!" The absence of the usual niceties shocked Westbrook, not that anyone could tell, but it did make him run and drop down the ship's ladders sliding only on his hands and arms.

Sheppard did not know what Hamblen had in mind, but the "urgent" was all he needed to make his communications staff move as fast as humanly possible.

— —

Amiral D'Aubigné and Admiral Hamblen walked into the wardroom onboard *Languedoc* where the assembled French officers rose as they entered. Quickly, *Amiral* D'Aubigné began the meeting. "Gentlemen, let me introduce a dear friend of mine from the United States—Admiral John Hamblen, former Commander in Chief United States Fleet and current special emissary from President Roosevelt. His arrival this morning was something I am sure you are all aware of. Besides sending us a former head of the United States Navy, President Roosevelt chose to doubly honor us by sending their most famous battle cruiser, the *Argonne*, still currently commanded by the hero of the Battle of Cape Vilan. She currently cruises off of *Mers el Kébir* awaiting our decision on President Roosevelt's offer."

There were murmurings throughout the crowded wardroom that obviously something had significantly changed since their last meeting. The talking died off quickly as *Amiral* D'Aubigné frowned at the interruption and waited for silence.

"President Roosevelt has requested that we take the fleet to Martinique in the Caribbean and remain there until the end of the war. He has offered to supply all our needs in fuel and food until we are able to return to France upon liberation. He has even positioned tankers in Gibraltar to replenish what we need to make the journey as soon as we decide to go. I am certain that the gesture of sending my friend Admiral Hamblen is both a sign of respect and of the genuine nature of the offer."

Contre-Amiral Bertrand stood. "*Amiral*, I do not understand why you would call this meeting. This seems the answer to our prayers. We get to keep the fleet and return to France with honor and without the English."

"Yes, Verne, it is a wonderful offer. Unfortunately, it was not the only communiqué that I received today." With that he read the telegram from the *Kriegsmarine* Admiral Klaus Schröder delivered by the Spanish consulate only hours before.

There was stunned silence in *Languedoc's* wardroom. For several moments not a man spoke as they all thought of their families wasting away to slow horrible deaths in the German slave labor camps.

Finally *Capitaine de Vaisseau* Fournier stood and spate on the deck. "*Boches*! What manner of men make war on women and children to blackmail men of honor." The wardroom rumbled with hate until finally Phillipe raised his hand for quiet.

He began again. "It is clear both from President Roosevelt's letter and the actions of the Germans that they both assess the situation the same. If our fleet is given to the Germans, they will win the war. If the allies can keep it out of German hands, then perhaps they will achieve victory. So my friends, if we do as the Germans ask, we will be able to live with our families in France but without honor. If we do as Roosevelt asks, we sacrifice our families. I do not see other alternatives."

Capitaine de Frégate Destin Moreau stood. "*Amiral*, do you think that this will be the only demand that the *Boches* make or are they then going to demand we fight against the Allies?"

Deliberately using his first name as a father would talk to a beloved son. "Destin, I do not think for a moment that this will be the last demand they make. They do not know our guns, our ships, or our machinery. They do not have the men to operate our ships. No, they will demand more. If we give in, I for one am convinced that the demands will only grow and having once given in for the sake of my Daphne and my son Étienne, I will have to make a habit of it." *Amiral* D'Aubigné sat. The stress of the last few days and the emotion of contemplating the death of his family overcame his professional demeanor and he wept.

Phillipe D'Aubigné was loved and respected by his officers. He had kept them together when France fell. He had defied the English, fought and repaired his fleet. He had found ways to keep them supplied with food and fuel purchased with his own family fortune. It was impossible for John Hamblen to tell whether his weeping or the contents of Schröder's telegram had affected the French officers more.

— —

The Deputy Assistant Attaché for Intercultural Development at the United States Embassy in Bern Switzerland was alerted to the high priority message being received by the embassy's communications center. Located in a secure area, it was perhaps the one group of embassy staff personnel that knew Bernie Smith's real job was with the OSS even if no one knew his real name. When he arrived, Bernie immediately went to his personal safe, to which he alone had the combination, to unlock it. He then pulled out a code book.

As the embassy radiomen recorded the five letter groups of the message, Bernie began to figure out the anagram that would tell him which settings to make for his cryptographic machine. A relatively simple device, it relied more on the one time use of keys than on a complex stepping sequence as naval ciphers did.

When Bernie finished decoding the message he carefully drew a line through the cipher that had been used and replaced the code book in his safe. Spinning the tumbler several times, he left, shredding the message that he had memorized before he left the communications center. Returning to his office he called Martin Lautens, the Swiss merchant that shopped for the Americans in Marseilles to meet their incessant cravings for sea food and placed an order for squid, bass, and tuna. Martin said he would try but was not hopeful for the bass. Bernie insisted on the bass, letting on that the Ambassador's wife was pregnant (true) and was craving sea bass. Martin laughed and said he would try hard.

The German Gestapo *ScharFührer* (Sergeant) listening to the tapped telephone line never suspected anything other than another crazy request from the Americans. They so spoiled their women when they were pregnant. Men that easily manipulated by their wives would never win the war.

— —

Admiral Hamblen knew that the meeting was at a critical point. He had followed the discussion in French as best he could, but what wording he missed was reasonably clear to him from universal human expressions. *Languedoc's* wardroom had fallen silent when he decided to try and speak.

"My friends, I cannot think of the right words to say and excuse me if I say something wrong. I can only think of the pain this message has brought you. It is clear to me that if not for this telegram; you would have decided to say yes to my President's offer. The swine Schröder has given you till the morning of the twenty-sixth. Please let me see what I and my country can do to help you between now and then."

Charles Fournier of the *Aquitaine* interrupted, rapidly exclaiming, "What could you possibly do to help us? Our families are as good as dead unless we take our ships to the Germans."

Admiral Hamblen wasn't sure what he said but answered, "I have all the things that my country has at my use. I only ask you let me try to help."

John Hamblen had not noticed that Phillipe D'Aubigné had recovered his composure, stood, and moved behind him. He put a hand on John's shoulder and said in English, "My friend, let me convince them."

Phillipe started. "I have known this man for over sixteen years. He has never told me anything but the truth. He has never misled me. I know his family as he knows mine. He has commanded the greatest fleets the world has ever seen." Phillipe paused.

Naval gunfire shattered the silence.

— —

The Italian Fiat CR.25 reconnaissance aircraft from the *Strategic Reconnoitre 173a Squadriglia* based in Sicily was nearing the end of its search of the North African coast. As Rommel had advanced westward along Algeria, fewer and fewer contacts had been found and the crews of the aircraft had become bored. Today's mission was not expected to be any different than yesterdays nor was tomorrow's likely to be any change either. Just one more beautiful Mediterranean morning's flight and a half dozen more hours for the crew's log books.

That is until they reached the end of the flight at *Mers el Kébir*. The crew was always careful to stay outside the anti-aircraft gun range of the French fleet, though it had been months since the French had wasted ammunition on the speedy Fiat.

The pilot had given the controls to his copilot as he raised his binoculars to begin counting the French warships contained in the harbor when he noticed the largest ship he had ever seen slowly cruising close to the port. It did not look like any warship he had ever seen before. It certainly wasn't French or Italian. The pilot had always prided himself on his knowledge of English ships and this one did not look like any of theirs either. Could it be a German? The Germans never told the Italian Regia Aeronautica anything. He decided to take a closer look before he reported the presence of this capital ship in Mare Nostrum.

As he flew toward the ship staying well out to sea away from the French guns, he noticed the huge American flags flying from both masts. It was the last thing he ever saw.

— —

Lieutenant Commander Jonathan Becker's Combat Information Center aboard *Argonne* had been tracking the air contact on the (Sugar King) SK radars for almost twenty minutes. He had coaxed the forward Mark 37 director called sky one onto the contact at a range of over twenty two miles. It had only taken a few more minutes until they had a fire-control solution.

Sheppard's real problem was deciding what the contact was. He was sure it was not an English search plane based on what Ollie Halverson had told him of their search patterns. What he wasn't sure of was whether it might be French. He had directed the on watch gunnery officer to track the contact. Beside sky one, sky two was also generating an accurate solution using optical bearings and elevation angles along with Mark 4 radar ranges. Both Ford Mark 1 computers had excellent solutions when Lieutenant Commander Gerry Archinbald had directed, "Sky One, Control Mounts five-zero-two, five-zero-four, five-two-zero, and five-two-two. Mounts five-zero-two, five-zero-four, five-two-zero, and five-two-two load special anti-aircraft common."

Finally one of the air search lookouts four decks above Sheppard saw the three rods and axes symbol of the Regia

Aeronautica using the 36 power spotting binoculars. Sheppard's order to, *"Commence firing!"* was quickly followed by Gerry's on the 1JC phones, *"Master Key, Continuous Fire, ten rounds per gun!"* The crack of the 5"/54s immediately followed as the mount crews raced each other to load and fire the ordered ten rounds faster than any other mount crew. As the 70 pound projectiles passed by the Fiat the small radar set in the nose fuse was activated by the rapidly increasing frequency of the return echoes. The 7.59 pounds of picric acid (Explosive D) detonated, shattering the projectile into hundreds of red hot shards of steel. They sliced into the aircraft's skin, wings, tail, engines, fuel tanks, and crew of the CR.25, turning the sleek twin engine plane into a flaming meteor of melting aluminum, exploding ammunition, and burning flesh.

Most of the eighty projectiles were wasted, but Sheppard was not taking any chances on a snooper surviving to call in bombers. He walked back into the conning station from where he watched the performance of his guns on the port conning platform. His ears were ringing badly from the crack of the 5-inch guns when he ordered, "Signal Bridge, make to the French flagship, 'Destroyed Italian reconnaissance aircraft,'" in a voice much too load for the quiet inside.

— —

Anthony Pennyman needed better photos. The ones that had been taken yesterday by the photo reconnaissance Mosquito were from high altitude. Good enough for counting ships and confirming classifications, they were not adequate for troops and tanks. He passed the information that he had developed thus far to the station commander and RAF intelligence with a request for a low level mission over the Wilhelmshaven docks.

The request was quickly ordered in view of the obvious implication that the Germans were getting ready for an amphibious assault somewhere. Better photographs might very well be able to determine where that was going to be. With advanced warning, the Home Fleet would probably be able to stop it.

It took less than a half hour before the De Havilland Mosquito I was on its way. It was just as well it was a low altitude mission, as a cloud layer was developing over the north German coast.

— —

Sheppard's message arrived in the *Languedoc's* wardroom not long after the reports from *Amiral* D'Aubigné's staff watch officer. The *Amiral* turned to John Hamblen and whispered, "An Italian reconnaissance aircraft has been destroyed by your ship."

Equally quiet so as not to engage the assembled French officers, Hamblen replied, "Thank you, Phillipe. Do you know if the Italian reported *Argonne*'s presence before they were shot down?"

"I do not think so. We monitor their frequencies and there was no transmission prior their destruction."

"Phillippe, I certainly hope that your communications people did not miss something. *Argonne* is a powerful ship, but like any single unit, she can be overwhelmed by numbers. Until she can be supported by your ships, she must remain undetected or at least unreported."

As *Amiral* D'Aubigné turned back to the meeting, Admiral Hamblen quietly worried why the Fleet Air Arm had not intercepted the snooper well before it got into the range of *Argonne's* guns. He could not imagine why Force H would not have had a Combat Air Patrol up from *Ark Royal* or *Splendid*. What had gone wrong with all the coordination plans that had been worked out with the British Admiralty? *Argonne* was in a very exposed position without the support that had been promised.

— —

The Sugar George surface search radar operator on the conning station reported, "Small intermittent skunk bearing zero-one-three degrees range one-one-oh-double oh yards." The surface lookouts three decks above were immediately alerted, but failed to see a contact. Sheppard went to the microphone for the VHF radio aircraft spotting network. "Mustang Zero-One, Panther; investigate skunk bearing zero-one-three range one-one-thousand yards from Panther."

Bronco knew that Sheppard would not be telling him what to do if he was not concerned that it was a submarine. He banked hard toward the reported location before he acknowledged, "Panther, Mustang Zero-One; Roger!"

He also alerted his radioman gunner, "Miller, keep a sharp lookout, *Argonne* may have detected a submarine's periscope. Don't worry about air contacts; we'll let Panther watch our backs."

The OS2U-5 began a rapid climb to an altitude of a 1,000 feet. The bright Mediterranean sun had climbed higher in the sky than his first search of the area. They both stood a better chance of spotting a submarine now in the clear blue water beneath at the higher altitude.

— —

Amiral D'Aubigné got the meeting back under control from the interruption. "My comrades in arms, we have just seen the extent to which the Americans are prepared to go in their assistance. They have risked their most famous ship to bring us a message. They are not fools. Think of the victory for the Germans, if they could avenge the Battle of Cape Vilan. Can there be any greater proof of American sincerity? Can you possibly doubt the offer of Admiral Hamblen to assist us in finding a solution?"

Capitaine Fournier stood. "My *Amiral*, no one doubts the intentions of the Americans, but what could they possibly do that we could not?"

Amiral D'Aubigné paused. He did not know the answer to the question, nor could John Hamblen tell the officers present.

Admiral Hamblen rose. "Your *Amiral* has said many kind things about me. I have not told him all the things that I have from President Roosevelt to use. What you see off the harbor is a very fast, powerful ship, with fuel to go anywhere quickly. What you do not see is what I cannot tell you. You must believe me when I ask to use those things to find a solution. I ask you, let me try."

Amiral D'Aubigné said, "I for one wish to let my friend try. The Germans have given us two days to get to Toulon. If we delay until tomorrow to send an answer we will still be able to reach port in time."

The rumble of exploding depth charges interrupted the meeting for a second time.

— —

Bronco spotted the shadow about 10,500 yards from *Argonne*. It was pointed at his home and he knew enough about submarines to know that this one was trying to close on *Argonne* for an attack. "Panther, Mustang Zero-One, sub one-zero-five-hundred yards from you; attacking!"

He dove on the shadow and dropped his two 325 pound depth charges. One detonated at 25 feet of water depth and the 224 pounds of TNT in the second exploded at 50 feet. In his haste, Bronco had failed to consider the refraction of the submarine's image by the glass calm surface of the Mediterranean.

The Italian submarine *Nicoló Macchiavelli* was badly shaken by the twin explosions, some leaks started and a fuel ballast tank began to spread an oil slick. Her captain immediately ordered 75 meters depth and two thirds speed. As interesting as this large American warship had been, *Capitano di Corvetto* Luigi Bergamini knew that his orders were to destroy French warships attempting to escape from *Mers el Kébir* when the Italian fleet attacked in two days. His orders were mute on the Americans.

— —

John Hamblen could wait no longer. He had to find out what had happened to Force H. *Argonne* was clearly in danger and the longer he kept her virtually immobile off of *Mers el Kébir*, the greater the danger. He either had to abandon his mission or risk losing the battle cruiser.

He turned to his host. "Phillipe, I must leave. My flagship is in grave danger. Please have my barge and signalman called. I will ask you for one last favor—buy me time to see what I can do."

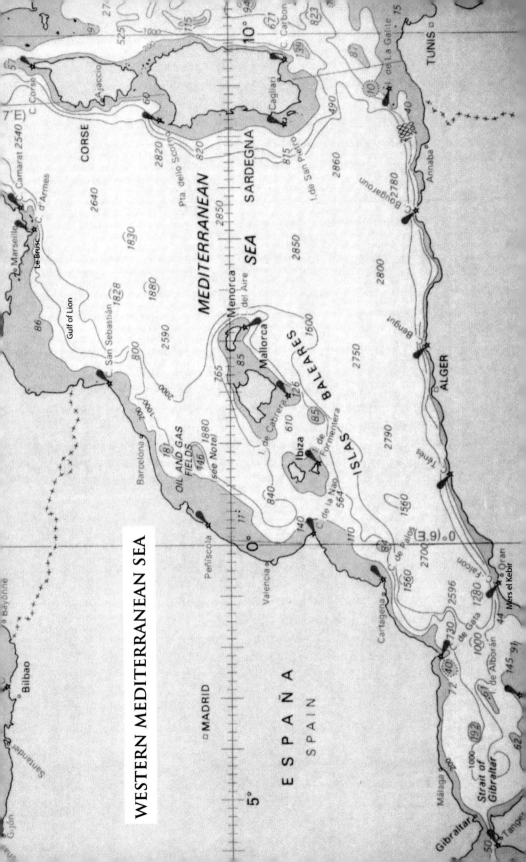

WESTERN MEDITERRANEAN SEA

5

INVASION

Boatswain's Mate second class Cruz wasted no time in heading back to *Argonne*. He had heard the gunfire and thud of the depth charges too. Unlike Admiral Hamblen, he could not see over the mole at *Mers el Kébir*. All he knew for sure was that his ship had destroyed the aircraft he had seen fall in flames. Johansen and Goldstein were obviously also anxious, having muffed the last movement of their routine with the boathooks.

Admiral Hamblen too was concerned. As they rounded the end of the mole, where he could get a clear view of *Argonne,* he stood. All six men on the gig breathed a sigh of relief when they saw she was not listing or burning.

More than anything, that also meant to Petty Officer Cruz that Captain McCloud was most likely unhurt.

——

Bronco knew immediately as he banked around after his attack that he had not sunk the submarine. There was no debris. There were no individuals struggling, nor dead in the water. There was only an oil slick and it was moving to the north away from the *Argonne*. Since he could no longer see the submarine, he knew it had gone deeper, outside the settings of his wingman's depth charges. As far as this submarine was concerned all Bronco could do was keep a watchful eye on its location relative to *Argonne.*

"Panther, Mustang Zero-One, submarine is damaged and moving to the north. Oil slick marks its location."

What Bronco really worried about was that if there was one submarine here, there probably would be more. He needed to get back up in altitude where he could get a good look down into the water. He also needed reinforcements.

"Panther, Mustang Zero-One, request additional mustangs!"

— —

Sheppard had heard Bronco's report on his attack result. Disappointed, he raised his binoculars and noted the oil slick for himself. He directed his Officer of the Deck to reverse course. There wasn't much he could do but stay away from the location of that moving slick. If Force H had been present, they could have sent a destroyer or two to gain sonar (ASDIC as they called it) contact and destroy the menace. He had also ordered the additional aircraft readied shortly after the first Kingfishers had been launched and well before Bronco's request came over the VHF spotting net radio. Looking aft, preparations were proceeding but Sheppard's order had caught his people by surprise and things were moving too slowly.

The OOD had relayed Sheppard's original order to *Argonne*'s airdales on the fantail. Less than a minute later the armored hatch had moved aft on its tracks in response to the slowly rotating pinion gears, opening the hangar. The hangar crew quickly positioned an OS2U-5 Kingfisher under the opening for the aircraft and boat crane to lift and place it on a catapult. Once placed on the catapult trolley, the wings needed to be unfolded and locked, the aircraft fueled, two depth charges loaded, and then the crew would climb in.

No sooner had the first Kingfisher been placed on the starboard catapult, than the crane was lowered into the hangar and retrieved a second. Placed on the port Mark 7 gun powder catapult; the second Kingfisher also began to be readied for launch. Now Sheppard idly watched his crew ready the aircraft, waiting for the report that would cause him to increase speed and launch them.

— —

He was not the only person intermittently watching. *Capitano di Corvetta* Placido Castiglione of the Italian submarine *Guiseppe Mazzini* was being very careful in the near glass calm sea as he closed in on this large American warship, first seen off in the distance when the sun came up. Having been picked specifically for his previous successes against the English, Placido was one of the key parts of Operation *Guardare al Futuro*. He knew how to stalk a contact that was not moving rapidly. The six bow tubes of his *Marconi* class boat could each fire a 48 knot steam torpedo to a range of 4 kilometers. With warheads of 270 kilograms, they packed a considerable charge that most ship's defenses could not withstand.

He decided to come up to periscope depth and verify that his target remained off of the entrance to *Mers el Kébir*. He slowed to the absolute minimum speed needed to control the depth of his boat preventing the periscope from leaving a visible wake on the surface when he made his observation. This had to be done very carefully. If there had been any large change in the trim of the submarine, he would either rise uncontrollably to the surface or sink to the bottom. It took speed for the diving planes to have sufficient force to overcome any deviation from perfect neutral buoyancy; speed that he could not use without his periscope's wake being detected.

— —

As Bronco climbed, his head, as usual, was constantly moving. The white silk scarf that he always wore was not a sign of bravado or ego, but rather an absolutely necessary item to keep his neck from being chaffed raw on this flight suit. That did not keep him from thinking about his attack on the submarine. He was certain he had laid his depth bombs exactly on target. Suddenly, he realized that was the problem. His target was not where he saw it in the water. The glass smooth sea created a perfect boundary layer. The refraction of light bent away from the vertical as submarine's image came out of the water. That made the target appear farther away than it was. The effect wasn't all that great, but it had been enough for him to only damage his enemy. If he got another chance, he vowed not to make that mistake again.

What was that, his subconscious registered it first—a shadow, a whale. It had not been there a few seconds ago. As he looked it became more distinct—another submarine. The ocean was lousy with them.

"Panther, Mustang Zero-One, submarine bearing three-three-eight degrees, range six thousand from you." Bronco did not wait for an answer. He needed Barry Jensen to get over here and attack that submarine before it closed any further on *Argonne*.

"Mustang Zero-Five, this is Mustang Zero-One, submarine spotted, my vicinity, attack from out of the sun, aim five yards short."

Barry Jensen wasn't sure why Bronco had added the last part of the order, but whatever Bronco's reason, he knew it was a good one. Barry banked around to the east of the reported position and started a shallow glide toward the spot that Bronco was circling. He throttled back the Pratt & Whitney engine to slow the Kingfisher enough that the depth bombs would not skip off the water when they hit. As he continued his approach, he couldn't see the submarine.

— —

Sheppard saw Admiral Hamblen's approach. Cruz was obviously in a big hurry which probably meant that the Admiral was in a big hurry. Had the meeting gone badly? Where the French about to open fire on him? Was there something vital that the Admiral needed *Argonne* to do right now? He couldn't maneuver toward the port entrance any closer and still have enough sea room to avoid torpedoes—if he spotted them in time.

Like a thunderbolt, Bronco's report of a second submarine, this one much closer, frightened him. *Argonne* was being hunted and Sheppard did not even know how many hunters were in this neck of the woods. Suddenly he felt very vulnerable.

"Where the hell is Force H?"

He needed to slow to a crawl to be able to pick up the Admiral, but that was going to leave him even more vulnerable to the submarines. He still needed a few more minutes before additional Kingfishers would be ready to launch. Sheppard knew that Bronco had called on Barry Jensen to make an attack, but Barry represented the last depth charges that he had airborne for defense.

— —

Martin Lautens had made the rounds of the local fish mongers. As expected, none had the requested fresh sea bass. They all agreed to place signs that requested the local fisherman to provide the desired fish as soon as possible, promising to call Martin whenever one was delivered. He thanked the fish mongers and went on his way to wait by the telephone for one of them to call with the good news of a supply of sea bass for the ambassador's wife.

It was not long before Pierre Ferres noticed one of the blue ink signs. He hurried off making sure that none of the local Gestapo agents were following him. Ducking into a back alley, he waited for any sign of a tail. None appeared. Certain now that he was not being followed, he went to the small one room apartment over a barn that he had rented on the outskirts of Marseilles. Checking surreptitiously placed telltales for any evidence his apartment or barn had been searched, he concluded that he was still undiscovered.

In a stall occupied by a skittish stallion that was well acquainted with him and docile in his presence, Pierre went to the farthest corner of the stall, brushed away the straw on the floor, and removed a few planks that were only laid in place. There was his radio and the battery that provided the power. He carefully made up the connections and tuned the frequency to the specified wave length for that day. Placing the earphones on his head, he first listened for any interference. Hearing none, he carefully took out the key to transmit; sending, "— — —, ·· —, — ."

— —

Capitano di Corvetta Placido Castiglione prided himself on how quickly he could make an observation on a target. It would normally only take seven seconds from the time the head window of the periscope broke the surface until he had the bearing, range, angle on the bow and was sending the periscope back down under the surface. This time was no different except he became mesmerized with the proportions and beauty of this American battle cruiser. A full fifteen seconds passed before Placido had the target information and lowered the scope to go deep and continue his approach. He was still outside optimum range for his 21 inch W270/533.4 x 7.2 'F' torpedoes in high speed.

He could shoot now, but that would give his target more than enough time to observe the bubbling wakes of the torpedoes and take avoiding action. On the other hand the closer he came, the greater possibility that a sharp eyed lookout might see his scope or its wake, even at 2 knots. He decided to continue closing. One more observation to confirm course and speed and he would increase speed to reach the optimum launch point for a six torpedo salvo.

— —

Barry Jensen saw the periscope off to his right. "Henry, there it is!" Barry said on the intercom to his radioman-gunner. "Do you see it?"

"No, Mr. Jensen," Hargrove responded. He had been searching off the Kingfisher's port side.

Barry kicked the rudder of the *Kingfisher* and pushed the stick to bank in that direction. Before the periscope disappeared he had leveled out, pointed directly at it. Closing quickly, at the last instant, he saw the submarine's shape before it disappeared beneath the cowling of his Wasp Junior nine cylinder radial engine. Barry pulled the bomb release levers as Bronco had instructed attempting to hit the water five yards short of the target. "Hang on, Harry!" he added on the intercom. *I think I did it.*

Lightened by over 600 pounds and responding to Barry's fire walling the throttle, the Kingfisher climbed away as the charges sank and detonated.

— —

Sheppard saw the twin columns of water rise from the exploding depth charges. They were only a little more than five thousand yards from *Argonne*—outside the range of a high speed torpedo. He began to do some quick calculations in his head on how long he had till the submarine would be within torpedo range. Unlikely as it was, if that captain had seen his aircraft and counted the explosions of their depth charges, he would know that *Argonne* was now defenseless except for gunfire.

He turned to look at the gig and estimated that it was no more than a thousand yards away—two minutes at the rate Cruz was pushing it; two more minutes to hook on to the aircraft and boat crane; one to lift it clear of the water—five minutes total. It would take the submarine twice that long to get within range.

He turned to his Conning Officer and commanded, "Back as needed, but stop the ship." To the OOD, he ordered, "Hook on and hoist the gig as quickly as you can." Sheppard knew he was taking a huge risk stopping his ship with an enemy submarine so close. Everything depended on his crew aft and on the gig flawlessly executing the hook up and retrieval.

Sheppard then went out on to the conning platform to check on the progress of readying the Kingfishers for launch. He had to calm the gnawing doubts that his orders were the best course of action.

Looking aft, he was satisfied that his men were working as fast as they could. Sheppard thought of one other thing he should do and returned to the conning station 21MC squawk box. "Engineering, we will be increasing speed rapidly to full ahead in about four minutes." Whatever the results of Jensen's attack, hopefully, no prayerfully, he could get *Argonne* out of danger before the submarine reached its attack point.

— —

Sheppard need not have worried about the submarine that Barry Jensen had attacked. His drop wasn't perfect since he was approaching from the submarine's beam, rather than along its axis, but his timing was great. The 25-foot fused depth charge actually bounced off the side of the bridge fairing of the *Guiseppe Mazzini*, lodged between a pressure cylinder for a 'maiale' and the hull, before exploding. The 50-foot one detonated just under the turn of the bilge outboard of the diesel engine room. Either one would have been fatal.

With both the control room and the engine room flooding rapidly, the *Mazzini* sank like a stone. The men in those two compartments including Placido Castiglione never had a chance. The Italian submarine came to rest on the sand bottom at a depth of 120 meters. The impact with the sand was just enough to collapse the forward torpedo room bulkhead. The men in that compartment too were lucky. Theirs was a quick death. The men in the aft torpedo room were not as fortunate. There was no way out. The lighting failed leaving them to wait in darkness for a slow suffocation.

— —

Radioman first class Miller in the rear seat of mustang-zero-one yelled, "Got him!"

Bronco turned his head to watch the oil and debris as well as water fall back into the ocean. Included were pieces of a two man torpedo, but no one other than an Italian knowledgeable of the *maiale* would recognize them—no American could.

"Good shooting, Barry," he called on the radio.

There was no doubt about this kill. Barry and his radioman could paint a broken submarine on the side of mustang zero-five. Bronco continued to circle for five minutes searching, hoping that there might be a survivor or two that could be rescued and taken back to *Argonne*. They had learned much from the German they had captured off of Norfolk and Bronco badly wanted to repeat that success.

It wasn't going to be. There weren't even any bodies. The huge oil slick and the bits and pieces of the *Mazzini* that were floating to the surface were all that marked the grave of the four crews for the 'pigs' and the crew of 58 Italian officers and men—most dead, the others about to die, but not soon enough for those unlucky enough to be still alive.

— —

"Admiral Hamblin, *Argonne* is readying to lift us directly out of the water."

"Thank you, Cruz. Well done with the French." Hamblin took one look over his shoulder and recognized exactly what Sheppard was planning when he saw the aircraft and boat crane swing out with the gig's lifting bridle attached. He beat a hasty retreat below to the safety of the gig's aft weather shelter as Johansen and Goldstein took their positions fore and aft with boathooks. Not for display this time, but the very important task of snagging the bridle and attaching the shackles to the lifting points for the gig.

Cruz backed full to check the gig's speed slowing the gig immediately under the dangling bridle. It was tricky because of the swirl from *Argonne's* backing down, but he managed to hold the gig steady enough for the four shackles to be attached. The moment that was seen by Aviation Chief Boatswain's Mate Bledsoe, he gave the hand signal for his assistant at the winch control to haul away—lifting the gig smartly out of the water. Clearing the lifelines and the port Kingfisher and catapult, the crane swung the gig over the yawning opening for the hangar, lowering it to rest snuggly in its cradle.

Ted Grabowski was standing by with eight side boys to assist Admiral Hamblen as a ladder was placed against the side of the gig for him to disembark. Hamblen waved the side boys away, quickly demonstrating that he was reasonably spry for a man of sixty-three years. He did something else Ted was not expecting when he touched the armored deck that formed the floor of the hangar.

"Commander, my compliments to Captain McCloud and request that he not launch additional aircraft and recovers the ones airborne as soon as possible."

Ted, dumbfounded at the order to leave *Argonne* defenseless, nevertheless complied, passing the information to the conning station via a JA phone talker in the hangar.

Admiral Hamblen then turned to the Marine orderly standing by. "Take me to Captain McCloud!"

— —

Pierre Ferres had to wait the proscribed eleven minutes for today's date before the American embassy in Switzerland began sending a long coded message. Pierre carefully wrote down the five letter groups that he would later decode in his apartment. He had long experience in copying the fist of this radioman and was certain that he had copied the message correctly. At the end he transmitted one short dot of acknowledgement—too short for the German radio direction finder net to detect let alone gain a line of position on.

Pierre then disconnected the battery terminal wires and stored the radio carefully. Replacing the loose boards and straw, he satisfied himself that the stall had been returned to its normal appearance. He did one last item of his routine in giving his best friend an apple as a reward for the stallion guarding his secret.

Ferres then went to his apartment, carefully checking the surrounding area for any sign of German intrusion. He had learned his field craft well in Virginia at Camp Smith and knew that survival was dependent on care with every aspect. Finally he sat at his small desk; and opened his copy of Voltaire's *The Age of Louis XIV* from among his other favorite books. He turned to page 145 since today was the 145th day of 1942. Starting at the top of the page he took the position of the letter in the alphabet of the text, and since today was an odd number subtracted it from the position of the letter in the message. The resulting number adjusted for any wrap-around gave him the position of the decoded letter of the message. He then moved to the second letter of the text and so on until he had finished the message.

The communiqué from the embassy was long, but since Pierre was practiced, he finished the decoding in only thirty minutes, quickly memorized the text, and placed the message and the decoded copy in his pocket. He always smiled to himself when he put his code book back on his desk—hidden in plain sight. He descended into the barn once more and feed both papers to a goat before he stepped outside and started off to a rendezvous where he could meet the *Maquis.*

— —

With a flat calm sea, Sheppard did not have to maneuver *Argonne* to create a slick for his Kingfishers to land. He still needed to worry about the target he was creating for any lurking submarines. Though he did not know if the subs were German or Italian, the Axis had clearly concentrated several off of *Mers el Kébir.* How many he did not know? He also did not know why they were here. He was also about to lose his airborne eyes to see down into the clear Mediterranean. Why was Hamblen demanding that he lose his airborne eyes and anti-submarine defense? All he could hope for was trying to prevent his enemy from gaining a fire control solution on his course and speed until he recovered his aircraft. Accordingly, he directed the Conning Officer to start a broad weave using a constant rudder angle to port and then back to starboard as *Argonne* moved away from the coast.

Sheppard directed the airdales to set up the recovery sled aft. Just a large matt of loosely woven steel cables, it was designed to be towed (port, starboard, or aft) by *Argonne* and allow the projecting hook on the pontoon of the Kingfishers to grab the wires. The airplane could then cut its engine and remain alongside being towed while the radioman connected the lifting cable to the aircraft and boat crane hook. The system worked well, but was much slower than the arrested landing system on carriers. It was also much more subject to the vagaries of weather.

Bronco had directed Barry Jensen to land first as he continued his lazy circles at 1,000 feet keeping a wary eye for additional submarines. He could not attack, but at least he could warn. Barry circled at low altitude astern of Argonne waiting for the rigging of the recovery sled to be completed. One of the great things about being assigned to the ship for long periods was the ability to work out coordination issues through practice, practice, and more practice. Evolutions like recovery could then be conducted rapidly without radio chatter cluttering the airwaves or disclosing information to an enemy.

— —

Capitano di Fregata Pietro Pasquale, commander of the Forty-eighth Submarine Squadron, was such an enemy. Stationed twelve nautical miles to the northeast of *Mers el Kébir*, he had listened to all the radio transmissions on the spotter network aboard the submarine *Cosimo De' Medici*. He could barely see the tops of *Argonne*'s mastheads, but he saw the Kingfishers flying low on the horizon. He also guessed that both the *Mazzini* had been sunk and the *Macchiavelli* had either been sunk or damaged. Back in Naples, he had argued against deploying the *maiale* fitted submarines this early in Operation *Guardare al Futuro*, but he had been overruled. Now the plan to attack the French destroyers would have to be aborted. Without eight of the twelve submersibles, there were not enough to make the necessary impact on the French anti-submarine screen when they deployed from *Mers el Kébir*. As long as the screen remained mostly intact, the thirty-two first class submarines covering the route out of the Mediterranean would have a difficult time attacking the French battleships should they try to escape before the Italian fleet arrived.

There was nothing Pietro could do except report cancelling the special attack after sundown.

— —

The Conning Officer had ordered, "Steady as you go," to allow Barry to hook on to the recovery sled as Admiral Hamblen arrived in the conning station. The Boatswain's Mate of the Watch sounded off with, "Admiral on deck," causing everyone to stiffen and the whispers between watch standers in the course of their duties to end. Sheppard turned to Admiral Hamblen with a cheerful, "Good morning, Admiral," trying to read the expression on his face.

Winded from the long climb, the Admiral went to Sheppard's chair and sat to catch his breath. "Admiral, would you like a cup of coffee or some water?" Sheppard solicitously asked.

"No, thank you." The Admiral gasped for a breath. "I am only staying a minute," gasping again.

Their conversation was interrupted by a report that the first Kingfisher had hooked on and was being lifted aboard. Sheppard ducked out of the conning station for a moment to verify that all was well, noting that Bronco was landing.

"Sheppard, have you enough fuel for another high speed run, this time to Toulon and back?"

With no idea what the Admiral had in mind, Sheppard could only rely on his memory of the last noon fuel, oil, and water report. "Admiral, I should be around 37 percent. Another two thousand miles will barely leave enough for a cruise to Gibraltar."

Hamblen's stare hardened. "But you will have enough!"

Recognizing the right answer when told, Sheppard could only say, "Yes sir!"

"Good, get going as soon as your last Kingfisher is aboard!'

"Aye, aye, sir!" Sheppard answered remembering why he

hated serving in flagships. You were never the master of your own command and frequently had no idea what the Admiral was thinking.

"Shep (using his academy nickname), I'll explain as soon as I can change my uniform and recover from this climb. Please have your Marine Major also present and send this message for me." Taking a message blank from chair side pocket he said, "*Argonne* is an immense ship; it is a long climb for an old Admiral." With that the Admiral quickly wrote out a message on a signal pad, left, and headed down to his stateroom on the port side opposite the Captain's.

Captain McCloud went to the 21MC to alert Engineering to the impending need for maximum power—again. At least Mr. Hess's new propellers were really getting a work out. If this trip didn't prove their worth Sheppard didn't know what would. *Argonne* had not slowed in the Atlantic crossing and he suspected that the propellers had not eroded much based on her continued high speed.

A minute later, Bronco was hooked on, lowered into the hangar, and the recovery sled lifted back aboard. With Captain McCloud's permission, the Conning Officer ordered, "All ahead flank," and turned to course 022° to pass to the west of the Balearic Islands. At least at this speed Sheppard would not have to worry about a submarine gaining a firing solution on the *Argonne*. There was just not enough time between sighting her masts and when she would be past the firing point, even if the submarine was in the perfect position by chance. Sheppard would never really discover and no one would ever tell him that from this moment on, his crew referred to him respectfully as "Ol' Shep."

— —

Pilot Officer Archie Willoughby with his navigator/photographer banked low over the island of Langeoog avoiding the German Freya and Würzburg radar sites by crossing the coast between Esens and Neuharlingersiel. The two Merlin twenty series engines pushed the Mosquito I at over 300 miles per hour, faster than German fighters could catch at low altitudes. They continued southeast passing over farmland west of Wittmund until they were nearly to Friedeburg. Turning east, they passed south of Schortens and climbed to just under the base of the clouds at about 1,500 feet.

As they climbed, the docks at Wilhelmshaven lay directly in front of them for their photo run. The only thing that Archie noticed was the surprisingly light anti-aircraft fire from the German fleet in the Jade Estuary. He had been briefed that it would be much heavier. "Bout time for some bloody luck," he commented as the Mosquito I completed the run from west to east and dove back to wave hugging heights.

Having gotten what he had been ordered to acquire, Archie banked hard left flying over the shallow section of the Estuary until he passed east of the Island of Mellum. He took a departure fix from the Roter Sand light house and headed south of Helgoland enroute to RAF Benson and the Photographic Development Unit based there. It wasn't until he climbed back into the comforting embrace of the cloud layer that the two men breathed a sigh of relief.

— —

Sheppard, Ted Grabowski, Ollie Halverson, and Major Morris Jenkins were waiting in the conning station when Admiral Hamblen returned. Proceeding again directly to Sheppard's chair, he sat and recovered from the long climb. From his own days in command of the battleship *Illinois,* he knew better than to ask a Captain to leave his bridge underway, particularly now in wartime. Climbing the twelve decks to meet Sheppard was a small price to pay for not interfering in the operation of the best battle cruiser the Navy had.

It did not take the Admiral long to brief what had happened in his meeting with the French. Sheppard, Ted, and Morris had stiffened with bitter expressions of silent rage when the Admiral relayed Schröder's ultimatum. Sheppard recognized the name immediately as the German Admiral he had defeated at Cape Vilan. It was a total surprise that he was now an Admiral in the *Kriegsmarine.* As he continued, it was clear to Sheppard why the Admiral had sent the message he had to the American Embassy in Switzerland.

But it wasn't clear to Ted or Morris, who had not read the message until the Admiral laid out his plan of action. Everything would rely on the *Maquis*. Even though Hamblen had no idea what the answer to his message might be, there just didn't exist the time to wait for the answer before getting close enough to Toulon to carry out *Argonne*'s part of the plan.

Before long the Admiral asked the gathered officers if they saw any holes in what he wanted to accomplish. The plan's success totally relied on the speed of *Argonne* in both the approach and withdrawal to avoid German or Italian countermeasures. Charts of the area were broken out and the water depth carefully surveyed as well as the pilot charts of the Mediterranean to check on the tides and currents in the area. Those were the critical considerations in determining the likelihood of the waters being mined. There was nothing they could do about the moon except hope for cloud cover.

Ted Grabowski said, "Admiral, Captain, we are going to have to move two more Kingfishers out of the hanger to make room for the boats."

Sheppard quickly added, "We will have to wait until we slow. Fifty knots wind across the deck is much too great for handling an OS2U dangling from the end of a cable."

Sheppard turned to Major Jenkins whose gaze was fixed at some far off place probably thinking rapidly about things only a Marine would understand. "Major, what are you thinking?"

"Captain, I will need all my Marines to accomplish the mission ashore. Request that they be removed from the watch-bill for the 5-inch mounts as soon as possible. I will need to brief them on the mission."

"Certainly, Ted, please see to it."

Commander Grabowski left to make the necessary arrangements. It would be difficult to be sure all the watches had enough rest.

Captain McCloud immediately sent for Commander Williamson, Commander Roberts and Lieutenant Commander Becker to inform them and discuss the navigation and communication requirements that needed to be put in place. The small meeting with Admiral Hamblen was turning into one of Sheppard's famous counsels of war. With the watch standers present, it took less than an hour before every man in *Argonne* knew what was going to happen. When Ted finally got back to his office on the second deck there was a line of over three hundred men who wanted to volunteer for the mission ashore.

— —

André Sorentino did not consider himself a resistance fighter. As a goat herder in the mountains of Corsica, he hadn't even seen a German soldier let alone understood that France was no longer a sovereign country. He only knew that his uncle had asked him to keep a watchful eye out for ships and had provided him with a telescope and a book of pictures to compare with what he saw.

Every once in a while he saw a ship, most of which he did not recognize, but he dutifully wrote them down and told his uncle when he returned home at the end of the day. Today he saw many ships from the summit of Capo d' Occi near the town of Calvi. Even more exciting to him, he was able to match them with some of the pictures in the book. He was very proud of that and ran immediately to see his uncle concerning the Italian aircraft carriers of the *Aquila* class and the battle cruisers that he had seen.

His uncle was a member of the resistance and went to where he had a radio hidden to send the report to the English. He did not worry about the Germans. As soon as he finished sending the message, he packed up the radio and moved it to another hiding place in the mountains around Calvi. There just weren't enough Germans or Italians in Corsica to chase down everything the resistance was doing.

— —

Pierre Ferres had finished his meeting with the *Maquis*. It had gone much better than he could have hoped. Now he had to get the information back to the embassy. He walked as quickly as he could through the outskirts of Marseilles. Once he got to the city proper where the likelihood of Gestapo agents was greater, he ducked into alleys and occasionally doubled back behind his own route to verify that he was not being followed. All that took time, but he could not afford to be arrested now.

Finally he reached his goal—one of the fishmongers who still displayed the sign asking for sea bass. He drew on his own experience as a fisherman off the coast of Maine in pretending to be the brother of the captain of a boat out of Le Brusc, a small fishing village to the East of Marseilles. He negotiated a price for the requested sea bass, claiming that his brother always had some in his catch. Pierre knew that anyone who wanted a special order would pay a hefty price and managed to extract a high price from the fishmonger for his brother's entire catch.

He told the fishmonger that his brother would be coming back into Le Brusc a little after midnight and would get the catch to him as quickly as he could. The fishmonger agreed and Pierre hurried off to his apartment.

— —

Martin Lautens was delighted with the message from the fishmonger. He casually inquired as to how he had managed to get the sea bass so quickly. The fishmonger relayed the story of the brother of a fishing boat's captain promising that his brother always had sea bass in his catch. They haggled over the cost of the sea bass until they settled on a price which, unknown to Martin, was more than double what the fishmonger was paying. Martin had to ask what port the boat was fishing from. The fishmonger would not give that information for fear of being cut out of the very profitable deal unless Martin promised to only deal with him in the future.

Once the long term arrangement had been settled, the fishmonger told Martin the remaining details of when and where the boat would dock. He confirmed the details of the long term relationship for the fishmonger and promised that he would be at his shop first thing in the morning to pick up the fish. He emphasized that the fish must be iced well as he had to deliver them to Geneva.

Martin then picked up his telephone again and called the international operator to be connected with the American Embassy in Geneva. As he waited, he heard the expected double click signifying that the Gestapo was listening to the phone call. When connected to the Embassy switch board he asked to be put through to the Deputy Assistant Attaché for Intercultural

Development. When Bernie Smith picked up, Martin gave him the good news concerning the sea bass with all the details of when the boat would arrive at Le Brusc. He closed the conversation with a comment hoping to be remembered to the Ambassador and his wife and wishing her a safe delivery.

The Gestapo *HauptscharFührer* (technical sergeant) who was listening wondered why the Swiss merchant would pass so many details to the American Embassy. International phone rates in wartime were very expensive. There had to be more to this than idle conversation. He decided to tell his *HauptsturmFührer* (captain) of his suspicions.

— —

Flight Lieutenant Anthony Pennyman was studying the photographs that had just been developed of Wilhelmshaven's piers. There were the usual assortment of tanks, half-tracks, trucks, and supplies. He needed to look closer to find out where they might be going. He took out his best magnifying glass, wiping it carefully, and began to examine the supply crates closer. He could just make out some of the wording that indicated what was contained in most.

Munitions and rations were not unexpected. Clothing, tents and bedding were more meaningful. As he studied them, one thing jumped out. The items were all labeled for cold weather.

So the Germans were getting ready to go someplace cold with perhaps three maybe four brigades of mechanized infantry and armor. Summer was just beginning, so it was unlikely that they would bring the supplies to sustain themselves long term in the initial loading. Four brigades were too much for someplace like Greenland. There just wasn't anything there. Armor made no sense for Jan Mayen or Svalbard. The Faroe Island's terrain also was far too bad for armor. That left the Shetland Islands and Iceland. In both cases the terrain could support armor, but the Shetlands would be under continuous air attack from the Orkney's and was very close to the Royal Navy's base at Scapa Flow.

Anthony picked up the telephone to Bomber Command Headquarters Intelligence at High Wycombe to relay what he had deduced of the German intentions. Bomber Command immediately forwarded it to White Hall recognizing the significance a successful invasion of Iceland would have on the fate of Great Britain. Admiral of the Fleet Dudley Pound phoned Downing Street to let the Prime Minister know. It did not make sense to Churchill who wanted to see the photos for himself at White Hall.

When Flight Lieutenant Pennyman was told to report immediately to White Hall with his photographs in order to brief the Prime Minister, his only thought was of the British Museum and the safe solitude of studying old bones. He fervently wished he had never joined the RAF.

— —

Pierre Ferres returned to the barn and his apartment by another route. He exercised more care than usual, doubling back three times and pausing long enough in a side alley twice to confirm that he was not being followed. He even approached the barn from a different path than usual. Entering the barn he repeated his checks of the telltales he had left to discover any surreptitious searches that may have been conducted by the Gestapo in his absence.

Finding none, he went to the stallion's stall and connected his radio. Having already used the frequency for today's date, he had to tune to the first of several emergency wave lengths. Again hearing no interference, he transmitted his *oui* and waited. It was fifteen minutes before the American Embassy responded; beginning a relatively short message. He transmitted the short dot of acknowledgement, carefully stored and hid the radio, making certain to reward his four legged guard, and went to his apartment to decode the message. This was somewhat harder since it was the second message of the day. He had to count 145 pages of Voltaire backward from the end to get the correct page.

When he read the message, he smiled that the American Embassy had understood what had been sent to them. He closed his book, went down to the barn and fed the goat. Now he had to maintain his cover. He hitched the stallion up to his little cart and set off toward an ice house he knew on the other side of Marseilles. He would then go to La Ciotat where he knew the fisherman and would be able to buy what he needed. He absentmindedly wondered as he drove the cart, which would come first—France's liberation or a hangman's noose—perhaps a firing squad if he was lucky?

— —

Admiral Hardy stood on the compass platform of *Renown* with his Flag Captain Sir Phillip Kelley as the capstans for Prince of Wales dock slowly pulled the old battle cruiser into the dry dock in Gibraltar Harbor. Both officers hoped it would take no longer than the day estimated by the base commander to repair the damage caused by the American 18-inch armor piercing projectile. Over by the air station, HMS *Ark Royal* and *Splendid* were still moored to the pier where they were loading aircraft and uncrating some new Albacores for *Splendid*'s strike/ reconnaissance squadrons.

Both his carriers were still armed with the venerable Fairey Fulmar fighters, though all four squadrons had upgraded to the Fulmar II with a more powerful Merlin XXX engine. Stealing from *Splendid*'s Swordfish, HMS *Ark Royal* was back up to her compliment of 36 of the biplane torpedo bombers. *Splendid*'s two squadrons were reequipping with the Fairey Albacore which had a higher speed and greater range despite still being biplanes.

Outside the mole, the four American tankers and two supply ships swung at their anchors. In spite of their value to the mission of preventing the French fleet from falling into Axis hands, there was just not enough room inside the mole for them and their destroyer division escort. The addition of the *Invincible* class battle cruisers and their destroyer flotilla to Force H had filled the small harbor. Hardy thought that they would be safe enough before he sortied and could then bring them inside the anti-submarine nets if need be. Until then he had ordered the patrols at the entrance to the bay doubled.

The two officers had received the latest intelligence report from London concerning the sortie of the Italian scouting force under *Ammiraglio* Moretti. Sir Phillipe commented that Moretti never went anywhere that the battle fleet did not also go. Hardy could only nod in agreement. It would have been a relatively even fight with Moretti's six battle cruisers and four carriers against Hardy's five and two. When you added in *Ammiraglio* Romano's battleships it was imperative that the HMS *Renown* be repaired and available. Even then Sir Bruce was going to have to be "creative" in how he handled the Italians. Neither officer knew how they would accomplish that yet—but they would have to.

— —

The messages arrived aboard at about 1800 when *Argonne* was on course 043° north of the Balearic Islands. Sheppard had needed to avoid some of the local fishing traffic, but so far there had been no air contacts or warships. After he read the messages, he realized that he needed to consult with Admiral Hamblen and Major Morris again. Sheppard sent Corporal Westbrook with the message:

> *Captain McCloud sends his respects; wishes to inform the Admiral of intelligence and rendezvous instructions being received; and requests the Admiral's and Commander Halverson's presence on the conning station for consultations.*

Sheppard sent the messenger of the watch with his "complements" and a request for the Executive Officer and Department Heads to join him in his sea cabin.

While they were gone Sheppard had the quartermaster of the watch find the relevant charts of the area. He took a quick look at them to familiarize himself with the waters and land areas where *Argonne* would be operating before he briefed the others. Surprisingly, Admiral Hamblen was the first to arrive, proceeding directly to Sheppard's chair. Sheppard handed the Admiral the message boards with the two messages of concern for him to read for himself. He deliberately did not discuss them before the Admiral read them to insure that Hamblen's interpretation would not be colored by Sheppard's own.

It wasn't long before everyone had arrived. Admiral Hamblen led the way to Sheppard's sea cabin behind the conning station where the quartermaster had laid out the charts. Sheppard began. "Admiral with your permission I would like to brief a plan that has been developing in my mind and then open the meeting for discussion of problems, factors I failed to consider, or improvements. Admiral you are also the only one who has seen the messages other than myself. I am relying on you to immediately correct any misunderstandings I may have."

"Certainly, Captain. I realize we are in an unusual circumstance where I do not have staff support. I think this arrangement is a good one."

Sheppard briefed the latest intelligence on the movement of the Italian fleet, laid chart number 53060 Palamoś to Saint Raphail on top of his bunk, and began. "Gentlemen, we are currently located at approximately forty-one degrees north latitude, three degrees east longitude, on course zero-four-three. In approximately one hour we will pass Cape San Sebastian and enter the Gulf of Lion. Our destination is a rendezvous with the *Maquis* off the fishing village of Le Brusc at midnight. At our current speed we will get there much too early. I propose that we slow after sunset, which will allow us to complete our preparations in the hangar before we reach Le Brusc. Are there any comments on that part?"

Art Roberts interjected. "Captain, if you will excuse me for a moment, I'll get my quartermasters working on the details with the OOD so we are not pressed for time in this meeting?"

"Good idea, Art." Sheppard continued. "Up here in the Gulf of Lion, I would not expect any submarines but with the developing cloud cover we will also have darkness on our side. Mr. Becker, is there any way that your radiomen or radar technicians can rig a device to alert us to any German radar?"

"Sir, we might be able to do that. I think I can detune one of the SK search radars and use it as a rotating receiver. If there is a German radar operating close to its frequency that radar will show up as a dotted line pointed directly at the source. All the German radars that are in my intelligence pubs for coastal surveillance and air search are close to the SK's operating wave length. The only problem is that I will need to keep the other SK in standby to prevent interference."

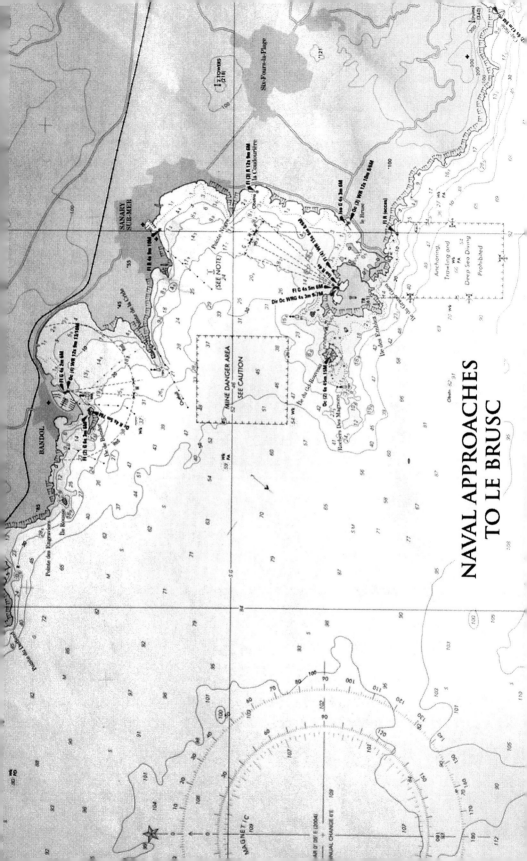

NAVAL APPROACHES
TO LE BRUSC

"Understood, Admiral, gentlemen, with the increasing cloud cover do you think that is an acceptable risk?

Ted Grabowski said, "Captain, if we double the lookouts with instructions to listen for aircraft as well, once we slow, I think it will be okay. Jonathan, how long will it take to bring the SK back up to operation if we need the air search?"

"Less than a minute from standby!"

"Jonathan, if we can set that up before we close the last forty miles, I think that is settled. Now," Sheppard continued laying the next chart Number 53081 Bec-de-L'Aigle to Presqu' Île de Giens on the top of his bunk. "If we lay about four miles off shore, here east by southeast of Île du Grand Rouveau we can remain in water that is too deep for mines. Art, we should be able to get good SG radar returns off of the cliffs at Pointe de la Cride and Île des Embiez for navigation."

"Morris, I want to send you and your headquarters group in the gig to make contact with the *Maquis*. We will use the gig since the dark blue paint should help avoid detection. Morris, make sure you have two field radios tuned to the spotter network in the gig. We'll use that VHF radio network for communicating with your Marines. I would not expect the Germans to be either listening on VHF or be able to direction find the signals. It is just too short range and near line-of-sight.

"I intend to put each of your platoons in a 50 foot utility launch ready to come ashore if you need them. I want each platoon to also have a radio. Your heavy weapons platoon will be in the 40-footer as a contingency, but I think *Argonne* can provide everything you need for general fire support."

Major Jenkins interrupted. "Captain, are we invading France?"

Sheppard smiled. "As much as I would like to, not at this time. I just don't know how suspicious the Gestapo might become of civilians moving toward the port at night and how successful the *Maquis* might be at keeping them at bay. Remember, we have no idea how many dependents of the French fleet may need to be evacuated or how long it will take."

Chuck Williamson then said, "Captain, I don't see a problem using the spotting network for gunfire support and it appears we have a good plan if German troops try to intervene, but what about the *Kriegsmarine* or this report that the Italian fleet has sailed?"

— —

Winston Churchill was not happy. "How could they possibly be planning an invasion of Iceland and we not know of it? Have they discovered that we can decode their enigma messages?"

Admiral of the Fleet Dudley Pound could only reply, "Prime Minister, we have not seen anything to indicate that in the messages to the U-boats. If the Germans were on to our capabilities, the first indication would be attacks on convoys from submarines that were reporting their positions elsewhere. We have not seen that. I believe our most vital source of intelligence is still secure."

"Then what are we to make of these photographs?"

"Prime Minister, if we take them at face value, Lütjens is planning an invasion in conjunction with the sortie of his fleet. The latest air reconnaissance sortie shows a German carrier fleet still heading north along the Norwegian coast. Based on what we have seen of tanker movements, they are probably going to refuel in Trondheim. That should take at least thirty-six hours. Whatever Lütjens does he will do in conjunction with that force."

"Flight Lieutenant Pennyman, how certain are you that Lütjens's objective is Iceland?"

"S-S-Sir, I can't be ce-ce-certain. There are to-o many unknowns. How-However, Iceland is the only objective that fits what we know."

Admiral Pound continued. "Prime Minister, there are only two possibilities. Either Lütjens will sortie in support of that force commanded by an admiral named Moeller and invade or this is a ruse to mask another breakout into the Atlantic by Moeller's fleet. For the first, the Home Fleet must engage Lütjens and destroy the transports before they get to Iceland. For the latter, Tovey should move north and destroy Moeller before he reaches the Denmark Strait.

"Prime Minister, the problem is that the Home Fleet is not strong enough or fast enough to do both."

"Dudley, can the American's cover the Denmark Strait?"

"Prime Minister, the only Task Force they have in the Atlantic is en route to Gibraltar to escort D'Aubigné to Martinique. That is, if John Hamblen is able to convince them to go. If the Americans are not successful, that Task Force in conjunction with Force H must destroy the French fleet at *Mers el Kébir*, or we will lose the war.

"It also appears that the Italians are attempting a breakout on their own or at least make a decisive blow to our base at Gibraltar. Force H and the Americans will have to deal with that threat even if the French cooperate with Hamblen."

"Admiral, it seems clear that we have three threats and only assets to cover two. Am I correct?"

"Yes, Prime Minister."

"Then of the three which is the least damaging?"

"Prime Minister, the German objective is the same in all cases—sink our convoys to force surrender. If they take Iceland, that is inevitable. If Gibraltar is destroyed giving the Italians access to the Atlantic it is also inevitable. If the French fleet comes under axis control, again, it is inevitable.

"If Moeller has freedom of action in the Atlantic, we will also lose the convoys. The results are the same in all cases."

"Admiral of the Fleet, what do you recommend?!"

6

RESCUE

KAPITÄNLEUTNANT GERHARD HAYNER, COMMANDER of the Thirtieth *Schnellboote* Squadron and *S-49*, was getting frustrated by the Gestapo's concerns about allied agents being landed or picked up by submarine in southern France. Based out of Toulon, this was the sixth time this month he had been ordered to sea on a mission to intercept one of their phantoms. They always wanted a maximum patrol effort and frankly his boats were wearing out without accomplishing anything useful. Of course the Gestapo and SS were nowhere to be found when it came to arguing for more fuel or spare parts from the supply offices of *Marineoberkommando Süd*. More than anything he would like to tell them and those black uniformed SS egomaniacs to get out from behind their desks and go to sea on a cold dark night on the open bridge of one of his torpedo boats.

He knew he had to go, but at least the Gestapo didn't specifically order him to take every boat with him. Even if they found a submarine, two boats would be more than enough to deal with it, if the English were stupid enough to try and complete their mission. Beside his own *S-49*, he would take *Oberleutnant zur See* Dietrich Werden's *S-52* giving the rest of his squadron a chance to do some long overdue maintenance on their 2,000 horsepower Daimler-Benz diesel engines.

— —

It was time to slow. Without the protection of high speed Sheppard hoped, prayed was more like it, that he had been correct in his assessment of the submarine threat in the Gulf of Lion. The conning station was black except for the dull red glow of the binnacle illumination reflecting off of the overhead. The SG radar operator had the rubber hood in place with its cutout to fit on his face, shielding the bright white glow of the rotating trace from being seen or reflected from the surrounding equipment, reflections that might be seen by an enemy up to two miles away.

As the pitometer log repeater showed *Argonne* slowing to less than 30 knots Sheppard gave permission to place two additional Kingfishers on cradles supported by the port and starboard catapults. Removing the OS2U-5s from the hanger was not hard. Placing them on the catapults delicately enough to prevent the centerline float from being holed was the hard part. Once completed, the airdales had been ordered to ensure that the four aircraft were drained of all the volatile aviation gasoline. Sheppard did not want a fire if one was damaged by enemy action or his own gunfire. He also did not want any of the bombs or depth charges to inadvertently be detonated. The only way to prevent that was removing and storing them in the magazine.

It was slow work with the remaining wind over the deck and the darkness of the overcast sky. No one complained. The darkness was a warm blanket to embrace *Argonne*'s passage in stealth other than the sound of her bow wave and whine of the forced draft blowers feeding air to her boilers. Sheppard had never liked waiting. The plan was in place but there were too many unknowns.

— —

ObersturmFührer (First Lieutenant) Rudolph Blauvelt had spent a long afternoon uselessly breaking in doors at the homes of the people on the list that SS Headquarters in Paris had wired down to Marseilles. He only knew that Headquarters wanted those people taken into protective custody. After finding none of the first ten on the list at home, he had become suspicious and reported his findings back to headquarters in Marseilles. It was not the first time that the *Maquis* had a better intelligence system in France than the SS, hiding away the people he was searching for.

He was tired after a long day of fruitless effort and wished that he could doze off the way his platoon riding in the trucks behind his small staff car were able to. Well, he hadn't expected an easy path when he joined the Hitler youth in order to help preserve the thousand year Reich. One last mission tonight and then he could return to Marseilles and get some sleep. Perhaps Yvette would be waiting in his apartment when he returned. He was never really sure about her loyalties, but she was beautiful and that was all he cared about for a mistress.

His platoon had been ordered to Le Brusc to intercept saboteurs that were supposed to be landed by submarine or fishing boat—headquarters didn't know which. The *Kriegsmarine* was going to be patrolling offshore, but the Gestapo had insisted on ground forces, to search the town if the *Schnellboote* failed to locate anything suspicious. Rudy really didn't have enough troops to be thorough, but that was an issue for headquarters. He knew he would not find anything. He never did. This was the sixth time this month that he had been sent out chasing ghosts.

— —

He was only known to his close friends and family as Émile Mallery; to the *Maquis* of southern France he was known as Commandant César and the less the men knew of him, the better, as far as he was concerned. The Gestapo had placed a high price on his head—too high not to tempt those whose loyalty might waiver under duress. He was intelligent, a surgeon in a hospital outside of Marseilles, which gave him a perfect reason to wear a mask for most of the day.

When the *Maquis* found out the SS was compiling a list of the families of French naval officers in the Toulon area, he knew immediately that the real objective was the fleet at *Mers el Kébir*. The Germans were going to try to blackmail the French into delivering the fleet to them without a fight. He listened to the BBC at night for instructions as well as information and knew that the war was not going well for the allies. It was Commandant César who had issued the orders to hide all of the families in the rough terrain east southeast of Le Brusc. He had personally seen to the safety of the French *Amiral* D'Aubigné's family. But Émile knew that hiding the families was only a temporary measure until he found a way to smuggle them out of France.

It had been a surprise when the American called Pierre Ferres had met with one of his Lieutenants and inquired about the safety of the naval families. His men had been watching Ferres for months. No family; lived alone; never sought the company of a woman. He had to be an agent. The only question that the *Maquis* was unable to answer until recently was whose. Once it was clear which side he was on in the war, it was easy for the *Maquis* to give him a method of contact that still protected his men if Émile's assessment of his loyalties was wrong.

Pierre had stated that he wished to help with the "evacuation" as he put it. He hadn't even reacted when told that there were hundreds of women and children that had to be moved. He only wanted to know how soon it could be arranged for the families to be moved to the vicinity of the town of Le Brusc. Émile had been impressed with his composure and confidence as he had talked with his lieutenant. A quick nod from Émile, when Pierre was distracted was all that his lieutenant needed to agree.

Émile had used the fishing village at Le Brusc before to smuggle people out of France and English weapons in. The shore batteries overlooking that section of the coast had been spiked before the Germans had captured them. They had not yet replaced the guns in the casemates between Cap Sicié and Île des Embiez. Le Brusc's great advantage was the rough terrain to the east with numerous caves to hide people or cache weapons. Those were the reasons that Émile had decided to hide the French officer's families there. Also, there were only two roads leading into the town. He had personally surveyed locations to ambush German troops if for any reason they became suspicious. Other than mines and the old French coast defenses, the Germans had yet to add fortifications to this section of the coast. The fishermen were all sympathetic to the *Maquis*, chafing under the restrictions the Germans were placing on their boats, fuel, and fishing locations. Émile still did not have a plan on how he was going to move the families to whatever it was the Americans were bringing. That could be a problem.

Sheppard knew it was time to begin. Major Jenkins had come to the conning station for any last minute instructions. Captain McCloud had never seen him in battle dress before. He always thought of Morris as just another of his officers dressed in khaki. Seeing the steel helmet, web belt, and .45 caliber Model 1911 automatic with extra ammunition clips only added to Sheppard's uneasiness. Like any father, he feared those times when his children were headed into danger without him to guide them. That was how Sheppard had always looked at his men. His men were his responsibility, just as his children were before they matured.

The only thing he could think to say sounded trite. "Don't do anything stupid. Just get the civilians and get back to *Argonne* as quickly as you can."

As an afterthought he added, "Don't leave anyone behind!" He didn't add "dead or alive." The thought was too much for him to contemplate openly, but he hoped Morris understood what he meant.

In his heart he knew there was no better man for the job. Morris's fluent German and French would be invaluable ashore. But he still was going to worry. He prayed for Morris's and his Marines' safe return as the Major quickly left the conning station headed to the hanger. Sheppard thought that at least the night was dark with a complete cloud cover. That should help conceal the evacuation.

Argonne had glided up to the position Sheppard had picked four miles from Le Brusc. With the exception of the SK radars all the rest were searching for any threats. The gun directors too were sweeping back and forth in their sectors ready to lock on to any target. The crew was at battle stations with every gun manned and the hoists filled with high capacity shells. Ted Grabowski and Senior Chief Hancock had juggled the watch bills to get the boat crews and Marines off and yet keep all the guns manned. Some of the repair parties were under strength but that had to be accepted.

Sheppard ordered the Conning Officer to back down and twist *Argonne* so that her stern pointed the shore. He wanted to be able to leave in a hurry as well as shorten the distance even by just the length of the ship that the boats would have to travel to bring the French families back. He had deliberately arrived ten minutes early. If there was a trap, being early might allow him to discover it before the enemy was ready.

— ▪ —

Kapitänleutnant Gerhard Hayner rounded Pointe du Rascas and headed west by southwest enroute to Le Brusc in *S-49* in company with *S-52*. He had no reason to suspect anything. The German garrison at Fort Saint-Elme, as well as the shore batteries nearby, had not reported any suspicious activity. He was a little late, but it would not matter. There wasn't anything there anyway.

In the dim moonlight filtering through the clouds, the only thing he could see of the *S-52* was her bow wave conveniently highlighted by the phosphorescence of disturbed plankton. He might complain about the SS's incessant demands for patrols, but Gerhard didn't really mind the beauty of the night and the thrill of an open cockpit—particularly at high speed.

— ▪ —

The Sugar George radar operator in the conning station was the first to notice the two blips heading toward *Argonne*. "Intermittent contacts bearing zero-eight-three degrees range two-two-seven double oh yards. Designate skunks Peter and Queen."

Sheppard got out of his chair and went over to the SG radar operator. "What do you see?"

"Captain, two small contacts moving at about 25 knots. They are being masked occasionally by Cap Sicié. That is why I am only getting intermittent returns."

"Very well, don't get focused on them. I'll have gunnery search that area."

Sheppard went to the 21MC "Guns, Captain, there are two small high speed contacts bearing zero-eight-three, use your forward directors and track skunks Peter and Queen."

Chuck Williamson quickly answered, "Guns, Roger."

In less than two minutes he reported, "Captain, guns tracking skunks Peter and Queen. Targets are on course two-six-zero speed two-eight knots. The targets are most likely hostile."

"Guns, Captain, prepare to illuminate with searchlights and engage when positively identified."

Chuck began the process of designating directors. Sky one and spot three would take the leading contact skunk Peter. Sky two would take skunk 'Queen.' He assigned both Turret 6-2 and 6-4 to spot three. Mounts 5-0-2, 5-0-4, 5-0-6, 5-0-8, and 5-1-0 were assigned to sky one. The remaining port side 5-inch mounts, 5-1-2, 5-1-4, 5-1-6, 5-1-8, 5-2-0, and 5-2-2, were assigned to sky two. He assigned searchlight number 2 to skunk Peter and number 4 to skunk Queen. The command, "Prepare to illuminate bearing zero-eight-three by searchlight," caused the searchlight operators to strike the carbon arcs in the 44-inch lights but keep the shutters closed, preventing the escape of any light.

— —

Morris had been lowered in the gig with his headquarters team. Goldstein and Johansen had quickly disconnected and Cruz raced toward the shore as the utility launches were being off loaded by *Argonne*. He had gone less than a mile when the gig was hailed by a French fishing boat. They must have been part of the *Maquis* since they knew the gig was American. Morris was told to proceed directly into the port where he would be greeted by an individual named Commandant César.

As the gig passed the corner of the mole at the little harbor's entrance the sound of gunfire could be heard from the coast road. A fire began to burn, and then another as the automatic weapons fire stopped as quickly as it started. What was happening?

Petty Officer Cruz told him that the water depth should be sufficient for the gig. That he had checked the chart but there wasn't much detail inside the harbor. As they pulled alongside the quay near a group of men, Major Jenkins leaped out.

"I am Major Jenkins, United States Marine Corp, assigned to the United States Ship *Argonne*." Morris spoke in fluent French.

"I am Commandant César, I am glad to make your acquaintance. Do you have boats to start moving the naval families to your ship?"

Morris turned to his Marines. "Bring the gear ashore. Call in the platoons immediately." Turning back to this tall Frenchman with the small hands he said, "Is there trouble?"

Before Émile could answer, two brilliant shafts of light originating from *Argonne* stabbed the night to the east.

— —

Chuck Williamson had reported, "Tracking skunks 'Peter' and 'Queen' range one five oh double oh yards." Sheppard did not want to let them close within torpedo range if they were S-boats. He also did not want to give away the element of surprise if the boats turned back to Toulon at the end of a patrol pattern. He would wait as Chuck called off the closing ranges—"one-three thousand"; "one-two thousand"; "one-one thousand." Sheppard could wait no longer these two contacts were not turning away. He had no choice but to protect *Argonne* and his mission.

"Guns, Captain, illuminate!" The shutters for the searchlights snapped open and binoculars, spotting glasses, turret periscopes and telescopic sights all confirmed that the two contacts were German *Schnellboote.*

"Commence Firing!"

Now Argonne's port side erupted as the 6-inch turrets and 5-inch mounts all fired in response to Chuck's order. "Fire continuous, master key." The loaders raced, as did the handling room crews to feed the guns as quickly as possible.

— —

From the moment the blinding lights hit them, *Kapitänleutnant* Gerhard Hayne and *Oberleutnant zur See* Dietrich Werden had less than a minute to live. They could see nothing but the carbon arcs and were stunned into inactivity. *Marineoberkommando Süd* would claim that they had boldly attacked a superior enemy force. Launching their torpedoes in a desperate bid to prevent the escape of French saboteurs and avenge the deaths of loyal German soldiers. The citations were all lies. Neither *S-49* nor *S-52* fired a gun or launched a torpedo before *Argonne*'s shells tore the two boats apart. Both boats sank in under 30 seconds. There were no survivors to tell the truth about what happened.

It could be said that they accomplished their mission. Alarm klaxons rang out along the entire south coast of France. Every German soldier and sailor in the maritime provinces of France was alerted to the presence of a powerful ship with numerous heavy guns. The operable coast defense batteries were manned and guns began searching for a target.

— —

"Cease Firing, Break Arcs!" were Sheppard's immediate orders; when he saw that further gunfire was unnecessary. The lights instantly were extinguished. Two additional salvos were yet to land, but the only thing they accomplished was to rearrange the wreckage—and the dead.

Admiral Hamblen and Commander Halverson had had enough of being by themselves on the flag bridge and quickly arrived on the conning station. Admiral Hamblen going directly to Sheppard's chair.

"Captain, what has happened?"

"Admiral, I am sorry for not informing you, there was no time. Two German S-Boats were rounding the point and within torpedo range. I had no choice but to destroy them."

"I understand. If you don't mind, Commander Halverson and I will stay up here with you. It will be easier for us to keep informed and make suggestions."

"Certainly, Admiral," was all Sheppard could say, thinking again how much he hated being on a flagship.

— —

Émile turned to Morris with a slight smile, "It appears there is trouble," he said in response to Morris. "I would suggest we begin loading the families." The first of the huge crowd of women and children were already walking toward the men—pushing and shoving, clearly agitated by the gunfire and apparent naval battle. "Major, let me introduce you to Madame D'Aubigné; her husband commands the French fleet at *Mers el Kébir.* Madame, this is Major Jenkins of the United States Marines."

"Major, do you have a doctor here? This is my son Étienne, his wife Marie is in, how do you say, *labor.*" She turned to a small cart with a young woman inside. Étienne stood next to it trying to comfort his wife.

"No, Madame, I do not. There are several fine doctors on the *Argonne*. We need to get her there as quickly as we can." The first utility launch was disembarking the 1st platoon and Major Jenkins ordered two of their men to rig a stretcher and take Marie D'Aubigné to the gig. He shouted to Cruz that as soon as she was aboard, the gig was to shove off and make to *Argonne* at best speed. Madame D'Aubigné and Étienne went with her as the two Marines gently handed her to Johansen and Goldstein. They gently laid her across the gap between the seats in the cabin and jumped up to shove off with their boathooks.

Major Jenkins called *Argonne* on the radio. "Panther, this is Cub, have doctor standing by when gig arrives."

Morris then turned back to Émile. "Commandant César, It would appear that we will be having visitors before the night is out. I would appreciate your help in positioning my three platoons of infantry in the best possible defensive positions. I only have some mortars and heavy machine guns with me for support; but if there is a steeple or hill close by where I might set up a radio, I should be able to bring *Argonne*'s guns to bear."

— —

Sheppard had anticipated that some of the French might need medical attention, but Morris's request came as a shock. He had heard the faint automatic weapons fire earlier while standing on the conning platform. Was it one of his men? How badly were they hurt? Had any been killed? It was easy to not worry when he had something to do. Sheppard's attention had been focused on the German S-boats until they were destroyed. Now his mind was free to wander and consider all the possibilities that he dreaded. In some respects he hoped that additional German forces would come; just give him something to do other than worry and think of the American lives his decisions had already ended on *Shenandoah*. Would his Marines be joining them?

What were the possibilities? What did he need to plan for? That was what he needed to do. If the Germans came again it would likely be by land. He needed his broadside pointed at Le Brusc. He was certain that they could not match his will—or his firepower. There were other considerations, too. His guns were naval rifles designed to send shells far over the horizon. At the range to the town and countryside surrounding, the trajectory was too flat for accuracy. A small error in elevation would make a huge error in range. The answer was to shoot at much lower velocities.

He went to the 21MC, "Guns, Captain, load high capacity in the main battery with reduced charges."

Chuck Williamson knew exactly what was on Sheppard's mind when he got the order. "Captain, Guns, Roger. Do you want reduced charges in the 6-inch as well?"

"Guns load high capacity and reduced charges in the 6-inch."

— —

Major Jenkins and his platoon officers were with Commandant César near the ambush that the French had executed against the SS. One of the Commandant's men approached. "Commandant, one of the swine still lives. He was riding in the lead car. I think he is the commanding officer. The radio in the car was not destroyed. It was saying help was coming from Fort Lamalgue and Fort Napoléon."

Émile walked over to where *ObersturmFührer* Rudolph Blauvelt lay on the ground. He was shot through the abdomen and both legs. The French member of the *Maquis* had disarmed him and handed the Commandant the German's 9mm Lugar. Émile thought he might have an hour to live by looking at his abdominal wound. Émile spoke to him in German to be certain he understood. "You are a dead man. You know this, of course. The only question is how long it will take and how much pain you can endure? Now, what forces are coming from Lamalgue and Napoléon?"

Rudy spat at Émile.

Émile shrugged and raised the Lugar. He shot the SS officer in his left shoulder, shattering the bones in the joint. Rudy screamed in agony.

"Now I will ask again, what forces are coming from Lamalgue and Napoléon?"

Through spit and screams Rudy answered, "Go to hell!"

Émile shrugged again and stuck the barrel of the Lugar into the wound in Rudy's shoulder. Just far enough so that the front sight rested in what was left of the ball socket. He then slowly began to twist the Lugar back and forth as Rudy screamed.

"I'll repeat my question once more. What forces are coming from Lamalgue and Napoléon?"

"There are two regular army mechanized infantry companies at Napoléon and a panzer company at Lamalgue."

Émile casually shot him in the other shoulder and asked, "Why should I believe you, swine?"

"I tell the truth. They are part of the 351st *panzer grenadier* battalion. That is everything that is in Toulon. You know this."

Indeed, Émile did. He bent down as if to work over the left shoulder and whispered to Rudy. "This is for my daughter Yvette!" Only a doctor knew how to inflict pain and keep the victim conscious.

Quickly Rudy passed out from the pain—the shocked expression that his mistress was a spy frozen for all eternity when Émile shot him in the head. Commandant César turned to his men. "Leave him here as a reminder of the fate that awaits the SS."

"Major Jenkins, it would appear we are going to need your ship's firepower before the night is out."

"That I can arrange, Commandant, but I must insist that you do not torture prisoners nor execute wounded."

Commandant César stared at the American major. What a fool this American was. Well, he would learn the ways that Germany wages war. There was only one way to treat them.

— —

Boatswain's Mate second class Raymondo Cruz was no doctor. Growing up as one of the oldest of a large family in a West Texas border town, he had seen his mother give birth to his younger brother and his younger sisters. This woman, Marie D'Aubigné, was not going to wait until they got back to *Argonne*. He ordered Goldstein and Johansen to give him their undershirts and turned the helm of the gig over to Goldstein. Cruz wouldn't dare use a snipe's shirt and let fireman Russert keep his while he took off his own and put his dungaree shirt back on.

He did not know what to do with Étienne; there was no place to boil water on the gig. He asked Madame D'Aubigné if she felt comfortable assisting him and would she please ask her son if he would help his crew get the gig ready to be hoisted aboard the battle cruiser. She said she would but like most French aristocrats had limited knowledge of the more base parts of life.

Cruz took out his Boatswain's knife and asked Johansen for his lighter. Being careful to keep below the gunnel, he struck a flame and sterilized the blade of the knife.

Fearing the worst of this American sailor, Madame D'Aubigné exclaimed, "What are you doing?"

"Don't worry, madame, I will need the knife to cut the baby's cord. Please, Madame D'Aubigné will you hold up your daughter-in-law's shoulders and tell Marie to spread her legs." At the next contraction, he said, "Madame, tell Marie to push with all her strength!"

She said something in French. It was enough, as Cruz caught the healthy baby boy, slapped him on the bottom to make him cry, and asked Madame D'Aubigné to let her daughter-in-law lay back down. Cruz cut the cord with his knife, asked Madame for her clasp to hold the folded over cord, wiped off the baby with one shirt, and then wrapped him in the other two to keep him warm. He gave Marie her son just as she discharged the placenta. Not knowing what to do with it (His father had always taken it outside and buried it.), Cruz wrapped it in the used undershirt, took it topside, and threw it overboard.

Étienne saw the bloody object thrown and thinking it was his baby that the barbaric Americans were murdering, passed out cold just as the gig reached *Argonne*.

— —

Sheppard saw the gig arrive standing on the conning platform with Admiral Hamblen and Commander Halverson. They all saw the sprawled body of a French civilian forward as Cruz came on deck with dark stains all over his uniform shirt and arms. It had to be bad. Cruz would never let Goldstein make a landing on his own, particularly at night in these circumstances. As Sheppard looked at his Coxswain through his 7 x 50 binoculars it was clear

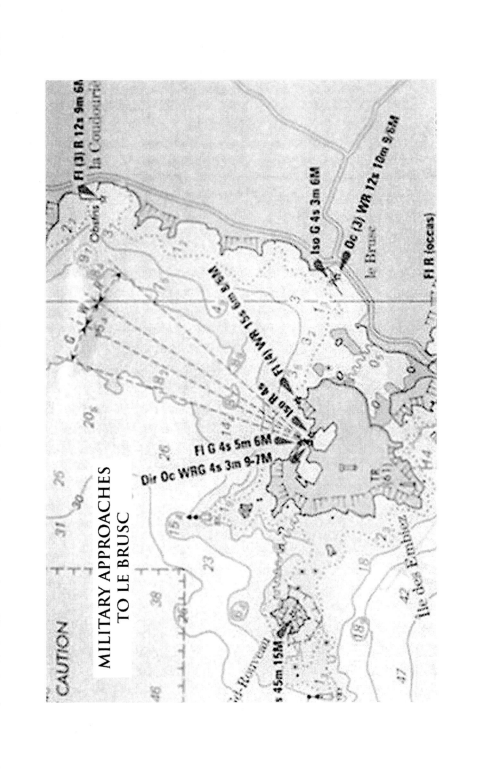

MILITARY APPROACHES
TO LE BRUSC

the man was not right, he was probably suffering from shock or was injured himself.

The *Argonne's* carpenters had built a platform in the hanger shaped to fit the port side of a 50 foot utility launch. When the gig was raised out of the water and then lowered into the hanger, Chief Bledsoe positioned the gig up against the platform. Members of the aviation repair party then boarded the gig and carried Marie D'Aubigné and her son off the gig. Doctor Blankenship examined Marie on the hanger deck for any signs of hemorrhaging. Finding none, he ordered his hospital apprentices to take the stretcher to sickbay. Doctor Blankenship then looked after Étienne, administered smelling salts to the new father and sent him off on another stretcher.

Sheppard was peppering the JA phone talker on the conning station with a staccato series of questions. "How many men were dead? Has Petty Officer Cruz been attended to? How badly was he wounded?"

It was all Ted could do to keep from laughing at the questions when he found out what had happened. He finally had the JA talker tell the conning station that everyone was fine and accounted for with one additional stowaway—male, blue eyes, approximately 7 pounds. For the remainder of Cruz's life no one in the Navy understood why a boatswain's mate would have the nickname of Doc.

It was the last lite moment in a night filled with death and destruction.

— —

Within ten minutes the first of the 50 foot utility launches returned to *Argonne* with a about sixty French citizens onboard. That was the maximum that Sheppard had decided he could risk as additional weight in the ten tons of the boat itself. The launch crew quickly attached the shackles of the lifting bridle to the hard points of the launch. Aviation Chief Boatswain's Mate Bledsoe then had the aircraft and boat crane lift the boat and its precious cargo into the lighted hanger where it was set on a cradle next to the wooden platform. Sailors assisted the French passengers out of the launch. When emptied the launch was lifted out of the hanger and placed back in the water. It wasn't the safest of procedures. Peace time would demand the passengers disembark before the launches were lifted, but it was the fastest way to move the numbers involved.

No sooner was the first launch disconnected than another full one took its place repeating the cycle. It took twelve minutes from the hook on of one launch till the hook on of the next. At first glance things were going very smoothly and about 300 French naval family members were coming aboard every hour. That meant that from the first load which arrived at 0030, it would take until at least 0300 to get them all onboard. That did not include another hour to recover the Marines.

There was no possible way that Sheppard was going to avoid an all-out battle before 0400. He knew he had better prepare for it in every way possible. He started by discussing the situation with Admiral Hamblen and Commander Halverson in a methodology the War College at Newport called a Commander's Estimate of the Situation.

— —

Commandant César agreed with Major Jenkins that they faced an all-out fight with everything that the Germans had in the Toulon area. As the Marines dug in setting up their mortars and machine guns to cover the two lines of approach, the *Maquis* went house to house to encourage the citizens of Le Brusc to take what they needed and retreat to the hills. Morris was surprised how readily they accepted the imminent destruction of their homes, some even volunteering to take up arms against the Germans on the spot. The intellectual in Morris wanted to know what the Germans had done to be hated so by ordinary civilians.

Once the French were clear and his two observation posts set, it was time to register *Argonne*'s guns. Not as simple as it sounds, both the spotters and the gunners had to have the same reference. The problem was that the only map that Morris and *Argonne* had was the same chart that Sheppard was looking at on the conning station. It had no elevations on it, which meant that it was useless as aim points for the firecontrol system.

The directors would concentrate on maintaining an accurate range and bearing to either Pointe de la Cride or the southern promontory of Île des Embiez Chuck Williamson would have to have both accurately in his computers in case *Argonne* had to begin taking evasive action and one or the other became masked. With spot one thru four and sky one, two, four, six and eight all getting accurate solutions on the two land marks it was time to determine the offsets in range, bearing, and elevation from those points to references the Marines ashore could see. There was no way to do that except by shooting and having the Marine spotters call corrections until both Chuck Williamson and Morris had the same reference on the ground even if Chuck's were just offsets from promontories.

— —

Oberstleutnant Dieter Fleischer, Commanding Officer of the 351st *Panzer Grenadier* Battalion, was determined to make an example of this latest attack by the *Maquis*. The Geneva Accords specifically prohibited civilians from attacking occupying forces. Should they take up arms they were combatants. Without distinctive markings recognizable at a distance, they could be considered saboteurs and summarily shot. In fact, German policy allowed him to kill ten civilians in reprisal for every soldier killed. Dieter was smart enough to know that would never work, but at times like these it was pleasant to contemplate.

He decided to have each of his mechanized infantry companies advance on the two roads into town until they met resistance. They would then dismount and advance in a frontal assault with platoons abreast. He would bring up his armor company with their PzKw IIIE and PzKw IVD tanks in support of the infantry once dismounted to overcome any obstacles too difficult for his grenadiers to handle on their own. He radioed his intentions to his company commanders to ensure that everyone knew the plan.

It was going to take his troops and tanks two hours to get into position, but Dieter still thought that he would be able to reach the town by 0245. With luck he would complete the roundup of all the townspeople by 0400.

— —

It didn't take *Argonne's* radiomen long to find the German wavelengths and listen in on their battle plan. But Sheppard had to think this through. If he passed everything he heard back to Morris on the spotter network the Germans could play this game also. Sheppard had to decide the importance of an intercept. But right now, outnumbered almost four to one, with no armor in support, his Marines needed every advantage possible to hold long enough to get the French civilians out of Le Brusc and onto *Argonne*. Sheppard would wait.

If nothing else, Morris should be able to control the location that the Germans would meet resistance and dismount from their trucks and halftracks. That was where Major Jenkins should register *Argonne*'s guns.

Sheppard knew he faced a moral dilemma. His Marines were badly outnumbered and he had a weapon in his magazines that would equalize the odds. However, he had been directly ordered to not use it over enemy held territory. He could save his men's lives but at the cost of untold numbers of allied airmen in the future.

His high capacity shells all had point detonating instantaneous fuses. That meant as soon as they hit anything they were supposed to explode. If that fuse failed, they all had auxiliary detonating fuses in the bases of the projectiles which should then set off the main charge. It sounded great in theory. The reality was that the shell would still move slightly beyond whatever it hit before exploding. If it hit the ground, the shell was slightly buried when it exploded. It was that slightly subsurface position that shielded troops from the deadly shrapnel if they were prone or dug in. To reach those troops the shell had to explode before it hit the ground. That was the advantage of his radar fuses.

The ability of those fuses to be set off by passing near the target was what also made them so deadly to aircraft.

Sheppard knew that 20 percent of the radar fuses would fail to function. One percent of the auxiliary detonating fuses would also fail. That meant that if Sheppard shot one thousand of the radar fused projectiles at the Germans ashore, two hundred would rely on the auxiliary fuse and of those statistically, two could be recovered intact by the enemy and analyzed. If duplicated, German radar fuses might mean the end of the Army Air Corps's plans for daylight precision bombardment. How many of *his* Marines' lives was the chance of that happening worth?

Sheppard went to the 21MC. "Guns, Captain. Gunnery officer, come to the conning station."

Chuck Williamson would probably suspect what was on his Captain's mind. He should have the same concern. Perhaps it was because he had more sleep than Sheppard; perhaps it was only because he was more junior; but he might approach the problem without a preconceived answer. His solution might not require compromising the radar fuses.

As soon as Chuck arrived, Sheppard stated. "I've decided to use the special anti-aircraft common fuses in support of the Marines."

"Captain, I have to strongly object."

"Commander Williamson, I understand your objection. I have carefully considered the problem and see no alternative to protect the Marines."

"Captain, if you will hear me out, before you order me to comply, I think I have an alternative." Chuck also knew the risks of the radar fuses being compromised this early in the war. He knew the direct orders to not use them over land, but he had to convince the Captain of this alternative.

"Very well, Commander, let's hear it."

Commander Williamson and Sheppard went to the quartermaster's chart table. Sensing that a major decision was going to be debated, Admiral Hamblen and Commander Halverson joined the two officers. "Captain, Morris thinks he knows the German plans. They intend to approach along these two roads (pointing to the chart). They will dismount when they meet resistance. If we move to this position (3.5 miles south southwest of Pointe de Deffend), we can fire along their front. If I use the 5-inch with timed fuses and full charges, the shallow trajectory and random variation in detonation times will spread the bursts over the heads of the German troops. I can also control the height of the bursts for best effect, which I can't do with the radar fuses."

Sheppard was intrigued, but his Gunnery Officer had overlooked one key item. "Chuck, unlike where we are now, those waters could be mined! We can't risk *Argonne*'s speed if we are going to avoid submarines on the way back."

Ollie Halverson joined in saying, "Captain, if anyone knows

the location of mines in this area, it will be the fishermen of Le Brusc, and all we have to do to avoid mined areas is ask them."

Sheppard was pleased. It might work. He went to the microphone for the Spotter radio. "Cub, this is Panther, send volunteer fisherman on next launch to identify German mined areas."

Major Jenkins, like any good Marine may not have understood everything that was on his Captain's mind, but he knew how to obey an order. With Émile's help the volunteer was quickly located and sent on the gig since it was faster.

— —

Oberleutnant zur See Lothar Reitemeyer of the *Schnellboote S-54* was the closest to getting his engines reassembled. The commanding officer of Batterie de la Verne had reported the destruction of *S-49* and *S-52*. It was not a surprise, when the orders came down from the Port Captain to get underway as soon as possible and engage the enemy ship. No one had any idea yet as to the identification of the ship or its type other than it was obviously large to have so many guns.

Lothar deduced that a direct high speed approach was hopeless. He would have to rely on stealth if he was to get within torpedo range of this ship. The water close in to the cliffs at Pointe du Rascas was deep enough for him to use the cliffs and land to shield his approach. The draft of his Schnellboot was less than the depth of the mine fields in the area. That was not a concern.

From there he could proceed to Pointe de Marégau, then to Cape Sicié. He would be out of sight of his enemy until he rounded the Cape. If he stayed close to the cliffs, he would be hard to spot until he cleared Île du Grand-Gaou. He should be within range of a high speed torpedo shot before he would be seen. He was certain it was the best plan, but he still did not know what his target was.

— —

Doc Cruz used his usual maximum speed to get the fisherman to *Argonne*, as the Major had ordered, "on the double." He landed the gig alongside a 50 foot utility launch that was just finishing making up the lifting bridle. Cruz told that coxswain to, "Get this man to the Captain ASAP (as soon as possible)," as the French fisherman nimbly jumped to the launch.

The moment the launch rested on its cradle the fisherman was the first to disembark. Ted Grabowski had been briefed by his JA talker on the fisherman's purpose and immediately sent him on to the conning station led by a member of the hanger repair party.

It took almost five minutes for him to arrive, breathless, but eager to help. Ollie Halverson greeted him in fluent French. As they both worked at the chart, the Frenchman was able to draw in the areas that the Germans had mined so far. He also showed where they had told the fishermen not to go in the future, indicating intent to mine those areas also. The information was priceless.

Sheppard could see that as long as *Argonne* stayed west of Île de Bendor, he had complete freedom of action. Sheppard knew enough French to thank the man. He then directed Ollie to ask if there was anything he wished for his help. The answer surprised them all. He wanted to go to England to fight the *Boches*. That was one request, that Sheppard with a nod from Admiral Hamblen was pleased to grant.

A few quick instructions to the Conning Officer and notification to the launches to stand clear sent *Argonne* on her way to the location requested by Chuck Williamson. In fact Sheppard could move even closer to the roads to get the flattest possible trajectories for his 5"/54s.

— —

Commandant César had stationed some of his men on the slope leading up to the 'six fours' fort with one of the Marine radios. It was their report of vehicles approaching from the north that gave Sheppard the initial indication of the German panzer battalion. He went to the spotter network and passed. "Cub, this is Panther. Panther will fire as cub directs." Sheppard had been debating with himself the wisdom of allowing Turret III to fire even with reduced charges. If nothing else the 18-inch guns shooting that close to the comings and goings of the launches would panic the French civilians.

There was another consideration in the safety of the four Kingfishers perched on his catapults. The blast from his after turret would damage them, leaving *Argonne* with only half of her aircraft for whatever else Hamblen had in store.

He ordered, "Guns, do not use Turret III."

He turned to his JA talker, "All stations have anti-aircraft gun crews forward of the superstructure lay below." That would protect them from the blast if he had to fire to seaward. It was good to keep his mind occupied.

— —

Major Walther Buhlers was leading his mechanized infantry company down the coast road. Expecting trouble he rode in the lead Sdkfz 251 halftrack. Armored against small arms fire, he knew the *Maquis* did not have anything heavier than 9mm Sten guns and old rifles. His men would make short work of them firing from behind the armor of his halftracks.

He was tired of writing the occasional letter to next of kin when the *Maquis* ambushed one of his men. They were all veterans of the fighting in Poland and France. Now he would have a chance to exact a measure of revenge.

"Stay alert," he told his men, but more importantly himself, those partisans knew this area far better than he.

— —

Sheppard knew Major Jenkins was waiting for the Germans when they broke into the clear along the beach just before town. "Panther, this is Cub, fire for effect on point one."

Chuck Williamson and Gerry Archinbald had already set up the correct offsets and assigned the turrets and mounts to directors. Chuck passed, "Fire continuous. Master key. Continuous aim." The stable element operators deep in *Argonne*'s bowels closed the master keys.

Argonne's starboard side erupted in flash and flame followed by billowing clouds of gun smoke.

Sheppard shut his eyes as the salvo warning bells sounded. If he did not, his night vision was going to be destroyed. The 18-inch three gun turrets forward turned night to day with the flash of the burning powder leaving the muzzles. Even with reduced charges the glowing balls of incandescent gases merged and reached the surface of the ocean. The sea boiled where it touched. The shock wave from the muzzles frothed the sea even further until the energy, dissipating as the pressure wave expanded, could no longer cause the spray to lift from the ocean. Just as it did the center guns of the two turrets fired creating a new pressure wave and spray. The bioluminescent plankton made the spreading arcs of the pressure pulses into glowing fans, eerily beautiful, out of place considering the death and destruction the projectiles represented. To a lesser extend the 6-inch and 5-inch guns contributed to the flash but neither had the energy to raise froth on the sea.

The noise was overwhelming. Surprisingly it was the 5"/54s that created the earsplitting blast as they fired. Using full charges their sound was closest to the sudden crack of a shattering tree hit by lightning or the report of a rifle. At the other extreme, the 18"/55s were distant rumbling growls only much louder than any sound of thunder. Their noise was more felt in the chest than heard in the ears. In all cases the whoosh of the shells departing grew fainter as they moved away—heavy for the 18 inch, lighter for the 5-inch and 6-inch. Within seconds the sounds came back echoing off the cliffs at Pointe de Deffend and Pointe des Engraviers. That was when Sheppard opened his eyes to see the dull red glow from the six 18-inch high capacity shells fly away toward the beach.

The 5-inch fired again. Sheppard knew it was useless to try and protect his vision. The vicinity of *Argonne* was now going to be continuously lit by the muzzle flashes. Some stronger some weaker, but no one on the conning station would have any effective night vision until the shooting stopped.

— —

Major Walther Buhlers on the beach road noticed the brilliant flashes off to his right. He didn't understand what they were. There were no reports on the army circuits of naval activity in conjunction with the *Maquis* attack on the SS. He felt a sharp blow as the 256 pounds of TNT from one of *Argonne*'s 18-inch high capacity shells exploded mostly under the right side of his halftrack. He could not fathom why he was flying. He was above the roof line of the houses in the town, but only for a moment before the Sdkfz 251 halftrack landed upside down killing him and his headquarters element instantly.

"*What is happening?*" was his last conscious thought.

— —

Morris was pleased with the registering of *Argonne*'s guns on this spot. The salvo had landed exactly where he wanted. Now it was time to move the impact point. "Panther, this is Cub, left spot one-hundred."

Gerry Archinbald, in the forward main battery plotting room adjusted his aim point accordingly. The next salvo of 18-inch shells headed for a point farther down the German column. More halftracks tumbled in the air as German soldiers began to abandon their doomed vehicles. Others urged drivers to get off the road and seek safety elsewhere. They could not move fast enough to avoid Morris's corrections.

Surviving German soldiers took shelter in the shell craters as *leutnants* and *feldwebels* (sergeants) tried to reorganize the survivors and see to the wounded. Now the most important thing that Morris needed was the ability to see.

"Panther, this is Cub. Illuminate!"

Chuck Williamson designated mount 5-1-9 to shoot the Mark 43 flares. The star shell computer automatically made the necessary corrections to the 5-inch guns' elevation. Within twenty-five seconds the twin mount barked. Night turned to day for forty-five seconds as the magnesium flares were ejected over the German positions; slowly descending on the attached parachutes.

The scene of wrecked halftracks and burning trucks showed Morris that he no longer needed the devastation of the heavier guns.

"Panther, this is Cub, Check fire eighteen and six-inch. Five-inch load anti-aircraft common."

Now *Argonne* would see if the gunnery officer's solution to Sheppard's dilemma was as effective.

In the light of the star shells, the anti-aircraft bursts looked like small black clouds even creating a shadow beneath them.

It wasn't the shadow that was important though. For a much wider circle the red hot shrapnel also impacted the ground and the Germans hiding in the shell craters.

Now panic set in and first a few, but then many of the German soldiers tried to scramble out of the shell craters that no longer offered any protection. Most of the Germans who rose, never made it out of their shell craters as more shells burst overhead.

As Morris adjusted the center of the aim point north and south along the strung out German column, the deadly shrapnel took its toll until Major Jenkins passed, "Panther, this is Cub, Check Fire!" The exploding shells stopped and shortly the flares burned themselves out leaving the scene dark filled only with the screams of the wounded German soldiers and the more prevalent silence of the dead.

— —

"*Wolf von Tiger.*" Major Günther von Lindenthal tried the radio again, "*Wolf von Tiger, kommen!*"

No answer! What had happened to his friend, Major Walther Buhlers? More importantly, what had happened to his company of *panzer grenadiers*?

Major Günther von Lindenthal halted his column on the inland road. He saw the fires and heard the thunderous explosions that lifted some of the halftracks into the air. He may not have been able to see the source of the artillery fire, but he suspected that it was a ship, a big one, offshore. This was obviously not a simple mission to root out some *Maquis* that had ambushed an SS platoon. To reach the town he needed armor and called for the reserve tank company before he proceeded further.

He grabbed the microphone again, "*Katze von Tiger, bitte um Panzer!*"

Now to deploy his grenadiers in line of platoons disembarked and wait for the reserves of the tank company to arrive.

— —

Commandant César's men by the "six fours" fort reported the clanking of the tank treads as Major Max Kühne's tank company closed on Günther's position. Riding in the lead PzKw IVD, Max should seek out the commander of the grenadier company in order to discuss what was turning into a difficult tactical problem. That bought Morris what he needed most—time!

Major Jenkins decided that it was unlikely the Germans would try to attack along the coast road again. He redeployed his platoons to concentrate on the inland road; leaving only a squad to cover the coast approach. He also did not expect them to be so stupid as to come at his Marines in a column. This time he would need to deal with dismounted infantry spread all along his front. He asked Commandant César to cover his right flank anchoring it in the rough terrain to the east.

The one problem that he knew he had was the lack of anti-tank weapons. The best he had were .50 caliber Browning M2 machine guns. They were capable of defeating the armor on the halftracks but that was it. *Argonne's* high capacity shells would have to achieve a direct hit except for the 18-inch ones. Even those would have to get very close to turn over a German Tank.

That was it!

It only took Morris two minutes to describe what he wanted to the *Argonne*. He could only hope that the Germans were not listening in to the spotter network. In a few minutes the forward main battery turrets split the night with flash and thunder.

— • —

Günther von Lindenthal wondered what the ship was shooting at. He had not yet advanced his infantry and Max's tanks were just coming up to his position. It didn't take either German company commander long to complete their preparations. Günther and Max just assumed that the enemy was shooting at the remnants of Major Walther Buhler's mechanized infantry company. If those troops had reorganized and were attacking it would make their job all the easier. That attack should also eliminate any forward observers.

Max had his two platoons of PzKw IIIE tanks in line abreast followed by his third platoon of PzKw IVDs. Each tank platoon was supported by a platoon of dismounted infantry. Major Kühne positioned his command tank between the three platoons in order to control the time and place for committing his reserve, as well as direct concentrations at enemy weaknesses. The job of the dismounted infantry was to prevent enemy ground forces from attacking the tanks with grenades or satchel charges.

— —

Morris was getting excellent information on the German movements telephoned from his spotters in the church steeple. He knew they were beginning to deploy. But he would now have to rely on the Gunnery Officer to issue the necessary orders. *Argonne* would have to shoot at several different targets or aim points all at the same time. She would also have to adjust the fire at Chuck's direction as Major Jenkins controlled the largest concentration of fire himself.

Two of the 5-inch mounts began firing smoke shells into the same area that had recently been covered by 18-inch high capacity and armor piercing shell bursts. Morris guessed where his enemy might be and began a barrage of main battery and 6-inch guns in the field that he would have used himself to deploy his forces for an assault. Using range spots of a hundred yards at a time, he was able to cover most of the area adjustments left and right expanded the devastation. He knew that the effect of the fire would be to make the German infantry take cover in the shell craters. That was Morris's only real goal. The occasional hit or disabling near miss on one of the tanks was an added benefit.

— —

The two German majors had anticipated the artillery barrage and knew that the troops had to move forward. The only way to avoid the shells was to get so close to the enemy that they would have to stop the shelling for fear of hitting their own men. It wasn't hard to get the tanks to press the attack, firing and machine-gunning to suppress the enemy, but the shelling, particularly the apparent randomness of those huge shells, was unnerving the *panzer grenadiers* of the mechanized infantry. Before two minutes had passed the German infantry was lagging behind the advance of the tanks.

Lindenthal grabbed his mike to urge his grenadiers to keep up with the tanks. *"Tiger vorwärts, marsch marsch! Schnell! Schell!"*

— —

"Conn, radio central, we have found the frequency that the Germans are using for their tactical communications. Do you want us to patch it through to the conning station?"

"Radio, Conn, patch it through," Sheppard quickly replied.

Turning to Commander Halverson he added, "Ollie, how is your German?"

"Captain, I fear it is only fair, but I think I can give you the drift of what they are saying. The German commander is ordering his men forward. I think he wants them to come to grips with your Marines."

"Don't look at me, Captain, my German is nonexistent," Admiral Hamblen interjected.

Sheppard turned to his JA phone talker, "Aft conning station, conn. XO send a fluent German speaker to the conning station." That would take time and in the interim, Ollie's ability would have to do. He could always pass it to Major Jenkins, but again, if the Germans were listening to his communications, then they would know he was intercepting theirs.

No, Sheppard would have to rely on his grasp of the tactical situation ashore and intervene only when it would be to his advantage. The other speaker demanded his attention.

"Panther, this is Cub, request 5-inch time-fused air bursts centered on area five zero yards north of last spot." Morris was calling for the death knell of hundreds of German soldiers as they struggled to move forward in the face of eighteen five inch guns firing as quickly as they could—nearly 200 70-pound projectiles a minute—over 12,000 pounds of red hot steel fragments propelled by 1,300 pounds of high explosive. Sheppard hardened his expression; there was no way to avoid this. His mission was to save the French. He recognized that this was unavoidable, but still his mind grappled with the reality of what was occurring ashore, and searched for an alternative.

— —

The German actions didn't matter. Whether they hid in shell craters or ran in the open, it did not matter. Morris's plan covered both possibilities. The shrapnel from the air bursts cut into the German soldiers. The men fell exposing more of their bodies to the jagged shards of steel. Some screamed in pain. Others quickly feel silent. Within less than a minute all of the fight had left the German grenadiers as Morris marched the aim point right and left, up and down in the field as *Argonne's* port sided erupted in a near continuous sheet of flame with the 5-inch gunners racing to load and fire as quickly as their tiring muscles would allow.

Major Jenkins was calling for more smoke and a few star shells all along the area that he had bombarded with 18-inch high capacity shells but only 25 yards north of and on the craters in addition to the shrapnel. Those smoke shell bursts were positioned so that the Germans could not see through the smoke to where his troops waited. Nor could they see the craters.

— —

Major Max Kühne and his platoon commanders were confronted with a wall of white when the star shells burst. Clearly the enemy was using smoke to cover their withdrawal. It was time to race ahead before they could get to the next line of prepared positions. Max urged his tanks forward to rush the enemy. He had to get closer to this enemy to avoid the artillery fire that had already destroyed two of his lead tanks.

"Vorwärts! Vorwärts in möglichst kurzer Zeit? he screamed into his radio. This artillery fire was devastating. The only answer was to go forward. How many of his men would be killed if they abandoned their tanks. *"Nicht stehen bleiben Vorwärts!"* Time was everything. The faster his tanks could advance, the fewer would be his losses. This had been a backwater assignment—a reward for the hard fighting in Poland and France. The French, except for the occasional attack by the *Maquis*, had been remarkably passive. What could be happening that would result in this level of military activity? Clearly, *OberkommandoSüd* had failed to anticipate this threat.

It was only two months ago that the 354th *Infanterie-Abteilung* had been transferred away from Marseilles. If we still had that division, this would be much easier.

— —

Morris split his fire. Half of the 5-inch guns continued to pepper the area that he hoped contained the pinned down German infantry while the other half joined the main and 6-inch turrets in shelling the area concealed by smoke. He knew that the German tanks had entered it from the sound of their treads triangulated by his platoon commanders. All he could do was hope that his plan would succeed.

When one of *Argonne*'s 18-inch high capacity projectiles exploded milliseconds after hitting the ground, it created a crater that was 25 feet across and 9 feet deep. The soil was loosened over even wider and deeper dimensions. The armor piercing projectiles didn't create as large a crater, but loosened a larger area of soil. If a tank entered either of those craters, it could not get out. Even if only one tread passed over the side of the hole, the tank would roll over and finish upside down in the bottom.

That was what Morris had hoped to accomplish by digging up a line across the front of his platoons, masking it with smoke and then blinding the German tankers with the reflected light of star shells from the white fog. None of the German tankers should be able to see the tank in front of them or on either side once they entered the white smoke. Until they got to the other side of the smoke they were all just individuals groping in the white cloud.

A few tanks were lucky enough to enter a shell hole directly and not roll over. When they got to the far side of the crater, the loose soil did not provide enough traction for the tank to pull itself out. The 18-inch craters made excellent tank traps that the Germans could not see. Hopelessly bogged down, the tankers' choices were to abandon their armored immobile fort or stay and wait for the inevitable grenades or satchel charge. Most chose to abandon their vehicles to be cut down by the anti-aircraft shell bursts.

When the clanking of approaching tanks stopped; Morris more than anything needed to see. He ordered check fire first of the smoke shells and then the main and 6-inch batteries. He wanted to keep the star shells and shrapnel coming until he could see what was happening with the Germans.

— —

Oberstleutnant Dieter Fleischer was desperate for information. He had lost contact with all of his company commanders and none of the platoon commanders were answering his radio calls. His radio operator swore that the equipment was functioning and that Dieter was transmitting. The last he knew, his left flank *panzer grenadier* company was pinned down and his tanks were advancing into a smoke screen.

That is until the survivors of his assault units began to trickle back to his command post. There were not many. Not one vehicle was among them. Dieter knew that artillery was the queen of the battlefield, but a destroyer just couldn't deal out this much devastation. The English would never be foolish enough to risk a cruiser or larger here off the coast of occupied France. Not under the bombs of the *Luftwaffe* or the torpedoes of the *Kriegsmarine*.

7

WITHDRAWAL

AS THE SMOKE CLEARED, Morris was confronted with a scene from Dante's Inferno. There were wrecked and burning vehicles everywhere. There did not appear to be any concerted effort on the part of the Germans to advance on his positions. He decided to end the bombardment. "Panther, this is cub, check fire!" There was an occasional burst of automatic weapons fire, but the lack of tracers meant that it was probably the *Maquis* mopping up.

Morris knew that the safety of a surrendered or wounded helpless enemy was now his responsibility. If he could not convince Commandant César to call off his men, he would also bear some of the responsibility for any slaughter the French might inflict.

"Commandant, what are your men doing?"

"Slaughtering Germans. Why do you care?"

"I can't let that happen! Those defeated and wounded soldiers are my responsibility to protect."

Émile, the leader of the *Maquis*, raised the Lugar he was holding. "Major, these men must die. I can't risk any surviving that may have seen one of my men."

Morris grabbed the grip of his .45. "Commandant, it is my duty under the Geneva Convention to protect these men. Failure to do so makes me guilty of a war crime. If that means I must fight for them, then so be it. We are not the same as Germans. We do not slaughter as the Gestapo does."

Émile spat in disgust. "It is stupid to fight over Germans. If they are so precious to you, take them with you!"

Major Jenkins quickly saw that was the only option that satisfied all concerned. Now he had to explain to Captain McCloud why *Argonne* would have to be risked waiting for Morris to evacuate wounded German POWs.

"Panther, this is Cub, send medical teams to stabilize wounded and extra stretchers."

———

Sheppard was still trying to clear the spots in front of his eyes to regain some semblance of night vision when Morris's radio call came in. He had been steeling himself all evening for this eventuality. From what Morris had said it was clear to Sheppard that his Marines had suffered a large number of casualties. His men, his Marines this time, had been wounded or killed as a result of his orders. How many and how severe only time would tell? Sheppard needed to apply himself to the problem of getting them back aboard *Argonne* where his surgeons stood the best chance of saving lives. He sent the messenger of the watch to find Doctor Blankenship with orders to send one of his Doctors, two Dentists, and six of his twelve Pharmacist's Mates ashore to triage and stabilize wounded. He vowed to do everything in his power to save all his men.

Sheppard went to the chart table and showed the Quartermaster of the Watch and the Conning Officer where he wanted *Argonne* positioned. He cautioned them about approaching the marked areas any closer than 500 yards. He also drew in an arrow to show how he wanted Argonne to be pointed. The position would mean that the launches would have to travel less than three and a half miles from the quay at Le Brusc to *Argonne's* stern.

He had to think. He knew fatigue was getting to him. *Radar!* He went to the 21MC. "Combat, Captain, search with both Sugar King radars." Jonathan Becker quickly acknowledged. If there were any German radars in the area: Jonathan would have found them by now.

He had to concentrate. His men were depending on him. He could not afford to relax. It was 0315. Why weren't all the French families onboard?

— —

Oberleutnant zur See Lothar Reitemeyer, Commanding Officer of the *Schnellboote S-54,* was rounding Cap Sicié. The gun fire had stopped a good ten minutes ago. All the star shells had also burned out returning the night to blackness that made hugging the cliffs east of Le Brusc dangerous. He knew he had about fifteen minutes until he passed Île des Embiez. That was when he expected to get a look at where the British warship might be. It had to be one of theirs, probably from Gibraltar. That would make the ship either a light cruiser or a *Renown* class battle cruiser. The latter was unlikely. Even the English were not so bold as to risk a warship that important within range of the *Luftwaffe.*

He needed to set his torpedoes for the shallower draft of a light cruiser. Five meters should ensure a hit. Even if the ship was one of the English battle cruisers, their torpedo defenses were too weak to prevent serious damage to vital machinery. If he could get two or even three hits, he might even sink it and avenge the deaths of his friends.

— —

Oberstleutnant Dieter Fleischer began to recognize that his command, the 351st *Panzer Grenadier* Battalion had been destroyed. There were fewer than twenty-five survivors that had made it back to his headquarters. There was nothing more that he could accomplish with what was left of his men. Reluctantly, he radioed Army headquarters in Marseilles to report the disaster. There were what seemed like hundreds of questions. Headquarters wanted the strength of the enemy forces. What kind of ship was it? Dieter knew that they were really building a case against him for use at his court martial as much as they were trying to decide how to handle this enemy.

He knew that if the *Maquis* was in the area his wounded would be quickly killed. Dieter had been with these men since the first operation to take Poland. He knew them all and some of their families. The fact that he could not save his wounded was what finally broke him. He didn't mind the fact that his career was over. He knew that whatever a court martial decided for his fate would probably be just in the circumstances. What he could not face was the families of the men he had abandoned on the battlefield to the *Maquis*. It was his last thought as the bullet from his 9mm Lugar automatic entered the right side of his skull.

— —

Commandant César came up to Major Jenkins with a sad expression. "Major, I must leave if I am to reach where I must be before I am missed."

"Commandant, you are a brave man; thank you for all of your help."

"Major, it was my pleasure to watch you kill the German occupiers of my home."

"Is there anything that I may do for you or your men before they go?"

"Thank you for the offer; but some of my men will search the German dead for what we need after you have taken their wounded. You are a good man. Perhaps there is hope for the future."

"Commandant, though I do not know your name, you must know that your actions today may have saved Great Britain from defeat. One day we will be back and France will be free. I hope someday to come back. Perhaps on an anniversary of today's events we can meet again here in Le Brusc?"

"That would be good. *Au revoir et merci!*" Émile turned and disappeared into the night. Morris feared that he would never see the intrepid French Commandant again.

— —

The Sugar George radar operator on the conning station called out, "Intermittent contact bearing one-two-six degrees, range five-four-double-oh yards. Designate skunk MIKE."

Sheppard jumped over to the radar.

"Captain, the contact is just coming out from behind Île des Embiez. Based on the size it might be another S-boat."

Sheppard knew that this enemy was already in range of a low speed torpedo shot. He went to the 21MC as quickly as he could. He had to engage and destroy the German, if it was a German, before he rounded Île du Grand-Rouveau. "Guns, Captain; track skunk MIKE bearing one-two-six range five-four hundred. Prepare to illuminate with searchlights."

Commander Williamson probably sensed the urgency in Sheppard's voice. His orders to the aft Mark 37 director were quick. "Sky Eight, track skunk MIKE bearing one-two-six range five-four hundred yards. Sky Eight, control all port mounts and searchlights." It was not in accordance with procedure, but time was too short. Fortunately, his men in the number four secondary battery plotting room understood and began turning the *J* switches as quickly as they could.

"Port mounts load high capacity contact fuses." As tired as the men were the gunners and loaders in the port 5-inch mounts and handling rooms jammed Mark 41 shells into the hoists, raised them to the mounts where they were loaded into the guns. Mount ready lights came on as soon as the breech blocks were shut.

Sheppard saw the 44-inch searchlight just aft and below the conning platform swing in the direction of the contact and heard the sizzle of the carbon arc being struck; *"Illuminate!"* He raised his binoculars as the *Schnellboote* rounded Île du Grand-Rouveau. Though not broadside, he saw enough to see that the contact was German. It took three steps to get back to the 21MC, *"Commence firing!"*

"Continuous fire, master key" was the last order that Chuck needed to get out. Now it was a question of how quickly the director personnel and the operators of the Mark 1 computer could get a solution good enough to make hits on the S-boat.

Sheppard had done what he could. Now he had a hard decision. If he accelerated and turned to avoid the German's torpedoes there was a good chance that he would swamp the launches waiting to be unloaded at the stern. He raised his binoculars. There was one launch that had just hooked on with civilians and another that looked empty. That one must be filled with wounded—his wounded Marines!

— —

Morris had split his platoons into squads abreast to search for German wounded. He had briefed all the squad leaders on what to say in German to demand surrender. He gave a final word of caution that there might be fanatical Nazis among the wounded more willing to die for the possibility of taking an enemy with them than the hope of living. Accordingly, it was with some trepidation that the Marines entered the landscape churned up by *Argonne*'s shells.

Most of the French had been evacuated though there appeared to still be a hundred of so remaining. Morris thought that this was going much too slowly. Determined to speed things up, he headed toward the port to remove any bottlenecks. He was surprised that there did not appear to be any.

The first of his stretcher bearers came to the port carrying the most badly injured of the German tank crews. *Argonne*'s medical personnel had not yet arrived. It was clear that many of these men were badly injured and needed immediate treatment. He loaded a launch and sent it off "on the double." The French civilians could wait. He knew that none would be left behind.

That wasn't the way the French saw it. They knew as well as Morris that dawn was approaching and with it the *Luftwaffe*. They feared that every launch was going to be the last for the French. It took all of Morris's linguistic powers to keep them from rushing the dock and hurling the German wounded into the sea. It did not help matters when the night was split by *Argonne*'s searchlights and her 5-inch guns began firing at a German torpedo boat less than a mile from them. Everyone had seen enough of combat this night.

— —

Oberleutnant zur See Lothar Reitemeyer had not. The *S-54* had just cleared Île des Embiez, when he got his first clear look at the warship. He still could not fire his G7a torpedoes. He was just outside their range in high speed. Besides, there was a reef between Île des Embiez and Rochers Des Magnons. If he fired now the torpedoes would dive into the reef before they settled on the running depth of five meters that he had set.

He was studying this immense warship that he had never seen before. It was beautifully proportioned though it was difficult to make out the lines in the darkness. In an instant it was gone. He was blinded by an incredibly bright white light. They must be searchlights from the warship.

Lothar became disoriented. He blinked trying to adjust his eyes to the light. His only reference was the light. He could see nothing else. Shells were coming—a lot of shells. They began to explode behind his *Schnellboote* where he had just been. He knew he did not have long and turned directly at the ship to launch his torpedoes. He might die, but he would launch at least the two torpedoes in his tubes.

The instant the *S-54* pointed the lights, he pulled the firing levers and the two G7a torpedoes leapt from the tubes. He could see them in the light as they hit the water to run on their deadly task. The shells were landing closer. Even though he had slammed the throttles of his Daimler-Benz diesels to the stops, his acceleration lasted for only a few moments.

— —

Sheppard saw the torpedoes leave the launching tubes of the German S-boat through his binoculars just before his guns found the range to the target. There was one hit. *Aft,* he thought, *perhaps in the engine room.* His fire control solution originally had the boat going too slowly as the shells were landing astern. Just as quickly as he achieved that one hit, now the solution was too fast. The 5-inch projectiles were now landing ahead of the German. The hit must have been in the engine room slowing the boat.

It took another ninety seconds before *Argonne*'s fire had torn the boat apart. Sheppard ordered, "Cease fire. Break arcs," wondering about the construction of this boat in comparison to the others. It had not yet sunk but was clearly a wreck and not capable of further offensive action. He coldly decided that *Argonne*'s torpedo defense system of liquid filled layers of tanks behind a "foam-filled" layer would just have to hold. If

Argonne was slowed by two hits, so be it. The wounded Marines in the launch astern were worth the risk. After all, the German *Schnellboote* captain may have anticipated him moving and aimed off accordingly.

— —

In Marine parlance, Morris's men were encountering light resistance as they searched for wounded Germans. He had been correct to warn his men about fanatics. An occasional shot from a German rifle or quick burst of submachine gun fire was followed by multiple shots from the Marine's Springfield bolt action rifles or a burst from one of their BARs (Browning Automatic Rifles). First one, then a few of the litters contained some of his Marines.

Perhaps Commandant César had the best idea. It would have saved some painful wounds among his Marines. It was a question that had plagued every military officer this century. Do acts of the enemy contrary to the Geneva Conventions justify you in committing further violations? There was no clear answer. On the one side, war would spiral quickly to unspeakable acts of barbarism. On the other, an immoral enemy gained an advantage. Morris wasn't able to resolve that dilemma, but he knew that his conscience was clear. Following the rules would let him sleep at night.

— —

Sheppard counted off the minutes. He knew the German steam torpedoes ran at 44 knots. It should take a little over three minutes for them to reach the *Argonne*. He had expected his lookouts to report the wakes of the torpedoes as the nitrogen contained in the air they used for an oxidizer and the combustion products reached the surface, disturbing the phosphorescent plankton. His lookouts had been alerted to watch for them and Lord knew they had the best motivation in the world at this point to do a good job. None had been reported.

That must mean the torpedoes were the wakeless electric type that had been used by the U-boat off the Delaware Bay entrance. Those were estimated to have a range of 5,000 meters, barely enough to reach *Argonne* from the S-boat's firing point. Their speed was less though; only 30 knots. Sheppard struggled to make his fatigued mind do the math. They would take four, not quite five minutes before they hit.

How long had it been? He checked the clock on the bulkhead 0338; before he realized that he didn't know the time that the German had fired. He just had to wait.

— —

All the firing had stopped ashore by the time that *Argonne's* medical team arrived with additional stretchers. One of the dentists did the triage while the lone doctor worked to save the more critically injured. One of Morris's Marines was among them. He was sent on the very next launch.

One of the standing jokes in the naval services, which included the Marines, was that if you got wounded in action make sure it was very minor or really bad. The minor ones a Pharmacist's Mate would work on. They were always very competent. If you were severely wounded, a real doctor would tend to your injuries with a good probability for recovery. It was the in between that you needed to be concerned about. Those were the injuries that the dentist would treat. Like most jokes it had no basis in reality.

— —

It was 0342. The German torpedoes regardless of the type should have been to *Argonne* by now if they were coming at all. Sheppard raised his binoculars to study the remains of the S-boat. It was still there without any signs of life. Why had it not sunk? His mind grappled with the imponderable that a heavily loaded torpedo boat so obviously riddled by his 5-inch high capacity shells could still float. As he stared, he saw the waves breaking at her bow on the Rochers Des Magnons.

Sheppard turned to Admiral Hamblen and Commander Halverson. Without the benefit of binoculars they were still marking time hoping the German torpedoes had missed. Neither officer could possibly understand why Sheppard was laughing hysterically. But Sheppard knew that his luck had held, or perhaps it was the ghosts of the 50,000 men who died along the Meuse-Argonne front in the Great War that were protecting his battle cruiser this night.

— —

It was 0400 before the last of the French civilians came aboard. There were three more launches of wounded before Morris began pulling back his Marines. First to return was the heavy weapons platoon. Then the line infantry platoons.

True to Marine tradition and Morris's promise to Captain McCloud, not one Marine or sailor assigned to *Argonne* was left behind. Morris had a formal muster from his First Sergeant in his hand as he stepped aboard the gig—the last American to leave Le Brusc. Morris marveled that a place so full of the thunder and flash of exploding shells just hours before could now be so peaceful. There was not one person stirring.

Boatswain's Mate second class 'Doc' Cruz brought Major Jenkins and his headquarters group to *Argonne* at his usual wide open speed as the first hint of dawn was brightening the eastern sky. That made it a little easier for Johansen and Goldstein to catch the bridle with their boathooks and in less than a minute the gig was lifted from the water at Chief Bledsoe's direction.

— —

Madame D'Aubigné somewhat bedraggled but still with the air of a French patrician was organizing the ever growing group of civilians in *Argonne*'s after mess decks. She had first followed Marie, her baby and her son Étienne to the ship's hospital. Reassured by a Commander Blankenship, that all three were strong and healthy, she then asked to be taken to where the French civilians were being gathered.

It did not take long before, with the help of Chevir, she began developing a list of all the evacuees and which of her husband's officers they were related to. The Navy families organized themselves quickly and naturally by ships and staffs, and an informal chain of command was rapidly established for the difficult coordination problems that lay ahead.

She was the first aboard *Argonne* to realize that the American battle cruiser was becoming a new home to the town of Le Brusc. Madame D'Aubigné feared that the Americans would send them ashore if their true identities were discovered. After all, it would not delay the evacuation if the launches took the residents of the town back on the boats' return trips.

Besides names, she also began collecting the skills that each individual brought. Daphne D'Aubigné decided that when the townspeople's presence became known, her only chance of saving them from the Gestapo was to quickly inform the captain or admiral of how they could help in the care of this immense group of civilians crammed into every corner of these eating spaces. Her task was made much easier when the mayor of the fishing village identified himself. With his help, every Nazi sympathizer was identified and placed under unarmed, but burley French guards.

Even the collaborators pleaded not to be sent back and thrown to the mercies of the Gestapo.

— —

Sheppard watched the gig start its rise at the end of the aircraft and boat crane hoist cable. He ducked his head into the conning station and directed his Conning Officer to work *Argonne* up to maximum speed as quickly as the Chief Engineer thought prudent. He also directed a course of 225° to clear the coast defenses at Toulon while still opening the French coast as directly as he could.

He needed to get his crew some rest. He ordered the Officer of the Deck to, "Secure from battle stations. Set the modified underway watch with one third of the anti-aircraft battery manned. Maintain condition *Zebra* below the second deck except for the passage of personnel on the third and fourth decks." That was the best compromise he thought prudent for the threats that they still faced and the enemy controlled waters that *Argonne* had to traverse.

There weren't standard orders to accomplish what he wanted; at least none that his foggy mind could think of at the moment. So he just told his OOD that he wanted the two Kingfishers at the aft ends of the catapults fueled, armed with depth charges and readied for launch except for their tie downs. He directed that the, what should he call it, disembarkation platform be broken down and the launches nested. He needed to make room to store two of the OS2U-5s back in the hanger in order to use the ones on the catapults.

— —

Major Jenkins in company with the *Argonne's* Executive Office made the long climb up to the conning station from the hanger. They each needed to report on the night's activities to the Captain. Neither of the two officers knew how Sheppard was going to react to the news that they brought.

As they entered the conning station Sheppard and Admiral Hamblen were discussing the need to get a message to the French fleet at *Mers el Kébir*. For all that Hamblen knew they might be raising steam to sortie for Toulon at this very moment. They had no way to know that their families were no longer in danger—at least not from the Gestapo or SS.

Major Jenkins and Commander Grabowski waited until recognized before they spoke. It was Admiral Hamblen who noticed them first, "Ah, Major. Well done!"

Morris knew there was no higher praise in the naval services. But at the moment he did not think it was earned; "Thank you, Admiral, but many lives were lost while we were ashore."

This was what Sheppard had been dreading all night—the report of the casualties among his Marines. "How many Marines did you lose?"

Morris did not understand the question. "Captain, do you know something that I don't. When I left Le Brusc, every one of my Marines was accounted for."

Two tired men were looking at the same events from different sides. "Yes, Morris, thank you for bringing them all back, but how many died?"

"Captain, they were all alive when I put them in the launches."

Sheppard was certain he had misheard his Marine Commanding Officer. He knew that all the launches were accounted for. None had looked damaged. "You mean you did not lose a man!"

"Yes, sir. My Marines suffered only five casualties—one very serious. A corporal took a submachine gun burst in the chest, but he was alive when we put him in the launch. I have not gone to sick bay to check on him yet."

"But all the stretchers. There must have been close to a hundred."

"Captain, there were ninety-two to be exact. Five were Marines. The other eighty-seven were German POWs."

"POWs?"

"Yes, sir. The French *Maquis* were going to execute them all for fear of being recognized later. I could not let that happen. The *Maquis* leader, a Commandant César, told me the only way I could live up to the requirements of the Geneva Accords was to take them with us. I thought they might be useful. We captured nine officers including two majors."

"Unbelievable." Sheppard looked at Admiral Hamblen, who just looked back at him. Ollie Halverson just smiled.

Admiral Hamblen asked, "Major, you said that many lives had been lost. What did you mean?"

"Admiral, we counted 649 German dead, including the SS platoon that the *Maquis* wiped out. We also destroyed sixteen tanks."

"Major, you did this with only five casualties?"

"No, Admiral, my Marines hardly fired a shot. *Argonne* did almost all the damage."

The only thing that Hamblen could say was, "Thank you."

Sheppard turned to Ted Grabowski. "XO, how did the evacuation turn out?"

"*Wellll,* Captain, I talked to Madame D'Aubigné when she came aboard. She said that there were about 730 family members with her. Captain, we owe her a lot. She has taken charge of all the civilians and is organizing them in the after mess deck as we speak."

"Ted, did we get them all?"

"Captain, the truth is I don't know. We have over a thousand French civilians onboard."

"What, I thought you said there were only about 730 family members" was all Sheppard could think of. His ship now had almost forty-five hundred people on board. It was big but this was stretching even *Argonne*'s seams. "How did that happen?"

"Captain, we could not tell who belonged and who didn't. It wasn't like we had a roster to check off. After you got underway, an old Frenchman came up to me in the hanger and identified himself as the mayor of Le Brusc. He said that when we started killing the German troops, his citizens came and asked him what to do? They knew that the German reprisals would be harsh on the town. He told them all just get in line. He thinks we evacuated the whole fishing village."

"I don't believe it."

"No, Captain, it's true."

"I am sorry, Ted. I do believe you. It's just an unbelievable turn of events, though the more I think about it, it is probably the best thing that could have happened. Major, keep your men off the gunnery watch bill. There may be Nazi sympathizers in this group. Until we can sort all this out, I want all the French kept where they can't do us any harm. Guard all the accesses to the fourth deck, the turrets, and the handling rooms."

"Captain, it seems that Madame D'Aubigné was thinking along the same lines. With the help of the mayor, they are confident that every potential saboteur has been identified and placed under French guard. Even the Nazi sympathizers are being very cooperative."

"Amazing!"

"Ted, get together with Senior Chief Hancock and figure out how we are going to feed and provide bunks for all these people. Oh, you had also better figure out how to entertain the kids."

"Admiral, I hope you don't think I am running a ferry!" Sheppard paused. "Alright you two get to it."

With that Morris and Ted headed to the ladder away from further questions. Sheppard, Admiral Hamblen and Ollie looked at each other, shook their heads and smiled.

Ollie said he had an idea on how they might be able to get the good news to *Amiral* D'Aubigné without jeopardizing any family members that might not have been able to get to *Argonne*. Both Hamblen and Sheppard thought it an excellent idea. Ollie raced off to send the message to the American Embassy in Switzerland. Admiral Hamblen then turned to Sheppard, held out his right hand to shake and told him, "Very well done!" Hamblen headed for the ladder with a last comment, "I'll be in my stateroom if you need me. Please keep me informed."

As the admiral was leaving, Sheppard noticed that his orderly, Corporal Pease, had been replaced by another Marine.

The shock that it was probably his orderly that lay among the wounded in sick bay drained the remaining strength from Sheppard. He went to his padded chair, sat, and wondered why it seemed that every success brought a measure of tragedy to him personally.

— —

Was it true? Had she lost him or was it the cacophony of noise, other's thoughts that were masking him? Everything had been so chaotic. Was he just too tired to think or even dream? He had been her strength, her rock. What now?

She knew in the depths of her soul that she had to sustain and support him. She had to will her endurance into him, even at a distance. Improve the bond that sustained them both, in this monstrous thing called war that threatened everyone.

— —

Gruppenführer Karl Bodermann read the plain language message that had been sent by the American Embassy in Switzerland on several of the French Navy frequencies for the third time trying to find a hidden meaning. There had to be one. He just could not believe that the *Maquis* could move people that fast from the south of France to the northeast corner of the occupied country without his knowledge. But there it was.

"Families safe in depths of Argonne Forest." He would send several companies of SS to search, but the forests were large and the terrain rough. It was easy for people to stay hidden. During World War I whole battalions got lost there for days. From that aspect it made sense that the *Maquis* would hide people in the Argonne. It also made sense that the French would move the families north for eventual evacuation to England.

Of course he knew of the annihilation of one of his platoons in the Toulon area. He had sent a company of SS soldiers to recover the bodies of Germany's heroes. The *Maquis* never left wounded alive. His men were also instructed to make an example of this fishing village of Le Brusc. It had been a source of smuggling on the south coast too long anyway. The occasional luxury items that were brought in from French North Africa no longer interested him. Even as profitable as the smuggling had been to him personally in satisfying Himmler's and Goering's appetites for the finer pieces of French art evacuated there before Germany occupied the remainder of France in 1941.

That man, Blauvelt, had been too impetuous to be a good officer anyway. Karl would not really miss him. Rounding up the French naval families was just one of many failures that Blauvelt had stumbled through. Karl smiled at the thought that he was not going to be embarrassed again with Blauvelt's shortcomings, but he still needed to be replaced. Karl decided to send *SturmbannFührer* Otto Reiniger to Marseilles and teach the south coast of France the price of resistance to the German occupation.

— —

Fregattenkapitän Bodermann hung up the receiver of his telephone. Now he had to face Admiral Schröder with the news that the French naval families had escaped the grasp of the SS. Karl had assured him that they knew generally where the *Maquis* was hiding them, but the area was large, rough, and heavily wooded. It would take time before they would be rounded up. Fritz never thought to ask where that might be. He only assumed that it would be in the Toulon area.

The one German who would have understood that the "depths of the Argonne" did not refer to a forest at all, but rather the American battle cruiser *Argonne* commanded by his personal nemesis Captain Sheppard McCloud, was never told what the message said.

Klaus Schröder took out a bottle of Schnapps to console himself and began reading the routine morning messages that the German Embassy had thoughtfully copied from the *Kriegsmarine* broadcasts.

— —

Sheppard must have dozed off. His Officer of the Deck was trying to get his attention. What time was it? How long had he been asleep on the conning station? Had he said anything in his sleep? He did not remember dreaming.

"Captain, Captain, combat is reporting a bogey (unidentified air contact) on the Sugar King radar bearing three-one-two range eight-zero miles. It looks like it is searching along the French coast."

As Sheppard shook his head trying to clear the fog he asked, "What time is it?"

"Zero-six-twenty-five, Captain."

Sheppard got up and went to the quartermaster's chart. *Argonne* was about sixty nautical miles south of Marseilles almost to the center of the Gulf of Lion.

"Captain, I sent for the Chief Engineer. He came earlier wanting to talk to you, but said it could wait until I woke you for some other reason. I have also alerted the duty gunnery officer concerning the bogey."

"Very well."

It didn't take long for Commander Chris Peterson to climb the sixteen decks from main control on *Argonne's* first platform deck to the conning station. He had brought Chief Machinist's Mate Greg Anderson, *Argonne's* fuel king with him. Greg's job with his assistants was to manage the hundreds of fuel tanks on the ship, keeping an accurate inventory of how much fuel was being used and how much remained available. Available was a key, since it was impossible to drain the last gallon of the heavy black 'Navy Special' out of any of the tanks. Some, in fact most, of the tanks were part of the torpedo defense system and remained filled with fluid, either oil or sea water, at all times. For those tanks, the heavy oil barely floated on top of the water pumped in to force the oil into what were called clean fuel oil tanks located in each boiler room. Twenty-four hours a day seven days a week, Chief Anderson's men worked in the bowels of *Argonne* to fill and refill those sixteen clean fuel oil tanks.

"Good morning, Captain."

Sheppard turned to face the two men. "Good morning, Engineer, good morning, Chief Anderson, it is good to see you again." Greg Anderson was one of the men that Captain Rogers of Sheppard's first battle cruiser command, the *Shenandoah,* had allowed to transfer to *Argonne* so that Captain McCloud had some men he could rely on immediately. Sheppard really hadn't needed them for that, but they had quickly made sure *Argonne* knew how Sheppard wanted to do business.

The fact that Chris had brought the fuel king meant that

there was trouble.

"Captain, you have to slow down! If we stay at Flank speed all the way to *Mers el Kébir*, we will be running on fumes by the time we get there. There will be nothing left to get to where the tankers should be at Gibraltar."

Many sailors think that ships run like cars. If you go faster, you burn more fuel. But your miles per gallon stays the same within reason. Unfortunately, on a ship, if you double the speed, it takes roughly eight times the power to drive it. That means eight times the rate of fuel consumption to only go twice as far per hour. What Chris was saying was that by slowing down, *Argonne* would significantly decrease the rate of fuel consumption and as a result go a much greater distance.

Slowing unfortunately meant that *Argonne* would become more vulnerable to submarines and would not clear away from the French coast as fast.

"I understand, Engineer. Here is a problem I want you to work out for me. I want to run at flank to get away from the French coast for two more hours. If I slow then, how slow do I need to run to get to Gibraltar with a layover of twelve hours in *Mers el Kébir* and a reserve of two hours at flank, if we run into trouble with the Italians?"

"Yes sir, we'll work out the numbers, but we have to make assumptions on how much oil we can get out of the tanks."

"I understand, take your best guesses. I'll see if we can't get a tanker or two to *Mers el Kébir*; but don't count on it."

— —

Feldwebel Siegfried Arnoldt was the FuG Rostock radar operator on the FW200C Kondor flying over the south coast of France. The *Kriegsmarine* had requested *Luftwaffe* assistance in locating a warship that had destroyed three *Schnellboote* off the fishing village of Le Brusc and then disappeared to the south. Flying out of Bordeaux, the Kondor had been airborne for almost ninety minutes, when Siegfried got his first returns on the Rostock. He immediately alerted his pilot *Oberleutnant* Otto Klöpffel to the possibility of a ship to the south east.

Otto banked the four-engine Kondor in that direction as Siegfried called off the ranges and bearings to the contact. There might well be some merchant ships in the Gulf of Lion operating between neutral Spain and France. The last thing that Otto wanted was to raise a false alarm that his buddies would leap on when he returned to base. The further that the FW200 flew, the less likely this contact looked like a merchant ship. It was moving much too fast. Otto decided that the winds aloft must have changed considerably from the last time they calculated them by radar fixes on the coast. No ship could move at 90 kilometers per hour.

Oberleutnant Klöpffel decided on two things. First, he would gamble and radio in his contact report to *IX Fliegerkorps* headquarters. Second, he was going to visually identify and photograph this contact. He doubted that any of his squadron mates in the first *staffel* of *Kampfgeschwarder 200* would ever believe him that a ship could go this fast unless he showed them proof.

— —

"Captain, combat, bogey has turned toward and is closing at approximately 200 knots. Bogey is hostile based upon Rostock radar emissions, single aircraft, designate *Raid One* bearing three-one-seven degrees, range six-zero miles, high."

Sheppard Acknowledged on the 21MC, "Roger, Combat."

"Guns, Captain, Track raid one!"

Chuck Williamson was in the command tower evidently giving one of his officers some sleep, "Guns roger, track raid one." He addressed his 1JC phone talker. "Sky Eight, track raid one, bearing three-one-seven degrees. Sky Eight, control mounts five-zero-one, five-zero-three, five-one-nine, and five-two-one. All designated mounts load special anti-aircraft common. Sky Seven, Sky Six, track raid one bearing three-one-seven."

"Captain, Combat, raid one bearing three-one-eight degrees, range five-zero miles, medium."

Sheppard knew that this was inevitable. The *Luftwaffe* had to find him eventually. He had just hoped to be further away from France before it happened. With any luck, he would be able to shoot this snooper down before he made a contact report. Even if he did though, he had to plan for the opposite possibility. The ranges that CIC was calling off kept decreasing until the sky lookouts on the O-16 level reported, "Contact bearing one-nine-three relative, position angle one, (meaning the aircraft was approximately 10° above the horizon) contact classified Foxtrot-Whiskey-Two-Zero-Zero."

"Guns, Captain, commence firing."

"Guns, roger."

"Continuous fire, master key, continuous aim," was relayed to the firecontrol system and guns.

— —

Oberleutnant Otto Klöpffel had never seen a ship that big or a wake that long. The ship had to be about 400 meters at least. There were three triple turrets—big ones. The British did not have such ships in Force H that he was aware of. He hoped it wasn't Italian. He would be the laughing stock of his squadron if that was the case. They had ships that had that turret arrangement.

The ship was shooting at him. He did not know what nationality it was, but even the Italians could not mistake the appearance of a German Kondor. The first explosion started a fire in his number four engine.

Otto banked hard to the left. All thought of photographs disappeared as he fought to keep control of his aircraft. He pulled the fire extinguisher lever for the number four engine and demanded a report from his copilot on its effectiveness. Whatever this ship was it had managed to hit him at a range of almost 20 kilometers. The next explosion was under the center of the Kondor's fuselage, breaking the main spars for the wing. The FW200 folded up like a falling house of cards in a fire ball of burning gasoline.

— —

Sheppard was on the starboard open conning platform fighting the wind. He saw the aircraft start to smoke and then disappear in a fireball. Returning to the shelter of the conning station he ordered, "Cease fire," on the 21MC. He went to the chart table and began to calculate how long it would take for the *Luftwaffe* to ready aircraft and organize a strike. Any reasonable estimate meant he could not escape.

— —

IX Fliegerkorps headquarters received the position report at about 0652. It took a few minutes to contact *General der Flieger* Joachim Coeler and get a decision on what units to use in the attack. By about 0704 the field orders went out to the airbases of the first *Gruppe* of *Kampfgeschwarder* 73 (I.KG 73) to attack with all three *staffeln* (squadrons) of JU-88A-4 bombers. Major Ludwig von Sichart, *Gruppenkommandeur* of I.KG 73, decided to attack with the first two *staffeln* (1.KG 73 & 2.KG 73) equipped with armor piercing bombs and his third *staffel* (3.KG 73) equipped with torpedoes. With his personal *stabsschwarm* of three more JU88s he would hit this target with 39 aircraft flying out of Toulouse.

It took an hour and a half to fuel and arm all the *JU*88s. The crew briefings were done at the same time so that takeoff was scheduled for 0845 GMT. It was going to be a long flight. As long as the target remained on the same course and speed it was a simple problem to predict the intercept point. The visibility was expected to improve the further south he went. At least that was the weather forecast from the data given by the Spanish.

IX Fliegerkorps headquarters had lost contact with the Kondor for some reason preventing Major von Sichart from gaining any additional intelligence on the target's classification other than a "huge three turret" warship. He had no idea of what type of flak defenses he was going to be facing; however, his men had never had any real problems with the feeble efforts of the British to defend their convoys; when they were foolish enough to come within range that is.

— —

There was no way around it. Sheppard had double checked Chief Anderson's calculations with Chris Peterson twice. He had to slow to only 24 knots. At that speed, a good submarine commander could make a successful attack. *Argonne* did not even have enough fuel to zigzag making the submarine firecontrol problem more difficult. The only thing he could do was try to make the submarines submerge by keeping his Kingfishers up continuously during daylight. In the open ocean it would be much harder to see them from the air, but it was all Sheppard could do.

"Conning Officer, slow to standard speed. Set standard speed at twenty-four knots. Officer of the Deck, as soon as we slow prepare to launch aircraft." The orders were issued. He went back to his chair to sit—and hope.

It was only fifteen minutes before the Kingfishers were ready to launch. A quick word from Sheppard and the powder charges hurled Bronco and Barry off the starboard and port catapults. Bronco climbed to get the best view into the clear Mediterranean waters that he could, in the ten miles ahead and on either beam of *Argonne*, while Barry flew ahead to drive any submarines under.

— —

It was going to be a near thing. If the warship maintained its speed, the JU88s would barely have enough fuel with their ordered bomb loads to make it to the target and back with little extra to safely search should the target change course or speed. Major von Sichart had always thought it was unnecessarily hard that he had to maintain this sham of Spanish neutrality. Several of his crews had made forced landings and the Spanish authorities had always repaired and refueled his bombers, sending them back as fast as if they had landed on German bases. Well, Ludwig had to comply with the field order from *IX Fliegerkorps* headquarters directing him to attack. They must have known that he could not comply unless he flew over the north east corner of Spain. So he did.

By his calculations he should intercept the ship at about 1045. At least the weather forecast had been accurate. The cloud layer was climbing and dissipating the further south he flew. He decided against a simultaneous attack. It was too easy for a warship to avoid his torpedoes. He needed to damage it first with his bombs, and then sink it with the underwater explosions of torpedoes.

— —

"Conning station, Combat, Sugar King, radar contact, many bogeys, designate raid two, bearing three-three-five, range six-zero miles." Sheppard knew that this was the expected raid from the *Luftwaffe* in revenge for what he had accomplished.

Sheppard answered it on the 21MC himself, "Combat, Captain. Roger . . . Officer of the Deck, man battle stations!"

"Guns, Captain. Action starboard, track raid two"

The Boatswain's Mate of the Watch passed the familiar *Word to be passed* followed by, "General quarters, general quarters; man your battle stations." The general alarm was then sounded with a final, "Man your battle stations!" Sheppard knew that the odds of *Argonne* escaping damage this time were very slim. It wasn't like there was only one aircraft or a few to concentrate his fire against.

"Captain, Combat. Estimate raid two at thirty-plus aircraft." He might be able to destroy half of them, but there were enough to saturate his directors and gun mounts. The 5-inch radar fuses were wonderful but they did not make up for escorts closer to the raid, more directors, or more guns. By the time the Germans reached the maximum effective range of his 40mm mounts, it was a given that some would get through.

— —

Major von Sichart was flying just under the overcast with his *stabsschwarm* at an altitude of 2,000 meters. Visibility was good and he should be seeing his target dead ahead in only 15 minutes. Whatever this ship was his 1,000 kilogram armor piercing bombs would take care of it. They might only have an explosive charge of 55 kilos of TNT, but they could penetrate over 17 centimeters of hardened steel from the release altitude and dive of his aircraft. Two *staffeln* of his JU88s were carrying two each.

His third *staffel* was armed with F5b 45cm torpedoes. He fully expected them to do the real damage with their 250-kilogram explosive charges. They had proven very effective against the British merchant ships in the Bay of Biscay until the convoys from Gibraltar to Britain had moved further out into the Atlantic. The torpedoes did have a limitation—they only had a range of 2,000 meters, but their high speed at 40 knots meant that the target had very limited time to try and maneuver away from their tracks. He might lose some aircraft and crews, but he was certain he would sink this ship.

— —

The familiar reports of stations being manned and then the department's reports of stations being ready were coming to the conning station. Admiral Hamblen and Commander Halverson had both decided to join Captain McCloud on the O-12 level. Curious the Admiral asked, "What do you have?"

"Air raid, Admiral, a large one! We are probably going to be hurt. I've ordered the civilians down to the fourth deck passage ways. I want them below armor when the bombs start dropping."

"Captain, Combat, raid two bears three-zero-nine, range three-seven miles and closing, altitude medium."

Sheppard answered, "Captain, roger," but something wasn't right. The raid was drawing to the left; "Combat, report raid two course and speed."

"Captain, Combat, working on it now."

"Captain, raid two is on course one-nine-one, speed two-hundred. Based on the speed, estimate those aircraft are JU88s sir." Jonathan Becker added, "I'll have a CPA (closest point of approach) in a minute."

"Captain, Combat. CPA bears two-five-eight, range three-three miles!" Sheppard had to think. What was the ceiling 7, no, 8 thousand feet? The Germans might not be able to see *Argonne* now that she had slowed, without that broad white wake behind her.

It hit him with the force of a right hook. He had slowed and he had shot down the German reconnaissance aircraft. The German bombers were headed to where he would have been had he not needed to conserve fuel. "Chief Anderson, I could kiss you," he stated to no one in particular, but raised puzzled looks among the personnel on the conning station.

"Combat, let me know the instant raid two changes course."

Now he had to ponder the mind of his enemy. What would cause him to change course? When would he do it? How could he influence him to turn away from *Argonne?* Did he dare reverse course and waste fuel, but open the range even further?

— —

Ludwig was getting concerned. It wasn't just his fuel state—it was the fact that he had not sighted his enemy yet. In ten minutes he would be at the predicted intercept point. If he had not sighted the ship by then, he needed to have a plan to search. At the speed the Kondor had reported it seemed unlikely that the ship could be further down its track than the intercept point. That left the possibilities of it slowing, or changing course. The former seemed unlikely. The enemy commander knew that the *Luftwaffe* would be coming, after the FW200 likely had been shot down. He needed as much distance from the coast as he could get, as quickly as he could get it. That argued for him to have turned south away from Spain.

— —

Barry Jensen really did not understand what Bronco had told him to do. Not that it was hard. It just didn't make sense to him. *Argonne* was on course 225° and he was almost 50 miles directly ahead. Why would Bronco tell him to fly on course 136° for a half hour until he was south of Cabo de la Mola on Mallorca and then turn east for another half an hour until south of Cabo de Pera? Oh well, ours not to reason why, the saying went.

"Mr. Jensen," it was his radioman Henry Hargrove on the intercom.

"Yeah, Henry, what is it?"

"Mr. Jensen, we've got company—JU88s six o'clock high."

— —

Major von Sichart had seen the small float plane flying to the southeast. He knew it wasn't German or Italian—neither had monoplane floatplanes with a single centerline float. It wasn't British either. Their heavy ships carried the Supermarine Walrus biplane flying boats. Ludwig wasn't sure what it was, but it had to belong to his target and it was heading southeast. Either it was scouting ahead of its ship or it was returning to it. Major von Sichart knew it wasn't the former; he had just covered that area of the ocean.

He ordered his three *staffeln* above the cloud layer while he stayed with the floatplane. He smiled at the thought of this pilot leading him to the destruction of his home. This floatplane had made his decision for him.

— —

"Captain, Combat, raid two has turned to course one-three-six, bearing two-one-eight, range four-one miles, altitude now high."

"Roger, Combat." Sheppard did not really want to believe in ghosts, but *Argonne*'s luck was too good. Now he was glad he had not decided to change course. But *Argonne* was not clear yet. If the Germans turned for home before Barry was half way through his east bound leg, they would still pass close enough to *Argonne* to spot the battle cruiser even at this speed. He had also potentially sacrificed Lieutenant Jensen and his radioman, if the JU88s decided to shoot them down before heading home.

He needed to reconstitute his anti-submarine patrol. "Officer of the Deck, prepare to launch aircraft."

— —

It was after 1130 hours when it suddenly dawned on Barry Jensen what Bronco had ordered him to do. The German bombers, three of them, were still flying high above him at his six o'clock. Radioman second class Hargrove had been giving him continuous updates on their location relative to mustang zero-five. He understood he was a decoy and was pulling the *Luftwaffe* bombers away from *Argonne*. He knew where she was supposed to be by her DR, but what he did not know was where the German bombers were based. When they finally got tired of following him, he assumed they would fly home. He was determined to keep leading them further away at all costs, even though Bronco had only required him to stay on course zero-nine-zero until he was south of Cabo de Pera.

Barry was afraid that the Germans would not be far enough to the east if they broke off when he had to return to *Argonne* or run out of fuel. He decided to keep luring them on even if it meant he would be unable to return. He did not bother to tell Radioman Hargrove of his plan.

— —

"Captain, Combat, lost contact on raid two bearing one-five-five, range eight-one miles due to masking returns from Majorca Island." Sheppard checked the clock on the bulkhead. It was 1125. He decided to keep the crew at battle stations until he knew that the German raid would not pass in his vicinity on their route home.

Admiral Hamblen expressed the thought that was on everyone's mind. "It looks like they took the bait."

"Yes, Admiral, I just hope my young pilot doesn't try to do anything stupid. He has barely enough fuel to return. He is much lower than the German JU88s, and we lost contact on him twenty minutes ago."

— —

Major von Sichart finally gave up. He did not have the fuel to continue chasing this slow float plane. The weaving back and forth to keep pace with the slower aircraft was draining his fuel. He suspected that the warship had turned south soon after it shot down the FW200, which fit with where the float plane was headed. That would place it now to the southeast of Minorca. But, why was it searching so far to the west when he discovered it. Well, it did not matter, he had to return anyway. At 1209 he turned back to his base at Toulouse and climbed above the cloud layer for best fuel efficiency to rejoin his Gruppe.

— —

Captain, Combat, Sugar King, radar contact, many bogeys bearing zero-eight-seven range, one-zero-four miles; designate raid three, working on course, speed and CPA."

"Combat, Captain, roger." Sheppard checked the clock again. It was 1219. If this was the same group of German aircraft, Lieutenant Jensen had pulled them to the east well beyond what they had planned.

"Captain, Combat, raid three on course three-four-zero, speed two-hundred; redesignate raid three as raid two. Raid two is at CPA and opening." This was the confirmation that Sheppard needed to breathe a sigh of relief.

"Officer of the Deck, secure from General Quarters, set the modified underway watch, set condition *Yoke* above the third deck. Get the civilians back up above the third deck. My compliments to Major Jenkins and request his men make a thorough search for unauthorized personnel below the third deck, in all turrets, and handling rooms." Sheppard had had enough surprises for one day and did not want anymore.

"Captain," it was Ollie Halverson, "if you and Admiral Hamblen could step over to the chart table for a moment, I would like to show you something I have been working on."

"Certainly." Sheppard's curiosity was peaked. He knew enough about Commander Halverson to know that, if he was going to raise a concern, it was something Sheppard needed to listen to.

"Admiral, Captain, the last position information we have on Moretti and the Italian scouting force was here at 1400 yesterday," pointing to the northwest corner of Corsica. "We have never seen the Italians sortie only a portion of their main fleet units. In all likelihood that means he will rendezvous with Romano and the Italian battle fleet before either conducts a major operation. I am well aware that it is always dangerous to make decisions on the absence of information, but it seems odd that we have heard nothing from Malta or the air searches out of Haifa. It also only makes sense for Moretti to be observed here, if the Italians were headed west.

"Intelligence has known for a long time that the Italians are short of fuel oil. That fact argues against a training exercise west of Sardinia. If it was just for training, they would do it in the Tyrrhenian Sea, and we would not have seen Moretti."

"Commander, so far I do not see a flaw in your analysis," Admiral Hamblen interjected.

"Thank you, Admiral," Ollie took a deep breath and continued. "That leads to the imponderable. Why are the Italians coming west now? There are only two targets that they could be interested in. The first is Gibraltar. The timing argues against that objective. All the Italians would have to do is wait for Rommel to move further west and soften our base with the Desert *Luftwaffe*. I believe the key is Rommel's advance through Algeria. That fact and the potential capture of the fleet by the Germans is what is driving the Italian action. Their objective is the capture or destruction of the French Fleet at *Mers el Kébir!*"

Admiral Hamblen and Sheppard looked at each other. Everything they had been working for this past week, all the risks that had been taken, was going to be for naught.

8

COORDINATION

THE BALEARIC SEA WAS fairly well sheltered by Spain and the off shore islands that gave it its name. Without the long rollers from the Mediterranean, conditions allowed for Bronco to land and taxi up to the *Argonne* without Sheppard having to make a slick. All he needed to facilitate the recovery of mustang zero-one was to rig the sled and slow to 18 knots. No sooner was Bronco aboard at one bell in the afternoon watch (1230) than he started asking if *Argonne* had heard from Barry Jensen.

No one had. Bronco was the last man to talk to the young pilot when he gave him the courses he was to fly for the decoy mission. Scout-Observation Squadron 68 saw a new side of their Commanding Officer that was totally unexpected. Bronco proceeded directly to CIC, grabbed a stool and sat down—concerned and anxious. He figured that Barry would run out of fuel at 1250, maybe 1300 at the outside. As the minutes dragged on with no radar returns he got up and began checking the two Sugar King Radar repeaters personally.

At two bells he called, "Mustang Zero-Five, Panther; over," on the VHF spotter radio. There was no answer.

— —

Radioman second class Hargrove told Barry immediately

when the JU88s banked to the north and climbed above the clouds at 1209. Being part of one decoy, Barry was suspicious of a ruse and maintained his course and speed until 1215. He knew he really didn't have a chance to get back, but decided that he would try everything he could to make it. He finally told Harry what they had been doing for the last hour and half and why he decided against following orders and turning back at 1145.

Now they both set to work trying to make the fuel last as long as they could. Barry jettisoned both of the Mark 17 depth bombs without arming them. Freeing the Kingfisher of 650 pounds of dead weight and the air resistance of charges slung under the wings, helped considerably. Harry Hargrove asked permission to jettison his browning .30 caliber machine gun, all his ammo, and his armor plates, figuring that if they were going to crash anyway, they really weren't worth keeping. Barry worked on leaning back the mixture of gasoline to air ratio in the nine cylinder Pratt & Whitney Wasp Junior engine until it started to misfire. He inched the mixture control forward ever so slightly until the engine just stopped misfiring.

It was Harry that suggested the last item. They both shut their sliding canopies. Besides making it quieter flying it also reduced the drag of the Kingfisher moving through the air. Neither could think of anything more they could do as Barry worked out the shortest path back to *Argonne* taking advantage of the slight tail wind from the east.

— —

Having gotten no answer from Barry Jensen, Bronco was really worried. Every pilot fears the epitaph, 'Missing, presumed dead.'

"Mustang Zero-Two, Panther, any sign of zero-five?"

"This is Zero-Two, negative."

"Mustang Zero-Six, Panther, what about you?"

"Negative."

Bronco really hadn't expected that they would. The Sugar King radars stood a much better chance of finding Barry than either of his other two pilots did visually. But he had to try.

— —

At 1252 Barry passed between Isla de Cabrera and Punta Salinas at the southern tip of Mallorca. Trying to stay just out of any anti-aircraft batteries the Spanish might have. It really didn't matter if they saw him. The German strike would be too far and too low on fuel to take advantage of the information.

"What do you think, Mister Jensen?" Hargrove asked plaintively.

"Well, Harry, all I can do is guess. I don't think we'll make it." Mustang zero-five changed course to 292°.

"At least the sea is smooth. It will be easy to land when we run out of fuel," he added hopefully.

If Argonne stayed on course, 292° was Barry's best estimate of an intercept point along *Argonne's* track. There were still 75 nautical miles to go and the fuel gauges were bouncing off the low pegs.

— —

Bronco made the long climb up to the conning station to inform the Captain that in all likelihood Kingfisher mustang zero-five had either been shot down or had run out of fuel. With luck Lieutenant Jensen and Radioman Hargrove had made a successful open ocean landing. Sheppard agreed with Bronco's assessment.

Unexpectedly, Bronco asked, "Captain, request permission to launch two OS2Us for search and rescue."

Sheppard knew that he owed both Bronco and Barry a great deal. Each had sunk an axis submarine saving *Argonne* from crippling damage. He knew that next to Bronco, Barry was probably his best pilot. Sheppard also had to face the possibility that Jensen and Hargrove might already be dead and with Commander Halverson's analysis, it may have been the Italians that were responsible. Sending two more Kingfishers could easily mean the loss of two more crews. Sheppard had to steel himself to that probability.

"Sorry, Bronco, but I can't afford the loss of four more of your men on what might be a fruitless search." Sheppard knew that it was he who was really responsible, not Bronco. He turned away from his squadron commander alone in his thoughts and guilt.

— —

It was 1311 when the Kingfisher passed Cabo de la Mola at the western tip of Mallorca. Barry only had 41 miles to reach *Argonne*, but more importantly, mustang zero-five was clear of the island and the ship's radars should now be able to see them, or so Barry hoped.

Forty miles didn't seem like a long way, but with all his fuel gauges on zero, they were never going to make it home.

"Harry, check your life vest and survival gear. She isn't going to last much longer."

"Roger, Mister Jensen."

— —

"Conning station, Combat, bogey bearing one-two-zero, range four-zero miles. Bogey is identified as friendly by IFF."

Sheppard acknowledged the report while Bronco grabbed the microphone for the Spotter network. "Mustang Zero-Five, Panther, over," Bronco could not hide the hope in his voice.

"Panther, this is Mustang Zero-Five, hear you loud and clear!" Bronco knew what Barry needed most at that moment, "Mustang Zero-Five, Panther, vector two-nine-nine, range four-zero over."

"Panther, Mustang Zero-Five, roger, thank you, fuel state is critical." Both Sheppard and Bronco smiled at the understatement of the century.

"Officer of the Deck, prepare to recover aircraft on the port side," was the happiest order that Sheppard had given all day—if only the Kingfisher's fuel would last.

— —

The nine-cylinder Pratt & Whitney R-985-AN-2 engine coughed and died four miles short of *Argonne*. Barry managed to glide another mile and a half before he ran out of air speed and altitude all at the same time. He confirmed the assessment of being *Argonne's* second best pilot by executing a perfect dead stick, open ocean, downwind landing—stopping two miles short of the battle cruiser.

In another surprise for the day, as soon as Sheppard told his Conning Officer Lieutenant Hamblen to, "Go get him," John Hamblen the fourth quickly approached the drifting Kingfisher upwind, created a lee, and then twisted the stern close enough for Coxswain Bergman to throw a heaving line to Radioman Hargrove. Bronco was waiting in the hanger when Chief Bledsoe lowered mustang zero-five onto an aircraft dolly. Barry came down the ladder ecstatic, having made it back to *Argonne* with his crewman alive, to see his squadron commander.

Bronco held out his hand to shake Barry's. "Nice flying! You're grounded for disobeying an order."

— —

Sheppard had called the counsel of war for 1400 to give him time to think and his department heads time to sleep. He was so tired, but a plan of action had to be formulated to deal with the Italians. He knew the odds were impossible to fight a conventional battle even at long range—there were just too many enemies. They would overwhelm *Argonne* even if help arrived from Force H. That was another problem. There had not been any messages explaining the failure to meet off of *Mers el Kébir*. For all anyone on *Argonne* knew they might never come.

Sheppard was struck by Sun Tsu's statement in *The Art of War* that the best policy was "to attack the enemy's plans." The Italians had organized their forces into a scouting force of battle cruisers and aircraft carriers—that was now for certain. He assumed that the battleships would be separate. If the Italians had wanted a single force then it was logical that they would have rendezvoused in the Tyrrhenian before the scouting force was seen northeast of Corsica.

Why would they organize as two forces? Did they have two missions? Assuming that the battleships were going to deliver the overpowering threat or killing blows to the French warships, then what was the purpose of the other force? Was it cover, a completely separate mission, deception, or a guard against interference? Interference by whom? Clearly they knew about Force H. They might know that *Argonne* had been at *Mers el Kébir* yesterday. The carriers meant air cover and long range strike. The battle cruisers meant the need for high speed heavy guns. The Italian scouting force had to be a guard against Force H. Hardy was the only air power they needed to worry about and the guns of his battle cruisers required the Italian battle cruisers to defend the carriers.

How to attack the plan? Sheppard did not have the airpower to attack the Italian ships directly. In addition unlike the Germans, some of their anti-aircraft guns were shielded preventing the tactic he had used at Cape Vilan. His only effective asset was the long range 18-inch guns on *Argonne*. *How to attack the plan?*

Another of Sun Tsu's quotes came to mind, "to subdue the enemy's army without fighting is the acme of skill." Nice— Sheppard did not think he would be able to do that. His only option was to fight—unless!

— —

Vizeadmiral Joachim Moeller was on the flag bridge of the aircraft carrier *Peter Strasser* as she passed Tostoya Island in the Trondheimsleia on course 064° at 12 knots. It was a long difficult passage to reach the anchorage at Trondheim, but the very length of the passage was what made it ideal as a base. The outlying islands afforded sufficient patches of level ground for the *Luftwaffe* airfields making air attack all but impossible. Those occupied islands also afforded sufficient warning of British reconnaissance flights to start the smoke pots ashore blanketing the anchorage with a thick white fog before the Spitfires or Mosquitoes reached the ships.

He had received the latest intelligence updates from Admiral Lütjens. Force H was still in Gibraltar and the reinforcement from the Home Fleet had arrived. That was good news as it further restricted Admiral Tovey's ability to detach squadrons to block the Denmark Strait. On the other hand there was a report from the U-boats off the American coast that a Task Force had sailed from Norfolk. Again containing two *Brandywine* class carriers, that Task Force must be the same one that had destroyed *Vizeadmiral* Schröder's planned sortie from Brest in April. At least this time it only had one of the American's new *Santiago* class battle cruisers. Two of those ships had been responsible for the German defeat at Cape Vilan, but one had been badly damaged. With only one left, even if that Task Force tried to interfere, his ships would be more than enough to defeat them. There would be no Force H to save them.

Gibraltar Harbor

lgeciras

BAY OF GIBRALTAR

Admiral Hardy was frustrated. There was still no method by which he could get messages directly to the Americans he was supposed to "coordinate" with. The Admiralty was really dropping the ball on this one. At least the repairs to *Renown* had proceeded on schedule and his flag captain had reported that the Prince of Wales dock basin had been inspected and flooding of the dry dock would commence momentarily. His flagship would certainly be able to meet the underway time that he had ordered.

Hardy had decided to leave after sunset and hope to avoid the prying eyes of the German and Italian spies that infested Algeciras. It was a constant struggle to keep his movements a secret. His was a unique position. He faced threats in both the Atlantic and the Mediterranean. If the Germans in the Atlantic knew he sortied east against the Italians, they were likely to try something. Similarly, the opposite was also a concern. He had been successful before the Battle of Cape Vilan by appearing to go one way and then actually going the other, but he did not have time tonight for a deception. He could only hope that his absence would not be detected until morning leaving both his enemies feeling threatened by his unknown location.

— —

Across the Bay of Gibraltar in Algeciras *Capitano di Corvetta* Leonardo Marchesani was supervising the suiting up of six of his men for an attack on the British shipping anchored in the Bay. Hidden in the forward compartment of the Italian tanker *Olterra*, that had been interned in Algeciras, a secret base for the deployment of the Italian two man submersibles *maiale* had been surreptitiously constructed. Periodically shipments of repair parts had been received by the *Olterra* that in fact were parts to assemble the pigs.

Once assembled, it was only a question of smuggling in shipments of 'farm machinery' that actually were the 300 kilogram warheads to be carried by the submersibles and attached to the targets by clamps. This afternoon would be the first use of the secret base to attack the shipping in Gibraltar.

Leonardo, casually dressed as a merchant seaman, went up on deck with a compass identical to the one used on the submersibles in order to take bearings on the targets that he intended his men to attack. Unknowingly, he failed to consider the compass deviation caused by the steel hull of *Olterra* that would not affect his crews once they launched.

There were four huge tankers, obviously fully loaded that were his priority targets. He did not know, nor would he have cared if he had learned that they were American. As far as he was concerned any ship on the east side of the bay was a potential target for his men, and the sooner he could attack them the better. The bay was nearly filled with the arrival of a convoy this morning, but these ships were the biggest outside the protection of the mole and submarine nets at the British base. His only limitation on how many and how often he could attack was how fast pigs and warheads could be smuggled into his base.

— —

Sheppard, Admiral Hamblen, Ollie Halverson and the *Argonne's* Department Heads made for a tightly packed sea cabin behind the conning station. Sheppard first asked Commander Halverson to review for everyone present the assessment of Italian options and the reasoning behind his estimate of their intentions. As expected there were only a few questions, though it was clear to everyone that the size of the Italian fleet enroute to *Mers el Kébir* (4CVs, 12BBs, & 6CCs with cruisers and destroyers) had made *Argonne's* mission to protect the French suicidal at best.

Sheppard then began by discussing his analysis of the strengths that *Argonne* possessed to use against the Italians. It wasn't a surprise to anyone that the advantages were long range 18"/55 guns, a large inventory of shells, exceptional firecontrol equipment with analog computers, and radar for both search and firecontrol. Captain McCloud made a point of mentioning that unlike the German battle cruisers that *Argonne* had fought off of Cape Vilan, the Italian heavy anti-aircraft guns had shields and were therefore not susceptible to shell bursts above.

Sheppard now had to begin by giving his officers a short tutorial on some of the items that he had learned in Newport. First was the concept of where the enemy's power came from. It was pretty obvious that it was the Italian Battle Fleet and not the Scouting Group. Then he analyzed the "Center of Gravity" as

Clausewitz had called it from the standpoint of how to attack it. Without much effort it was clear to all of the officers that *Argonne* did not have the power to attack it directly. Accordingly, if they were going to accomplish their mission, they would have to use the indirect approach through some other vulnerability that the Italians had.

To the delight of the Captain, it was Art Roberts who pointed out that the weakest part of their fleet was in the air. He said that since they only had aircraft carriers for a few years and the Italians were chronically short of fuel oil, those ships were probably not proficient at launching and recovering their planes. It also meant that the Italians would not be flying at night; the most difficult of all carrier evolutions. Nor would their doctrine for the use of aircraft on carriers and the employment of those planes be very advanced.

Sheppard asked, "Why do you think the Italians brought them since the Germans are close enough to provide air cover?"

That sparked discussion with opposing views being freely exchanged as Sheppard had intended until the Department Heads settled on two possibilities; the first was that the Italians were not coordinating with the Germans; the second, that the Italians wanted the air cover further than the Bf109s could range. That was when Sheppard reminded everyone that the Italian goal was fundamentally different than the German. There was no possibility of the Italians letting the Germans in on their plans to capture or destroy the French fleet when the German goal was its capture and incorporation into the *Kriegsmarine*.

"So, Ollie, why would air cover be so important to the Italians?"

"Captain, it has to be Force H. The Italians fear what Admiral Hardy can do to their battleships, particularly after what Admiral Cunningham did to them at Taranto."

"Good show, old chap," Sheppard injected with his best attempt at a British accent. He knew he had to keep the meeting light if he was to get everyone's best input, and Ollie was the perfect foil—unimpeachable performance of duty and widely respected.

Sheppard had already spent more time at this meeting than he had intended and began to summarize, 'Okay, if air is their weakness, and our advantage is gunnery, what do we do?" Sheppard knew he had been successful when Doctor Blankenship offered, "Why, Captain, it is obvious, we get Force H and we attack their carriers."

To the group as a whole, Sheppard asked, "And how do we 'get Force H'?"

Admiral Hamblen replied, "Captain, leave that to me." He then turned to Lieutenant Commander Burdick and said, "Bronco, I am going to need a ride." After thinking for a moment he also said, "I am also going to need a signalman. Bronco, can your Kingfishers hold three people?"

The answer was immediate, "Not really, Admiral. Cramming three in a Kingfisher can only be done for a water takeoff. The third man would never survive a catapult launch without significant injuries. The radios get in the way of any additional space and even with the .30 cal. removed the gunner's seat is not very comfortable."

"Well, that seat will just have to do, and I guess my Morse code is going to be good enough."

Knowing the way admirals think, Sheppard interjected, "Admiral, do you have anyone in particular in mind that you would like to be your pilot?" Sheppard turned to his squadron commander, "Bronco, who is your best pilot with a signal lamp?"

"I'm afraid it is Barry, but he is grounded."

"Bronco, if you can see a way to let him fly, I'd like to take that young lieutenant. He showed good initiative in leading the German strike away from us," Admiral Hamblen softly added so that only Bronco and Sheppard could hear.

Sheppard smiled. One of Hamblen's more endearing qualities was creating opportunities for young officers in need of redemption in the eyes of their superiors. Sheppard knew that this also created a dilemma for Bronco in how to maintain his authority at the same time he acquiesced to the Admiral's wishes.

Art Taylor spoke up. "You know we are in a waxing gibbous situation."

Chuck Williamson jumped in, "Okay what does that mean for gunnery types?"

Art continued, "Sorry, the moon is at seventy-two percent of its maximum illumination. Moonrise has already occurred and it will reach its highest point in the sky at twenty-oh-nine. It will set at zero-two-nineteen tomorrow and we will have two hours of maximum darkness before twilight at zero-four-twenty-two in the morning."

Sheppard was struck that his request of his oil king matched exactly the time he would have of blackness to engage and defeat the Italians. "Anything else, gentlemen?"

"Yes, Captain," said Jonathan Becker. "I just wanted to make sure everyone knew that the Italians do not have radar."

Sheppard looked at his CIC officer dumbfounded. That information meant that the only way the Italians could detect him was the flash of his guns. As bad as that was, they could not get a range from it. The flash would also blind the range takers using the Italian optics. Even Sheppard was beginning to think they might pull it off.

"Captain, if it is going to be as light as Art says it is and if the sea state holds for landing, I think a few of my pilots are good enough to do a little recon for you after sunset. I am sure we will be able to find things, but we probably won't be able to identify them all that well."

With Bronco's statement and an agreement on many of the details, the meeting broke up without discussing the world's fourth largest submarine fleet—all in the Mediterranean.

— —

The Italian two man crews of the pigs had been moving toward their targets at a little over 3 knots for an hour. Breathing pure oxygen they had to stay within 13 meters of the surface to avoid oxygen poisoning. At the same time they needed daylight to find their targets while submerged; they had to stay deep enough to avoid being spotted by the numerous British patrol boats.

Capitano di Corvetta Leonardo Marchesani had thoroughly briefed his crews on their targets and what they could expect in terms of identifying characteristics of the hulls. Obviously large, they would be square bilged, not rounded like some merchants; importantly engines aft implying the main circulating water systems for the condensers would be close to the stern, and finally that they would have single screws.

As the crews began to see the shapes of hulls before them, some unknown current or problem had caused them to encounter the wrong ships initially. Undeterred, each crew began to search in the vicinity until they located hulls with the characteristics described by Marchesani. It had taken time, but the closed cycle breathing devices they wore had an endurance of six hours and each crew had found a hull with the correct characteristics within three and half hours of the start of the mission.

Now with the pigs resting gently against the targets' hulls with slight positive buoyancy, the second operators (swimmers) disembarked and removed clamps from the storage locker. Without much difficulty they found suitable gratings in the sea water discharges or bilge keels to attach the clamps, providing anchor points for the ropes that were then strung between the two tie points. This allowed optimum positioning of the 300 kilogram explosive charge directly under the center of the engine rooms; tied off and suspended about a meter below the hull.

Having detached the warheads from the pigs, optimally positioned them, and secured them in place; the swimmers armed the charge and set the timers to detonate at 2100, allowing plenty of time for all the crews to make their returns to the *Olterra*. It was on the return trip that the oxygen breathing apparatus of one of the pilots began to malfunction. Becoming disoriented with a splitting head ache, he surfaced his pig and pulled off his mask. That was when a British patrol boat spotted them and investigated. Both men were captured but not until after they had scuttled their pig. Suspecting that they had been launched from submarines, the British doubled their patrols and made a thorough but fruitless ASDIC search of the harbor. Every ship in the harbor was alerted to the possibility of swimmers in their vicinity.

— —

"Ted," Sheppard called after his executive officer as the others left. "How about keeping an eye on things up here for a while? There is something I have to do."

"Sure, Captain," was Commander Grabowski's answer with a puzzled look. What would demand his Captain's attention on the eve of a major battle somewhere other than on the conn?

Sheppard with Corporal Chase in tow began the long climb down the forward tower of *Argonne* to the main deck. Sheppard was beginning to know his way around the ship and went directly to the athwartships passage down two decks and forward. There were French civilians everywhere. He found the access trunk leading below the third deck. The Marine guard, watching for any attempt by a civilian to go below, stiffened to attention as he approached. The armored hatch never failed to impress Sheppard concerning how well *Argonne* had been designed to resist long range gun fire—nearly a foot thick of the best steel American industry could provide. Fortunately for Sheppard and Corporal Chase, it was open.

One deck down and forward, Sheppard first stuck his head into the combat information center or CIC. Jonathan Becker saw him enter, thought for a moment and sounded the "Attention on Deck."

Sheppard quickly gave them, "As you were," pleased that Jonathan might be beginning to adapt to the Navy ways and asked politely, "How is everything going?" Lieutenant Commander Becker proceeded to give a detailed status report on every radar and communication circuit in his domain. He then went over every radar return from Cabo de la Nao on the Spanish coast as well as Islota Vedrá, Ibiza and Formentera in the Balearic Islands. He covered every air contact over Spain and the numerous fishing vessels off of the coast lines. It was a thorough briefing, but Sheppard quickly concluded that his effort to turn Jonathan into a naval officer still had a long way to go.

Sheppard and Corporal Chase escaped eventually and continued forward past the firecontrol plotting rooms until they reached sick bay. Doctor Blankenship must have been warned that he was coming as Sheppard was greeted by his friend as they entered.

"Ah, Captain, ready for that proctology exam that I've been promising?" Hugh joked. He was the only American onboard junior to him that Sheppard let get away with teasing and Blankenship reveled in the opportunity to humor the man they all depended upon for their safety.

"Today I'm kind of busy. I think I'll pass until we get a doctor with smaller fingers. Besides, there are more than enough second opinions onboard that think I am still a perfect asshole," Sheppard joked back reasonably certain that there might not be too many, if the crew was surveyed. Several pharmacist mates nearby unsuccessfully tried to suppress laughs and snickers. Turning serious he asked, "Where are my Marines?"

Doctor Blankenship took him to the isolation ward. It was the only portion of sickbay without armed Marines standing with fixed bayonets. Four of the five men inside began to struggle to rise. Sheppard, shocked that his orderly was not among them, recovered and quickly gave them, "As you were." He chatted with each for a few minutes, inquiring if the doctor was treating them well? Was there anything that they needed? Discussed their wounds and when they would be able to return to duty. That left his visit to the more seriously wounded Corporal Pease for last.

He was grateful that the young Marine was conscious, though it was also apparent that Doctor Blankenship had him comfortable with morphine injections. "I managed to remove the bullets. None hit his heart or he wouldn't be here, but his right lung was hit and he has lost a considerable amount of blood," Hugh whispered to Sheppard. Sheppard whispered,"Is he going to make it?" Hugh answered with a shrug and a shake of his head—indicating probably not.

Sheppard knew at that point that Pease's attitude was going to be the principle factor in determining the outcome. He would do everything he could to help him.

"Good afternoon, corporal," Sheppard began.

Pease rolled his head and looked at Sheppard, "Oh, Captain, sorry I let you down. The kraut had a Schmeisser." He coughed and flecks of blood stained the white blanket.

"Corporal, you did your duty. I am proud of you." Sheppard meant it. He wished that he had a stock of Purple Hearts and the authority to award them on the spot. His five Marines had been injured trying to save lives.

Corporal Pease smiled and looked at the Captain. "What do I look like, *cough*, a female sheep?"

Sheppard's eyes glazed over and a tear formed in each corner. Here was his orderly close to death, teasing him. "Get well, Marine! I need my orderly back." Gesturing to Corporal Chase, he said "This one can't limp worth a lick—can't stay in step with me."

Pease smiled as Sheppard turned to leave sickbay before his emotions got the better of him. Doctor Blankenship smiled at him and reported, "I lost two of the POWs, but I think the rest will make it. The two majors wanted to thank you for saving most of their wounded from the *Maquis*."

"Tell them to thank Major Jenkins. I had nothing to do with it."

"Captain, they are insisting."

"Very well," Sheppard followed the doctor into the main part of sickbay where the officers were being cared for off in a corner.

"*Herr Kapitän*," Major Max Kühne spoke in heavily accented English as Major Günther von Lindenthal looked on through a heavily bandaged face. "We wanted to thank you for caring for our men. We have been together since Poland, and it means a lot to us."

"You're welcome," Sheppard curtly answered.

"*Herr Kapitän*, don't think the *Heer* (Army) or the *Wehrmacht* are the same as the Gestapo or SS. We are soldiers, not thugs in uniform. You and your Marines fought by the Geneva Accords. So did we. Your soldiers could have left us to the *Maquis*, but I understand that your Major was prepared to fight the French resistance on our behalf. We owe you our lives."

Softening his tone, Sheppard simply answered, "We all need to remind ourselves that most of the men on the other side of the battle are honorable professionals, the same as ourselves."

"*Herr Kapitän*, two of our men have died, what will happen to them?"

"We will hold a burial at sea tomorrow with full military honors, if we survive the night's battle." Seeing the concern on Max's face, Sheppard added, "Don't worry, you and your men will be safe here below the armored deck." He did not add, "I hope." He turned to go, almost running over Madame D'Aubigné.

She spoke in perfect English, "Captain, thank you for rescuing the families of my husband's officers from the SS. You have treated us well. I have been talking with your ship's surgeon and ask that we be allowed to help with the wounded. I have a few doctors and many trained nurses among my charges."

"Thank you, if my doctor has no objections, I would be pleased to accept." Sheppard paused, "I ask that you pay special attention to my young orderly Corporal Pease. He may not survive, and I am sure a pleasant female voice would comfort him." Sheppard added again, "Thank you," fighting back his emotions as his eyes moistened. Hugh indicated that he would appreciate the help for his physicians and Pharmacist's Mates.

"Madame, I have one request of you."

"Certainly, Captain, what is it?"

"Madame is your daughter-in-law strong enough to bring your grandson to a special place in the ship?"

"Why, I believe so." Sheppard outlined what he had in mind as Madame D'Aubigné smiled and readily agreed to his request.

With that Sheppard was finally able to escape sickbay and start the climb back to the conning station. On the way he stopped into Admiral Hamblen's stateroom to inform him of the idea. Hamblen thought it a tremendous idea, saying he would enthusiastically support it.

— —

Ammiraglio di Squadra Moretti knew from the Italian spies in Algeciras that Force H was still in port as well as the visiting battle cruiser squadron from the Home Fleet. They had also informed Supermarina that the British flagship HMS *Renown* was in dry dock. All good news as far as Leonardo Moretti was concerned. He would take up his blocking position west of *Mers el Kébir* and wait for Force H's attack from the west. They obviously would approach from Gibraltar. It was an easy decision to plan his deployment—a line of light cruisers closest to the British base, but out of air attack range, to ensure he was not surprised. They would warn and shadow Force H, then his battle cruisers patrolling on a north-south line would be close enough for support. By using a north south line he would cap the British 'T' as Togo had demonstrated at Tsushima. Finally, his carriers would be safely positioned closer to *Mers el Kébir* to provide fighter cover for both his and Romano's forces. They would be optimally positioned to support both with air-cover in daylight as well as provide bombers to attack the French or British.

Leonardo knew that *Ammiraglio di Armata* Romano would arrive to threaten the French fleet shortly after dawn. It seemed strange to throw away the advantage of surprise, but if Operation *Guardare al Futuro* was to achieve its objective, Italy needed to give the French the opportunity to surrender to the Regia Marina. If not those French capital ships must be allowed to reach open water. If they were sunk while moored in *Mers el Kébir* it would be too easy to salvage the ships after the war. Any remnants that escaped Romano heading either north or west would have to face lines of Italian submarines. The French ships were not going to be allowed to reach the Straits of Gibraltar or the open water of the western Mediterranean.

— —

It was well into the second dog watch by the time that Sheppard limped back to the conning station with Corporal Henderson now in tow. It was time to put the plan into effect. First *Argonne* would have to change course to 249°. Without the ability to see down into the clear waters of the Mediterranean from his scout-observation planes, Captain McCloud would have to rely on the Sugar George radars to find the submarines. In all likelihood they would be surfacing after twilight faded at 1936 GMT. Between now and then the best approach was to hug the Spanish coast just outside territorial waters and hope to avoid them.

"Officer of the Deck, prepare to launch aircraft."

In no time the JA phone talker had passed the order to V-Division on the fantail.

— —

Aft, Barry Jensen was pleading with Bronco to reinstate him to flight status unaware of the Admiral's request. Barry argued that his action was totally justified to save *Argonne* from the *Luftwaffe*'s attack. Had he turned back at the time Bronco specified, he would have lead the Germans directly to the ship. It was a conscious decision to go beyond his fuel supply limit to accomplish his decoy mission. Bronco had to agree when Barry showed him on the chart what would have happened had he not disobeyed orders.

"Okay, Barry, I am assigning you to fly Admiral Hamblen to Gibraltar, but for God's sake be careful! You won't be having a gunner with you. And take some extra starter cartridges with you in case you have to lay over there," he yelled out as an afterthought as Barry ran off to get his flight gear.

— —

No sooner had the port catapult fired sending the Kingfisher with Admiral Hamblen off into the setting sun, than the armored hatch was opened to load mustang zero-one in its place. Just as mustang zero-five had not been armed with Mark 17 depth charges, neither of the next two Kingfishers would carry them, but also had the slipper fuel tanks in place of the bombs. This was strictly a search mission and the key factor was long range and long loiter times to maintain contact, if they found the Italian forces.

As Sheppard watched the setting sun he thought back to a similar time over six months earlier. He had watched that twilight from the bridge of *Shenandoah* also on the eve of battle. He had been so supremely confident of his ship and men then. He had recklessly attacked the Japanese carrier force achieving surprise as they celebrated their success at Pearl Harbor. It had cost him one hundred-eighty-seven men dead. As he lay with the wounded in the forward battle dressing station he had vowed to never be over confident again. This time, his guns were better and so to *Argonne's* radar. CIC was a definite advantage, but where was the line between believing in a good ship with a well-trained crew and foolhardiness? Sheppard concluded as the sun vanished into the sea that it lay in hindsight alone. He wondered what history would say of this battle and his actions. *What new demons of guilt would he have to bear?*

"Captain, ready to launch aircraft."

"Very well, Officer of the Deck," he answered and stepped out on the open conning platform to check for himself.

Returning, it was a simple order to send four men off into the night sky, searching for a far superior enemy, "Officer of the Deck, launch aircraft." The pilots had been given the location of where they could expect to find *Argonne* when they returned. Everyone knew it was fiction, her location would be dependent on what they reported, the location of the moon, and the success or failure of Hamblen's latest mission at diplomacy.

— —

Admiral Hardy watched as the little net tender labored to move the anti-submarine net away from the southern break in the mole at Gibraltar. His two destroyer flotillas were already taking in lines one after the other to lead his fleet to sea. It would have been a grand sight in daylight with six battle cruisers, two carriers, and a light cruiser squadron filing out of the harbor. Force H had not been this strong since 1940 when his predecessor had set to sea bent on destroying the French at *Mers el Kébir*. Now his mission was to save it. Ironic how war could change things.

He raised his binoculars to check on the American tankers in the Bay of Gibraltar. They were all the new American type T3-S2-A1 with strange names undoubtedly of American Indian origin—*Ashtabula, Aucilla, Caliente,* and *Chikaskia*. At least now, they and the four destroyers of their escort could enter the safety of the inner harbor with its net defenses once Force H cleared creating enough space. The two man swimmer scare earlier worried Hardy. His search for the launching submarine had yielded nothing as had the interrogation of the two prisoners of war.

With smoke rising from their funnels aft the tankers showed their readiness to get underway in addition to the near vertical angle their anchor chains made with the water. The four American destroyers also had steam up. More than anything Hardy knew that success always boiled down to logistics and without those tankers and two supply ships all his efforts as well as the American efforts would be for naught.

His destroyers were clear of the mole and fanning out to conduct an ASDIC search ahead of the fleet as the tugs were straining to pull his flagship into a position fair with the opening in the mole. Sequentially they would do the same for each of his battle cruisers and carriers—all just too ponderous to maneuver inside the breakwater. His light cruisers would wait their turn, but their captains were only one step removed from the brashness of destroyer command and would make their way to sea without the tugs.

His Flag Lieutenant demanded his attention. "Admiral, signal tower reporting unidentified aircraft to east!"

Hardy knew his fleet was at its most vulnerable. What night fighters he had were on his carriers HMS *Ark Royal* and *Splendid*. It could not possibly be Moretti's carriers or could it?

The first tanker in the Bay exploded in a fireball of burning aviation gasoline.

— —

Sheppard had changed course again at 2100 to 180° and slowed to 16 knots. He wanted to get further away from the Spanish coast, in the belief that any submarines would be surfaced and vulnerable to detection by radar. He had personally cautioned the SG operator on the bridge to be alert for new contacts inside of 20,000 yards—that close could only mean a surfacing sub. He really did not want to engage them with gunfire and told his Officer of the Deck to avoid the contacts with a minimum CPA of at least 13,000 yards. A query of Jonathan Becker confirmed that no Italian submarine was capable of 20 knots on the surface let alone the 24 knots he could safely use with his limited fuel supply, meaning he could control the range in all circumstances. Maneuvering would cost more fuel, but it would maintain the element of surprise when he did battle with this Admiral Moretti.

Satisfied with his intercept course for the moment, Sheppard had Art Roberts write some night orders and retired to his sea cabin trying to sleep before the early morning's battle. Not surprisingly, he would be unsuccessful.

— —

"Miller, what do you make of those ships?" Lieutenant Commander Burdick said on the intercom of mustang zero-one. Bronco was being careful not to tell his radioman/gunner his own thoughts so that Miller's assessment would be untainted by his.

"Skipper, I see four carriers and six more big ships with a bunch of smaller ones. I am not sure how many."

"Miller, I agree, I think this is the Italian scouting force. Those big ships should be battle cruisers." He looked at his plotting board in the dull red light of the cockpit. "Miller let me know when you are ready to write down my best guess of their position."

"Ready, skipper."

"Thirty-six, forty-seven point five North. Zero-zero-zero, thirty-eight East. Did you get it?"

"Yes sir, Thirty-six, forty-seven point five North, Zero-zero-zero, thirty-eight East."

"Right, now encode it with, 'four carriers, six battle cruisers, many destroyers,' and send it to *Argonne*.

Bronco circled around to an up moon position until he confirmed the composition of the force. His next report of estimated course and speed told Sheppard all he needed to know that this was Moretti's Scouting Force with all four Italian aircraft carriers. Having closed in to identify the force Bronco now wisely opened out to a position where he could maintain contact but not alert the Italians to his presence. From this time on as far as Bronco was concerned it was just more boring flight hours for his log book until a replacement came to take over the shadowing duties. But both he and Miller had their heads on swivels constantly looking for any other contacts or worse, aircraft.

— —

Admiral Hamblen saw the lights of Gibraltar go out and the searchlights come on. The British base must be under air attack. Where were the aircraft? He had told Lieutenant Jensen to skirt around "the rock" to the south anyway and avoid flying close to Spanish air space, if they could help it. Now the Admiral had a better reason to remain clear. As they rounded the mountain and saw the bay, three huge fires were burning. He wasn't very superstitious, but he got a really bad feeling that if they flew over that bay, the British might not be very friendly right about now.

"Admiral, I am worried that the British might shoot at an unidentified aircraft," Barry said on the intercom.

"Lieutenant, I agree. Keep our distance until we can sort this out."

"Aye, aye, sir."

As Admiral Hamblen studied the Bay of Gibraltar through his binoculars, he was struck by two things. First the fires were burning tankers. Were they his? That would end his mission in failure without the ability to refuel the French on their way out of the Mediterranean. The second was that there was a line of heavy ships standing out to sea from the inner harbor. That had to be Force H. How to get close enough for them to see the small Aldis Lamp for signaling, was going to be a problem with an axis air attack in progress.

"Lieutenant, do you see the line of heavy ships standing out of the harbor?

"Yes, sir."

"Get me close enough to that lead battle cruiser to communicate." John Hamblen didn't have a clue as to how his pilot was supposed to accomplish it without getting them both killed.

Neither did Barry until he was struck by the thought that the British were under *air* attack.

— —

Renown's Type 281 radar operator had been tracking and reporting the aircraft flying around to the southeast outside the range of the ship's 4.5-inch heavy anti-aircraft guns. It wasn't particularly fast; only about 120 miles per hour and it was only at about 500 feet of altitude. As he was continuously reporting, those parameters created considerable confusion as to the reason that this plane was in the vicinity. It certainly was not following any previously observed German or Italian attack profile. Suddenly it slowed and he lost contact. His mate on the Type 279 surface warning radar still held it, but its speed had dropped to less than 20 knots and turned toward the flagship.

If the radar operators were confused, so were Admiral Hardy and Captain Kelley standing on the compass platform. As the range decreased, Admiral Hardy ordered his Flag Captain to illuminate the contact with one of *Renown's* 44-inch searchlights. Hopefully the Spanish and Italian spies would not see the directional light aimed to port.

It was an American float plane—the same type that they had seen before the Battle of Cape Vilan. The pilot turned the aircraft clearly showing the rudder 'flash' of red and white horizontal stripes and the large white star in a blue circle confirming its identity. More importantly, it reminded Kelley to dowse the blinding light as it was no longer necessary.

It wasn't long before the Kingfisher floatplane had closed and paralleled *Renown*'s course. An Aldis Lamp began to slowly exchange flashing light messages with the British flagship for almost 20 minutes as Hardy formed his fleet and turned east into the Alborán Sea. Finally, he wished Admiral Hamblen well and watched the Kingfisher take off heading east.

— —

It was after 2200 when Sheppard's Officer of the Deck woke him, unfortunately just after he had managed to finally drop off to his usual tormented sleep, with the last piece of the puzzle. Mustang zero-two flown by Lieutenant Richard Bigelow, Bronco's Executive Officer, with Radioman second class Waldo Jones had found the Italian battle fleet at 37° 25.0' N, 003° 13.0' E. The Italian battleships were on course 257° at a speed of twenty knots. What amazed Sheppard when he got up to look at the chart with the plotted positions of the two enemy formations was that they were 135 miles apart. As he looked at the chart he tried to understand why they would do that?

The carriers provided air cover and long range strike; being that far away meant the Italians were not expecting any interference in their plan other than from Force H confirming his previous estimate. The latest report from Bronco stated that the carriers and battle cruisers were still operating in the same formation. That did not make sense to him. The carriers were too tender to keep in the vicinity of the battle cruisers if you were expecting a gunfight at night against other high speed ships— specifically Force H. They must be planning to break off. That would be his opportunity. But he still had time and sleep was what he needed most so he headed back to his sea cabin.

— —

Ammiraglio Moretti onboard *Aquila* got the message from Supermarina informing the fleet that Force H had sailed in company with the four battle cruisers that had been detached from the Home Fleet. He had to assume that they would be coming east and needed to prepare his plans accordingly. The British would not be expecting him this far west, creating an opportunity for him to deliver the all-important first blow of a carrier battle.

He issued orders for his carriers to prepare their RE.2001 *Ariete* fighter bombers for a dawn strike. He also ordered his cruisers to fly off their Ro.43 reconnaissance float planes at morning twilight and search to the west for Force H. He had no doubt that he would find the British before they found him. The first strike would cripple or sink their two carriers forcing the English battle cruisers to withdraw or face continuing air attack by his carrier aviation.

Moretti, in a further confirmation of the inexperience of the Italians with aircraft carrier operations, never considered how vulnerable his carriers would be with fueled and armed aircraft on their flight decks and hangers waiting to take off, nor did he consider the possible "furthest on point" of Force H in setting his cruiser scouting line.

— —

Barry had been flying on a course of 093° for almost an hour when they sighted Isla de Alborán. It was an excellent confirmation that they were on course to *Mers el Kébir*.

"Lieutenant Jensen, can you identify the island on our port side," Admiral Hamblen asked on the intercom.

Barry wasn't use to having anyone second guess his navigation, but his passenger was a four star admiral. "Alboran Island admiral," he spoke politely into the intercom. "We should be at *Mers el Kébir* in a little over an hour or so."

ALBORAN SEA

"Thank you."

At least Barry hoped they would be. His fuel state was again causing concern. *I hope the French can give me some gas*, he said to himself. In another hour he should be seeing Îles Habibas and Cap Falcon beyond it, with their destination just beyond. At least that was what his chart said. He had to be careful to shut his canopy before he took it out or it would be quickly lost. It was hard to read in the faint light. The admiral had been doing his best to understand and decode Bronco's reports on the location of the Italian scouting force and give the location to Barry. He wasn't sure how reliable the information decoded was, but it made sense looking at the chart. The location of those ships was a major concern, he did not want to be known as the pilot that killed a four star admiral by stupidly flying over an Italian fleet. Flying well to the south would give those a wide berth but waste more of his precious fuel. In his own mind, there were two possibilities if he was detected. First, they might shoot at him. The second was worse—they might have night fighters up. Either way, it was important to avoid their location. Of course the third alternative of running out of fuel was equally as devastating to their mission.

— —

The bulkhead clock struck two bells in the midwatch when the messenger entered Sheppard's sea cabin to wake him. "Captain, Captain, two bells, sir!"

As the fog of his abbreviated sleep began to clear, Sheppard realized that his rest had been untroubled by any of the usual nightmares. Was it the anticipation of battle? Could it have been what the German majors had told him? Whatever the cause, he felt somewhat refreshed for the first time at sea since he had been carried off the bridge of *Shenandoah*. He carried out his morning routine. Dressed in a clean uniform, freshly shaved, he stepped back out on the conning station to be briefed by his Officer of the Deck at the chart table.

"Captain, here are the latest positions of the Italian forces. We believe we have radar contact on the last two ships in the Italian Scouting Fleet bearing two-seven-zero at a range of forty-nine thousand yards. In accordance with the night orders, as soon as we had confirmed with mustang zero-one that we had contact on the carrier force, I turned to parallel and commenced shadowing them. I decided not to wake you since your night orders anticipated everything that happened."

"Very well, Officer of the Deck." Sheppard took out a pair of dividers and noted that the Italian battle fleet was now 167 miles to the west of Moretti. He had not guessed that they would be this far away. It would take six hours for them to get to a supporting position even at maximum speed. If they decided to do that, they would be silhouetted against the dawn. "Officer of the Deck, prepare to launch aircraft and recall Mustang Zero-One and Zero-Two." It was simple to contact Bronco well within line of sight range of the VHF spotter network; there was a delay in coding the low power HF Morse transmission to Dick Bigelow.

It did not take long to ready the Kingfishers perched on the Mark 7 catapults. Commander Roberts had included in the night orders an item to have them ready at 0100. This time they would be armed with depth charges as they would be needed for *Argonne*'s defense against submarines. Both pilots had been briefed that they would be observing *Argonne*'s gunfire and not trying to maintain contact on Romano's battleships. A quick check aft, when the Officer of the Deck reported "Ready to launch aircraft," and Sheppard gave the order, "Launch aircraft."

With mustang zero-three and zero-seven safely away, it was time to recover Bronco. It was going to be after moonset before Dick Bigelow would make it back. He was going to have to be vectored to find *Argonne,* and it would be impossible for him to land in the blackness. Sheppard cursed his stupidity at not recognizing the danger posed by the battle fleet's greater range. He needed to think through how to safely get Dick landed and back on board.

After slowing slightly, the sled was rigged and Bronco was recovered, hoisted aboard, and mustang zero-one as safely stored in the hanger at Chief Bledsoe's skilled direction. At Sheppard's request, Bronco made his way to the conning station wondering where his XO was. When he arrived, Sheppard briefed him and solicited his opinions on how to make Dick Bigelow's landing a safe one.

It was after 0100 when Barry and Admiral Hamblen flew past Cap Falcon. Mustang zero-five settled into the gentle chop and easterly breeze not far from the western entrance to *Mers el Kébir*. They taxied into the harbor and made to *Languedoc's* vicinity. It was fortunate that the Kingfishers had been flying in the vicinity of the French fleet the morning of two days earlier as it was quickly recognized by the French lookouts and reported to the flagship. Barry shut down the Pratt & Whitney radial as a launch approached the Kingfisher.

Admiral Hamblen nimbly climbed down from the aft gunner's seat, and showing amazing dexterity for a man of his age carefully made his way to the front of the pontoon. What appeared to be an admiral's barge approached and Hamblen jumped for it. He did not quit make it, but two French sailors caught his arms and hauled him up to the deck only half drenched.

Another launch slowly approached the floatplane, threw Barry a line which he attached to the Kingfisher's small cleat on the nose of the pontoon and towed them to a small mooring buoy, to which the French tied their end of the tow line. Before long, a launch with a refueling tank came carefully up to the Kingfisher which must have been in response to what Hamblen told them as Barry spoke not a word of French.

— —

Amiral D'Aubigné greeted his old friend following the twittering of the boatswain's pipe. "John, this is an unexpected surprise, though after your message I should not be, by anything you do. Can I offer you some dry clothes?"

"Phillipe, you and your ships are in grave danger. May we go to your stateroom and discuss the situation."

Concerned at the suddenness of his friend's desire to get down to business, Phillipe led the way to his cabin with both his Chief of Staff and Flag Lieutenant.

When they arrived, Admiral Hamblen began immediately. "Phillipe, before I begin, I want to prove to you that I speak from the heart and do not mislead." He took out a photograph and presented it to *Amiral* D'Aubigné. "Congratulations on your first grandson."

Stunned, as if shot, *Amiral* D'Aubigné collapsed into one of the overstuffed wingback chairs.

"John, how? When?"

With a big grin John Hamblen explained how his daughter-in-law had delivered a healthy baby boy during the evacuation of the French naval families. He added impishly, "Of course, there is a significant problem."

"What, I thought you said he was healthy. Is his mother not well?"

"Phillipe, everyone is fine, it is just . . ."

"John, for the sake of God what is wrong?"

"Phillipe, I don't know how you are going to explain that your grandson is . . . well, you see . . . *Argonne* and her boats are sovereign territory of my country. The grandson of the ranking French Admiral is a . . . citizen of the United States."

Amiral D'Aubigné laughed at having been duped into thinking there was a problem. His officers gave their congratulations and Phillipe directed his steward to get his finest cigars and champagne. "I am a grandfather" was all he could keep saying.

Admiral Hamblen had to break the moment by bringing up the more important reason for his visit. "Phillipe, I have in this envelope both a letter from Madame Daphne D'Aubigné attesting to the accuracy of this list of French naval families that are currently onboard *Argonne*. They are well, though it appears we evacuated the fishing village of Le Brusc in addition. Now I need a favor from you. We have intelligence that the Italian battle fleet will be off *Mers el Kébir* at dawn. We fear that their purpose is to either block your escape or destroy all of your ships. *Argonne*, though heavily outnumbered, will engage the Italian scouting forces to the west opening a path for you to escape. I implore you to take it."

Amiral D'Aubigné's stateroom fell silent knowing that the fate of the families of all the officers present was tied to *Argonne*'s survival.

9

TIPPING POINT

SHEPPARD HAD TO THINK this through. If he closed on the Italians even though the moon had set, he would likely lose the element of surprise when he went to recover Dick Bigelow. As usual, Bronco had an excellent idea on how to do it, but to make it work without giving away his advantage he had to be over 50,000 yards distant. The Italian Scouting Force had split into two groups at 0200 with the carriers now lagging behind the battle cruisers and light cruisers, which made sense if they were only concerned about Force H.

Argonne had manned battle stations a good ten minutes ago and was as ready for action as Sheppard could make her. All the Marines except the POW guards and wounded were back at their normal assignments. Every French civilian had been vetted by Madame D'Aubigné or the Mayor of Le Brusc with everyone below the third deck, Nazi sympathizers under heavy French guard even though they were unarmed. The hoists were filled with high capacity shells to do as much damage as possible to the carrier flight decks and hangers. At this point his objective was to start fires and put all four out of the business of operating aircraft. If he managed to sink any of them so much the better, but it wasn't necessary at this point.

Dick Bigelow had been given a vector to get him back to *Argonne's* vicinity and Sheppard was waiting on the conning platform hoping to hear the approaching Kingfisher. The wind was out of the east at about 10 knots, which was ideal for both Dick and the tactical situation he hoped to achieve. Sheppard also noted that there was slight phosphorescence in the water where *Argonne* disturbed the plankton. That should help Dick find his home.

"Conning station, sky lookouts, aircraft, bearing zero-eight-zero," was reported by the JA phone talker.

He turned and acknowledged, "Very well. Conning Officer, come left to course one-nine-zero smartly." *Argonne* was moving too slowly to worry about excessive vibration aft. He went to the 21MC and ordered, "Guns, Captain, prepare to illuminate on a bearing of zero-nine-zero." Sheppard then went back to the conning platform to listen. Yes, he could hear the drone of the Kingfisher's Pratt & Whitney Wasp Junior radial engine just as the sizzle of the carbon arcs in the searchlights punctuated the developing plan.

Chuck Williamson reported, "Ready to illuminate!"

"Guns, Captain, illuminate," caused the shutters on his port searchlights to snap open splitting the night sky. Pointed away from the Italians, Sheppard hoped they would not see the loom of the lights as he lit a landing area for Dick. They shouldn't as the night was clear, free of fog or a low cloud layer.

The growl of the Wasp Junior grew until mustang zero-two passed directly over *Argonne* at masthead height. Lieutenant Bigelow had recognized the plan without spotter network chatter to reveal their presence to the Italians. The Kingfisher then made a perfect landing in the illuminated path. No sooner had it slowed enough to stop planing, when Sheppard ordered, "Break arcs" to extinguish the lights and not blind Dick when he turned back in *Argonne's* direction.

"Conning Officer, come smartly to course two-six-zero," Sheppard ordered as he went to the 21MC.

"Signal Bridge, Captain, train a 24-inch signal lamp on the fantail and illuminate it."

"Officer of the Deck, prepare to recover aircraft on the port side," completed what needed to be done.

It all worked well and shortly mustang zero-two was safely lowered into the hanger by Aviation Chief Boatswain's Mate Bledsoe. As the armored hatch shut with a clang the aircraft and boat crane was lowered and clamped to stretch out on the hatch like a sleeping giant, further reinforcing the armored hatch from the blast of Turret III. Sheppard ordered all the anti-aircraft gun crews forward and aft of the superstructure below the third deck to avoid the blast of the main battery when it fired with full charges.

It was time to close and attack, but first he had to refresh his airborne eyes to spot for the guns.

"Officer of the Deck; prepare to launch aircraft."

— —

Sheppard was successful in preventing *Ammiraglio di Squadra* Leonardo Moretti from seeing the loom of his searchlights, but they did not escape the attention of *Capitano di Corvetto* Adriana Luzzatto of the submarine *Giulio dé Medici*. He was assigned the western end of the first northern patrol line guarding against the escape of French ships headed toward Toulon or Marseilles. Like any good submariner, Adriana was curious and unafraid. He knew that there were no other Italian submarines to the west of him. He did not think anyone would criticize him for "expanding" his area. Those lights might have originated with *Ammiraglio* Moretti's scouting force, but if that was the case why had he not heard any gunfire. He decided to turn and close it at his best speed of 18 knots.

If it is the Scouting Force, I can always just come back to my patrol area. Then again perhaps the French were trying to escape now that the moon had set, but that meant that they had already passed many of his fellow Italian submariners. Adriana was proud enough of his fellow submariners to believe that was impossible.

The more he thought, the more curious he became standing in the cutout on the large sail of *Giulio dé Medici*.

— —

Argonne had closed until the forward Sugar George radar was painting a clear picture of the Italian carriers to the southwest and their closest destroyer escorts when the Captain's voice began issuing orders to gunnery on the 21MC. "Guns, Captain, action port; we'll take the far carrier first. That contact is designated ABLE-ONE. Track ABLE-ONE."

"Captain, Guns, roger track ABLE-ONE." Chuck passed the orders on the 1JC for Lieutenant Hamblen in spot one to track the carrier and control turrets I thru III. He directed Spot three, the forward Mark 34 director, to track the leading carrier designated BAKER-ONE. The aft Mark 38 director was assigned to the trailing carrier designated CHARLIE-ONE. And finally the aft Mark 34 was assigned to the closest carrier DOG-ONE. He wasn't sure if the lower after directors could see the targets, but it would be good practice for them to try. Lieutenant Commander Becker had been tracking the formation for over an hour using the SG radars and it was a simple task to transfer the course and speed solution to the firecontrol computers from CIC. That information coupled with the accurate ranges and bearings from the Mark 8 radars on each director was all the information needed for an excellent solution devoid of only the imponderables.

"Guns, Captain, load high capacity."

Chuck directed his turrets in turn to *Load*. The hoists were already full of high capacity shells.

Standing on the top level of the command tower even behind 2 feet of face hardened steel, Chuck could hear the clangs as the projectiles were rammed home in each of the guns. The battle cruiser's "hell's bells" signaling more death and destruction. The turrets turned to point in the direction of where the shells should intercept the target. A few more moments to roll the eight powder bags out of their hoists onto the shell transfer trays and they were quickly rammed into the breeches. Each gun captain closed his breech and turned his gun ready switch to ready. The instant he did the muzzles rose into the night, malevolent fingers reaching to grab an unseen enemy.

The last command needed to attack came from the Captain on the 21MC, "Commence firing!"

Chuck's order was not nearly as dramatic. "Salvo fire, continuous aim, master key." That would cause Lieutenant Commander Gerry Archinbald, in the forward main battery plotting room, to direct his Fire Controlman at the Mark 41 stable vertical to, "Shoot!"

The salvo alarm rang a second before the firing key was closed. Sheppard closed his eyes at the alarm trying to save his night vision. He had seen the night turn to day before as the growing balls of incandescent gas blossomed from each gun muzzle, now much more ferocious than last night off of the French south coast, as the guns were shooting with full charges. The guns jumped 4.5 feet in half a second as the recoil and counter recoil cylinders absorbed the momentum of the gun and transferred it to the hull. *Argonne* shook under the force of the full charge salvo of six guns followed quickly by three more when the center naval rifles in each turret fired two seconds later. The glowing gas expanded and each turret's merged until the gas touched the water and boiled the sea stimulating the plankton to a stunning display of iridescent water. In five seconds it had cooled sufficiently to no longer glow, but the hot breathe of the guns was felt by everyone in the open as the expanding cloud of hot gas enveloped *Argonne,* challenging the light easterly breeze, until nature overcame the actions of man. The smell of burned smokeless powder, silk, oil, titanium oxide, and hot steel assaulted the nostrils. Sheppard opened his eyes to watch the nine dull red spots of tracers recede into the night sky, the center of each group of three trailing well behind, the delay coils designed to prevent interference in their flight from the super-sonic shock waves produced. As the projectiles flew there was a great tearing sound as if the projectiles were rending the atmosphere itself. Sheppard knew that those carriers would hear a similar sound but louder as the overs passed.

At this range it would take 83 seconds before the fall of shot alarm sounded, alerting all to watch optics and radar scopes as well as the pilots and observers of the Kingfishers, since the alarm automatically sounded on the VHF radio network also, that *Argonne's* nine projectiles were raising columns of red tinted white water. Tonight those columns would also be phosphorescent from the plankton, as they rose more than 500 feet high in the vicinity of the target at the sound of the alarm. While the men manning the firecontrol instruments waited, the gunners reloaded in less than 30 seconds. For all the modern technology, there were still too many unknowns that could only be discovered by experiment. Those experiments were the salvos that indicated the sum of all errors. Assumed constant, a spot of right or left, add or drop range would be used to center the splashes of the next salvo on the target. The best place to see the placement of a salvo was from above—God's view. The Kingfishers would provide it.

If done well the second salvo would be perfectly centered on the target and then the laws of probability dictated the number of hits. At this range with these targets that translated to a 5 percent chance that any given shell might hit the target. Combined, *Argonne* had a little less than a 50-50 chance with each salvo; as long as the target did not maneuver. When the enemy recovered from the initial surprise of being under attack, that became a bad assumption. A target could move a long way from its predicted location in 83 seconds. It was up to the directors and their Mark 8 radar operators carefully watching any change in the range return or differences from the two radar lobes, to quickly see the maneuvers and transmit the information below to the fire control computers controlling the main battery guns. The falling shells would stay on target. *But with each salvo Sheppard knew the result—the screaming wounded, twisted steel, fire and silent dead.*

— —

Sixteen decks below Sheppard, French women screamed and children cried. It is easy to be brave when you know what is happening. It is impossible when you don't. All the French civilians were packed into the fourth deck passageways—barely enough room for them to sit, propped against the bulkheads where mounted equipment allowed. Repair parties stepped over them to correct the minor casualties caused by the recoil of the main battery. *Argonne* shook with each salvo, the thunder of the guns reverberated through the dimly lit caverns, dust and paint chips rained from the overhead above the families of the French fleet.

Madame Daphne D'Aubigné walked quickly among her friends and countrymen trying to reassure everyone that what they were experiencing was normal for a ship in battle. There was no need for alarm. They were all perfectly safe below the thick steel they had seen when they passed through the armored deck hatches.

She prayed that was the truth.

— —

Aboard the Italian carrier *Sparviero,* most of the crew were sleeping. The *Ariete* fighter bombers were fueled and loaded with the 250 kilogram semi-armor piercing bombs—demanding work, but completing it allowed a launch the moment that Force H was found. The watch officers were maintaining *Sparviero*'s position 2800 meters on the port quarter of the flagship in a diamond formation that allowed each carrier to conduct air operations without interference to the others. It had taken three days to arrive at this blocking position in the event Force H tried to intervene and save the French. Now about 20 miles ahead, Italy's battle cruisers and a light cruiser squadron were providing a protective scouting line,while *Soldati* class destroyers provided protection in the unlikely event that a British submarine might be transiting through the area.

The sea was calm with a light breeze from the east raising only friendly waves, barely noticeable from the bridge. The gentle swish of the bow wave and rumbling hum of the forced draft blowers was broken by the unmistakable rending tear of heavy shells and the sight of eight mountainous phosphorescent columns of water climbing to the sky mostly off the starboard bow, completely hiding *Sparviero* from the flagship and hiding the reason for only eight from the Kingfishers. To everyone topside; the red fountains of the gates of hell beckoned.

— —

"Panther, Mustang Zero-Three, drop two hundred, left two hundred," came on the spotter network. Commander Williamson knew Gerry Archinbald would enter the spot in the Mark 8 range keeper in the forward main battery plotting room. Gerry then turned to the stable element operator commanding, "Shoot!"

Both he and the Gunnery Officer knew how to capitalize on the element of surprise. They were going to put as many shells on the Italian carrier as they could before the Italians reacted to *Argonne*'s salvos. The first salvo was only off by the width of the 18-inch pattern. Gerry knew his next would be on target with little likelihood that the Italian carrier would yet react. Williamson's command, "Fire continuous, five rounds, master key," would make the gunners in the turrets load and shoot as fast as they could. There would not really be salvos, as such, just a bunched stream of two ton projectiles; forty-five in all. At least two should hit by probability with devastating results.

At the command master key, Gerry Archinbald ordered the firing key locked. The moment any gunner indicated his gun was ready, it would elevate to the correct angle and when matched, the computer in forward main battery plot would fire it. With the exception of the physical act of loading, *Argonne* was in full automatic. Adjustments to the *solution* as well as spots could still be made, but were not likely to improve the probability of hits until the battle cruiser went back to salvos. What would help most were the continuous inputs of range from the Mark 8 firecontrol radar in spot one. If Lieutenant Hamblen could get a point of aim visually, that in combination provided everything needed to keep the solution perfectly updated for every twist and turn the target used trying to evade the rain of steel and explosives.

— —

Argonne's first salvo, actually the left gun of Turret III, though no human could know that, hit the starboard bow of *Sparviero* about two meters above the waterline. When the shell detonated milliseconds later, the hull plating and bulkheads within 10 meters were pierced, torn, bent, and the seams between plates broken over an area 10 meters by 8 meters. The sea rushed into void spaces and store rooms. Shrapnel from the ship and shell reached a berthing compartment tearing flesh and bone alike. *Sparviero* took a slight list to starboard and settled deeper into the sea at her bow. In the berthing compartment lights failed, the injured screamed for help as the dead and dying lay silent.

Ninety seconds later more shells arrived; more hits occurred; more men died. A hit on the flight deck sealed *Sparviero*'s fate, as a raging fire fueled by the gasoline in the aircraft illuminated the surrounding sea.

— —

Ammiraglio Moretti arrived on the flag bridge of the carrier *Aquila* dressed only in his pants, undershirt, and shoes. He was surprised that he could see the mountainous columns of water as the shells landed near *Sparviero*. Initially thinking it was the phosphorescence, as he looked closer he saw that the water columns were lit from fires burning the life out of the carrier. In the flickering light the water appeared blood red unnerving him for more than a moment.

Regaining his composure, he asked his staff officers, "Who was shooting at them and where was the enemy?" They did not know. Finally the *Falco* reported gun flashes bearing 025° by flashing light. That solved the problem of where, but there was no answer to who? Moretti needed to save his carriers. He ordered his flag lieutenant to radio the battle cruisers to immediately come to his assistance. He ordered his ships to turn away from the enemy and increase speed to 30 knots. The 5th Destroyer Squadron under *Capitano di Vascello* Piero Sabbatini was directed to counterattack.

Examining *Sparviero* through his binoculars, he ordered two other destroyers to stand by and help with fighting the fires that were rapidly wrecking a quarter of his aviation assets. As he watched, the first of the bombs attached to the burning *Ariete* fighter-bombers detonated hurling pieces of aircraft and men over the side of the carrier. He saw that she was lower in the water and falling out of formation—slowing as the fires consumed her fighting ability.

— —

Sheppard watched the loom of the fires on his target grow until he could see the leaping flames with his binoculars. That carrier was no longer a threat. "Guns, Captain, check fire, shift targets to skunk BAKER-ONE. When ready, commence firing."

Now it was Chuck Williamson's turn to transfer solutions. The desirable alignment was always to use Spot One at the very top of the forward tower and the forward main battery plotting room. He could use any of them, but Spot One had the best view causing Chuck to delay 30 seconds while J-switches were realigned to connect the Mark 38 director to the other computer in the forward main battery room. The director jumped as it trained to the bearing of the second carrier. "Spot One, control turrets I, II, III, track BAKER-ONE." After he received acknowledgements and a report of tracking BAKER-ONE, he added, "Salvo fire, master key."

Ollie Halverson looked at Sheppard. "You bloody yanks and your technology. The Italians don't have a chance."

Sheppard looked at him. "They're not supposed to have a chance, like we didn't have a chance at Pearl Harbor or your convoys wouldn't have had a chance if Schröder had broken out. Besides, tell me that in an hour when the dawn breaks and the Italian battle cruisers are chasing us into it. If your buddy Hardy doesn't show up, it will be a short fight at effectively thirty-six to one odds."

He really wasn't in the mood to joke when he was killing people, even if he could not see them. The salvo alarm warned him to shut his eyes before a broadside shattered the night sending nine high capacity shells at *Aquila*.

— —

Capitano Sabbatini formed his four *Soldati* class destroyers into a column, increasing speed to 42 knots. They would dutifully follow in the wake of *Lanciere* as he refined his approach angle to hold constant the relative bearing of those gun flashes. Destroyer squadron command was always his great ambition ever since graduating high up in his class at *L'Accademia Navale* in Livorno thereby gaining a choice of assignments. Piero had chosen destroyers with the allure of early responsibility, ship handling, and ultimately command before his classmates.

He had a general idea of where the enemy was located by the flashes from the heavy guns. He had trained his whole life for this moment. His *Soldati* class destroyers were optimally designed for this moment too with high speed and two triple 533mm trainable torpedo tubes. The twenty-four torpedoes of his squadron would sink any warship afloat. The only requirement was skill. As the 5th Destroyer Squadron approached, each captain began to solve the target motion of this warship by the bearing drift of the gun flashes. An area of expertise in the Regia Marina, torpedo attack training was rigorous and frequent. At least as frequent as the fuel shortage would allow.

— —

"Captain, Combat, four skunks approaching in column. Course zero-one-eight; range three-two-oh-double oh, speed four-zero. Designate skunks, EASY-ONE thru HOW-ONE"

Sheppard answered on the 21MC, "Roger Combat," the inevitable counter attack by destroyers. They would launch their torpedoes at no more than twelve thousand yards. He had until that point to stop their approach.

"Guns, Captain. Track EASY-ONE; commence firing with turrets six-two and six-four when ready." Sheppard did not want to give rudder orders to Commander Williamson on how to do his job, but he did not want his direction to result in the main battery being pulled off of the carriers, at least not yet. "Prepare to illuminate EASY-ONE with star shells." Those destroyers, if they were destroyers, were still well outside the range of his 5-inch battery, but his command would alert the Gunnery Officer to his plan.

"Captain, Guns, roger!" It wasn't long before Sheppard could see the forward Mark 34 director, Spot Three, train round to face the leading destroyer. That also meant that the other Mark 1 Ford computer in the main battery plotting room would be tracking the target.

Sheppard knew that his Gunnery Officer had passed the order, "Spot three control turrets six-two and six-four, continuous aim, fire continuous, master key." He saw the port 6-inch turrets face the destroyers and the guns elevate. There was no salvo alarm to alert him as both turrets fired their first salvo. Six empty brass powder cases flew from the floors of the two turrets, clanging against the deck and each other—more bells from hell. That first salvo would be the only defined for them until the check fire. Each gun's crew was now loading and shooting as fast as man-handling the 105-pound Mark 34 high capacity projectiles and sixty pound Mark 4 brass cartridges into the gun loading trays would allow. Milliseconds after the vertical sliding breech block closed and the gun elevation aligned, the gun was fired by the computer in the plotting room. There was no need to return the gun to a loading angle for the next round's loading cycle just as with the 5-inch, though as the target closed;

loading became progressively easier on the crews struggling with the heavy shells. The spent cartridge cases began to accumulate in piles beneath each turret on *Argonne's* weather decks, the shiny brass reflecting the flash of her guns.

— —

Piero Sabbatini could see that *Aquila* was also now burning. He knew the business of torpedo attack better than most squadron commanders; perhaps that was the reason Moretti had sent him. His flagship would probably be destroyed, he knew with some certainty. But the success of a torpedo attack particularly one such as this, that had to be executed on the spur of the moment, depended on overloading the defenses of the target or in a fleet action the enemy battle line. It was to do that and compound the enemy's firecontrol problem that he ordered his squadron into a line abreast and opened the distance between ships to 750 meters. Too far and they could not concentrate the attack; too close and the enemy might get cheap hits on one of his ships while actually aiming at another.

His poor understanding of the technical nature of this battle was reflected in his order to make smoke in an effort to shield the carriers from further attack in addition to making a screen his destroyers could withdraw behind after launching their torpedoes. It would deny an optical bearing to the targets but accomplished nothing against the spotting of the Kingfishers or the ranging of the radars. *Capitano di Vascello* Piero Sabbatini was not surprised as the projectiles began to fall around his flagship *Lanciere*. At least the enemy now knew he was under attack.

— —

Lieutenant John Hamblen high in *Argonne's* fore tower saw the second carrier burning and the start of the secondary explosions. It was pointless to keep bombarding that ship when there were still two undamaged to deal with. "Request permission to shift targets to DOG-ONE." John knew that the aft Mark 38 director and the after plotting room were tracking CHARLIE-ONE. If he were the Gunnery Officer he would assign the turrets to spot two and give them practice on a live target.

You never knew when the backup system would be needed.

"Spot One Guns, shift targets. Track DOG-ONE," was the swift reply on the 1JC phones. That gave Hamblen pause. Why so quick? Did it mean that he was finally over the reputation that he had earned from his first ship? Whatever the reason, he set to work with his six men to shift to the left hand target that had been trailing the formation. It was only a minute before he could report, "Tracking DOG-ONE," to Commander Williamson in gunnery control.

The Gunnery Officer issued the commands to assign the turrets to the director and resume salvo firing until he had a good straddle of the third carrier. Again he would order rapid fire to smother the carrier before it could chase his correcting salvos thereby avoiding hits.

— —

Capitano Piero Sabbatini's last conscious thought was that he could see the dull red shell that was coming at his flagship's bridge. The Mark 29 point detonating fuse functioned as designed only a few milliseconds after impact with the forward face of the superstructure. The 13 pounds of Explosive D in the 6-inch Mark 34 projectile turned the 90-odd pounds of steel shell into hundreds of pieces of shrapnel, some large, some small, but all deadly. The explosion destroyed the helm, engine order telegraph, communication circuits, charts, gyro compass repeater, alidades and dozens of other bits and pieces of equipment that provided for the proper direction and control of *Lanciere*. Every individual there from the Commanding Officer to the most junior phone talker was killed outright. *Lanciere* was without direction or leadership. There would be no more orders to the 5th Destroyer Squadron.

— —

Ollie Halverson watched the bravery of the Italian destroyer-men with mixed emotions. They were attempting every dashing officer's dream of an all-out charge against a capital ship in executing a torpedo attack. Many times in command of *Swift*, he had dreamed of the same thing, pitting his small, fast, lightly armed ship against the fire power and bulk of a battleship or battle cruiser. There would always be damage and casualties. Some of your squadron mates might even be sunk, but for sheer excitement and the rush of adrenaline there was nothing to compare with this desperate act to turn a superior enemy into the hunted prey.

The right hand destroyer had been obviously hit several times. It was burning and in the light of the flames Ollie could see the ruined bridge through his 7 x 50 binoculars. Thankfully the inevitable carnage was too distant for even the magnification of his binoculars to bring into focus. He really didn't need to see it. He had lived it and would remember the names and positions of every one of his men when the German shells had cut them down. How did God decide who lived and who died? Just as there are no atheists in foxholes, there are no atheists in sea battles, but men would die even as they prayed. How was the decision made?

— —

Sheppard could see what was going through his mind. He knew that Ollie was reliving the Battle of Dover Straits as he had relived Pearl Harbor almost every night since. "We did not start this war, Ollie. If we could get Mussolini and Hitler under our guns this minute, it would give me no greater pleasure than to end it—right here, right now! But we can't. We have to work our way through their minions until we can. I am only certain of one thing—eventually we will."

Ollie turned and looked at Sheppard. What did Sheppard see in his eyes? Ollie was a decorated hero of a battle for the survival of his country a Knight of the realm. Was he actually admiring the determination, resolve, and humanity of another warrior?

— —

It was time to get the 5-inch batteries involved. *Lanciere* was slowing, listing heavily, afire and down by the bow. Undoubtedly she would soon sink and was not likely a threat. Chuck shifted Spot Three and the forward 6-inch computer to the new right hand target, while he ordered the foremost Mark 37 director, Sky One, to track skunk GEORGE-ONE. The next most forward

Mark 37 on the port side, Sky Two, was assigned to HOW-ONE. With the exception of Mount 5-2-2 which he directed to shoot star shells for illumination, the remaining 5-inch mounts were split evenly between the two Mk 37 directors—five each, ten guns on each remaining destroyer.

He immediately recommenced shooting at what turned out to be *Artigliere* with the 6- inch turrets 6-2 and 6-4 in continuous aim, continuous fire, with the master firing key for the 6-inch computer in the forward main battery plotting room closed and locked. Again, other computers were in charge of *Argonne*. At 22,000 yards he directed the same for the port side 5-inch mounts. As the range closed the guns did not have to elevate as high and two things helped *Argonne*. First, the trajectory of the shells was flatter which improved the probability of hits both by increasing the danger space of the target and reducing the dispersion caused by the random variations in shells and powder. Second, with less elevation the guns were becoming easier to load which improved the rate of fire. In less than 45 seconds, shells were falling around *Fuciliere* and *Carabiniere* as well as *Artigliere*.

— —

The bulkhead clock had struck eight bells in the mid-watch (0400) almost ten minutes earlier when spot one reported that skunk DOG-ONE was burning heavily. Sheppard's phone talkers on the conning station keep him advised of every order or report on each of their circuits, even if he had not given it. Following Hamblen's recommendation the Gunnery Officer had ordered, "Check fire turrets I, II, and III. Spot two, control turrets I, II, and III. Salvo fire, master key," beginning the process to destroy the last Italian aircraft carrier—*Falco*. The secondary explosions from the burning Italian bombs onboard *Pegaso* had begun when the first salvo was fired at *Falco*.

"Panther, this is Mustang Zero-Seven, six large ships in column headed your way at high speed, bearing roughly two-eight-zero from you."

Those would be the Italian battle cruisers coming to try and save the carriers, Sheppard thought. He needed to wait and get a course and speed on them before he decided on his ultimate plan of action. Captain McCloud walked out on the port conning platform to examine his targets through his binoculars. He had closed on the burning carriers in the process of chasing the undamaged ones. They would not present a threat. The three remaining destroyers were rapidly absorbing hits, ending the possibility of a torpedo attack from them. There had been four that had split up, but he would have to look at the SG radar to see where they were.

The 21MC demanded his attention, "Captain, Combat, skunks KING-ONE through PETER-ONE are on course One-zero-nine at speed four-two knots. KING-ONE bears two-eight-one degrees;range four-eight-five-double-oh yards. Gained contact on skunks ITEM-ONE in the vicinity of ABLE-ONE and JIG-ONE in the vicinity of BAKER-ONE."

"Roger Combat," the Italian battle cruisers were coming fast. He was going to have to take a risk with the damaged destroyers.

"Guns, Captain, coming left to course one-five-zero." Sheppard paused, "Conning Officer, drag the outboard starboard shaft and come left smartly to new course one-five-zero." Both officers acknowledged his orders and *Argonne* heeled to starboard as she turned with a bone in her teeth. Dragging the shaft outboard of the turn minimized the vibration caused by the propeller race entering the flow to the inboard shaft while still keeping maximum propeller wash on the starboard rudder. The moment the helmsman reported, "Steady course one-five-zero," the Conning Officer went back to 'Ahead Full' on the starboard outboard shaft.

"Guns, Captain, track KING-ONE," the JA phone talker relayed to the Gunnery Officer. Sheppard looked up from the conning platform where he stood fighting the wind of *Argonne*'s passage with Ollie, pleased that the younger Hamblen had already trained his director in that direction. He caught Ollie's eye and pointed at the director. Ollie quizzically looked at Sheppard.

"He's already on target." That brought the same smile to Ollie. Sheppard wished that the Admiral was also standing with them on the platform outside of the conning station to see his son's actions in battle.

— · —

Contrammiraglio Dante Falzone stood on the flag bridge of the Italian battle cruiser *Coraggio*. He could easily see three of his nation's aircraft carriers burning in the night. How could that happen? It was impossible for Force H to have gotten past his light cruisers let alone his battle cruiser patrol line. Who was this enemy capital ship?

"Gun flashes bearing one-zero-one degrees." That solved the problem of where, but still who?

His enemy was almost directly ahead and in the prefect position to cap his T. That was unavoidable. He had to close and relieve the pressure on Moretti's ships, even if it meant accepting a tactical disadvantage in the process. He still had four turrets of his most powerful ships pointed at the enemy. Those twelve 45cm/50 guns should be more than enough to worry his opponent until he could close and turn to unmask the after turrets as well as bring the 40cm turrets of his other four ships within range. Dante also knew that the eastern sky would begin to brighten momentarily and silhouette his target. That was an advantage worth keeping while he remained cloaked in darkness.

— —

Capitano di Vascello Giorgio Sciambra had been in command of the carrier *Falco* longer than any of the other commanding officers in *Ammiraglio* Moretti's squadron. He had seen the initial salvos destroy the *Sparviero* when he arrived on the bridge. Recognizing what was happening to his sister ships, on his own initiative, he broke the spot on his flight deck. Fostering his own sense of desperation in his crew, they worked like men possessed to remove the bombs from each of the *Ariete* fighter bombers, either sending them below to the magazines or just pushing them overboard as desperation took hold. Simultaneously with that task the crew set to work defueling the aircraft of the volatile aviation gasoline. As the work on each Re.2001 aircraft was completed, *Capitano* Sciambra had it pushed to the forward end of the flight deck as far as possible from those aircraft that remained fueled and armed.

— —

Capitano Luzzatto was getting very frustrated. This contact, obviously a very large heavy gun warship was moving away from him as he ran at the best speed his submarine *Giulio dé Medici* could make. On the verge of giving up and returning to his patrol box before the sun forced him to submerge, he was surprised when the ship suddenly turned and the bearing began drawing to the left. Something had made his contact turn and perhaps that same thing would keep his target moving to the west. He decided to take an intercepting course of 180°. If he could not hold the bearing steady, he would have to give up, but if he could there was hope he might be able to attack it after all. The coast of North Africa would box in his target.

— —

Sheppard wasn't sure if he had hit this last carrier or not. He thought he had seen the glow of two exploding shells, but with all of the brilliant flashes of his own guns, what he had seen, or thought he saw, may just have been the spots in front of his eyes as he had blinked. He wanted that last carrier, but he had to think of the Italian battle cruisers and trying to save *Argonne* from them. He knew he had the advantage of position and radar. With luck he might be able to inflict enough damage that his speed would allow him to escape. As long, that is, as he avoided the damage that had crippled *Belleau Wood* at Cape Vilan

"Guns, Captain, check fire on DOG-ONE, load armor piercing! Shift targets to KING-ONE." Sheppard wanted the punishment of the destroyers continued until they sank. He was going to have to pass close to them on this course and did not want a hero on one of those ships making a desperation launch of their 21-inch torpedoes.

"Captain, Guns, roger," Chuck knew that there would be a delay. He directed his 1JC talker to, "Turrets I, II, and III, discharge guns through the muzzle, then check fire." Nine more shots left *Argonne* before the main battery was silent. "Turrets I, II, and III, load armor piercing." This was the item that would delay the most. In each turret the hoists were put into lower and one by one the high capacity shells were parbuckled back to the rotating shell ring. Once the hoist was empty the shell deck crews worked as fast as humanly possible to fill the hoists with the black and yellow armor piercing projectiles. As soon as one reached the top of the hoist and entered the tilting bucket, the gun captains loaded the two-ton shells and eight powder bags into the breeches. Chuck could hear the projectiles being rammed home and ordered, "Spot one control Turrets I, II, and III, salvo fire, continuous aim, master key."

Sheppard passed the word to his Kingfishers that *Argonne* was shifting targets to KING-ONE. "Mustang Zero-Three and Zero-Seven, Panther, shifting targets to the leading battle cruiser."

Both pilots quickly acknowledged. Sheppard went out onto the open platform as the turrets trained round to starboard well aft of the beam. This time when the salvo alarm sounded, Sheppard had to duck as well as close his eyes. The fireball of white-hot gases was much closer. The turrets could actually train 15 degrees further and still fire but at that extreme, they would blister the paint on the bridge and fore tower. He raised his binoculars in time to see the first Italian salvo of six shots land about 700 yards off his starboard quarter. Discretion was definitely the better part of valor, if he was not going to be singed by Turret II. Deciding to return to the safety of the forty pound plating on the conning station, he ordered his Conning Officer to increase speed to 42 knots. As he watched the large spread of the Italian fall of shot, a plan was developing on how he would avoid their salvos.

The fall of shot alarm sounded and Sheppard raised his binoculars to see the mountainous splashes rise over the horizon. He still could not see the target as the first rays of civil twilight began to illuminate the high clouds.

"Panther, Mustang Zero-Four; drop three hundred, right two hundred," was the observation from on high.

Gerry Archinbald entered the spot in the firecontrol computer and commanded the Mark 41 stable vertical operator to, "Shoot!" All nine guns fired another broadside as *Argonne* shook with the arrested recoil's momentum.

No sooner had the guns fired and Chuck Williamson commanded, "Continuous aim, three rounds, fire continuous, master key," than the answering Italian salvo plowed the ocean just aft of *Argonne*. Sheppard's speed increase had caused that one to fall astern. He knew that the Italian gunnery officer would make another adjustment for the new speed. This time he ordered the Conning Officer to come right to course one-seven-zero smartly dragging the outboard port shaft until they were steady on course.

Another Italian six shot salvo landed more than 1,000 yards beyond *Argonne*. A second battle cruiser was beginning to engage. Sheppard had a decision to make. It was really fairly easy. He knew from experience that if he tried to chase every fall of shot, his maneuvering would be less effective than if he concentrated on just one ship's shooting. He had to make sure that he did not put two maneuvers together that had the effect of not maneuvering at all for his second antagonist. At least that was the doctrine that had been worked out on the gaming floors at Newport. As the fall of shot alarm sounded, he raised his glasses to observe.

— —

He reached out to steady himself against the inner surface of the armored command tower, the shock of a shell hitting *Coraggio* causing him to lose his balance. A sharp metallic ring followed a moment later. *Contrammiraglio* Dante Falzone then listened to the shell splinters rattle off of the command tower aboard *Coraggio*. The hit was clearly forward but where?

He couldn't know, but God did. The armor piercing projectile had hit the right hand lip of the forward turret skirt penetrating between the turret face plate and the barbette. It then followed the inside surface of the barbette for 30 feet before the 58.25 pounds of explosive D detonated. The forward turret rose a half a meter before settling back irrevocably jammed. That was all Dante could see. He gasped at what would happen next but fortunately none of the powder bags inside the hoist tubes were ignited by the shrapnel. Had they, the Italian admiral knew seeing the turret rise would have been his last conscious thought on this Earth.

Dante had no idea how many of the turret's crew had been killed or injured. What was more important to him at the moment was the loss of twenty-five percent of the 45 centimeter guns that could bear on the target. He was actively considering a column course change to bring his after turrets to bear when he was totally surprised by the arrival of more projectiles about 30 seconds after the hit.

— —

Sheppard thought he saw the flash of a hit, but it was hard to tell with armor piercing. He was still looking when the third Italian salvo landed over by 800 yards, almost exactly where Sheppard had planned by his course change. He now had another decision to make. He wanted to come back to the left but that would have the effect of cancelling his first course change for the second ship that was shooting. He decided to go beyond his original course and ordered the Conning Officer to come left to course one-four-zero smartly with the usual dragging of the outboard shaft on the outside of the turn.

"Captain, Guns, spot one reports a hit on the forward turret of KING-ONE. Hamblen also reported that KING-ONE is classified a *Coraggio* class battle cruiser. Sheppard did not know how his young lieutenant did it, but he had yet to be wrong.

Ollie Halverson was also watching the enemy battle cruiser without the distraction of trying to second guess the Italian gunnery officers. "Hit," he sang out in time for Sheppard to raise his binoculars and see the flash of burning powder light the starboard side of his target. Just then the mountains of water rose only a hundred yards over but 300 yards aft of *Argonne* from the second salvo of *Argonne's* other antagonist. Sheppard made a quick mental calculation that if he was that gunnery officer he would 'down' spot again as well as right spot to hit. He should miss based on the last maneuver.

Cat and mouse, think and double think, *Who would be wrong first?*

— —

Dante Falzone was worried. Now the guns of his 152mm starboard turrets were pointed at crazy angles. Eventually the reports came informing him that the third hit had gone through the face plate of his flagship's forward starboard 152mm turret. After wrecking the interior it exited the barbette continued aft, penetrating the barbette of the adjacent 152mm turret. It came to rest against the inside aft surface of that barbette where it detonated, igniting the powder charges in the turret; burning it out; and killing every man of the crew.

The second one was an inconsequential underwater hit on the port torpedo bulge. It flooded a few tanks, but the small list was quickly corrected by counter flooding.

The fourth hit, which no American observed, was the most devastating. Plunging downward, it hit aft of the tower foremast, barely missing both funnels. Penetrating the superstructure deck, main deck, and second deck the soft cap on the body of the projectile did its job of stressing the point of impact on the deck armor—interstitially welding itself to the Italian steel, it cradled and supported the hardened tool steel of the shell's body allowing it to penetrate the armor. The protective deck did accomplish one thing—it activated the fuse. Four hundredths of a second later after the shell had reached the bottom of the aft port engine room, it exploded. The shrapnel from the shell perforated the centerline bulkhead dividing port and starboard turbine compartments.

An unusual effect of the American super heavy armor piercing projectiles occurred after detonation. The explosion drove the intact armor piercing nose, actually almost 25 percent of the projectile's mass onward at higher velocities. That effect virtually guaranteed that any hit would result in the hull being penetrated and damaged compartments would flood. That was the case here, as both inboard main engines were lost. *Coraggio* was slowing to 30 knots and there was nothing that Dante could do about it.

— —

Sheppard watched as the next salvo from the leading battle cruiser landed. He really could not tell where. There were only three water columns. That confirmed the report from Lieutenant Hamblen in spot one that he had severely damaged one of the lead ship's turrets, preventing it from firing. This changed things. The odds of being able to spot and adjust salvos accurately with only three shells were small, much smaller than with six. Six was much better, nine made it easy—as long as gun alignment had been done correctly. Captain McCloud decided to stop chasing the lead battle cruiser's fall of shot; instead he would chase those of the second.

The shock of *Argonne's* guns firing with full powder charges was taking a toll on the ship's electronics. Some of radio central's receivers were not working. Both of the air search radars had gone down with the first dozen salvos. The aft Sugar George radar had lost its PPI display. Sheppard had acknowledged each of the reports but the impact had not really registered until the forward surface search set stopped transmitting. Sheppard had not realized until that moment how accustomed he had gotten to having God's view of the battle space around *Argonne*. He felt blind with enemies all about trying to destroy him.

The worst part was he lost his focus when the report came from the SG operator. His immediate reaction was to go look— exactly the wrong thing to do. He was just so tired. He failed to maneuver and the next six shot salvo raised five water columns and one hit. The Italian 45-centimeter armor-piercing shell, hit just aft of Turret III. The 2-inch thick main deck took off the projectile's wind screen and the cap from the main part of the shell as well as activated the time delay fuse—just as the deck was designed to do. The projectile passed through the second deck wrecking many of the tables and benches in the after crew's mess in the process. Continuing on it entered a storeroom on the third deck where to the crew's delight it destroyed dozens and dozens of cases of canned meat—Spam. Hitting the HY80 of the armored deck, but without the cap it ricocheted off and sliced through the foundation bulkhead for the port belt armor. Detonating, it sprayed shrapnel into and through the hull at frame 265 port side.

— —

The two north of center Italian cruisers in Moretti's light cruiser scouting line, *Eugenio di Savoia*, and *Luigi di Savoia* were ideally suited as companions for Italy's battle cruisers. Equally as fast, they were well armored against destroyer or light cruiser gun fire. They were only modestly armed with 10- 152mm/55 guns in four turrets, but unlike many foreign cruisers they carried twelve 533 mm torpedo tubes; making them a potent threat to larger ships. Like every other ship in Moretti's fleet, they lacked radar and after a boring night of nothing happening as far as the scouting line was concerned, might be forgiven for not seeing the approaching ships in the pitch black of night following moonset.

The first they knew of the approaching ships was the dull glow of 'flashless' powder that sent dozens of 15- and 16.5-inch shells in their direction. As good as the Italian armor was against smaller caliber guns, it was no match for the heavy shells that rained down on them at short range. Almost half of all the shells fired found the hulls, superstructure, gun turrets, and torpedo mounts aboard the two light cruisers. Within five minutes they were both smoking, drifting, and sinking wrecks without having accomplished their fundamental task of alerting the Italian Admiral of the enemy's presence and maintaining contact on his force.

Their executioners moved on to the east at 18 knots.

Not unexpectedly, *Amedeo di Savoia* and *Ludivico di Savoia,* the last two light cruisers in the Italian scouting line, saw the fires from their sister ships and turned to investigate what had happened. Four 'enemy' light cruisers had been assigned to watch the two Italian ships. When they turned to investigate, forty-eight 6-inch guns opened fire at less than 9,000 yards range. At a rate of six rounds per minute per gun, it was but a few minutes indeed before the common pointed ballistic capped (CPBC) shells with nearly 4 pounds of explosive had devastated the two cruisers. Before the order to cease firing was given, the only remaining ships of Moretti's light cruiser scouting line were afire and sinking; the majority of the two crews dead or wounded. None had alerted the Italians to the presence of a major force moving west.

The four enemy light cruisers went to 28 knots hurrying to regain their position in the van of the heavy ships.

— —

Sheppard knew that he had been running generally southeast for a while. It was light enough to see the mountains of Algeria and the vague form of ships where there had only been radar contacts before. He ordered another course change to 165° to throw off the gunnery officer of the second Italian battle cruiser as his own guns continued to try and eliminate the leading ship. If he was successful the enemy flagship would no longer be able to control that squadron and he might be able to escape. He raised his binoculars to survey the enemy aircraft carriers. Three of the four were listing, down by the bow or stern and heavily afire. None of those would require any more attention on his part.

The last was not burning and only slightly listing. He estimated the range at about 28,000 yards—near the limit of effective 6-inch fire. "Guns, Captain, track DOG-ONE and prepare to engage with turrets six-one and six-three using armor piercing shells."

"Captain, Guns, roger," Chuck answered and set about getting spot three, the forward Mark 34 director and the 6-inch computer in the forward main battery plotting room to track the target. "Turrets six-one and six-three load armor piercing," would get them ready as soon as he received the report that DOG-ONE was being tracked. It would take some time as the hoists had to be emptied of the high capacity shells used earlier. If Sheppard could destroy or at least render that carrier combat ineffective he would be able to run away—but where?

"Mustang Zero-Three, Panther, spot fall of shot vicinity furthest carrier. Mustang Zero-Four, spot vicinity of leading Italian battle cruiser." Sheppard knew that was his best hope of eliminating the carrier quickly at the same time that his other Kingfisher was spotting on the leading *Coraggio* class battle cruiser. Hopefully the 6-inch 135 pound armor piercing projectiles would be heavy enough to penetrate the Italian's deck armor. If not, he did not know how he was going to accomplish his mission unless he shifted his main battery to the carrier.

— —

From *Contrammiraglio* Dante Falzone's perspective things were not going well. *Coraggio* was being hit with almost every salvo. Half of the sixteen Yarrow style boilers had been destroyed, though it had not affected his speed much since two engine rooms were already flooded. Besides half of her 152mm guns, five of the twelve 90mm anti-aircraft mounts had been destroyed. Despite his best efforts the range was still excessive for his firecontrol arrangements though he felt that the 40cm guns on his *Avanti* class ships should soon be coming within range. He needed to relieve the pressure on his flagship.

He ordered a column turn to a course of 065°—just enough to allow the aft turrets on all his ships to be brought to bear on this enemy capital ship. He still wasn't sure of the target's classification other than enemy. He could see the two widely spaced funnels and three main turrets. That did not fit anything that he was aware the British had and it certainly would not be a German ship. The Brits would never allow it to get past Gibraltar. It had to be American! "What were they doing in the Mediterranean?"

— —

John Hamblen in Spot One was the first to notice the course change away on the part of the Italian battle cruiser line. He quickly passed the information on the sound powered phones to the forward main battery plotting room to update their solution. It did not take long before the ranges reported by the Mark 8 radar operator confirmed the turn and Gerry Archinbald put in a 250 yard range spot to compensate for the delay in recognizing what had happened. It would be prescient.

Sheppard saw this course change too from his position on the conning station looking through the rotating glass portholes. The Italian Admiral had committed himself to a deployment to his left. It created the opportunity he needed to get around the enemy to the south.

"Conning Officer; go to maximum speed." Sheppard's next course change would be further to the left holding his enemy at the limit of his forward turrets ability to shoot aft of the beam. He had his opening to escape to the east. All he had to do was make sure the remaining Italian destroyers did not try to interfere before he got out of range. *Argonne* jumped again as nine more two ton armor piercing projectiles headed toward the *Coraggio*.

— —

Madame Denise Bertrand couldn't take any more. She screamed, stood and ran toward one of the trunks leading to an armored hatch. Chevir, ever the faithful servant of his mistress, grabbed her—bear hugging the distraught woman. All he could do was hold on. No words of calm or explanation registered behind Denise's eyes wild with terror.

Madame D'Aubigné did not know how to reach the kind American doctor that cared for her grandson, but she knew where her daughter and child were. What did they call it, 'sickbay'. She ran to it and saw the man she was looking for.

"Doctor, you must come at once."

"Why, madame, my duty requires me to remain here."

"One of our women is screaming with fear and has had to be held by my butler. She needs to be, how do you say it? Sedated."

"I understand, let me get what I need and I will follow you."

A few minutes later, Dr. Blankenship was injecting Madame Bertrand with seconal. Quickly taking effect, she slumped in Chevir's arms. With the help of several of the officer wives, she was laid comfortably next to a bulkhead and covered with a white and blue Navy hospital blanket.

When the screaming stopped, some of the other French visibly relaxed, not to mention the crew members of *Argonne* in the vicinity.

— —

The sun had not quite risen above the horizon, but it was high enough that the arching armor piercing shells caught the full illumination in the clear morning air. It was too early for the rising humidity to create the haze that would limit visibility later in the day. These lighting circumstances created one of the most unnerving of sights that was part of naval battle—the ability to see the incoming shells. In fact almost from the time they left the muzzles of *Argonne*'s guns, these nine projectiles could be clearly seen; first by the men of *Argonne*; then by the sailors of the Italian battle cruisers. For most of them it was clear that they were not going to hit their ship and could be ignored.

For *Contrammiraglio* Falzone and the men on *Coraggio* that was not the case. Throughout the later part of the shell's flight, they seemed to be coming at their ship as indeed they were. Normally at the last possible instant the shells appeared to veer off unless they were going to hit. Two of them looked like they would and did.

The first shell hit the firecontrol tower just below the directors and neatly sliced through all the electrical cables connecting both directors to the plotting rooms below. None of the plating that the shell encountered was sufficient to activate its fuse. It continued on eventually exploding in boiler rooms that were already flooded. To all the observers on *Argonne* and mustang zero-four it was a miss, but it effectively destroyed *Coraggio*'s ability to control her gunfire at any meaningful ranges.

The second destroyed *Coraggio*! It actually hit about ten meters inboard of the gunnel on the starboard side of the main deck slightly forward of the aft main battery 45cm three gun turret. It penetrated the main and second decks easily and then the soft cap welded itself to the third deck as it smashed through the thick armor. The base detonating fuse was activated by the projectile's impact with the armored deck. Forty milliseconds later, after the projectile had penetrated down to the second platform deck, the fuse detonated the 58 pounds of picric acid high explosive. The red hot shrapnel created by the explosion cut into dozens of powder cans holding the propellant designated by the three initials NAC for its components manufactured by a company appropriately named *Dinamite Nobel*. The white hot expanding gases from the explosion started the powder burning. As pressure in the first magazine rose, more powder was ignited destroying bulkheads to adjacent magazines and starting the powder cans contained there ablaze until the entire 225 tons of NAC was burning.

Occurring in only a few seconds from the hit; the aft turret, which weighed more than a destroyer, lifted a hundred meters into the sky from the force of the burning powder as the after third of *Coraggio* disintegrated. The ship slowed, sinking by the stern. In a little over three minutes the bow of the battle cruiser was pointed at the sky and then slide slowly out of sight as one bulkhead after another was crushed by the sea pressure. Surprisingly there were hundreds of survivors. Dante Falzone was not among them.

— —

Sheppard and Ollie stood transfixed by what they had just witnessed as a mushroom shaped cloud of gas—first incandescent, then just reflective of the red dawn, rose over the remains of the Italian battle cruiser. It was John Hamblen in spot one that took action first. "Guns, Spot One, shifting targets to the next battle cruiser LOVE-ONE."

Commander Williamson acknowledged setting everything in motion. "Spot One, control turrets I, II, and III. Track LOVE-ONE. Continuous aim, salvo fire, master key." He then passed on the radio, "Mustang Zero-Four, Panther, shifting targets to next battle cruiser in line."

Sheppard heard mustang zero-four acknowledge as the next Italian salvo landed off of *Argonne's* port quarter. As he turned to the Conning Officer to direct a course change of fifteen degrees to the right the JA phone talker reported, "Many aircraft bearing two-nine-zero, range three-five-oh-double-oh yards, position angle one." Captain McCloud raised his glasses to look but was unable to make them out yet. What he did see bothered him as both of his Kingfishers were flying in the vicinity of the Italian battle cruisers. "Mustang Zero-Three, Panther, report your position," was a polite way of reprimanding his pilot for sightseeing rather than paying attention to the fall of shot around the last carrier.

The answer, "Panther, Mustang Zero-Three, vicinity of carrier DOG-ONE," totally surprised him. Sure enough when he looked there was a Kingfisher circling in the area of the Italian aircraft carrier just out of anti-aircraft range. His fatigue must be getting to him. He thought he saw two near his main battery targets—the Italian scouting force.

— —

Barry Jensen and Admiral Hamblen knew the real reason for Sheppard's confusion. "Panther, this is Mustang Zero-Five, radio check."

Ollie Halverson's cry, "They're Swordfish!" was not nearly as surprising as the JA phone talker's report. The gathering dawn was allowing the surface search lookouts to finally see clearly to the horizon and beyond. It was their report that the JA talker relayed of ships bearing zero-nine-two, range four-one-oh-double-oh yards. Sheppard would have to wait for the usual classification—Lieutenant Hamblen's director was pointed at the Italian scouting fleet.

"Ships bearing zero-nine-zero include at least five capital ships and many others based upon masts on the horizon." Another report by the JA talker. *More bad news,* Sheppard thought. The Italian battle fleet must be racing west to try and save the day. *Argonne* was trapped between two forces with only a few antique biplanes to help. There was nothing he could do but plan to face them both until he and his beloved—yes she was loved—ship fought on until they both were inevitably destroyed. *At least I will be finally free of these nightmares,* he thought.

— —

Contrammiraglio Achille Birindelli was the last surviving flag officer in the Italian scouting force. As the commander of the 2nd battle cruiser squadron with his flag in *Avanti* he had watched the running gun battle with this American capital ship. Unable to contribute to the battle as the American remained out of range of his 40cm guns, he had helplessly witnessed the stunning destruction of the *Coraggio*. Salvos were now falling around her sister ship *Potente*. He knew that he was falling into a defeatist attitude, but the fact that three of his nations four aircraft carriers were burning and the fourth being surrounded by shell splashes was clear evidence of the scouting force's failure to provide the absolutely required air cover for Operation *Guardare al Futuro* to succeed. His lookouts were reporting the very thing that they were supposed to guard against—an air strike by force H.

Reluctantly, he ordered a simultaneous turn of his remaining five battle cruisers to a course of 030° and an increase in speed to 42 knots. That would make a long slow approach for the ancient British biplanes and an impossible run for their slower torpedoes. He ordered his flag lieutenant to send a radio message to the light cruisers ordering them to withdraw to a rendezvous north of Corsica. None would answer. That left the two destroyer squadrons. He could not make out the hull letters of the ones with the carriers but it was evident that there were only four *Soldati* class destroyers visible. He recalled both of the squadrons hoping that some might be over the horizon, relying on the honorable nature of his British adversaries to rescue the crews of the sinking ships. One thing he failed to consider was the geometry forced upon the destroyer commanding officers by his recall order. The other thing he failed to do was notify *Ammiraglio di Armata* Gugliehno Romano of what was happening, assuming that Moretti had done so.

— —

Admiral Hamblen knew from reading the messages from mustang zero-two while Barry Jensen was flying toward the French at *Mers el Kébir* that the Italian battle fleet was about a 100 miles to the east. Now he saw the turn away together by the Italian battle cruisers and rightfully guessed that they were a beaten force. He also knew that *Amiral* D'Aubigné did not have the fuel to escape if the Italian battle fleet chose to pursue.

Without a second thought he directed Barry Jensen to fly alongside the approaching British torpedo planes hoping to reach them before they deployed for attack. The Italian battle fleet had to be stopped at all costs if *Argonne* and the French were to be saved.

— —

"Captain, Engineer. If you don't slow down, *now,* we will run out of fuel before we reach Gibraltar." That was not what Sheppard wanted to hear over the 21MC. He knew that the Italian battle cruisers had turned away together from him, without knowing why.

"Captain," it was Ollie, "it looks like those destroyers are heading our way." More bad news. Sheppard had hoped that they would continue their support mission of rendering assistance to the carriers until he was clear. He raised his binoculars to study the Italian carrier that was not burning. She was lower in the water with a noticeable list and hardly moving.

There wasn't time for the usual niceties of not issuing rudder orders to Chuck Williamson. "Guns, Captain, assign spot three and six-inch turrets to closest destroyer; assign sky one, two and four to the other three. Load high capacity and engage as quickly as you can." He needn't have worried.

Chuck was just as aware that the destroyers were coming *Argonne*'s way. It did not take long for him to get the correct orders issued. Sheppard saw the effects as the Mark 34 and the Mark 37 directors trained at the advancing destroyers. The one thing he lost track of was the next course change he needed to make in chasing the Italian 45cm salvos.

— —

Capitano Adriana Luzzatto of the submarine *Giulio dé Medici* had been forced to submerge by the growing light. At this point he was absolutely determined to attack this enemy. His nickname inside the service was *torello* (bull) for his stubbornness. Adriana was going to get this target if it was the last thing he did. *Giulio dé Medici* certainly had the firepower with six bow tubes loaded with 53.3 cm steam torpedoes manufactured in Fiume, Italy. Like all Italian large diameter torpedoes, they had a 270-kilogram TNT warhead. What he was most pleased about was looking at the chart; he had his target pinned against the North African coast. At some point that ship would have to come to where he was slowly closing in.

— —

The Gunnery Officer of the Italian battle cruiser *Potente* had observed his last nine shot salvo land about 300 meters aft of his target. Of the six modern battle cruisers that were originally part of the scouting force, his was the gunnery champion. He knew how to get the most out of the simple analog calculating machine and directors high on the fore tower. Thinking not just of the spot that he had to enter to center his pattern on the enemy; he was more concerned with analyzing the why. What had caused that salvo to miss? It was those corrections to his computer that had made *Potente* the gunnery champion.

Following his routine, when he entered the right spot of 300 meters, he also changed the target speed to the limit of his machine—50 knots. Skeptical that a ship could go that fast he nevertheless had confidence in the mental calculations that led him to a seemingly impossible conclusion.

The moment that his system operators reported they had entered the corrections. He gave the command to "Shoot!"

He counted himself lucky that he was able to shoot before his forward turrets reached the limit of their train. Future salvos would be limited to the three guns of his after turret because of *Potente*'s course change. Nine 1,530-kilogram armor-piercing projectiles flew to intercept *Argonne*'s position 70 seconds into the future. It would be the last Italian salvo of the Battle of the Alborán Sea as *Contrammiraglio* Achille Birindelli hoisted the signal to cease firing.

10

TRADITIONS

SHEPPARD KNEW HE HAD made a mistake when he saw the nine Italian 18-inch shells arcing down toward *Argonne* in the morning light. How many men were going to die? Would any of the French civilians be injured because he had gotten distracted? Would *Argonne's* luck hold one more time? He did not have long to wait. There was the rending tear of the air as the first few overs passed. The ocean heaved as mountainous water columns began to form on all sides of *Argonne*. The sickening sound of tearing steel and shattering wood joined the sound of the water rising. There were seven columns of water. *Argonne* had been hit twice. One was serious.

The first hit about 4 feet above the waterline on the starboard side at frame 232 abreast the after engine room. Its fuse shattered as it ricocheted off the armor belt. Then the shell continued downward, penetrating tanks in the torpedo defense system including the outer foam-filled layer. Exiting through the thin steel of the hull below the belt, the lack of an explosion prevented shrapnel from creating additional holes, flooding additional tanks.

The second shell slammed into the main deck forward between the two 18-inch turrets slightly to starboard but directly above his forward magazines. Sheppard could see the hole from the conning station walkway. He held his breath expecting any moment to be his and *Argonne*'s last, erupting in a fireball as Turret I and II's magazines exploded to be joined by the hundreds of projectiles stored inside the barbettes.

— —

What happened? Why was he suddenly filled with fear? Had her love been wounded again? Was it a more serious wound this time—fatal? What did he know that endangered him? Would he triumph again or would his enemies prevail this time? She knew it was a dangerous mission. After his meeting at the White House he had been somber, reflective, and reticent. He had not divulged what was to come unlike before when he had sailed against the Germans. This was different. She had never before felt this level of trepidation in the connection of their souls that they shared for what seemed to be a lifetime.

She knew that she had been hurt. She could feel his pain, but why. What more must they both endure?

— —

The 2-inch main deck accomplished its design purpose of removing both the ballistic wind screen and the cap as well as activating the fuse to start its 0.035 second delay. The shell continued downward wrecking two berthing compartments in its passage until it hit the HY80 of the third deck. The sharp tip tried to dig into the armor deck but only succeeded in causing the shell to rotate and slap the deck in a thunderous earthquake heard and felt throughout *Argonne*, but especially in the sickbay directly below the point of impact. Sheppard may have caused the hit by not staying focused on chasing the Italian salvos, but he had managed to remain in the "immunity zone" where the Italian projectiles could neither penetrate *Argonne*'s deck armor nor her belt armor.

The shell ricocheted off the deck, exploding above the third deck in a berthing compartment just before it would have safely exited the ship. Bedding, clothing, personal items and the paint caught fire. The compartment was destroyed and the bulkheads outboard were perforated by the larger steel fragments. It was only minutes before the repair party entered the adjacent spaces with fire hoses and breathing apparatus to combat the damage. *Argonne* was hurt again, but not threatened.

Sheppard waited for the personnel casualty reports, dreading the confirmation that his mistake had again caused death and injury to his crew. He knew that he wasn't yet paralyzed by the fear of making a mistake but he absolutely knew that every mistake he made was paid for in the blood and lives of his men.

— —

Capitano Luzzatto needed to check on his target again. As he closed the range, it was vital that he keep track of any course changes that would prevent him from reaching a firing point before this target escaped. With the growing dawn that meant slowing before he raised his periscope. Five, four, three knots . . . he would risk the small wake that the scope would leave. He knew the sea state, even if only a slight chop, would mask the wake particularly at this range.

As the water drained from the head window Torello smiled. His target had been damaged and smoke was rising from the area forward of the superstructure. The range was still too far to shoot, but a second observation a minute later confirmed that the bearing was not changing rapidly. He should be able to engage this target. It would only take his determination and patience. He had both and he knew it.

— —

In the days of sail, where voyages could last months, even merchant ships were armed with cannon to deter uncivilized savages and the more brutal pirates born in European countries; it was not uncommon for women to give birth at sea. For the more refined ladies of Europe that was obviously a traumatic event, the first of which they were not likely to be well prepared for without parents or friends in attendance. Among ship's surgeons more attuned to amputations of shattered limbs than obstetrics, there arose a rather unique custom to assist a woman in delivery during the later stages of labor. It was really quite a simple method of encouraging her to push with all her might at the correct time in a contraction.

The solution entailed frightening her out of her wits by firing a cannon to leeward from a location as close as practical to where she was suffering. Not being accustomed to the blast of the gun's discharge, the noise was quite effective in encouraging that last little bit of extra muscle contraction needed to deliver. The age of steam, however, had shortened sea voyages to days or at the outside weeks allowing prudence to avoid the necessity of delivery at sea and the traditional remedy had rarely if ever been needed since well before the turn of the century.

— —

Dr. Hugh Blankenship, *Argonne's* Medical Department Head, began the long climb up fourteen decks to the conning station. He was bone tired from over 48 hours without sleep operating on first wounded Marines and German POWs, and then seeing to the care of the French evacuees. When the main battery had begun firing, a few, he was too tired to count, but at least several had become hysterical. For the sake of the others and the few injured among the French, he had sedated them. The gunfire had created another problem for his surgeons in causing three of the pregnant French wives; at least he hoped they were wives, to begin their labor.

Like any good doctor he had tried everything in his power to save all his patients. Unfortunately, it had not been humanly possible. Where they had died, he had to tell himself it was God's will. The other possibility that he had overlooked something was too painful to bear. It was that aspect of his personality that had allowed him to recognize a kindred compassionate soul in his Captain. Hugh wished he knew how Captain McCloud escaped the psychological damage of his mistakes, if there were any. If he made an error in judgment, at most one individual paid the price. With Sheppard a mistake could lead to hundreds of dead or maimed.

As he reached the conning platform, he was winded and knew Sheppard would tease him about it, which he would try to return. His admiration and respect for his Captain showed as he waited patiently to be recognized by the man they all depended upon to be *right*.

— —

Sheppard raised his binoculars to confirm that the four remaining *Soldati* class destroyers were on fire, but more importantly sinking. He had to slow and two of them were within range of low speed torpedo shots. His lookouts would give him more than sufficient warning when they sighted the frothy wakes from the combustion steam engines, but only if he was at a high speed. Slowing to conserve fuel would make it harder to avoid the torpedoes even when seen. His lookouts could no longer see any of the Italian battle cruisers and assumed that they had disappeared over the horizon out of range.

"Cease fire," was the most pleasant order he had given all day and for once in the hours since he had first started shooting at the Italian aircraft carriers, *Argonne*'s guns fell silent. Their blackened muzzles lowered for rest.

God, he was tired!

"Ah, the good Doctor Blankenship, and how was your monthly exercise today?"

As Hugh studied Sheppard's face he could see the fatigue clearly, "Well, Captain, I think we both could use a rest."

"You have that correct. 'But I have promises to keep and miles to go before I sleep'," he said, quoting Robert Frost.

"Captain, as your doctor, I advise you to get some sleep. We need you rested, not dead on your feet keeping your promises."

"Okay, doctor. I'll take that under advisement. Please give me a report about the casualties," as he steeled himself for the answer.

"We were lucky, Captain. We will only have three dead to bury—two you already know about. The last died only a few minutes ago, but we never expected him to survive. From the battle, we have lots of flash burns and shrapnel wounds among the anti-aircraft crews, but nothing serious. One member of the repair party fell through the second deck in the smoke and broke his ankle. They should all make a full recovery. Captain, you know that old tradition of firing a gun to leeward for pregnancies."

"Yes, Doctor, what of it?"

"Well, Captain, when that Italian shell hit the deck over sickbay, the overhead bounced with a horrendous noise and then there was an explosion above. Three of the French women were in labor from the battle and delivered at that moment. It seems we have a baby boom on *Argonne*."

Three dead, four born including the D'Aubigné child. Sheppard thought that at least in the ugly calculus of war he had come out ahead this time. His heart was heavy, but duty still required more action.

"Doctor, please give my compliments to the XO and head chaplain and inform them that we will bury the dead as soon as all the preparations are completed."

Hugh wanted to stay and convince Sheppard to rest, but he knew it was futile. After all, he had just been given a direct order. With an, "Aye aye, sir" he turned and left.

— —

Commander Robert Bruce-MacLeod RN was the senior aircraft squadron commander aboard *Splendid*. As such, it fell to him to lead the Fleet Air Arm strike on the Italian scouting force. Flying in a Fairey Albacore it was only about thirty minutes after he had formed up with his squadron and set off to the east that the American Kingfisher had pulled up alongside and began sending a flashing light message on an Aldis lamp. There was no doubt about its nationality from the white stars on the fuselage and red and white stripes on the rudder flash. What surprised him the most was when the man sitting in the gunner's seat held up the blue flag with four white stars. Robert knew enough about the American Navy that it was an Admiral's flag, a *full* Admiral's flag, and assumed that the elderly man in that seat was that man.

As the American blinked out a message, he had a decision to make. This Admiral wanted him to do something other than what he had been ordered to accomplish in the preflight briefing. He had no reason to doubt what he was being told. He could see that his assigned target was moving rapidly to the east-northeast, presenting him with an extremely difficult tactical situation. Undoubtedly loses of several aircraft from each of the four squadrons he was leading would occur in the long slow approach that the Italians had forced upon him. It was also perfectly clear that the French had sailed and were headed toward Gibraltar at too leisurely a pace to escape, if what this Admiral told him was true concerning what lay over the eastern horizon.

Well, he had always been told by his admiral father that he was a bloody fool. "If you want to make something of yourself in the service, you have to do it on the compass platform of His Majesty's ships in command." He may have been right, but then his father never experienced that absolute joy of flying. That was his passion. He had decided to remain the bloody fool.

— —

"Panther, this is Mustang Zero-Four; request permission to land and come aboard."

The spotting network shocked Sheppard back to reality. He shook his head twice trying to clear the cobwebs. His spotters must be running very low on fuel for them to make this request. Could he risk it now, sending more aloft for the new threat to the east? Was he going to have to fight again—in spite of his critical fuel state?

Going to the 21MC Sheppard ordered, "Officer of the Deck; prepare to recover aircraft using the astern method. Prepare to launch aircraft. Secure from Battle stations. Set the modified underway watch. Feed the crew." What did he have, half an hour at the most until his guns would have to roar again? How much was left of the aft crew's mess?

"Conning Officer, come to course two-seven-zero, slow to one third." One more thing he had to make sure of: "JA talker, Fantail,Captain, load Kingfishers with depth charges." With the dawn again he had to worry about the Italian submarines. At least they could try to open the Italian battleships while he recovered and launched aircraft.

"Captain, Guns, spot one reports. The contacts to the east are French!'"

Sheppard thought for a few moments. The Italians were abandoning their survivors. Where they now his responsibility?

"Signal Bridge, when you can establish contact, make to the French flagship. Request destroyers recover Italian survivors."

The water was warm and there had been enough time for the destroyers' and carriers' wounded to be evacuated to boats with the rest seeing to their own life preservers. As soon as he had his pilots back on board *Argonne* he would return and assist them, but for now, his men came first.

The danger passed, Sheppard slumped like a deflating balloon, the fatigue hitting suddenly like the left hook that had broken his nose.

But I am going the wrong way.

"Officer of the deck. Shift your rudder. Steady course zero-eight-zero." *I'm issuing rudder orders—no backup. I've got to think—will myself to concentrate. God I want to sleep. Am I now the Conning Officer? I told my order to the Officer of the Deck. Well at least the Conning Officer is now issuing the order to the helm.*

— —

The sound man aboard the Italian submarine *Giulio dé Medici* called out, "Capitano, the ship is slowing." Torello Luzzatto smiled as he slowed his boat to take another look through the periscope. There was nothing like the hunt for a submariner, the quarry oblivious to the stalker.

When he finally slowed sufficiently to prevent a visible wake, the sight that greeted him made his determination worthwhile. The ship had not only slowed, but was now coming back toward him. He took some observations at specific time intervals so that his men at the plotting table could determine the target's course and speed from the bearings and ranges he gave them. The more he looked at the ship the more he realized that there was something different about it.

The crane had not been there before. They were hoisting out aircraft and getting ready to launch them. That was when he saw the first float plane land astern, then another, finally one more. There were three waiting to be lifted back onboard all lined up astern like ducklings following their mother. He lazily swept the periscope around the horizon to check for other ships or aircraft before he lowered it. *Destroyers!*

— —

The American Admiral had been correct. Stretching out ahead of Commander Bruce-MacLeod was the Italian battle fleet. Lead by a destroyer screen, the twelve capital ships were in a column coming right at him. It was a perfect tactical position for his slow biplanes. There were a few floatplanes being launched, but his escort of Fulmar fighters would make short work of them as soon as he signaled the attack.

Using hand signals and his radio, he began to deploy his four attack squadrons two on either side of the approaching Italian column for an 'anvil' attack. The Albacore squadrons would attack the last six battleships in column using their higher maximum speed, still only 159 mph, but more than the Swordfish's maximum of 139 mph, to go the greater distance. With the stringbags attacking the leading six, all the torpedo squadrons would be dropping at about the same time, spreading the anti-aircraft fire out among all seventy-two of the biplanes. As they began their attack runs, he would release his eighteen fighters of the escort to both strafe the AA gunners and deal with the Italian aircraft.

It was a great plan, limited only by the poor capability of the Mark XII* 45 cm torpedoes. With a warhead of less than 400 pounds of TNT it would be a miracle if the torpedo defenses designed into the battleships was breached and any significant damage could be achieved.

Just in time he completed the deployment of the squadrons as the black puffs of exploding 90 mm shells began to appear near the British.

— —

Torello Luzzatto began to make a series of mental calculations on the speed of the destroyers, their range from *Giulio dé Medici* in comparison to the distance he needed to travel to a launching point for his torpedoes. They were only capable of four kilometers at the high speed setting of 48 knots. It was too far. The destroyers would be on him before he got to the firing point for his steam torpedoes. All they had to do was look back along the visible wakes to see his location and increase speed to attack

They wouldn't even need to drop depth charges. *Giulio dé Medici* would not be able to go deep fast enough to avoid being rammed. No, he would have to take a low speed shot using the 36-knot setting. That gave him 8 kilometers and he was already within that range. He could shoot but the likelihood of his target evading was high.

Adriana calculated that his target would have about five and a half minutes to spot the torpedo wakes and take avoiding action before his weapons arrived at the intercept point. It was too long, but the only other answer was to not attack at all. Go deep to avoid the destroyers and hope for better luck another day. Torello Luzzatto would never do that!

He took one more observation of his target to confirm his solution of the course speed and range. When his torpedo firecontrol system operator reported, "Ready," he began to fire the narrow spread of six—only one degree separation for the gyro angle offsets. As long as the target did not maneuver, he was certain all six would hit on the port side of that huge ship. With any luck that much damage all on only one side would capsize the target before counter flooding could control the list. Torello smiled as the fish left his forward tubes.

— —

Worse than the fact that fatigue was getting to Sheppard was the fact that he knew it. He stepped out on the conning platform hoping the morning breeze would help clear his head, but the warm sun only made it worse. He had to concentrate and stay sharp until *Argonne* was comfortably inside a destroyer screen in formation with the French fleet. Perhaps then he could doze off in the conning station chair.

He decided to concentrate on the recovery of his Kingfishers. Zero-five, zero-three, and zero-four had landed and were waiting astern. Depth charges were being hoisted into position on the wings of mustang zero-six and zero-seven as they rested on the catapults. The aircraft and boat crane had put the sled into *Argonne's* wake to snag the hook of the first OS2U-5 when it ran up on the landing mat. He raised his binoculars to identify which of his aircraft was the first in line for recovery and saw that it was Barry Jensen and Admiral Hamblen's mustang zero-five. Sheppard was pleased with that; he actually looked forward to seeing the Admiral back on board. If he had to pick, Hamblen was probably one of the better flag officers he had ever worked with.

Barry had managed to get hooked onto the sled on his first

try and quickly shut down his Pratt & Whitney engine. Without his gunner, it was Barry's job to climb out onto the wing to attach the crane's hook to the lifting cable on the bulkhead behind his seat. He was definitely not as agile or familiar with the evolution as his usual gunner Radioman Hargrove was. This was taking more time.

Everything else was all going like the well-oiled machine that Bronco had trained when Sheppard's thoughts were interrupted by, "Torpedoes bearing Two-Nine-Zero relative." Instinctively he ordered, "Conning Officer, come to flank with left full rudder. Have the signal bridge raise the submarine alarm on the port halyard."

Something whispered *No!* Was it his fatigued mind? Was it Evelyn trying to warn him from thousands of miles away? He felt her presence in his mind or did he?

— —

Two French squadrons of large destroyers called *Contre-torpilleurs* were building speed to recover Italian survivors. After all *Amiral* D'Aubigné had ordered "expedite" in spite of their shortage of fuel, when the lookouts aboard the *Contre-torpilleur Mogador* also saw the torpedo tracks begin off of the French ship's starboard bow. *Capitaine de Frégate* Destin Moreau was on the bridge of his destroyer and knew instantly that the *Argonne* was in grave danger.

He knew exactly what to do, having had experience with Italian torpedoes before when *Mogador* had been hit off of LaSpezia in 1940. Destin relieved his Officer of the Deck of both the administration of the ship and the direction of her movements immediately by issuing his first order directly to the helmsman. He would now only have to issue orders to the helm and crew for what he needed to quickly accomplish. There would be no unnecessary delays. Though in all honesty, if asked, he would say that he had forgotten or that it did not concern him. But when *Amiral* D'Aubigné had passed around the list of French dependents on *Argonne*, he had seen that his pregnant wife Angélique was safely on board the American battle cruiser.

Mogador was lightly loaded with little fuel oil or stores onboard. She had proven capable of over 43 knots on her sea trials with well over a hundred thousand shaft horsepower, and at this loading she would be even faster. That was what Destin was counting on as he ordered maximum speed and began issuing rudder orders to the helm. He also proved himself again as one of France's greatest young naval leaders by ordering all hands not required in the engine and boiler rooms onto the weather decks in their life jackets.

Then he ordered, "Standby the depth charges."

— —

"*Belay my last!* Maintain course zero-eight-zero and one-third speed! Suspend aircraft recover after zero-five is aboard. Signal zero-three and zero-four to stand clear. Pass the word, 'collision imminent, collision port side, and sound the collision alarm.'"

There is nothing like nearly killing six men in the *Kingfisher*s to shock you back to focus. If Sheppard's original order had been acted upon, the wash from *Argonne*'s over half-million shaft horse power would have destroyed the aircraft astern and drowned their crews. For the sake of his air crews he could not increase speed. If he turned before mustang zero-five was lifted, the crane would drag the *Kingfisher* sideways and swamp it. The younger man might swim clear, but someone of Hamblen's age weighed down with flight gear, and unfamiliar with the "Mae West" inflatable life jacket would drown.

His torpedo defense system should be capable of absorbing the blows, without endangering *Argonne*'s vitals. There would be broken ankles and frightened French but no one should die. He did have to worry about one thing and went to the 21MC.

"Damage Control Central, Captain, begin counter flooding the starboard outboard voids. Fantail, Captain, warn Mustang zero-three and zero-four to remain well clear of the propeller wash." He was so tired, was he repeating himself? Would his men notice?

If it was a full salvo from an Italian submarine, six or eight hits might capsize *Argonne* if he did not get ahead of the list caused by the resulting flooding. The down side was that if set as deep as his draft the torpedoes might hit below the turn of the bilge, under his torpedo defense system with catastrophic results to the engineering plant. He went back out on the conning platform to check on mustang zero-five and the torpedoes.

— —

The Italian anti-aircraft fire was beginning to take a toll on the British biplanes as they pressed home their attack. Shrapnel from the bursting 90mm shells, as well as 37mm and 20mm projectiles, were hitting the obsolete aircraft. Holes were appearing in the fabric of the wings and fuselages. Despite their age, in one respect the Albacores and Swordfish had an advantage. The fabric did not offer enough resistance to activate the fuses of the lighter Italian AA projectiles. Occasionally one of the planes fell when a pilot was killed or an engine was hit; however, for the most part they reached their drop points about a thousand yards from the Italians.

It was a beautifully executed attack. The Fulmar fighters even managed to do some strafing of the light anti-aircraft guns on some of the ships after they had destroyed the Ro43 float planes. Of the seventy two torpedo bombers that had launched from *Splendid* and *Ark Royal,* Bruce-MacLeod saw sixty-seven reach the drop points for their torpedoes. Only two more were destroyed as they escaped.

There was very little that the Italian admiral could do other than signal a simultaneous turn toward the port group after they dropped. That left the starboard group perfectly positioned to make beam attacks on the battleships.

As he jinked and skidded his Albacore, Commander Bruce-MacLeod's gunner reported water columns alongside nearly every Italian battleship with some suffering two and one three hits.

He had every reason to be pleased as he signaled the attack results back to *Renown*. The final determination of the exact number of hits would have to wait until the flight crews were debriefed, but as the biplanes and Fulmars headed back west nearly every battleship was listing, slowing, and almost all were trailing a heavy oil slick.

— —

Destin had been in command of *Mogador* when she engaged an Italian destroyer squadron in company with her sister ships *Volta* and *Marceau*. The victim of a well-executed torpedo attack that ended the fight, *Mogador* had suffered a hit that kept the ship in repair at Toulon until just before the Germans occupied the rest of France in late 1941. That damage was not what caught Destin's attention.

It was the two torpedoes that had not hit his ship. Both missed astern as he had accelerated to avoid them. Both had also exploded in *Mogador's* wake without hitting anything solid. The whole time in the shipyard he had badgered the engineers at the torpedo design shop in the Toulon Navy Yard for the reason. It had taken a considerable amount of good will and cognac to finally get them to devote the time for an engineering determination of the forces involved and the causes of the detonations.

The explanation in retrospect was fairly simple. The Italians had to be using an inertia switch to activate the warhead rather than the more conventional contact exploder. It was the only possible explanation. That was the genesis of *Capitaine de Frégate* Destin Moreau's plan; that and his ability to do mathematics quickly in his head. It would work only if *Mogador* could outrun the Italian torpedoes.

— —

Sheppard was back out on the port conning platform watching the progress of the recovery of mustang zero-five as well as the torpedoes coming his way. *Argonne* was starting to list to starboard as Damage Control Central orchestrated the filling of the starboard side voids in the torpedo defense system. Idly amused that everything seemed to be slowing down, he looked around at *Argonne* almost like a last look before leaving an old friend.

She appeared a wreck. The gun muzzles were blackened, blistered paint gave emphasis to their deadly work. There were hundreds and hundreds of shell casings from the 5 and 6-inch guns knee deep on the main and O-1 decks. As he looked closer the weather decks were covered with the residue of the silk powder bags and cork powder cartridge closures. Pieces of shrapnel from the near misses of exploding Italian shells littered those same decks and turret tops. The teak decks were scared here and there from shrapnel gouging light marks in the dark blue camouflage.

He could see the ugly furrow in the starboard side of the main deck between turret I and II; still smoking from the last of the fire below decks. Sheppard could not see the holes in the port side of the hull cut by the shell fragments of the two hits that had detonated onboard, or the neat round entry hole abreast the aft starboard engine room. He also could not see the burned and blistered paint on the starboard side of the bridge and forward tower where the muzzle flash from the main battery had scorched the superstructure.

That is when he saw the large French destroyer accelerating and racing at him akin to an outfielder trying to snag a fly ball before it hit the wall in Yankee Stadium. What was that captain trying to do? Sheppard prayed he wasn't trying to sacrifice his ship by having the torpedoes hit him rather than *Argonne*. His battle cruiser could withstand the blows, a destroyer could not. Sheppard looked aft to check on mustang zero-five.

— —

Captain Moreau had briefed *Mogador's* Weapons Officer on his plan and the vital role he had. So vital, that the Weapons Officer was running aft now, at breakneck speed. It would be his job to supervise the depth charge racks and perfectly place some of the drop points. When he breathlessly arrived, his men had already set the charges to thirty meters; the shallowest possible setting for their two-hundred kilograms of explosive.

Destin had to get ahead of the Italian torpedoes to make his plan work. The limiting item was the sink rate of his depth charges which he knew to be three meters per second. As *Mogador* pulled abreast the silver colored underwater missiles, Destin estimated that they were moving at about 35 knots—say eleven-hundred meters per minute. He had to drop the first charge about two-hundred meters ahead of the torpedo for the charge to explode just alongside and beneath it when the weapon passed the drop point. He would roll the charge two seconds after he could look straight down the wake from the bridge of *Mogador* compensating for most of the ship's length. To be sure in case his estimate was off, his Weapons Officer would drop a second charge when he was looking directly down the wake from the fantail. The first charge should create a lateral motion the second a vertical one. The last try was *Mogador's* wake itself as she strained every fiber of her being at over 44 knots.

One thing was working in his favor. The Italian submariner had spread his shots from aft to forward on his target achieving the maximum separation between torpedo hits in his planned attack, even though the gyro offset appeared to be small between weapons. Most of the fan shaped spread probably was caused by *Argonne's* motion between launches. The first torpedo that Destin needed to attack was the closest to him, but to reach the farthest he had to continue racing at top speed. He did not think he would get to it in time.

— —

Chief Bledsoe should have hoisted the Kingfisher by now. Sheppard went into the conning station and demanded of the JA talker, "Fantail, Captain, report delay in hoisting aircraft!"

When he got the answer, Sheppard had to struggle to hold his anger. The crane operator was reporting that the landing sled was hung up on the hook beneath the pontoon of mustang zero-five. Chief Bledsoe was seeing to the arming of zero-six and seven. Try as they could, the airdales had been unsuccessful in their attempts to free it.

Sheppard's order was quick and to the point, "Hoist both together!" A quick check from the conning platform for the results of his order and he barked, "All ahead, flank, left full rudder!"

He had a dozen things to estimate in trying to determine if his actions were going to swing *Argonne* clear of the danger. How fast was the ship going to accelerate? Not very! How fast would she turn with the wash of the inboard racing propellers hitting the rudders? Not fast enough! How many boilers were on line—he had forgotten? Where were the torpedoes? Which ones were the most dangerous? What was that destroyer trying to do? Would her captain keep her clear?

There was no time for instruments or measurements of the variables. It all came down to his twenty-four years of service mostly at sea and the seaman's eye that he had honed during that time. Like so many things, too many for Sheppard as tired as he was, the safety of his ship and the crew rested on his judgment in a crisis. It was no wonder that the service saying was, "... *at sea the Captain is God!*"

He wasn't going to make it. Something else was needed!

— —

Destin had ordered two depth charges dropped as *Mogador* had crossed the first two torpedo paths and his weapons officer had dropped one, when the first detonated two hundred and fifty meters astern of the racing destroyer. The first blast of high explosive from the depth charge was followed by a larger explosion immediately after as the first Italian torpedo was destroyed by its own warhead. It was working!

Now all that Destin and *Mogador*, for the action of the two were inseparable, needed was continue rolling the charges as the *Contre-torpilleur* raced on—as long as there was enough sea room to complete the plan. Destin looked at the American ship. Finally she was trying to evade. What had taken her so long? There was a gigantic swirl of white water forming at her stern. Captain Moreau could only guess at the power that could create such a wash.

Mogador was pointed only slightly aft of amidships of the American battle cruiser. There was not enough room for him to complete his plan as he dropped another charge and another torpedo was destroyed. He would collide with the *Argonne* just aft of her after turret at almost the exact moment he needed to drop the last of his charges. Destin knew the results of his three thousand ton *Contre-torpilleur* hitting that monster of a ship at nearly 45 knots. *Mogador* would be destroyed but what of the American?

— —

Sheppard jumped back into the conning station and barked, "Port outboard main engine. Back emergency!" He was now the Conning Officer and Lieutenant Cunningham's, "The Captain has the conn," confirmed it.

The port lee helmsman grabbed the handle for the outboard engine order telegraph and yanked it aft as far as it would go, went all the way forward and then back again leaving it indicating the Captain's order.

Sixteen decks below in the forward port engine room the throttleman at the gage board Machinist Mate second class Milton DeLong answered the order by matching his handle to the indicated order and started spinning the ahead throttle valve hand wheel shut as fast as he could.

The port lee helmsman reported, "Port outboard main engine answers; back emergency, sir." There was nothing more for Sheppard to do but go out to the conning platform and watch the onrushing French destroyer, bracing for the inevitable explosions of one or more Italian torpedoes. *Argonne's* two stacks were erupting in volcanoes of superheated combustion gases and smoke. Well, the smoke did not matter now. Sheppard needed power. The Italians, the French, and whoever's submarine that was shooting at him already knew where he was.

No sooner had the throttleman shut the ahead guarding valve than he began to spin the astern throttle fully counterclockwise until the 3 foot diameter hand wheel came up to the hard stop. Main engines were designed to provide maximum power going ahead and Petty Officer Delong was well aware that he controlled well over a hundred thousand horsepower going ahead. The backing turbine elements were almost an afterthought. Despite having the maximum possible steam flow going to the engine, it would only generate about one fifth the ahead horsepower when going astern.

The 40-inch diameter shaft slowed and stopped rotating in the ahead direction; reversing from counter clockwise when viewed from astern to clockwise as the astern engine began to generate power. As it did so the wash from its propeller began to create a swirl of water on *Argonne's* port side moving toward the bow and building up against the forward motion of the ship. There was nowhere near enough power to substantially slow *Argonne's* mass or even significantly slow her acceleration, but the effect was to cause the stern to swing faster to starboard.

— —

Chief Bledsoe stopped worrying about loading depth charges on the two Kingfisher's resting snugly on the catapult launch cars and ran aft shouting at the crane operator, "Smitty, two-block that Kingfisher and swing her forward as quickly as you can!"

"Roger, Chief," the reply almost lost in the increasing whine of the forced draft blowers.

As Chief Bledsoe ran aft leaping up on the armored hatch to the hanger, it was getting harder to keep his balance. *Argonne's* stern was starting to buck like a rodeo bronco with three shafts accelerating ahead and one spinning astern. Would the Kingfishers spotted for launch with their tie-downs removed fall off the catapults?

"Smitty, you are rotating the wrong way; swing to starboard, not to port."

"Sorry, Chief," the chastened crane operator replied.

Chief Bledsoe caught a glimpse of the racing French destroyer, aiming it seemed directly at him as he moved aft. There was no time to reverse the crane's rotation. That destroyer would hit the Kingfisher if it tried to veer off at the last moment. "Smitty, keep rotating to port!"

"Okay, Chief," what was his boss thinking—first one way and then back again as he again reversed the hand-wheel controlling the crane's rotation machinery on the deck below.

"You boys with the hold-off poles, do your best to keep that plane from swinging into the crane as she's hoisted above the other planes." It probably won't do much good, the angles are all wrong for them to be able to control the Kingfisher. "Jonesie, use your pole to knock that landing mat free. If it comes aboard with that plane, it's going to wreck the tail on zero-six!"

— —

Destin and his weapons officer had dropped their ninth and tenth charges trying to destroy the fifth Italian torpedo. They had run out of time and space.

"Weapons Officer, place all depth charges on safe."

Destin passed, "Brace for large angles."

There was one last desperate gamble to take. This time he was thinking of his wife and unborn child.

He ordered, "Right full rudder," knowing full well that at this speed with *Mogador* lightly loaded, that she might very well heel over onto her beam ends and founder.

"All back emergency,"

"Brace for impact."

His engineering personnel did their best to comply with their Captain's engine order but the rapidly tilting deck made it all but impossible.

Mogador's bow cleared the port quarter 40mm quadruple mount gun tub on *Argonne* by less than a meter as her bridge clinometer passed a list angle of 50 degrees. Her starboard propeller came out of the water and the starboard main engine raced to its limiter set point. The *Contre-torpilleur*'s stern was swinging rapidly toward *Argonne* with the port side of her main deck under water.

A collision seemed certain when Destin issued his last order in command of *Mogador*, "Shift your rudder;" as he lost his grip and fell. The bridge clinometer reached 65 degrees and hung there as the rudder machinery strained to go from right full to left full at a list angle it was never designed for.

— —

Sheppard watched what he had to admit was the finest example of ship handling he had ever seen. He had always prided himself on how well he could handle his destroyer when he had his first command, but this French commanding officer was more than his equal. He watched with grateful admiration as the exploding depth charges and Italian torpedoes had come closer and closer to *Argonne*. He had seen the wakes and knew that there was but one more that was yet to be accounted for.

Once more Sheppard's mind raced. *Would it miss? Would it hit the destroyer? Would it hit Argonne in her most vulnerable place by his port shafts and rudder? Should he stop the port shafts to prevent a bent one from opening all the bulkhead seals to his forward engine room? That would be catastrophic!* That torpedo wake looked to be aimed directly amidships of that French destroyer. What was its running depth? Would it detonate on that ship or continue on to hit *Argonne*?

The torpedo detonated about 50 feet from *Argonne*, far enough that the battle cruiser—his ship—should not suffer any significant damage. Sheppard waited in dread of the reports that the rudders were not responding to the helmsman's orders, or the reports of flooding where the hull might be breached from Damage Control Central. He prayed there might only be some dishing in of the thin outer skin at his stern.

But those damage reports did not come, *Argonne* was functional and essentially undamaged. The same was not true of *Mogador* as she drifted to a stop slowly righting herself, settling by the stern. There were men—French sailors in the water. "All stop, stop the shafts!" He had to prevent them being sucked under by that swirling mass of water aft; at least it looked like they all had lifejackets on.

Chief Bledsoe was reporting that the Kingfisher's appeared undamaged, but Sheppard would not take any chances. He went to the 21MC, "Officer of the Deck, secure attempts to ready aircraft until all OS2Us onboard have been inspected for damage. Away the rescue and assistance detail."

No one could possibly know if that last torpedo exploded as a result of *Mogador*'s last desperate act or as result of Sheppard's backing the outboard port shaft. Perhaps it was the combination of both acts creating the maelstrom of swirling water needed to activate the Italian detonator. No one would know, but to be honest, no one cared. Sheppard would give sole credit to *Mogador* in his report making it certain that *Amiral* D'Aubigné would give full credit to this unknown French officer in all the official reports of the action. *Capitaine de Frégate* Destin Moreau would take his rightful place in the pantheon of France's naval heroes.

— —

It did not take long for *Mogador's* squadron mates to dispatch the *Giulio dé Medici*. Torello Luzzatto had taken his submarine down to her test depth of 100 meters in an effort to get away. It was exactly the wrong thing to do in the spring Mediterranean morning. Without a storm having passed through the area recently, there was a sharp enough temperature gradient at about 15 meters to create a fairly safe shadow zone that would limit the sound equipment on the *Contre-torpilleurs* if he had stayed at 30 meters. By going deeper he left himself more vulnerable to detection and localization.

Sheppard was watching as the air bubble, oil, and debris rose to the surface following their second attack, marking the end of *Argonne*'s assailant. He had stopped *Argonne* using only the starboard shafts. There were men struggling in the water and *Mogador* was sinking lower every minute. "Conning Officer, I am ready to be relieved, answering all stop, no course ordered."

"I relieve you, sir, answering stop on all shafts, no course ordered," replied Lieutenant Cunningham.

Sheppard smiled that the young officer had expanded on what his Captain had stated without concern that he would get recrimination.

The first-repeat pennant had been lowered from the starboard yardarm as soon as mustang zero-five settled into a cradle in the hanger and Admiral Hamblen, none the worse for wear, deplaned. The OS2U-5 had its wings folded and was pushed to a storage position on the forward port side of the hanger while boat crews and damage control personnel mustered. Lieutenant Barry Jensen was rumored to have kissed the third deck again as soon as he exited the Kingfisher. He had seen *Mogador* pass almost directly under his aircraft as it swung at the end of the hoist cable from the aircraft and boat crane with the mast passing on one side and the superstructure passing on the other.

The first launch lifted from the hanger set about rescuing the French sailors swimming nearby. Chief Bledsoe sent one of his men up to the top of the crane where he had the best view for locating men in the water. Using hand signals, every Frenchman living and dead that floated nearby was recovered.

The second and third 50-foot utility launches packed with damage control personnel and equipment were lowered and quickly set off to assist *Mogador* by the time the first returned. The lifting bridle was attached and the boat carefully hoisted to *Argonne*'s gunnel where stretcher parties and one of the Medical Department's doctors were standing by to assist. Three sailors were pronounced dead at the scene, with another dozen suffering from internal injuries caused by the explosive concussion of the detonating Italian torpedo as they struggled in the water nearby. The stretcher parties rushed those to sick bay where *Argonne*'s surgical teams were waiting. By now every man, woman, and child aboard *Argonne* knew of the heroics of *Mogador* in saving them from the Italian submarine.

— —

Admiral Hardy stood on the compass platform of *Renown*, reading the blinker light messages from *Splendid* and *Ark Royal*. The report of damage inflicted by the strike group was encouraging. The Italian battle fleet had been damaged for a second time. Hardy knew that just as they had been repaired following the strike at Taranto, they would be repaired again, though it might take a year or more. Nothing would give him greater pleasure than to pursue the damaged battleships and finish them off, but both his Flag Captain and he recognized that it would be foolhardy in the extreme to pursue. His ships were outnumbered twelve to six and however fine their gunnery and crews, *Renown* and *Repulse* were no match for any modern capital ship, let alone the pride of the Italian Navy. Besides, by the time he overhauled them, they would be well within the range of the *Règia Aeronautica's* exceptional torpedo bombers flying out of Sardinia.

Another air strike to concentrate on sinking a few was out of the question. Every Swordfish and Albacore that returned was damaged. *Ark Royal* had estimated that it would take 36 hours in her report of the engagement before her remaining biplanes would be ready for a second strike and Hardy's Flag Captain Sir Philip Kelley rightfully believed that *Splendid* would need the same amount for her Albacores.

The only other option was the Italian Scouting Force, but they were retiring at a much greater speed than his elderly ships could hope to achieve on the best of days. Second guessing himself, he could not find an answer. Perhaps if he had not been hampered by the 18 knot maximum speed of the American tankers and supply ships, he could have intercepted the Scouting Force. He began to curse his decision to bring them along, safe from more Italian swimmers. Though he would achieve his mission of safeguarding the withdrawal of the French as Admiral Hamblen had requested, he was bitterly disappointed that the major units of the Italian fleet had again escaped destruction. At that moment a lookout reported, "Smoke bearing green one-five."

— —

It was the SG radar operator that cried out as soon as his radar came back on line, "Contacts bearing Two-Nine-Five about two-five miles. It looks like six large warships in column."

Admiral Hamblen had just finished the long climb up to the conning station when the report came. He quickly stated, "That is Force H."

Sheppard could not hide either his joy or the sarcasm in his voice as he looked at Ollie, "Better late than never. I just hope they brought a tanker or two, or we are going to have to row."

"Sheppard, have you gotten any reports from your rescue and assistance teams on *Mogador* yet?

"Yes, Admiral, most of her crew are hurt, maybe a third suffering broken bones. Besides the men that we recovered from the water, there are many severely injured including the Captain. Admiral, in all honesty, he is the best ship handler I have ever seen. Do you know his name?"

"His name is Destin Moreau. What about *Mogador?*

"It looks like they can save the ship, but *Mogador* is a floating wreck. The Italian torpedo warped her shafts, damaged the rudders, and flooded several compartments aft; but the worst part was trying to answer emergency engine orders at that list angle you saw. There was severe carryover of boiler water down the steam headers that destroyed the turbines. She doesn't even have a functional generator for electric power. Lieutenant Schneider found the French stability diagram. By all rights *Mogador* should have capsized. Had her captain not shifted his rudder when he did, she would have, as well as collided with *Argonne.*"

As Hamblen and Sheppard were talking they watched the litters being carried forward from where the hoisted utility launch was resting against the gunnel. Some of the French sailors were walking with splinted arms or blood soaked bandages. Oddly one Stokes litter was being carried by four French sailors being exceptionally careful. There was a man under a white Navy hospital blanket who obviously had their respect. A blood soaked bandage wrapped around his head. There was no sign of movement.

— —

She was so tired. The accolades of previous weeks were gone. The excitement of her recent events had died away in the humdrum of routine. She sensed from long experience that her beloved was bone tired too. He would drive himself to beyond human endurance for the sole sake of responsibility to his men. There was nothing she could do to stop that to convince him that he needed to look out for himself. At least that man Jefferson looked after him.

Was he condemning himself once more for decisions made and not made? Was he grieving for men dead or injured—at his hand or others? Didn't he understand that this was war and in war human life is at risk—ships are at risk? Didn't he realize that he could make mistakes; that for all the good he accomplished, it would not be perfect?

— —

He could not put his finger on it. Something just did not feel right to him. He had that same feeling in the British museum when he was examining a bone classified as one species when after thorough study it turned out to be something else. Flight Lieutenant Anthony Pennyman cleaned his magnifying glass again and studied yesterday's photos of the Wilhelmshaven docks for what must have been the twentieth time. He just could not determine what it was that was giving him that prickly feeling he knew was self-doubt. It is not often that a Flight Lieutenant briefs the Prime Minister and decisions of national survival are made. What if he had been wrong? He knew what he had read on the sides of the crates, but why did that little voice inside not let him believe it?

There was only one way to get a definitive answer. He was going to have to ask RAF Benson for another low level mission. The only problem was the weather was worse than the day before yesterday. A cold front had moved in and the forecast was for rain and a low ceiling over the north German coast. It would be a dicey mission for the Mosquito I.

— —

It had taken several hours, but the spent brass removed from the weather decks had been struck below. That was the easy part. Re-stowing the magazines was a much harder task. The cartridge cases had to be put back into their aluminum ammunition cans and the magazine contents rearranged so that the empties were in the farthest reaches. Each 5- and 6-inch powder space was sequentially emptied into the fourth deck fore and aft passages and then the thousands of powder tanks put back being careful to store the same lot numbers in the same sequence for each. The vetted French townsmen demanded that they be allowed to help in this labor intensive task. Sheppard was glad for the help as his gunners and magazine personnel were dead on their feet.

At least there was nothing to do in the 18-inch magazines except put the covers back in place and mark them as empty. The shell rings were refilled from the fixed storage in the main battery turrets again setting up the maximum firing rate for the longest possible time.

Once the after deck was swept and cleaned and preparation completed, Sheppard ordered the Boatswain's Mate of the Watch to pass the order he hated most.

Petty officer Bergman went to the 1MC microphone and piped the call *Word to be Passed*, "s^s-s-s-sssssssssss," followed by a solemn, "All Hands not on watch, bury the dead."

Sheppard had arranged for the Navigator Commander Art Roberts to come to the Conning Station and back up the Officer of the Deck while Sheppard was on the quarterdeck. Petty Officer Jefferson had brought his number one set of blues, freshly pressed, a starched white shirt, spotless black tie, morning band for the left sleeve of his blouse and spit-shined shoes for *Argonne*'s Captain to change into; honor the fallen.

When Sheppard and his orderly reached the quarterdeck all hands not on watch had been assembled as well as the ambulatory members of the *Mogador*'s crew, German POWs, and the French civilians. Many of the crew stood atop the aft turret. Eight flag draped stretchers—five French, two German, and one American—were arrayed along the starboard lifelines with six body-bearers each in their best dress uniforms; the body bearers holding the national flags as they billowed up in the swirling air aft. Major Jenkins with his sword and seven armed Marines formed the firing squad also in their dress blues. Commander Grabowski, the senior Chaplain, Senior Chief Hancock, and the ship's best bugler completed the official party. Sheppard knew that his boatswain's mates had prepared the bodies in the traditional manner—sewn into a white canvas shroud with a 5-inch projectile between their legs. Sheppard did not know what type, but it really didn't matter, any of them were heavy enough. By nautical tradition the last stitch was always through the nose—a tradition based on need, when ships rarely had doctors, it occasionally prevented tragic accidents of consigning a living person to the deep.

Major Jenkins gave the commands, "*Crew, a—tten—shun,*" followed by, "*Pa—rade rest!*" The senior Chaplain then read the service. Major Jenkins brought everyone back to attention.

At his command, "*Firing party, Pre—sent arms.*" every service member regardless of nation saluted. Sheppard noted that not one German gave the Nazi stiff arm. If only someone could get rid of the German leadership, this war would be over.

Sheppard following the old tradition had reserved the next part of the service for himself as the Captain of the ship.

He somberly began, "Unto Almighty God we commend the souls of our shipmates departed, and we commit their bodies to the deep . . ."

One at a time each stretcher tilted until the canvas wrapped body slid from beneath the flag. " . . . in the sure and certain hope of the resurrection unto eternal life when the sea shall give up its dead, through our Lord, Jesus Christ, Amen." Sheppard could not watch as it became the turn for the American; lifting his eyes to the heavens in a silent prayer for his loyal orderly. It was too painful to see Corporal Pease consigned to an undeserved and early grave.

Major Jenkins brought the assembled military members back to parade rest for the Chaplain's benediction. As a final respect by the assembled crew, the Major returned everyone back to attention ordered a hand salute, and then barked the orders, "*Firing party, fire three volleys.*" "*Ready, aim, fire; aim, fire; aim, fire. Present arms!*"

As the last crack of the rifle fire echoed off the nearest ships, the bugler began playing *Taps*. Originally composed by General

Butterworth in the Civil War to mark the end of the day, it had become the traditional piece to mark the death of brave men in service to their country.

On the last note of the melancholy call, Major Jenkins ended the service with the commands, *"Or—der arms. Dismissed!"*

Sheppard stared at the swirl of water serving as the only headstones the sailors, soldiers, and marine from three nations would ever have for eternity. They would lie next to each other on the ocean floor of the Alborán Basin, comrades in death that they could not be in life. War seemed so utterly pointless to the men that fought it. Everyone knew the lofty speeches, the inspiring words of the four freedoms, but here—now—warriors of three nations, one an ally, one an enemy, fighting that their cause would emerge victorious were disgustingly equal.

Honored were the dead. Grieving for fallen comrades in arms needed to end. With the stars and stripes 'two-blocked' at the truck, *Argonne* had to get back to the unfinished business of war—the unfinished business of death and destruction.

END NOTE

FROM NOVEMBER 1921 TO FEBRUARY 1922, nine nations—the United States, Great Britain, Japan, China, France, Italy, Belgium, Netherlands, and Portugal—met in Washington DC as part of the Washington Naval Conference. The main goal of the conference was to come to an agreement on naval disarmament in the aftermath of the Great War, making it the first disarmament conference in history. By its end, the conference had produced three international treaties, including the historic Five-Power Treaty (aka, the Washington Naval Treaty) that was signed by the US, Great Britain, Japan, Italy, and France. The Five-Power Treaty strangled naval construction, ship and armament sizes, while flooding the world's scrap-metal markets with banned warships—all helping to avert a naval arms race among the great powers of that age for over a decade.

But what if the Washington Naval Conference hadn't transpired as history recorded it? What if one lone incident— an assassination, common in the politics of one participating nation—occurred and changed the conference . . . and thus irrevocably altered all military history in the following years and ultimately World War II itself? What would history have looked like then?

What if . . .

— —

Baron Tomosaburō Katō—Admiral Imperial Japanese Navy, Naval Minister, and the head of his nation's delegation to the Washington Naval Conference—sat in his hotel room alone late on the evening of November 14, 1921. He listened to his favorite phonographic recording of traditional music while rereading staff notes on the position Japan would take for the conference's most important second plenary session the next day. At that moment, someone knocked on the door, entered the room, and bowed. Two minutes later, Baron Katō lay on the floor in a pool of blood—dead. The murder remained unsolved despite the unfettered efforts of the DC metropolitan police and all the resources the United States government could bring to bear.

Calling it an assassination, and accusing the Americans of collusion, the remaining members of the Japanese delegation walked out of the conference fearful for their own lives since Baron Katō had been strongly in favor of a treaty limiting naval expansion, opposing his own militarists. Without Japanese agreement to stop their 8-8-8 building program enshrined in Japanese law, the United States continued the naval expansion it had begun with the 1916 and 1919 naval appropriations. Faced with growing Japanese and American fleets, Great Britain had no option but to continue its own construction programs of battle cruisers and battleships. Italy chose to restart building the *Caracciolo* class, sparking a renewed interest in the *Lyon* class by France. Finally, Germany renounced the Treaty of Versailles, collapsing the League of Nations. The former Allies acquiesced, unwilling to return to the trenches as Germany, too, began rearming.

Around the world, shipyards rang as riveters joined steel to hulls. New mines, mills, and factories sprang up to feed the growing demand for naval rearmament. Huge government arsenals continued the development of 18 inch and larger guns started in the Great War to defeat the thicker and better armor at longer and longer ranges. Industry hired more tradesmen to meet the endless government contracts. Laboratories accelerated the development of all manner of naval technology and metallurgy, perhaps at the expense of aviation—perhaps not. Flotillas of dredges slaved endlessly on shallow harbors; building ways gave way to construction dry docks and expanding shipyards as warships grew too large for traditional launching methods, further bolstering civilian construction trades. Unfettered, warships grew ever larger, remaining immune to the weapons of all but their own breed.

The Roaring Twenties roared on into the thirties as consumerism fueled continued economic expansion. Growing tax revenues satisfied the financial needs of the fleets' expansion. Plentiful jobs and rising living standards, as well as enhanced job opportunities in the growing navies, obviated the pressure on politicians for social programs. Empires flourished, although the Soviet Union's command economy lagged behind the other international powers. Still, Hitler, Stalin, Mussolini, and Hirohito all dreamed of and plotted greater empires, replacing the old order, until the world erupted once more in global conflict.

CPSIA information can be obtained
at www.ICGtesting.com
Printed in the USA
FSOW01n0433180217
30810FS